THE NELSON TOUCH

The Nelson Touch

by

Len Manwaring

© Len Manwaring 2001

First Published in 2001 by
Marionette Books
1 Hutton Close
South Church
Bishop Auckland
Durham

British Library Cataloguing in Publication Data.
A catalogue record for this book is available
from the British Library.

ISBN 1 84039 015 8

Typeset by George Wishart & Associates, Whitley Bay.
Printed and bound by Antony Rowe Ltd., Chippenham.

Author's Note and Acknowledgements

Some of the events in this story actually took place. Most did not for they come from my imagination although set against the background of a few years during World War II. Research for Part III of this story revealed little in the way of detail regarding the momentous days at Habbaniya in 1941. Books covering the history of the Second World War scarcely mention such a brief and little known episode. It seemed almost as though it was deliberately suppressed at the time for security reasons and since then has been forgotten. Even accounts covering that area of operations give little importance to the battle waged by the RAF against the Iraqi army. I am indebted to the following publications for some details even though they often conflict with each other.

Armitage, Michael. (Air Chief Marshal) *The Royal Air Force: an illustrated history.* Arms and Armour, 1993.

Bowyer, Chaz. *The Encyclopedia of British Military Aircraft.* Bison, 1982.

Churchill, Winston S. *The Second World War.* Cassell, 1959.

Keegan, John. *The Second World War.* Pimlico. 1997.

Keegan, John. ed. *The Times Atlas of the Second World War.* Times Books, 1995.

Pitt, Barrie and Frances. *The Chronological Atlas of World War II.* Macmillan, 1989.

I had just about completed my story when a friend gave me a copy of *Air Mail: Journal of the Royal Air Forces Association. Vol. 52, No. 1. January – March 1999.* In it was a brief account of the Habbaniya siege some 58 years ago and it mentioned the one important reference which had so far eluded me. Indeed I never knew it existed. Air Vice-Marshal Tony Dudgeon, Sqn/Ldr as he was then, had actually taken part in the desperate hours of my story. He records in graphic detail his part and that of the officers, Flying Instructors, pupil pilots and ground staff who defended Habbaniya in *Dudgeon, Air Vice-Marshal A.G. The war that never was. Airlife, 1991.*

Even with this new information I decided not to alter my story as it is fictional about a character called Harry Nelson. It is surprising how closely my 'hero' mirrors some of the 'blind eye' exploits of Sqn/Ldr Dudgeon. I hope he would have approved of Harry Nelson on his team.

To the best of my knowledge the senior officers and other personnel in my story did not exist. The British Ambassador in Baghdad and his niece are also figments of my imagination.

I wish to acknowledge the considerable help from Joan who suggested vital changes in the draft and helped with proof correcting.

Finally a personal note of thanks to Jack Hill who not only gave me the copy of *Air Mail* but who also gave me personal recollections of his posting to Habbaniya. He was based there a few months after the battle had been won although signs of earlier German occupation were still visible at Mosul. Nick Carter, another RAF officer, kindly agreed to read the final draft of my novel and I am obliged for his pithy comments.

L.M.

Dedication

Many of the young men who were at Habbanyia in May 1941 received no recognition for the stand they made against the uprising. It is a credit to their steadfastness against all odds that they won the day. This story, fictional in many respects, is a small tribute to their valiant efforts and sacrifices so long ago.

Contents

Prologue   Cyrenaica June 1940 9

Part One: Preparation

Map 1   The Red Sea 7

Chapter 1   Manchester 1936 9

Chapter 2   Flying Badge 1937 15

Chapter 3   Another Posting: Aden 22

Chapter 4   A New Toy 27

Chapter 5   Operation 'Expedience' 34

Chapter 6   Decision at Gunpoint 42

Chapter 7   First 'Op' 47

Chapter 8   Safe Landing 51

Chapter 9   Luxor 58

Chapter 10 Return to Aden 67

Chapter 11 As You Were 75

Chapter 12 Roll on the Boat 84

Part Two: A Testing Time

Map 2   The Western Desert 101

Chapter 13 Egypt and Preparation For War 103

Chapter 14 Into Battle: June 1940 112

Chapter 15 Strategic Withdrawal 119

Map 3   The Takoradi Route 127

Chapter 16 Fighter Pilot to Ferryman 128

Chapter 17 Attack! Attack! 139

Chapter 18 Down In The Desert 147

Chapter 19 Rescue Mission 152

Chapter 20 A Court Martial Offence 160

Chapter 21 Promotion 168

Chapter 22 To Aid The Greeks 174

Chapter 23 One Final Effort. 181

Chapter 24 Everyone Back 187

Part Three: Desperate Hours

Map 4   Iraq 201

Chapter 25 Convalescence 203

Chapter 26 Promotion Confirmed – And A Gong 211

Chapter 27 No. 4 F. T. S. Habbanyia 222

Chapter 28 Diplomatic Diversion 236

Chapter 29 The Nelson Touch 250

Chapter 30 New Planes For Old 262

Chapter 31 Help From India 274

Chapter 32 Final Preparations 282

Chapter 33 A Calculated Risk 293

Chapter 34 Pre-Emptive Strike 303

Chapter 35 Desperate Hours 313

Chapter 36 Final Account 327

             Happy Landings 339

C   )

Cyrenaica June 1940

It was the best time of the day – the silence which spread across the land in such dramatic contrast to the noise and bustle which had just ended was a welcome relief. It seemed as though the whole world was holding its breath. Yet it was but a brief respite while opposing forces waited quietly – recovering – gathering energy and resources to resume the onslaught the following day. Harry knew this but was nevertheless relaxed. It was cool now contrasting sharply with the searing heat of the day when every breath seemed barely enough to keep the lungs functioning and the body obeying the brain.

However the greatest change from day to night was in the sky. The stars in their thousands cast their twinkling light against the midnight dark of the heavens. They seemed so near one could almost reach out and touch them. Yet they were where they had always been – totally out of reach. Their magic still remained – and the silence.

It was in the solitude of such moments that Flying Officer Harry Nelson wondered which side God was really supporting in this conflict. Soon the desert night would be like ice and he would wake up in the morning cold and stiff until the heat of the new day warmed his bones and the whole process would begin anew. He had survived another day and for that he must be grateful. He wondered how long his luck would hold out. He already knew what the squadron would be doing as soon as it was light; the same as it had done yesterday and for several days before that, attacking Italian troop concentrations in Cyrenaica, just west of the Egyptian border with Libya.

1

In the air this was such an impersonal war with no immediate contact with the enemy, strangely similar to the mock battles in training. Shooting at a plane several hundred yards away was exciting yet remote. Harry knew that they had inflicted heavy casualties on the Italians and destroyed huge dumps of equipment. However it was not until they counted the bullet holes in their own aircraft or failed to meet some of their own comrades in the mess that the grim reality of war became personal.

On the ground in North Africa the British army was completely outnumbered when the Italians declared war on Britain in June 1940. In the air the Italian Air Force outnumbered the RAF several times over. Although the biplanes of both combatants were similar the Italian aircraft were somewhat faster than the British. Even so the advantage lay with the RAF. They had the element of surprise and their training had been far more thorough. However, British replacements were not readily available whereas the Italians could call up new machines and pilots from Sicily and Southern Italy. Because of the huge supplies held in readiness it was obvious that Mussolini was intent on capturing Egypt as quickly as possible. Some additional RAF squadrons had arrived to support the few already in the fray but without further supplies it was obvious that they could not continue their present onslaught much longer.

For all their global knowledge and the information readily available to them the British War Cabinet seemed to treat the war in the Western Desert as a side-show. After the fall of France the British were hard pressed to hold on to anything yet all the time calls were made for their help either in response to fulfilling a treaty obligation or because the German war machine continued to swallow up region after region. Now with the Italians in the conflict and Vichy France not remaining neutral but actively helping the Germans the British resolve was stretched to the limit.

Normal supply routes through the Mediterranean were difficult. Freighters ran the gauntlet of attacks by the Italian forces based in Libya and Sicily making the voyage through the Mediterranean hazardous. New supply routes from India, Australia, New Zealand and even South Africa were extremely long while munitions, food and personnel took weeks or even months to arrive. It was all such a mess. The troops on the ground and the RAF Units wherever they were deployed felt that they had a much more accurate picture of the situation than the War Office back in London where it seemed that theoretical forces on bits of paper were moved from one catastrophe to another.

Harry Nelson reckoned he was entitled to a bit of innocent treason in his thoughts while he tried to catch what sleep he could before the throb of engines and the chatter of machine guns once more destroyed the silence. What would the new day bring? Would they continue the advance to the west or make a strategic withdrawal to the east? His thoughts drifted back to the events which had brought him to this tent in the desert, hastily erected with many others and which formed his makeshift home for a few days or maybe just a few hours.

PART ONE

Preparation

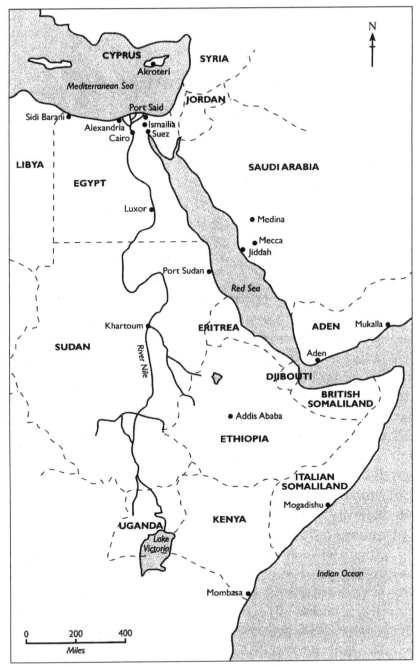

Map 1: The Red Sea and East Africa

THE NELSON TOUCH

CHAPTER 1

Manchester 1936

Everyone said how lucky he was to get a place at Manchester Medical School. Harry and the others who arrived in October, 1934 knew it was not luck but hard work especially over the past three years as the embryo doctors passed exam after exam in their progress through grammar school. The hectic first few weeks at University had given way to an acceptance of the hard slog ahead and at times their new life was even agreeable.

In 1936 and now well into his second year Harry Nelson and his immediate friends took more interest in the wider aspects of university life and like many young men aired their views in debating societies and wherever young people met and talked. In May of that year when the Italians entered Addis Ababa it served as just another reminder of the march of Fascism. He and a few of his close friends tried to transfer to Edinburgh University in order to join the University Air Squadron. No transfers were possible, but the naive and impressionable young men continued to be excited at the prospect of flying. With the impatience of youth they decided to leave university and apply to join the RAF. Much to their surprise the authorities made no serious objections and even promised to keep their places open for them. It was more surprising that all five were accepted by the RAF and in October that year instead of returning to Manchester they all reported for duty at RAF Uxbridge. Harry was 19 and the others the same age within a few months of each other. Their first few weeks were spent with 45 others of the new intake of pilots in training who, if successful, would pass out with the rank of Pilot Officer.

Harry Nelson had fair hair, blue eyes and an innocent open face which stayed with him as he grew older. He was about 5' 9" and by the time he was 19 had filled out nicely and more or less maintained his weight at 11 stone from then onwards. He had his share of troubles. His father died soon after Harry went to university and for a long time his young sister, Molly, was very ill. Although he took part in most games Harry would be the first to say he excelled at none. He began to do cross country running, not really because he liked it but because he wanted to keep fit especially at university where he spent so much time indoors. He was not a loner although he often seemed to prefer his own company. Yet when invited to join in with others he usually did so and in spite of rarely taking the initiative he was popular with most of his acquaintances and well liked.

Their first introduction to actual flying came twelve weeks later. It was too much to expect that the five friends would remain together although Harry, Tom Livingstone and George Lee did just that, being posted with nine others to RAF Cambridge. Alan Mackenzie and Sam Jordan, the other friends from Manchester were among the group who went to Donnington. The remainder of the initial intake were posted to flying schools at Grantham and Edinburgh, where they did far more flying than if any had managed to join the University Air Squadron.

Ahead of them stretched sixteen weeks of elementary flying, navigation and gunnery. This was done in the trainer workhorse of the RAF then in use. The Avro 504 J had a top speed of 95 mph and an endurance of only 3 hours and was almost a hangover from the Great War. Gradual improvements continued and a later version became the first RAF trainer to be fitted with blind flying instruments at the Central Flying School at Wittering. At the same time the trainee pilots continued to be indoctrinated into the very strict regime of becoming first class officers in the Royal Air

Force. 'You know', said Harry to no one in particular 'We've merely exchanged one set of exams and swotting for another.' Tom Livingstone agreed adding 'Yes, but if we fail here we can always return to Med. School sooner rather than later.'

At Cambridge the initial barriers of meeting new people had not taken long to be broken down. By now all the intake knew they had in their midst three budding doctors as well as two trainee solicitors, an ex-librarian and a college lecturer. One young man was the son of an Air Vice- Marshall and he was given a hard time by most of the training staff from the corporal armourer to the Station Warrant Officer. Two others were cousins, related by marriage to the proprietors of a chain of hardware stores. Another was an ex-policeman who after only six months in that force had decided that catching criminals was not the life for him. The last of their special friends in this intake, Arthur Knowles, remained something of a mystery and seems to have tried his hand at many things. He was obviously quite intelligent although he appeared not to have any formal qualifications. Nevertheless he sat the RAF entrance exam and passed easily.

Great emphasis was placed on sports and team games for the potential pilots while actual flying took second place at least for the first few months. Indeed, during the first few weeks Harry and his comrades learned more about keeping the machines airworthy than they did in actually flying them. Once flying had actually started they spent at least fifteen hours in the air before any of the new pilots flew solo. Even after having achieved that milestone they were not permitted to do much solo flying. It was back to careful coaching by their flying instructors to put into practice the navigation they had learned in the classroom.

The countryside around the aerodrome stretched for miles in a complex patchwork of fields and for the most part it was flat. The land itself showed almost black where it had been ploughed. A few lazy rivers carved their ways to the North Sea and everywhere there were canals for irrigation or drainage. Far away on the Suffolk coast the waves gently rolled in and out. In Norfolk it was much the same but here the Broads cut large lakes into the low lying country where occasionally the young pilots and hoards of holiday makers spent lazy days in the summer months. The cross country flights did not cover great distances and they usually consisted of a triangular course. Setting out from base to a point some 60 miles away the pilots would identify some feature on the ground and turn onto another course for a turning point some 40 miles away. From there the final leg would be back to base, the whole flight having taken no more than one and a half hours. The complexity of the rail and road system in England was demonstrated in these cross country exercises. So many features seemed to be duplicated, for example, where railways crossed roads, that at first the novice pilots felt that they would never master map reading. However, rivers, a few small lakes, the canals and some acres of woodland helped them to find their way around the countryside eventually.

With the coming of the New Year there was a flurry of activity. Fresh instructors arrived and a more advanced type of aircraft. The Avro Tutor was a newer version of the old trainer with a new Lynx engine of 180 hp which gave it a top speed of 120 mph. The second stage of the race to get their wings began. No reason was given for this new impetus. The Spanish Civil War was still in progress and rumours began to circulate that the British would be dragged into it.

The dangers of flying were brought home to all by a dramatic accident which happened in full view of everyone on the aerodrome. During a somewhat longer cross country exercise in which two pupil pilots were flying solo the wind direction at base changed completely round. Only one of the pupils noticed this on his return. The second, flying the same course though in the opposite direction failed to notice the wind change as indicated by the windsock and they both came in to land at the same time but from different directions. R/T not being available on these training planes it was the job of the ground control to fire a red Very light to warn approaching aircraft not to land. Only one pilot responded by attempting to go round again but before he could get clear the other aircraft flew straight into him. The planes crashed onto the aerodrome and both pilots were killed. It was several days before the black cloud of this incident lifted but the accident did serve as a salutary reminder to be extra vigilant at all times, more especially now that they were flying newer and more powerful machines.

At last the pupil pilots began flying what they called 'proper aeroplanes' which were in fact Hawker Harts. Originally designed as light day bombers they had a crew of two and with a 525 hp engine the top speed had been pushed up to 184 mph although their endurance in the air was only 3 hours. Tom Livingstone was the first of the group to fly solo in these machines and came back quite exhilarated from the experience. Approaching the airfield on his first solo landing he decided to extend the flight by going round again. Opening the throttle the engine responded immediately and he continued on the circuit, came down on his second approach and executed a perfect three point landing. He later explained to his instructor that his first approach didn't seem quite right but everyone knew why he'd done it, merely to extend his first solo flight.

Tom came from Musselburg. Occasionally and then usually for effect he spoke in a broad Scots accent although he had long since lost his native brogue. He was much the same build as Harry but had slightly darker hair leaning towards red though anyone who called him 'Ginger' experienced a tongue lashing out of all proportion to the implied nickname. He and Harry were often together, partly because they had the same instructor and partly because they had also been paired in practical sessions at medical school.

Much of their free time away from flying or classroom work was spent in games. However at the weekends it was the usual practice for them to go into Cambridge and compete with the university undergraduates for dancing partners at the local dance halls. Disagreements between the two main groups were frowned on by the university and the RAF although quarrels inevitably arose not necessarily always over girls. Tom, the quiet Scot could always be relied upon to step into any unpleasant argument and to break it up, barely raising his voice. George Lee, at over six feet and weighing over 15 stone was the quiet giant, rarely needing to say anything to restore calm.

CHAPTER 2

Flying Badge October 1937

The time passed quickly. They were all becoming more proficient in flying, navigation and gunnery as the first part of their advanced course drew to its close. The highlight was a dinner-dance before going home on leave for seven days. Following this short break they were all posted to the next station for the final part of their pilot training. If successful they would be awarded their 'Wings', correctly called in RAF parlance the Flying Badge.

The new aircraft which they had to fly after this leave were more powerful than the Avros and Harts in which they had become embryo pilots. Even so these Hawker Hinds were not much faster than the Harts although the engines were rated with a higher horsepower. Rumours of new single wing monoplanes spread throughout the mess but contained only a minute element of truth. The trainees, a few at a time were taken up for a short flight in a visiting Anson. True it was a single wing aeroplane but it had two engines and was no faster than the planes they had already been flying.

Sammy Jordan now back with the others from his initial training at Donnington was the first to appreciate that they might be experiencing a subtle form of psychology by dangling before them the possibility of becoming bomber pilots instead of the fighter pilots they had all assumed would be their role. Sure enough the next day they were asked to complete a questionnaire designed to show what type of aircraft they would prefer to fly, fighters or bombers. For the first time they were shown a film of the various types of aircraft at present in service, mostly with squadrons at home although a few were shown abroad and in glamorous settings throughout the Mediterranean and even further to the east. Nothing was ever heard about the results of the questionnaire or their preferences but maybe the seeds had been sown.

Sam Jordan came from London. While Harry could be described as well built Sam, by contrast was positively thin. Although only an inch shorter but with a much paler complexion he really looked undernourished. His black hair only served to accentuate the contrast. He was not a Cockney but could put on that accent at the drop of a hat. He knew all their peculiar sayings, their rhyming slang and their songs. Towards the end of their first year at university when concerts were being arranged he often performed and when, later, Harry volunteered to play the piano to accompany him their friendship was forged.

They hit it off at once and were a huge success at every party they attended. Sam had a wealth of stories, all with a grain of truth though Harry suspected that most were embroidered from Sam's fertile imagination.

Their training continued at a fairly leisurely pace on the Hinds and Harts with an occasional return to the old faithful Hawker Audax which Harry was to encounter later in his RAF postings overseas. At last the great day dawned for their passing out parade. It was held on a somewhat windy day with everyone in their best blue. Invited family members and friends sat on chairs placed in five ascending steps on a raised platform so that everyone could see the proceedings. The RAF band played a series of marches while a detachment of airmen marched and counter-marched prior to the presentation ceremony.

When this began the band played popular dance and light classical music and as each man's name was called out the band reduced the volume until he had been presented with his 'Wings'. As each candidate returned to his place so the music became louder until the next name was called. It was an impeccable piece of conducting. A short speech by the Commanding Officer followed the presentations and the whole company was invited to retire inside a hanger which had been specially cleaned. Each new pilot took his friends and family to one of the small tables set out at regular intervals. Tea, small sandwiches and even smaller cakes were then served with remarkable efficiency by the mess staff and the whole affair took on the semblance of a refined social gathering. For those who wished to remain there was also a dinner at 7.30 followed by a dance before families and friends dispersed at 11.30.

The following day the new pilots reported to the adjutant's office where they were given ten days' leave and told to what station they would be posted. Harry and George Lee were to go overseas to Kenya. Tom Livingstone and Sam Jordan were also posted overseas, to Aden. Arthur Knowles was posted to Ismailia. Three others went to Somaliland on the east coast of Africa and the remainder received home postings. Cyril Richardson and Arthur Osbourne went to Wittering to train as flying instructors.

After a hectic ten days' leave which went all too quickly and yet another medical, followed by various inoculations Harry and George waited at Tilbury for a ship. George Lee was born on a farm a few miles east of Norwich. He was the proverbial gentle giant at just over six feet tall and weighed in excess of fifteen stone. When the RAF medics first examined him they were concerned that his size would make him unsuitable for flying. Nobody argued with George although it was not just his size which may have put off would be aggressors. He had such a friendly disposition it was difficult to pick a quarrel with him.

From a distance it looked as though he was bald but close up he had very fine blond hair which he kept very short. When he first appeared in flying kit he looked huge. On one occasion as a joke his instructor pointed to a Wellesly bomber which had landed the previous night implying that he was too big to fit into the small training aircraft. George had endured all this before and started walking towards the large aircraft knowing this was not intended. Even the instructor appreciated that his joke had misfired.

George and Harry compared notes regarding their recent leave. Apart from being in different towns each had been remarkably similar, doing the rounds to say goodbye to aunts, uncles and cousins, families and friends. If they kept their promises to write to each and everyone it was obvious they would have little spare time to pursue any activity other than correspondence once they had settled in at their new station.

After waiting a week Harry and George finally set sail for Gibraltar on the first leg of their journey. Once having cleared the Thames estuary the ship was virtually on its own as it headed briefly into the North Sea before turning to starboard on its voyage down the English Channel. During summer holidays Harry had been to France a couple of times on a paddle steamer. Now going down the channel he experienced the full force of the choppy seas that can occur at any time of the year in this busy waterway. Having reached the most westerly part of France the ship headed almost due south across the Bay of Biscay which remained remarkably calm. Much later they waited with other vessels outside the port of Lisbon The Second Officer of their ship asked the RAF men if they'd like to accompany him ashore for a few hours. It seems that his sister had married a Portuguese Immigration Officer and when time permitted he visited her.

Harry and George were glad of the excuse to go ashore and once there Grahame Boulton telephoned his sister to warn her of additional guests. A slow ride on the tram up the long gradient brought them almost to the top of the hills overlooking the Tagus River. A short walk brought them to a pleasant villa and from there they could see the vast array of ships far below. Eleanor greeted her brother and was obviously pleased to see him yet welcomed the RAF men almost as long lost friends. Later Grahame revealed that she was always pleased to see people from England although such visits made her a bit weepy. They spent some time in the pleasant courtyard of the villa sipping refreshing drinks before the evening meal. As the sun set and it became cooler outside they went out onto the veranda and into the garden. All too soon it was time to return to the ship.

A day later they reached Gibraltar. 'It's not a bad life.' ventured George. 'We're seeing a bit more of the world each day and there's more to come.' Two days later the ship set out on the long voyage through the Mediterranean to Alexandria. It had taken them three weeks and they were still almost 1500 miles from Kenya. Two days later a lumbering Vickers Valentia transport plane ferried them on the final leg and they arrived at the main RAF station worn out and feeling anything but the so called elite of the RAF.

Having settled into the peacetime activities of the RAF overseas George and Harry soon found time hanging on their hands. This was their first operational station but they soon got to grips with their new aircraft. These planes were also manufactured by the Hawker company. An improved Kestrel engine increased the maximum speed to 223 mph. Even though flying each day they still seemed to have plenty of time on their hands. The sports, station dances, mess nights, standing patrols and war games still left a lot of hours to be filled. Harry wrote home for some of his medical textbooks and suggested that if his mother wished to send something special on birthdays and for Christmas new editions of some of the standard medical texts would be very welcome.

For their first break from RAF duties the two friends spent the time on the coast at Mombassa. On their next long leave they managed to get a flight in an RAF transport to a reserve airfield out in the bush and saw the Owen Falls at Lake Victoria. After only six months in Kenya they were both posted to Somaliland where they met up with some of their former comrades. There seemed to be no reason for this sudden move. Strategic posts had been created throughout the world to protect British interests, especially those in the Mediterranean and the Middle East. Suez at one end of the Red Sea and Aden at the other provided strong points and refuelling depots to guard this vital waterway.

In East Africa bases in Kenya and Somaliland guarded the routes to India and the Far East. The British Mandate in Egypt and Jordan took a great many resources while the agreement with Iraq allowed the RAF to have bases at Habbaniya and Shaibah near Basra. There was also for a time a base at Mosul near the oil fields, north of the Iraqi capital. Sadly, most lacked modern equipment in planes, tanks and guns and in some cases even personnel to man them adequately.

In British Somaliland the routine for the RAF was much as it had been in Kenya. Here though they were much closer to the Italian forces which had only recently subdued Abyssinia and were now making overtures to expand from Italian Somaliland into that part controlled by Britain. Routine patrols sent up to show the flag often met Italian aircraft on similar duties though so far no incidents had occurred. After they had been there about three months even these encounters ceased and the pilots in the RAF were left with a good deal of time on their hands.

Visiting aircraft en route to India and beyond and those returning to the UK often stopped off at the RAF base. Some stayed only to refuel. Others stayed overnight and even longer. It became the norm for any different type of visiting aircraft to take the resident pilots on a short flight. The station commander was much in favour of this unofficial arrangement and was usually among the first to try out any new type of plane. He actively encouraged all his pilots to fly as many different types of aircraft as possible. To date there had been no accidents while everyone benefited. The visiting pilots and crews liked the arrangement because they enjoyed the best food the station could offer while the station pilots gained valuable flying experience.

Like most C.O.s, Roger Braithwaite had on his charge a separate aeroplane which he could use for communications or small ferrying trips. No one enquired too closely how he had managed to obtain an almost new Airspeed Oxford, a twin-engined aircraft that had only entered the RAF in 1937 and which was used later as an advanced trainer. Wing Commander Braithwaite encouraged all his pilots to fly it but with a range of only 925 miles it had limited use in the long distances between RAF stations overseas. This was in addition to the Hawker Hart which most RAF stations overseas had on their strength as a relatively fast communications plane.

Harry often included little sketches of places he had visited in his letters to his sister and in reply, in her bold upright writing she kept him informed of local events. His mother's letters were much more personal. She invariably wrote of forthcoming marriages or births and frequently reminded him to write to various girl friends she had approved of during his adolescence. Harry merely put these reminders down to her being an incurable romantic. However when she questioned him in succeeding letters regarding his present female friends he was forced into creating imaginary girl friends and then had to continue the deception for some time. In the end he felt obliged to 'borrow' the less amorous adventures related by P/O Middleton, a pleasant and handsome new arrival who seemed to have a string of female companions. No one really believed his stories although everyone listened to the accounts of his conquests.

CHAPTER 3

Another Posting: Aden

Having served in Somaliland for eight months Harry Nelson, now promoted to Flying Officer, was posted, again with George, this time to Aden. He had only been there a day when Sam Jordan arrived back from leave. Almost at the same time Alan Mackenzie, Arthur Knowles and Tom Livingstone flew in from Ismailia having also been posted back to Aden. So for the first time since attending their 'wings' parade the old friends were back together. They greeted each other warmly until Sam managed to catch the eyes of all but Harry and he in unison with the others executed low bows and grovelling motions as they saluted the new Flying Officer. Harry laughed but hastened to assure them that their own promotion must surely be on the way soon.

He took an interest in each place he visited, a hang-over from the days when he used to go on holiday with his parents and sister Molly. At Aden he had no need to look up the local history. A few days after they had all settled in the new pilots were summoned to the C.O.s office for an informal chat. Wing Commander Kenneth Brandon welcomed them and put them at their ease with his first few words. 'Nice to have some new blood on the station. I'll gradually get to know you all. First I want to fill you in about Aden, why we're here and what we must do.'

They listened intently as he explained in an interesting though brief narrative. 'Aden was previously under Turkish rule but is now under British protection. We show the flag, are on reasonably good terms with the local ruler and our purpose is generally to demonstrate the British way of life.

Sometime during the last ten years Yemeni irregulars attacked Aden, when No. 8 Squadron, flying DH9As operated against them. Then a couple of years later, equipped with Fairey 111fs the same squadron was in action against the same lot. From then on its been as peaceful as it gets out here.'

He went on. 'In 1935 when the Italians in Somaliland invaded Abyssinia we weren't sure what to expect. We had a whole host of squadrons drafted in and even had 203 Squadron of Short Singapore flying boats. We also had two additional squadrons from England. Fortunately nothing came of it as far as we were concerned and by August the same year we were back to just one squadron, Number 8. Any questions?'

'Just one, Sir.' Harry explained that in Somaliland they had occasionally seen Italian aircraft on patrol. 'Do they ever come this side of the Red Sea?'

'Not so far. It's difficult to anticipate what's likely to happen. For years the whole of the Middle East has been in turmoil. Every so often dissenters break into open revolt and then settle down again usually after a few RAF raids. I'm sure they just try out our strength to see how far we are prepared to go. Nothing much changes. We do what we're told and don't take sides. The League of Nations in its wisdom carved up the map and gave various regions to be policed by us and the French. The Italians did their own carving and nobody took any notice.'

The history lesson was drawing to its close. 'One final point. We hear talk of marvellous, fast new monoplanes but so far no one east of Gib. has seen them. In the meantime all of you will be expected to keep your hand in flying my Maggie. It's a good little plane. Over the next few weeks I'll take you all up and once you've gone solo if ever we get some monoplanes the change over won't be so great. Thank you gentlemen. Let's go and have a drink before dinner and tomorrow it's back to work.'

In Europe a non-aggression pact signed between Russia and Poland relieved the growing tension somewhat. A similar pact between France and Germany removed the threat of war for the foreseeable future. In the Middle East and in northern India dissident tribesmen continued to show their grievances by occasional uprisings. Some of the older and more experienced RAF pilots now based at Aden told of bombing raids carried out in previous years especially on the North West Frontier. They were glad now to be in the relative safety of Aden. In recent years, unable to afford large numbers of ground troops, the British Government saved millions of pounds by employing a small RAF force to police huge areas and keep the tribesmen in check. Although it could not really be proved it was generally thought that both Russia and China cast envious eyes over India and took every opportunity to rouse local tribes against the British rule.

Those RAF pilots were generally not happy with that type of policing. It seemed that when orders came to attack the insurgents many senior Air Force commanders first carried out leaflet raids to warn of potential bombing raids if the tribesmen did not toe the line. Inevitably a few rebel leaders ignored these friendly warnings and as a consequence attacks were carried out with varying degrees of success. The one good thing which came out of these policing activities was that a few RAF pilots gained considerable flying experience. On the downside the raids promoted enormous resentment against Britain for years to come. In the Aden Protectorate the locals did not appreciate that Britain was acting as policeman for the League of Nations and periodically attacked the British garrison whom they saw as interlopers.

The immediate area around Aden, some 47 square miles, was virtually administered by the RAF. The land beyond and mainly to the east, although nominally under British protection was largely unknown to the British garrison. For the moment all was quiet and life for the RAF station continued more or less peacefully. For the pilots it meant keeping their hands in with flying, bombing and gunnery practice with the occasional navigation exercise. Horse riding, polo and other sports in which they all participated resulted in the occasional broken limb. When it became too hot they resorted to swimming in the warm sea during the day and cool drinks in the mess on the hot sultry nights. There were few hints that within months they would all be engulfed in a major war.

It was common knowledge on the station that Harry Nelson and his friends had cut short their medical training to join the Air Force and the C.O. put their limited medical knowledge to good use. Like most RAF stations, Aden was more or less self sufficient and equipped with sufficient resources to withstand a lengthy siege. Under the watchful eye of the Medical Officer, Harry and his friends were invited to help out at the sick bay. With the M.O., Sqn/Ldr Carter, acting as their supervisor they agreed to provide additional help if needed, one of them being on call at the sick bay a week at a time. They were rarely called upon to assist apart from two occasions when the station suffered a number of fever attacks and a few of the senior medical staff and most of the orderlies were stricken low.

To their credit the pilots knuckled down and at one point they were all on duty at the hospital until things returned to normal. Although they made light of the emergency they were relieved when everyone was back at their proper posts. Harry summed up their collective thoughts. 'There you are lads. Now aren't you glad you joined as pilots. We now have the best of both worlds.'

The station commander, Kenneth Brandon, had as his personal plane a Miles Magister trainer. He used it mainly to keep his hand in. Fitted with dual control he took a personal interest in teaching all his pilots how to fly the single engined monoplane. Even though its top speed was only 130 mph it was a rugged little aircraft with full aerobatic capabilities. It was in service with the RAF towards the end of 1937 as a basic trainer although far more pilots trained on the Tiger Moth.

The RAF station was several miles to the west of Aden. Almost due south were the extensive harbour installations which had served as a coaling station for many years. Now it also had huge oil storage facilities as well as warehouses for all manner of provisions. Wing Commander Brandon made sure he was on good terms with harbour authorities, the local police chief and the Major in charge of the small detachment of British troops.

Although the RAF station provided sufficient recreational facilities to satisfy most personnel the bright lights of Aden attracted everyone at some time or other. While most of the shops, bars and cafes were run by local people there were a few places run by ex pats. One bar was run by a Scot, an ex navy stoker who had called at the port on numerous occasions during his time with the fleet. He had married a local girl and while his bar could only be described as a dive it was always full. A more up market bar was managed by two ex army captains and in addition to drinks could be relied upon to provide quite passable English meals. There were also three small hotels, the Palace, the Southern and the Queen Victoria all owned by Molly Andrews, the wife of a sea captain who had long since departed this earth. Her favourite was the Palace and it was here that she resided leaving the others to be managed by a French woman at the Southern and an Italian, so called princess, at the Queen Victoria.

CHAPTER 4

A New Toy

The days passed slowly into weeks in the uneventful routine of a peace time RAF station overseas. Then a series of totally unrelated events occurred which had a great impact on Harry Nelson. He and two other pilots from C Flight had been out on a patrol. Along the coast for about 50 miles they had flown east, then south for half an hour, then west for the same time. Finally, turning north, if everything went to plan they should end up more or less within sight of base. During this practice of a square search they noted down the shipping they came across, the size and likely destination. They flew at varying heights from 5000 feet down to 250 feet above the waves and practised open and close formation flying.

Their first task on reaching base was to fly just to the north where they practised runs over their bombing targets. On each of four runs a plane released one bomb at a time, the first from 1000 feet. On each subsequent run a bomb was released 250 feet lower so that the final attack was carried out at 250 feet above the target. Checkers on the ground awarded marks for the closest hits and there were usually private wagers among the pilots taking part.

Usually after such an exercise the pilots returned to base and parked the aircraft outside their flight hanger. The ground staff then manhandled them inside to carry out maintenance checks. On this particular occasion there had been a small fire inside the hanger and until it was deemed safe they were directed to the maintenance hanger. The doors were wide open and almost invited inspection. Inside this slightly larger building Harry noted an odd assortment of spares for a variety of aircraft and in one corner shrouded in an enormous dust sheet he could see the outline of a twin engined low wing monoplane.

'Whose is that,' he enquired from W/O O'Brien

'That Sir, belongs to his Nibs.' was the quick reply.

'Who do you mean?'

'I don't know his correct title but we call him the King of Aden. He's the local ruler here.

Intrigued, Harry said, 'May I have a look?'

'Don't see why not. Corporal, get someone to help you take off these covers.'

In a few minutes this order had been carried out. Standing before him Harry saw his very first Airspeed Envoy – a silver, twin engined monoplane with a thin blue flash painted all along the fuselage enhancing its streamlined shape.

'There you are Sir.' W/O O'Brien held out a key. 'Have a look inside but please lock the door when you leave and give the key back to me.'

'Thanks.'

Inside Harry was surprised how roomy it was – seating for eight and in a small closed off section at the front seats for two pilots side by side. Apart from the passenger seats he thought the cockpit looked familiar and as he locked up and returned the key W/O O'Brien volunteered the information. 'This is really the civil version of the Oxford. Have you ever flown one?'

'Well yes. We had an Oxford on my previous station. Nice aircraft. Thanks for letting me see it.'

It was the practice for the C.O. to hold a mess dinner once every two months for his officers, who together with the very few wives and girl friends on the station brought a semblance of social life to it in stark contrast to the harsh environment. About once every six months an invitation was extended to a few of the local dignitaries – a deliberate policy to ensure that the local population, while being protected by the British might also feel that they were part of the larger family if they so wished.

A year earlier the Emir of Aden had persuaded the C.O. to house and maintain his aircraft. He was an accomplished pilot and in exchange for looking after the Airspeed Envoy he allowed the C.O. to use it whenever he wished. A signal sent to London and later a full report had ultimately been successful in achieving this goodwill gesture. Indeed the Emir and Wing Commander Brandon got on well with each other and often flew together. Harry took the first opportunity to ask the C.O. if he could accompany him next time he flew the Envoy.

'Yes. Why not. It's due for its 500 service next week and I always do a flight test afterwards. It's part of the deal with the Emir and it keeps my hand in. I'll give him a ring beforehand. He may like to accompany us but in any case I must get your name put on the list of those who fly in it.

So the following week Harry Nelson sat in the right hand seat of the Envoy while the C.O. took the controls in the pilot's seat on the left. The Emir could not join them but gave permission for Harry to go in his place. They taxied out, turned into wind and as he steadily opened the throttle the aircraft gathered speed until with an almost imperceptible bump it became airborne and climbed steadily into the clear sky. Selecting the undercarriage lever up the wheels retracted into the wings and after leaving the circuit they continued to climb up to 5000 feet. With a

cruising speed of 155 it was slower than the Oxford he had flown recently in Kenya but otherwise seemed almost the same aircraft. After ten minutes flying, over the intercom. the C.O. said. 'O.K. Harry. You have control.'

'Thank you Sir.' came the instant reply as he took over the controls.

'Just get the feel of it, no sharp manoeuvres, just gentle turns. Get the feel of the throttles and move them together.

Now, keeping a sharp lookout, increase the revs on both engines and make a gentle turn to port. Keep the nose level. Check with the horizon.'

The C.O. nodded his approval as Harry carried out these instructions.

'O.K. Straighten out, reduce the revs, get the speed down to 120. Once there alter the trim of the aircraft and tighten the throttle nut.'

'Very easy aircraft to handle Sir. What else can we try?'

'Ease back on the throttles, allow the nose to drop and descend about 500 feet a minute. When you reach 3000 feet, level off and maintain the speed at 120 mph.'

'O.K. Now climb back up to 5000 feet. Increase the throttle setting and climb at 95 mph. Level out at 5000 feet, make a gentle turn to the right and we'll go back to base.'

Once this height had been gained the C.O. said, 'I have control. This little plane will fly quite well on one engine.' The pilot demonstrated this by pulling back the throttle of the starboard engine and went on to alter the rudder trim by winding a small handle to ease the pressure required to keep the plane straight and level. The C.O. continued to check the flying capabilities of the Emir's plane on the way back to base. Once in the aerodrome circuit he gave a running commentary of what he was doing and made a perfect landing on the two main wheels and as the speed fell away the tail wheel gently touched the ground. Having raised the flaps he taxied the aircraft back to the hanger, switched off the engines and both pilots got out of the aircraft.

W/O O'Brien approached and the C.O. said 'She's O.K. I'll sign the log book and you can telephone the Emir that his aircraft's still in one piece and ready for him.'

This was the longest time Harry had been with the C.O. and felt that he should make some comment. 'Thanks very much Sir. From now on its twins for me.'

'In your dreams Son. But I will try to get permission for you to learn on this and be responsible for it. I'll ask the Emir next time I see him.'

'Thank you Sir.'

As good as his word the C.O. gave Harry a few more flying lessons and in just over nine hours he was allowed complete charge of the aircraft, in effect flying solo. Protocol demanded that he could not be strictly alone as the aircraft did not belong to the RAF. At the next mess dinner for local dignitaries Harry was introduced to the Emir as another pilot capable of flying the Envoy. They took to each other at once. Harry learned that the Emir had been educated in England and subsequently been to Sandhurst. It was two years after leaving the army establishment before he was able to fly but this was in his blood and he longed to be able to do more of it. With the death of his father responsibility for his people prevented him from being too foolhardy. He had married young, had three daughters and finally a son, now ten years old.

Although he had not realised it the C.O. had spoken privately to the Emir about Harry's flying ability. As his entourage were leaving after dinner the Emir asked to speak to Harry and they arranged to meet at the airfield the following week and fly to Al Mukalla, just over 300 miles along the coast in the Gulf of Aden and almost into so called 'enemy territory'. 'I've already got approval from your C.O. so if its alright with you I'll be here after breakfast next Tuesday.' Harry was pleased even flattered and could hardly explain that he had already arranged to go swimming on the coast a lot nearer home. The swimming would have to wait.

The airfield at Aden was about 20 miles inland from the coast and about the same distance to the west of Aden itself. The coastal strip was pleasant enough yet only a few miles inland the rocky, arid region stretched for miles to the east. Further inland the mountains rose to over 3000 feet and the peaks were in excess of 6000 feet. The whole area seemed remote and inhospitable – certainly no place for a plane to run out of fuel. Even if a landing could be effected and even if the pilot was alive it would be unlikely for him to survive the harsh conditions and make it back to civilization. Yet on the few occasions that he had flown close to the Hadramaut Range Harry had seen small groups of nomads. He looked forward with anticipation to a pleasant flight eastwards with the Emir and wondered what could be the purpose of the visit.

Early the following morning he asked Wing Commander Brandon if he might be permitted to have a few more flights in the Envoy before Tuesday and was pleased when the C.O. agreed and said he could fit in two more sessions.

The trip to Al Mukalla turned out to be something of a mystery. The Emir flew most of the way but asked Harry to land the plane while he changed into more traditional dress. Once on the ground Harry was escorted to the small building which did duty as airfield control, local shop, petrol station and police station. A smartly dressed man greeted the Emir. He carried a brief case in one hand while the other fingered a wicked looking ceremonial dagger. Harry suspected he also carried a pistol. The Emir told Harry he'd be about an hour and asked him to have the plane refuelled and ready to take off when he returned. The Emir waved goodby and was driven off towards the mountains inland.

The captain in charge of the airfield provided lunch while they waited but when the Emir was half an hour overdue Harry became concerned and asked about the delay.

'Don't worry. He will come when he comes. There have been problems.'

Harry persisted. 'I have to get back to my duties at Aden. Is there no way that we can find out what's keeping him. I need to let my C.O. know I may be late.'

'We are not on the telephone here. That's why it was necessary for the Emir to come in person to deal with quite a serious matter.'

With that Harry had to be content. The Emir arrived 15 minutes later, driving himself. He apologised for the delay and within five minutes they were on their way home with Harry at the controls. No explanation was forthcoming about the trip so Harry remained silent.

CHAPTER 5

Operation 'Expedience'

The station medical officer, Sqn/Ldr Michael Carter, returned to Aden from a short leave at Mombassa, immediately went down with a virulent fever and put himself in quarantine just to be on the safe side. He was quite advanced in his knowledge and management of tropical diseases and had fitted out a small building as an isolation unit about 50 yards from the main hospital. He had installed a series of doors and extractor fans to ensure a good degree of protection for the nursing staff who all had to be covered up when attending to patients. In a sense it was an experimental unit and though time consuming for the staff seemed to work efficiently in combating the spread of diseases.

Michael Carter was visited by Harry and a few other officers who spoke to him through glass panels. He seemed to be getting better almost at once before a relapse set in and it became obvious that the fever would need to run its course before the patient was finally restored to health and fit for duty. In spite of fairly rigorous precautions to prevent the spread of this disease several members of the medical staff and a few others on the station were affected. It put considerable pressure on the relatively small RAF hospital.

Then the Emir's son showed similar symptoms and when his own doctor couldn't pin point the trouble he turned to the RAF station for advice, unaware of the problems it was facing. Nevertheless the C.O. discussed over the phone the boy's symptoms, explained the situation at the camp and promised to speak to the S.M.O. Michael Carter, in spite of his own low state of health, realized the symptoms were not

34

exactly similar and asked Harry if he could go and have a look at the Emir's son.

Harry was not too happy about this additional responsibility, pointing out that although he was glad to help out with the crisis at the station he was not qualified as a locum doctor. He suggested they sought advice from another RAF station or army unit. In the end The C.O. persuaded Harry to go, see the boy and report back. Harry asked endless questions when he saw his young patient, checked temperature, pulse, breathing and the boy's general health. He left soon after, deciding he must get confirmation from Sqn/Ldr Carter before he gave his diagnosis.

'I think he's got appendicitis. In fact although I've only ever seen two cases and they were three years ago I'm pretty sure.'

'I think you're right son. From what I've been told and from your observation I'm sure you're correct. There's no way I can do anything about it whatever the Old Man suggests. It's an easy operation but I can hardly stand up let alone remove an appendix. It's a pity because he's such a nice fellow – the Emir I mean. It would be good to help him especially as the boy is his only son and heir.'

After more discussion Harry suggested that the C.O. should try to get the boy on the next boat going up the Red Sea to Cairo or even on the next RAF transport. Hasty enquiries revealed that no plane or ship was due for another week but so that the patient might be more comfortable in hospital he was moved the next morning to the RAF sick bay and put in a small ward on his own. The nursing staff saw their patient was getting worse. High temperature, pain and sallow complexion, all indicated a very sick young boy. Harry, who saw him in the evening, became concerned, and asked to see the C.O.

He didn't stand on ceremony. 'Sir. That boy is going to die unless we operate within the next 24 hours. Sometimes an appendicitis will carry on for a few days gradually getting worse. This one has accelerated and if it bursts the boy will die. I think there's only one thing for it. Someone will have to fly him to Alex. and hope to get there in time.'

Kenneth Brandon made his decision. Calling his adjutant he explained what he wanted him to do. 'Thomas, can you organise an emergency operation at Alex. Explain our problems and that we must try to help the Emir. Pull out all the stops. In the meantime I'll get hold of the Emir and see if this is what he wants. He may decide not to go but let us have everything in place and ready.'

'Yes Sir. Leave it with me. If its O.K. we'll need to get clearance from a couple of stations en route.'

'Right. Harry can file the flight plan and then hand it over to you to get the O.K. Alright Harry?'

'Yes Sir. What plane will you use?'

'Harry I can't order you but I'd like you to go along. I doubt if the Emir will want to fly but he'll definitely want to go. How soon can you be ready? We'll use his plane. I'm sure there will be no problem.'

'Well Sir. I'm happy to go along but I need Sam Jordan as co-pilot. If the Emir's not willing for him to take off and land I could do so. In any case we'd need to share the flying and as you know Sam has already flown Oxfords. It's a straight forward flight though we'll need to refuel on the way.' Glancing at the map which hung on a wall in the office he took a few minutes to calculate the distance as about 1600 miles. Can we land at Jiddah? That's 705 miles. Then on to Luxor in Egypt. Can we refuel there? That's 505 miles. The final leg to Alex is a short one, some 405 miles.' Harry was voicing out loud the thoughts that were crowding his mind.

'Yes. I can't see any problems there. Can you organise that Thomas?' The C.O. replied urgently.

'Yes. Is that the lot Sir? I'll get cracking and let you know when you get back with the Emir.'

'Just let me know if there are problems. Actually in spite of

36

the seriousness of the trip it will be a useful exercise. Can I leave you to organise the plane Harry.'

'Yes Sir. On my way. I'll tell Sam Jordan. One thing more. Could you ask at Jiddah and Luxor if they would be prepared to do the op. if necessary?'

Harry stayed a few minutes in the office working out the flight plan. It was not quite the straightforward route he had thought. True, he could fly almost in a straight line to Jiddah but first he would have to climb well over 6000 feet in order to clear the mountains north of Aden. To avoid them he could fly almost due west and then follow the shore of the Red Sea all the way. This would put almost an extra 200 miles on the journey. Balancing the time to reach a safe height and fuel consumption on the direct route against the much longer way he finally decided to fly over the mountain range. A visit to the Met Office to get the wind and likely conditions for the next 24 hours confirmed this as the better option. Allowing at least half an hour for each refuelling stop he reckoned that the first leg would take four hours and forty minutes, the second about three hours twenty minutes and the final leg, by far the shortest about two hours forty minutes. Although the wind might change during the 1600 mile trip, if it continued from the south for only part of the trip it would reduce the time even further. Even so it would be almost twelve hours before the patient could be in hospital.

Harry called in at the mess on the way to the large hanger. He explained as quickly as possible what was needed and Sam agreed without a moment's hesitation.

'Haven't been to Alex yet. Any chance of staying over to the next day?

'Not sure but if everything goes well I'm sure we can wangle an extra day.'

Warrant Officer O'Brien put forward no objections when Harry explained what was needed. He wanted three seats on the starboard side of the Envoy removed and a bench fitted in place with a mattress and straps to hold the patient secure while in flight. The ground staff worked quickly and almost silently as the seats were removed. Six steel brackets quickly took their place and were bolted into position and within the next thirty minutes a bed board with straps was in place and a mattress had been borrowed from sick bay. It was W/O O'Brien who suggested a supply of fresh water and rations for two days might also come in handy and before the C.O. came down to see what progress had been made these were on board, the plane had been wheeled out and refuelled. Harry explained the minor modifications regarding the Emir's plane and went on to demonstrate that all could be restored with little effort.

As far as the pilots were concerned it would be Sam Jordan who would take off while Harry did the navigating with occasional checks on the patient. Word had soon got round the station and a male nurse volunteered to accompany them and brought his emergency medical equipment and supplies. Harry had agreed to this in the C.O.s absence, who when he was told of the arrangement not only agreed but was obviously well pleased at the way everyone had helped. As soon as he arrived the Emir was informed of the arrangements in hand, the modification to his plane and that two pilots and a medical orderly would accompany him. He greeted Harry warmly and thanked everyone who was helping though all could see his main concern was for his son and heir.

When everything was ready W/O O'Brien remembered that beneath the two front seats on the port side were two compact medical kits. These were apparently checked twice a year. The first contained a supply of splints, a small cylinder of oxygen, various bandages, ointments and drugs. The second pack also contained an oxygen cylinder, a fairly basic kit of surgical instruments, together with a mask and a quantity of chloroform, ether, cocaine and syringes.

'Who on earth equipped this kite with a medical kit like this?' Harry asked the W.O.

'I think it was the Emir's First Minister. Apparently he doesn't like him flying anyway so they came to this peculiar compromise. The Emir does fly but always has the medical kit on board though there's never a doctor so I don't know what good they'd be.'

By 9.30 all was ready with the plane waiting outside the hanger. It was a beautiful day, not too hot as yet and they would have the benefit of a following wind from the south adding at least another 20 mph to the speed over the ground. Soon the ambulance arrived with the patient and another ten minutes went by as he was transferred and settled into his makeshift bed and strapped in. There had been some concern as to how the stretcher could be manhandled through the door. They need not have worried. The young prince was picked up bodily by his personal bodyguard and carried gently into the cabin and placed on the bed. He was a huge man who stood head and shoulders above everyone else in the party. As soon as his young charge had been settled in the big man sat in a seat on the port side making it obvious that he would also be travelling to Alex.

Sam Jordan and Cpl Jenkins, the orderly, were introduced to the Emir who settled down just behind the pilot and behind him the bodyguard. The next seat contained supplies for the trip securely strapped in, leaving the orderly the remaining seat on either the port or starboard side. The C.O. came along the cabin saying his goodbyes and said he would let Jiddah know that because of the helpful wind to expect them a little earlier. At 9.45 the plane taxied slowly into wind and took off. This would be the longest time Harry had flown in the Envoy though on this occasion he would share the duties with Sam Jordan. The first leg to Jiddah on the east coast of the Red Sea would take almost five hours, but with the two pilots alternately flying the plane and navigating there should be no fatigue problem. In fact the navigation merely consisted of watching the land and the sea pass slowly below as they headed north. An occasional check on drift allowed Harry to correct for the actual wind direction. Between them they had agreed to pilot for an hour at a time and as the plane was fitted with dual control there was no need for them to change places.

At 6500 feet there was still some turbulence from the effects of the land and the sea as the sun gradually heated up the earth so Sam took the plane up another 1500 feet. The first leg went well and with the benefit of the following wind in a little over four hours from take off they were approaching Jiddah where they intended to have a quick meal while the plane was refuelled.

Just to the south they could see crowds of people making their way northwards. The pilgrims were on their way to Jiddah where they would turn towards the east and head for Mecca to visit the birthplace of Mohammad. 'Infidel that you are there's no way they would let you in there.' Sam spoke into the intercom. to Harry though anyone on board would have heard him if they had been plugged in.

At Jiddah, Harry and Sam went for a meal first. As soon as they had returned to the aircraft the Emir and the RAF orderly went off while Harry checked on the patient who seemed to be fairly comfortable although he became concerned when he realised how high his temperature had risen. The bodyguard steadfastly refused to leave his charge. Harry put on what he assumed to be his best bedside manner and tried to reassure his patient that all would be well within a few hours.

The stop-over took longer than they had anticipated but soon they were on their way once more. Harry went back to speak to the Emir.

'Sir. I know you are worried about your son. I too am very concerned. I think we should try to get him into hospital at Luxor. His temperature is now very high and in my opinion his appendix needs to be removed as soon as possible. I don't think we should wait until we reach Alex. Although facilities are not quite as good at Luxor I think in an emergency you take what is available. I'm going to relieve Sam and do a bit of piloting.'

'Yes. Thank you.'

Back in the cockpit Harry voiced his concern about the patient and suggested an increase in airspeed to get there sooner. Sam was not too keen. 'We can cruise along nicely at 155. The maximum is only 180 and we shouldn't do that for long so all things considered we'll not gain very much on this shorter leg. At the higher speed we'll use a lot more fuel and the flight may not be so comfortable for the patient.'

'O.K. Sam. Would you mind having a look at the kid and let me know what you think.'

'Sure.' Sam left his seat and went aft to look in on the patient In the cabin Harry checked his instruments and the course. Flying at 8000 feet there was little turbulence and at this altitude as the Red Sea passed slowly below he could make out quite clearly the land on both sides of this stretch of water. In the distance the sea, the land and the horizon merged into one indistinct haze. For the moment Harry was alone in the cockpit. The steady beat of the engines was a comforting sound and just for a moment the reason for this flight became secondary in his mind as he absorbed the tranquil view. His reverie was cut short by the return of Sam who confirmed his worst fears.

'You're right. Our young patient is very ill. I think as soon as we are within R/T range of Luxor we should warn them of an emergency operation they will have to perform as soon as the plane touches down.'

'Thanks Sam. I agree. Did you tell the Emir.'

'No but I'm sure he knows.'

CHAPTER 6

Decision at Gunpoint

An hour and a half went by. The contours of the land below changed little as each check point came into view. From this height they could see both banks of the Red Sea and make out the small scattered places along the shores where a few nomadic people eked out an existence from the land. Sam had just remarked how inviting it looked from this distance when the medical orderly came forward to the pilots and shouted his concern for the patient above the noise of the engines.

'I'm sorry to interrupt Sir but I think you should come and see. He's burning up and seems to be very weak now.'

'Right Corporal. I'll come back.'

Harry followed the corporal as they made their way back to the patient. One look was enough for Harry to realise that the crisis was about to be reached. He plugged his R/T jack into a socket and spoke over the intercom. to the Emir, echoing the Corporal's remarks.

'Sir. I'm afraid your son's appendix is likely to burst soon. If this happens he may die and I'm afraid there's nothing we can do. We are too far to turn back to Jiddah and in any case they do not have the facilities. Also we are still too far away from Luxor even if we fly at maximum speed and we're also too far away for any clear R/T to advise them. I thought I should let you know.'

'Yes I understand and so would my son if he could speak.' The Emir continued, 'I know you have medical training. It is asking a lot from you but would you please operate on my son.'

Harry did not reply for what seemed like a long time. Much later when he recalled this moment he realised he had been anticipating such a request and had wondered what his answer would be. Now he replied, 'Sir I have had only two years at medical school and that was several years ago. I have at least another two to complete and possibly more before I qualify. In any case I have no experience as a surgeon. I really do understand your concern but I have to say No.'

'I thought that might be your answer. Can you just let him die without even trying? What can I offer you?'

'Nothing Sir. I would do it if at all possible. Do you not believe in Allah? Surely if he needs your son to live he will survive.' Harry wondered if he'd been too personal, impertinent even, though the Emir seemed not to notice.

'I have been brought up in the faith, of course, but when it comes to the crunch it has to be man's decision and at present this is mine. I beg you to perform the operation.' The Emir's voice was calm.

'I cannot do it. I have no experience. We do not have the facilities and even if we did I could be struck off the register even before I became a doctor.'

Harry felt helpless. He took a deep breath, sensing that the Emir was at his wits end. 'Let me discuss it with Sam Jordan. He's also had as much medical training as I have .....' The Emir nodded and Harry moved quickly forward.

'We have a problem.'

'You have a problem. Keep me out of it. I heard it all of course.'

'The boy's worse and I think he's going to die. I think the Emir's quite determined that I should do the op. He's quite calm at the moment. Almost too calm – probably at breaking point.'

Sam came straight to the point. 'You can never trust these people. They turn on you at the slightest whim. I wouldn't trust him an inch.'

'He's concerned for his son's life. There's no way we can reach a hospital in time. Go and have another look at him please Sam .....' Harry broke off abruptly realising that if the Emir had still got his R/T on he would have heard everything.

'O.K. if you think it'll do any good.' Sam released his straps and moved back towards the patient leaving Harry to pilot the plane. Checking pulse, temperature and general condition of the boy Sam was forced to the same conclusion and quickly returned to the cockpit to confirm his assessment.

'You're right Harry. It's curtains for the lad.' If nothing else Sam always spoke his mind. In situations like this there was little room for niceties.

As soon as Sam was at the controls Harry made his way back and spoke to the Emir. 'We both agree. There's little we can do except to press on and hope we are in time. We are both very sorry.'

'How do you respond to threats?' asked the Emir, looking Harry calmly in the eye.

'I suppose it depends on the circumstances.' replied Harry and glancing down found himself looking at a revolver touching his stomach, then back to the cold eyes of the Emir who said in a clear steady voice.

'This is not what I intended. I believe we are friends but if it comes to my son's life or yours you will lose.'

Harry sensed this was no idle threat. He also knew that the Emir had not gone over the edge. He realised with deadly calm it was his only way of bringing home to Harry just how much his son meant to him.

Harry summoned all the strength he could muster to control the fear mounting within him as he replied with a voice he scarcely recognised as his own. 'Sir there is no need for this and I'm sorry you felt it necessary. I will forget it and the orderly here will never speak of it. Now put your gun away or better still give it to me.'

'If I do will you operate?'

'You know I can't.'

'Then my threat remains.'

'From my point of view,' replied Harry, 'it is entirely unethical and being threatened makes it even worse. Behaving like this makes you no better than a common criminal or one of those tribesmen who attacked you three years ago. You showed considerable bravery then.'

Harry hoped he sounded firm and sure of himself though in reality he was beginning to feel afraid of the outcome. He realised he must continue in this vein. If he once weakened he would be finished. He heard the stifled intake of breath from the orderly during this strangely calm exchange of words. Harry sensed a lessening in the tension at the back of the plane and without another word the Emir reversed the revolver and handed it to Harry.

'Thank you Sir.'

'Tell me Harry. What are his chances.'

'To be honest very little although I'm no expert. I only know what I've read and I've only ever seen two cases.'

'Tell me,' went on the Emir now speaking quite deliberately, 'do you think you could perform the operation.'

'Possibly but we do not have the facilities and if we hit an air pocket at the wrong time with a scalpel in my hand it could be all over in any case. An appendix is only a small piece of tissue but when it becomes inflamed it can increase tremendously in size. In that case there is very little room for error.

'I'm begging you. It's a chance against no chance.

'You can't Sir,' called the orderly. 'You know you can't.'

Harry's mind raced. Every instinct told him 'No'. At the same time a small voice inside seemed to suggest he should ignore such instincts. 'After all', he thought, 'If I do nothing I'm sure the boy will die. If I operate I might just save him. All life is a gamble.' He tried to visualise the last time he had seen this operation performed. It had been in a well equipped

45

hospital by a surgeon who had done it hundreds of times. Here inside a noisy aircraft it was asking a lot. His mind made up Harry replied to the corporal's comment.

'I know I shouldn't.' replied Harry. 'However in certain circumstances one may have to look the other way or in this case concentrate. Will you help, Corporal. What have we got? Any chloroform, swabs, cloth, scalpels, needles and thread?'

'I've got my usual first aid kit that I always carry. There's more in the medical equipment under the seat. Let me take a look. Begging your pardon Sir. I think you're mad.'

'So do I. So do I.' replied Harry. 'We'll keep this to ourselves, shall we? Go along and tell the pilot to climb to 12000 feet, reduce speed to 110 mph and keep the plane as steady as possible, oh and tell him I'm going to operate with your help.'

'I heard all that Harry. I agree with the Corporal. I think you're both mad. For what its worth I'd probably do the same. Good luck.'

CHAPTER 7

First 'Op'

Turning to the Emir Harry said, 'While we're waiting Sir will you sign a document absolving me, Sam Jordan and Cpl Jenkins from any blame whatever the outcome of the operation?'

'Gladly.' came the immediate response as the Emir took out from his briefcase a sheet of headed notepaper and wrote,

To whom it may concern

F/O Harry Nelson operated on my son, Crown Prince Emil, who was diagnosed as having an inflamed appendix. He was assisted by Corporal Jenkins while F/O Sam Jordan continued to pilot and navigate the plane during this vital operation to save my son's life. I freely absolve them from any blame arising from this operation. Furthermore I freely admit that I threatened to kill Harry Nelson if he did not operate. Although I handed over my weapon before he agreed to operate I still accept responsibility for this unusual state of affairs. My only excuse is my love for my son. This operation is his only hope of surviving.

Signed. Abdul Emil, Emir of Aden Protectorate.'

'There, Harry. Is that in order?'

Harry read the letter and commented, 'Yes Sir. Thank you. Let's hope it goes well'

At last all was ready. Harry called over the intercom. to Sam. 'O.K. Sam. This is it. Everything is calm back here. The threat is no longer a problem. I alone will be responsible for the operation. Thanks old boy. Keep her as steady as you can.'

'Wilco.' came the only reply.

Harry's hands were a lot steadier than he thought they would be. With the orderly's help he carefully undressed the patient and prepared the instruments, thankful that at least the corporal had assisted at a number of operations at the base hospital. It was only later that he heard this was the first appendix operation and certainly the youngest patient in Cpl Jenkins' career. He was surprised by the comprehensive nature of the medical equipment carried in the plane. There was even a small tank for sterilising instruments. With the corporal's help they were all assembled. Even so it was a good fifteen minutes before Harry was ready. Putting off the first incision as long as possible he read again the instructions regarding body weight and anaesthesia dosage

With the patient sedated and breathing almost normally he could delay no longer. He asked the Emir to go forward and tell Sam that he was about to start the operation. This simple expedient gave him time to collect his thoughts and at the same time the Emir did not see him begin the operation. Carefully following the mark he had drawn on the small body he made the first incision and then cut deeply into the flesh with the scalpel. There was not as much blood as he had expected and with the orderly keeping the flesh apart and cleaning up as he probed even deeper it was five minutes before he was able to examine the offending appendix.

He called quietly to the Emir to see the problem and then with a deft cut removed the appendix quickly. The corporal cleaned away the blood and Harry commenced the process of sewing the ends of the wound together. He thought he heard the patient moan, glanced at the corporal who gave him a reassuring nod and carried on with the next stitch. He felt utterly calm, quite unlike he had expected to be and he wondered at his own composure. The thought suddenly flashed through his mind, "Fools rush in where angels fear to tread". It was at this point that his calmness left him.

'Would you like me to finish off Sir?'

'Yes. Thanks. Have you done this before?'

'No Sir. Only fingers and small surface wounds but I guess its much the same.'

'You'll either get a medal for this or the chop.'

'I'm glad I was here. Anyway Sir I guess we're both in the same boat.'

'I guess we are. I think we'd both better write up a report about this incident when we get down.'

Harry left the orderly to complete the closing of the wound, clean the instruments and generally tidy up. It wasn't until he sat down in the spare seat and the corporal joined him later that he began to shake and felt perspiration forming on his forehead. He saw that Jenkins was in much the same state. The Emir smiled his thanks, too overcome with emotion to speak and went to be with his son now sleeping peacefully. A little later the Emir appeared at Harry's side offering a small flask.

'One swallow and give one to the Corporal.'

Harry took the proffered flask and put it to his lips. The liquid burned his mouth and the back of his throat as he swallowed.

'Good God Sir. Did you make this yourself?'

'It's a family recipe, we aren't allowed alcohol you know.'

Five minutes later Harry was feeling more like his old self and went forward to take up his seat next to Sam.

'That was probably touch and go for a minute but I think the worst is over now.'

'Congratulations Harry. Does anyone need to know about this?'

'Well a few people do already. I think we'll have to tell the hospital as they are expecting to do the op. themselves.

'Harry, take over here for a moment will you. Get your hand in again with flying this kite. It will help steady your nerves doing something more normal.'

'Thanks. Have a look at the lad will you?'

Sam moved quickly to the rear of the plane. Over the intercom. he had heard the conversation that went on and could well imagine the strain Harry and Jenkins had been under. He was tempted to warn the Emir not to pull a stroke like that again. In the end he merely said how glad he was that everything seemed to have gone well.

CHAPTER 8

Safe Landing

In another half hour and they were able to pick out the landmarks as they approached Luxor. In a few more miles they were within R/T range of the airfield and Sam called them on the radio and received their reply.

'You are clear to land. The wind is from 050 at 20 mph. Taxi to the control tower.'

'Thank you. Could you please have an ambulance standing by to take a patient to hospital.'

'Understood. Wilco. Out.'

'Not by a long way you don't, old son.' muttered Sam under his breath.

'You O.K. to land Harry?'

'Yes thanks. I was sweating like a pig but I'm alright now. Let's get down and have a beer'

Losing height at a steady rate, Harry brought the plane lower, joined the circuit and made a wheeled landing keeping the power on. Once the main wheels had touched he cut the throttles and allowed the tail wheel to touch the ground. The heat of the day had created a heat haze which hit them as they approached the control tower.

An ambulance appeared quickly and within minutes the patient and the Emir had been whisked away before they had time to explain that the operation had already taken place.

Just before the ambulance had appeared the Emir had shaken hands with the two pilots and the corporal. 'Let me do the talking. Come to the hospital later if you wish. I cannot thank all of you enough.'

'We'll stay here for a while, get in touch with Aden and then go for a meal.'

Harry was content to remain in the relative cool of the control tower while Sam supervised the refuelling and signed the necessary documents. It seemed that the Emir and his plane had been there before. In fact the station welcomed him not only as a friendly dignitary but as a benefactor. He usually gave a large sum of money for use on station comforts and insisted it did not all go to the officers mess.

Sam returned to the control tower and accepted gratefully the cool drink which Harry had waiting for him. He approached the control officer. 'May I telephone Aden?'

'Not necessary. Signal's already been sent. It's normal procedure.'

'Yes. I appreciate that but F/O Nelson needs to speak to the C.O. there personally.'

'He'd better have a word with the duty officer, F/Lt Richards?'

Harry approached the duty officer. 'Good afternoon Sir. It's important that I contact my C.O. at Aden. Could you please ask him to come to the phone?'

'Bit unusual, but alright. I'll call you when we've located him.'

Ten minutes later he called Harry over and handed him the telephone. 'Good afternoon Sir. F/O Nelson here. Our patient has gone off to sick bay. There was an incident on the way here which I don't feel able to tell you about on the phone. However I will write a full report.'

'Are you alright.'

'Yes Sir.'

'And Jordan?'

'Yes, we're both alright Sir. Something very unusual happened on the way and I was afraid word might get back to you before we could report it in person.'

'O.K. Son. When are you coming back?'

'Not sure Sir. We think we'll have a meal then go to the hospital. If the Emir wants to come back with us we'll leave tomorrow morning.'

'Alright. Keep me posted. You haven't pranged the Emir's plane have you?'

'No, nothing like that. I think he's quite happy about the outcome. Goodbye Sir.'

'Nice work Harry.' was Sam's comment who had been listening to Harry's end of the conversation. 'The fewer people who know what actually happened the better. I wonder if we can manage a couple of days here. Let's see if His Nibs wants to stay until his son is able to be moved again.'

It was already beginning to get dark and Corporal Jenkins said he was going over to the sick bay to see if he knew anyone there. This reminded the two pilots that they should also find accommodation for the night. The Duty Officer asked them to sign the register, booked them in for an evening meal and then found them beds for the night in adjoining rooms in one of the unoccupied married quarters.

Once having bathed and made themselves presentable they joined other officers for drinks before going into dinner. It was not a formal evening meal so the officers were dressed in a variety of clothes from uniforms to civilian dress. They had all witnessed the arrival of the Airspeed Envoy and were surprised when the two Air Force officers had stepped down from the plane. Without giving too much away Harry explained how they came to be flying the Emir's private plane. His explanation seemed to be accepted and Sam remarked quietly, 'There you are. No problem. Stick as close to the truth as possible and you'll get away with it every time.'

After dinner the two men excused themselves and made their way over to the sick bay to visit the patient and see the Emir. They were met outside by Corporal Jenkins.

'He's not here Sir. As a civilian it was thought best to take him into town.'

'So, where's the patient and the Emir?'

'Gone to the civvy hospital in town.'

'Well I suppose we'd better go and see what's what. Do you want to come along Jenkins.'

'Yes please. The hospital is on the far side of town from here. We'll need a taxi.'

'You know this place do you?'

'Yes. I was stationed here before I came to Aden, but all my mates seem to have been posted elsewhere. Anyway I managed to get a meal and a bed for the night. I'll get a cab then shall I?'

'Yes. Thanks.' They left the corporal, who obviously knew his way around, to organise a local taxi.

It was fifteen minutes before it arrived and during that time the last of the sun had completely gone and it was getting cooler by the minute. The flickering headlights of the taxi as it made its way along the road heralded its approach and with little more than a nod from the driver the three men got in and were soon heading towards the town. Jenkins sat in the front with the driver while Sam and Harry suffered the experience of being bounced about on the back seat while being driven at breakneck speed towards the lights of Luxor.

The driver seemed unaware of the bad condition of the road and never attempted to avoid the pot holes that came at regular intervals. 'I've heard about these drivers.' said Sam. 'They have two speeds. Flat out and stop.' Apart from that one comment there was silence as both pilots mulled over the events of the day The corporal carried on an animated conversation with the driver but whatever was said was drowned out by the engine noise. The traffic in the centre of the town would have forced any normal driver to slow down. Not this one. He carried on at the same speed, merely weaving in and out of the traffic until they came to a screeching stop outside the hospital.

'Have you got any money Sir? He wants two pounds. I suggest you give him ten shillings.'

Sam handed over a ten shilling note to the corporal who passed it quickly to the driver. He nodded and scarcely giving his passengers time to get out he put the car in gear and raced off towards the centre of town.

'Are they all like that?' enquired Harry.

'More or less, Sir. The quicker they get one job done the sooner they can get on with the next.'

'If they live long enough.' was Sam's comment.

All three walked up the steps of the hospital, opened the door and stepped into the immaculate reception area. A young English nurse, obviously just going on duty, followed them up the steps and as they stopped to get their bearings she asked if she could help.

'Well yes. Thank you. We're hoping to see the Emir of Aden and his son who is a patient here.'

She turned, and pointing to a notice 'Enquiries' pressed a bell. Almost immediately the door slid to one side and a porter asked how he could help. The nurse asked where the patient could be located and after consulting a list he told her. Suggesting that all three follow her as she was going there herself she walked towards the far end of the wide corridor. At the end she turned to the left and stopped outside double doors. They swung inwards to reveal a typical small ward and nursing station.

'Wait just inside please and I'll see if he can receive visitors.' She smiled again, not at the officers but at the corporal. 'Are you Corporal Jenkins?'

'Yes.'

'Do you remember me?'

'Of course, although its some time since I was in Luxor and you look different.'

Then she was away enquiring about the patient. Sam took the opportunity to ask Jenkins if he really did know the nurse.

'Yes Sir. The face is familiar but I can't remember her name.'

'Look at her name badge when she comes back or you'll be in trouble'

The nurse, now without her outdoor cloak, returned and ushered them into the ward. 'The Emir is here and wishes to see you. His son is quite comfortable and now sleeping peacefully. I gather he had an emergency operation.' She took in the glances which passed between the three men but was unaware of their significance.

'Don't stay too long. If the patient wakes up please call me.'

Sam, Harry and Jenkins walked slowly into the ward and the Emir rose from a chair and came to meet them. 'So glad you could come. Have you eaten?'

'Yes thank you Sir. Is the Prince alright?'

'No problem thanks to you three.'

They all wanted to know what story the Emir had told the hospital.

'I merely told the doctor that, after his operation, I had been concerned because my son didn't seem to be recovering as quickly as I thought he should. He examined him thoroughly, said there was a little redness and bruising around the wound but that everything appeared to be normal and that we should let nature take its course. The only real comment he made was that two of the stitches appeared to be botched while the remainder were quite professional. He probably decided I was a doting father, worrying unnecessarily and let it go at that.'

It was all that Sam could do to restrain his laughter at the thought of Harry's poor stitches. Cpl Jenkins looked suitably pleased with himself while Harry felt himself getting redder. The Emir took all of this in and motioned them outside. Once in the main corridor he spoke quietly in a confidential manner.

'All is well. I will, of course, tell your Commanding Officer exactly what happened but I hope no one else need know.'

With nods of approval all round he went on. 'I shall be staying in town with an old friend. Do you think you could all come to this address tomorrow about ten o'clock. By that time I shall have spoken to your C.O. and I shall have asked him if you can all stay at Luxor for a few days so that we can all return to Aden together. From what the doctor said my son should be able to travel in three or four days and after three weeks he should be up and about again.'

Thanking the Emir and taking the address of his friend they left the hospital and made their way on foot towards the town centre.

CHAPTER 9

Luxor

'Now then Jenkins. You've been here before. What can we do till bedtime?'

'Well Sir. Strictly speaking I shouldn't be with you when not on duty but I do know a club where we can get a drink and there's dancing. Everyone seems to gravitate there some time or other. Its called *The Oasis.*'

'Lead on.'

Once inside they were greeted by an usherette, scantily clothed, who took their hats, gave them three tickets and held out her hand for money. Sam looked at Jenkins who whispered 'Thirty bob should be enough' and so it was. Almost immediately they were ushered to a table and three cool drinks appeared and three glasses. A few couples were dancing on a small square in the middle of the room. All around were tables at which sat a variety of customers and once they had become accustomed to the smoke-filled room they could see that most were in uniform, either air force or army. At the far end a couple of native dancers performed their complicated dances though few people seemed to appreciate their efforts. The beers went down well and Sam wanted to have another. As if by magic it appeared and so did two others for Harry and the corporal.

'That's what I call service.' said Sam. 'When do we pay.'

'You already have Sir. Make these last and we don't need to buy any more.'

At half past ten Jenkins suggested they should make their way back to camp. 'If we go now we'll get a taxi. Any later they'll all be gone and we'll have to walk.'

Outside the cool night air hit them. The atmosphere inside the club seemed not to affect Jenkins but the two pilots were glad to get outside and breathe fresh air. Jenkins disappeared round the side of The Oasis and a few minutes later a taxi arrived with him sitting next to the driver and calling to them to hurry up. They reached the RAF station before 11 o'clock, not in the same taxi they had used earlier but one driven just as fast.

The next morning they managed to persuade the Duty Driver to take them in an RAF transport to the Emir at Al Bara, a building set amid a small oasis a short distance from the town. Once they had been ushered into the imposing courtyard the Emir came forward to meet them.

'I'm so glad you could come. Your C.O. has arranged for you to have three days leave. It will of course be deducted from your annual entitlement but it will not start until this morning and will not include the day it takes us to return to Aden. I hope this is acceptable to all three of you.'

With a chorus of murmured thanks they all moved out on to the terrace where cool drinks were served. The Emir again expressed his thanks for all that they had done for his son.

'I hope you will accept these little gifts in appreciation. They are of no great value but they are well crafted and are supposed to bring you good health and luck. They come with my grateful thanks. And now I would prefer no one refers to the incident ever again.'

He offered them each a piece of carved jade, wrapped in red velvet. To the corporal he gave a goat. Sam received a dog while Harry had a cat. Their stunned silence as they looked at the exquisite carvings was thanks enough for the Emir.

'I'm sure none of you brought enough money with you for this extended trip so I ask you accept a small token to tide you over. I want no protestation from any of you. Just make me happy by taking it.' To each he gave a small envelope.

'Now you are free to do whatever you wish for the next

three days. Abdul Allahamir, my driver, will take you into town or wherever you want to go. If you need to get in touch you may telephone me here or at the hospital. All being well we shall return to Aden on Thursday morning.'

They realised they were dismissed so with murmured thanks they took their leave. The car when it came round to the front of the building was a huge American Studebaker, painted bright yellow and its tyres had white walls. As soon as they were settled in the back it started off towards Luxor and they opened the envelopes to reveal they had each been given a hundred pounds. For the moment no one said anything. For once even Jenkins was speechless.

'Can we really accept this?' Sam wanted to know.

'I'm think we have to.' Harry answered. 'Although it's money it is a gift and it would be the height of bad manners to refuse. He gave his reasons for giving it. We'd better clear it with the C.O. when we get back.'

'Sir. May I make a suggestion.' Jenkins spoke for the first time. 'There is a shop in town which sells really good civvies. We can't go round town in uniform all day. There's also a tailor at the back of the shop and he'll alter anything which doesn't fit.'

Harry and Sam, happy for Jenkins to take charge, followed him into the shop. They spent the best part of an hour choosing light-weight suits, shirts, somewhat garish ties and light shoes. Only Sam's trousers needed to be taken in at the waist and the corporal's jacket sleeves shortened. While these alterations were carried out the three men wandered around the central part of Luxor and stopped off at a restaurant for a light lunch. It was 3 o'clock by the time they returned to the tailor to collect their clothes. They spent the hottest part of the day wandering round the bazaar and each purchased a few small gifts as souvenirs. They returned by taxi to camp in time for dinner. Thoughts concerning recent events were left unsaid. They each felt, if not a sense of guilt, a sense of unease at the secret they all shared. The two officers could discuss their feelings later but Corporal Jenkins, so close to the others in one sense felt isolated, knowing yet unable to share the secret with anyone else.

The next morning while having breakfast Sam was given a note. It was from Jenkins who was waiting outside. Sam went to look for him and didn't recognise him at first as he was wearing civilian clothes. Jenkins smiled and came straight to the point.

'Sorry to bother you Sir but I have a suggestion. When I was here before I never had enough money or the opportunity to visit the ruins at Thebes. Now I have and I wondered if you and F/O Nelson would like to come with me. It would make a nice day out and who knows when another opportunity will occur.'

He had obviously rehearsed what he needed to say and Sam thought that it was a good idea. He would have given his answer at once but felt he should consult Harry first in case he had some other suggestion.

'What's your Christian name, Jenkins?'

'Jonathan, but I'm usually called John or JJ. Why?'

'Well if we are going to spend all day together we can't go on calling you Cpl Jenkins and you can call us by our Christian names while we're here.'

'Thanks Sir. Sam. I can have a car in say an hour.'

Sam hurried back to the mess just as Harry was about to sit down to his breakfast.

'Right lad. Get that lot down as soon as possible. Put your civvies on and we're going out to see somebody's tomb at Thebes. We have a new friend called John who is at this very moment organising a taxi to take us out there for the day.'

Puzzled for a second or too Harry soon made the connection between their new friend and Jenkins. 'O.K. Give me a few minutes.'

'No real hurry. You've got at least half an hour. I'll tell

Jenkins to get a taxi now you've agreed and I understand we can get a meal out there. We deserve a day out.'

The day started well and for the moment was pleasantly warm. Cpl Jenkins, John, at least for the day, arrived actually driving an Austin 12 saloon. He grinned as he drew up outside the officers mess, got out and opened the rear door for them to get in. Once they were comfortable he let in the clutch and moved away. He handed over a street map, saying, 'I hope you don't mind. The route is pretty straightforward once we leave town. Could you get me to the place marked START while I make sure we miss the locals wandering all over the road.'

'Where did you get the car?'

'I've borrowed it from the bloke where we got the clothes. It cost £10 and we have to pay for the petrol. I expect he's hoping we'll hire it again.'

'Right. We'll settle up at the end of the day. Let us know if you want us to share the driving.'

After a few stops to avoid various carts, other forms of transport and pedestrians they were soon clear of the town and on their way to the Valley of the Kings. Signs already indicated they were heading in the right direction and quite soon they saw in the distance the first of the ruins. A huge towering building showed bright yellow in the sun. The immense size of the temple and the nearby columns surprised them all.

'I think if we want to do any sightseeing we'd better do it now before it gets too hot. I'll park the car and we can maybe join the next party of visitors. It's probably better to have a guide.'

They spent far too long looking over the ruins and it was almost 2 o'clock when they went to get some lunch. Jenkins who had never been there before seemed to know his way around remarkably well and suggested they go by car towards the river where it might be cooler and where there would be many more eating places. It was 4 o'clock before they had finished their leisurely lunch and decided to visit the museum of Tutankhamun. It was dark by the time they arrived back in Luxor and Harry suggested they should round off the day by having dinner at the most luxurious hotel in town.

'Our treat.' He explained to Jenkins that it would be a little thank you for a most interesting day. 'When do you have to take the car back?'

'Tomorrow will be alright. He's probably hoping we'll buy some more clothes.'

'Well we might. In any case we'd better get a small suitcase each. We can't go back wearing civvies and a case will be easier to stow in the plane when we return to our proper duties. Thanks very much John. See you tomorrow and we'll come into town with you.'

'Goodnight Sir, er, Harry. Sam.'

The two officers waved goodbye and grinned at each other.

'He's a cheeky bugger, but nice with it. He'll go a long way.'

'Yes I'm sure he will. It's going to be a bit awkward when we first get back to Aden.'

'I doubt it. Today was just a pleasant interlude. It'll be back to normal in two days. I don't think he'll take advantage.

'We'd better give the Emir a ring and visit the hospital to find out how the boy is.'

'O.K. We'll do that tomorrow when we take the car back.'

The next day was spent in Luxor after returning the car. They bought a few more shirts, sandals and a suitcase each and visited the bazaar for the last time. They went to the hospital in the afternoon and actually saw the young patient, now sitting up in bed and looking very much better. While there they telephoned the Emir who said he would call at their mess in the evening. Then it was back to the RAF station by taxi. Cpl Jenkins disappeared into the sick bay and the officers went to their mess.

During their last morning at Luxor they were invited to

watch a few practice races on the river between RAF rowing teams. The actual regatta took place in two weeks' time when units from the army would also compete. There were no local teams taking part but apparently the local population lined both sides of the Nile to watch the various races. The river was quite wide at this point and flowed quite swiftly, the waters still swollen by the winter rains high up in the mountains far to the south. The races were usually held in the morning leaving the midday period for a siesta.

As soon as the heat of the day became bearable a few parties would be held on river barges. However, Sam and Harry would not be able to stay for any of these. Cpl Jenkins volunteered to go in person to the hospital, ostensibly to make sure he had the necessary medical supplies for the return trip. Sam and Harry guessed his main reason was to see the nurse again. Their final afternoon at Luxor saw them checking over the plane and arranging for it to be stocked with provisions. The return flight was scheduled to start at 9 o'clock the next day.

The pilots wore their civilian clothes for the last time at dinner in the mess, stood drinks all round and were invited to return anytime. Cpl Jenkins did not return to camp until almost 11 p.m. First, at the hospital he saw the patient and the Emir who promised to telephone the officers if there was any change to the take-off time. Jenkins then enquired about nurse Betty Smith and was told she would be back on duty in the evening. He also managed to find out where she was billeted – now having placed her as one of his dancing partners when both were stationed at Luxor.

She apparently had no plans for the afternoon and early evening so Jenkins borrowed the car once more and together they drove out to Isna, a small town to the south. They chatted casually and when it appeared that he was apparently on speaking terms with the Emir she wanted to know more about how this came to be.

'Oh well. It was a bit of an emergency. The Emir didn't want to fly himself so the two pilots volunteered. I wanted a trip to Luxor see some old friends. It's as simple as that. I thought we'd go to the RAF hospital but he was transferred to yours otherwise I might never have seen you again.' Jenkins knew how to turn on the charm but he wasn't entirely sure that Betty was convinced with his answer. They got back to Luxor late in the afternoon, had a meal in the same hotel and he then drove her to her billet, waited while she changed and then took her to the hospital. It had been a pleasant afternoon for both and as they parted they exchanged addresses with a promise to write to each other. Over 900 miles separated them so once John was back in Aden the chance of them seeing each other was remote. Yet unknown to Jenkins he was to see Betty Smith again and that was to be quite soon.

He returned the car and decided to walk back to camp, setting off at a fast pace. He soon caught up with two other airmen trying to get back before their passes expired at 11 p.m. Jenkins explained he was at Luxor only until the following morning when he would be returning to Aden.

'What's it like there?'

'Hot,' was his brief reply. Feeling that it was a bit too brusque he went on to explain in more detail what it was like for a corporal in the medical corps of the RAF. The other airmen were both fitters and when they learned that he had arrived in the Airspeed Envoy they were really envious. Just at that moment a huge American car drove past and then stopped. The sole passenger wound down the window and called out.

'Is that you Corporal Jenkins?'

'Yes sir,' replied Jenkins immediately recognising the Emir.

'Want a lift back to camp?'

'Thank you Sir but I've got two friends with me.'

'Ask them to get in as well.'

So Jenkins sat in the back with the Emir. The other two squashed up together on the front seat next to a huge man who took up more than his share of the seat and whom Jenkins recognised as the Prince's bodyguard.

'Off tomorrow then Sir, back to Aden?' Jenkins posed the question though he already knew the answer.

'Yes. I thought I'd better come personally to see the Duty Officer or even the C.O. I come here once or twice a year so they know me fairly well.'

'Will you be flying the plane back Sir?'

'Oh no. I'll leave it to the proper pilots and I'll sit at the back with you and my son.'

The two airmen in front said nothing, surprised that the corporal, and a medical bod at that, should be on speaking terms with the Emir. They arrived at the gate with half an hour to spare and dropped off the airmen while the Emir continued on to the officers mess where he asked to see F/O Nelson or F/O Jordan.

'They're both here Sir. I'll go and get them.'

When they arrived the Emir was invited in but he declined saying he only wanted to confirm that they would be available to return to Aden next day.

'Yes everything is in order. It's already refuelled and we've arranged for rations for tomorrow so we can take off whenever you wish. We suggest not later than 9.00 as we'll most likely have a head wind. We could make a longer stopover at Jiddah for lunch and with a bit of luck be back in Aden before nightfall. Would you like us to do the piloting?' Harry had done all the talking.

'That sounds fine to me,' replied the Emir. 'Goodnight gentlemen. Till tomorrow.'

He was gone before they could say any more. Harry and Sam saw the huge figure of Abdul opening the door of the Studebaker. With scarcely a murmur the big car headed back towards the lights of Luxor.

'That's what I call travelling in style,' was Sam's final comment as they headed towards their bungalow and beds.

CHAPTER 10

Return to Aden

The Emir and his party arrived early and by 9 o'clock next morning the silver Airspeed Envoy was airborne with its full complement of pilots, passengers and the young patient. As before the bodyguard had lifted him into his bed and strapped him in. The big man was silent as usual, only a slight smile indicating the great relief he felt that the young prince was recovering and that they were going home.

Sam did the take-off and flew the aircraft for the first hour while Harry did the navigating with an occasional visit to the patient. He was content to leave him in the capable hands of Jenkins. Everyone seemed in a happier frame of mind. The thought of returning to familiar surroundings, the obvious feeling of relief that the operation had been successful and the knowledge that they all shared a secret seemed to lend an air of intimacy and trust.

The slight headwind was no more than 15 mph so the 505 miles to Jiddah was completed in three and a half hours. Instead of having lunch in the mess they opted to have the sandwiches and fruit they had brought with them so the two pilots joined the others in the main cabin. While the plane was being refuelled they poured out cups of coffee from the thermos flasks. By the time the ground staff had completed their tasks and the Emir had signed for the fuel they had almost finished their lunch. Harry took over the flying and headed due south on the longer leg of their journey home.

After an hour the pilots changed over duties and Harry did the navigating for an hour. He then went along to the Emir. 'I wonder if you'd like to navigate or pilot your aircraft. We still have the same head wind but we are covering the ground at something like 140 mph so we still have three hours to go.'

'Yes, I think I will. It will be good to stretch my legs.'

Without another word the Emir went forward, tapped Sam on the shoulder and settled himself into the other dual seat. 'O.K. Sam. I have control.'

Sam took over the flight plan and made the appropriate note regarding the change of pilots and entered the time. After an hour or so the Emir asked Sam to take over as pilot and indicated that he would navigate. He soon asked Sam to alter course by three degrees to starboard to take account of a slight change in wind direction. Later Sam told Harry he was sure this slight change was only intended to demonstrate that the Emir could also calculate drift and was able to use the small hand-held calculator.

The Emir returned to the rear of the plane after about two hours and Harry took his place in the cockpit. As soon as they were within R/T range Harry called up control and asked for permission to join the circuit and land.

'Welcome home stranger,' came the reply. 'You are clear to land. The wind is gusting at 30 mph mostly from the east at present 065 degrees. Please call when you are closer to base. Use your landing lights if necessary. Out.'

'Lazy buggers,' said Sam. 'Can't be bothered to set out a few goose lamps. What would they do if we hadn't got lights on board and we were an hour later. It would be dark by then. Never mind. I think we'll be there in time but I'll use the landing lights just for the hell of it.'

The next hour seemed to drag and as they got closer to Aden a few lights appeared on both shores of the Red Sea and they could see quite clearly two large ships both sailing northwards. Lights blazed out from every porthole and the promenade decks. A few minutes further on and they passed through a rain storm. Sam switched on the navigation lights and the cabin lights and for a while outside it was very gloomy and threatening until they came out of the rain belt.

'They could have warned us about that. Now we know why there won't be any landing lights. They don't want to get wet setting out the flare path.' The lights of Aden came into view and Sam called control again.

'Is it raining in your part of the world?'

'No. Not at present. With luck you'll be down before it hits us again. Wind direction as before. You are clear to land.'

'Roger. Out'

Sam joined the circuit. It was not really dark but on the final approach he switched on the landing lights. Two beams of light spread out, one from each wing of the aircraft and as the plane came lower showed the landing area quite clearly – highlighting every little bump in the slightly uneven ground. Once down, flaps were raised and Sam taxied slowly towards the control tower where an ambulance was already waiting. As soon as the patient, the medical orderly and the other passengers had left the aircraft Sam taxied to the large hanger and switched off the engines. He and Harry gathered together their belongings and walked back to the control tower.

By the time they had taken their parachutes to the flight room, returned to their rooms for a shower and then had a late dinner it was nine o'clock. The C. O. found them relaxing in the mess after he had spoken to the Emir. It seemed that few people, apart from those in their own flight were aware that the two pilots had been away from the base for almost a week. Wing Commander Brandon nodded briefly to them and asked them to see him the following afternoon. Although everything had gone well on the return flight it had been a long day so the two friends decided to have an early night.

After breakfast it was back to work with a vengeance. Three days earlier two new pilots had been posted to Aden and had both been assigned to C Flight. When they reported for duty

Sqd/Ldr Clarkson, the flight commander, introduced the newcomers and asked Sam and Harry to look after them.

'Will you take them out and show them the various landmarks – not that its easy to get lost around here but we don't want them straying into non-friendly territory. Do one flight this morning to the south across the water as far as Somaliland. When you get back to this side of the Red Sea fly eastwards for about a hundred miles and then back to base. This afternoon go north as far as Abha. Make sure they know the boundaries of Djibuti and Eritrea. Show them the bombing range and the emergency landing grounds. By the way, welcome home. I gather it was a successful trip.'

They realised they had been dismissed and away from the flight commander's hearing Sam said 'So it looks as though nobody knows the whole story.'

'Let's keep it that way,' replied Harry.

Sqd/Ldr Clarkson came out into the flight room. 'The C.O.'s just been on the blower. He wants to see both of you at 14.00 hours today so you'd better make your afternoon flights at 15.00 or whenever you get back from seeing the Old Man.

Sam and P/O Fuller walked out to their aircraft and as soon as they were strapped in the mechanics started the engines of both planes. Sam led, taxiing to the take off path, swinging the aircraft to the left and then to the right to make sure nothing was in front of the aircraft. The nose of the Fury stuck up high into the air and prevented a forward view while still on the ground. The new pilot followed and once on the take off path into wind Sam gave the signal, eased the throttle forward and as the aircraft began to roll along the ground he gave more throttle until flying speed was reached and the little aircraft became airborne. Fuller followed straight away and within a few minutes Harry and his new pilot, P/O Tompkins, joined them.

As soon as they were settled into their patrol Harry pointed out the various landmarks. The important borders between

French possessions in east Africa, those of Italy and the British protectorates were not clearly defined so it was always a good policy to keep well within one's own region. If a pilot was forced to make an emergency landing in foreign territory he was advised to stay with his machine and offer no resistance. All the aircraft in the squadron had been fitted with R/T. One channel allowed them to speak to base if they were within a few miles. Another ensured that no one apart from aircraft fitted with the same crystal could hear the conversation. In this way pilots in the same flight could talk to each other without interrupting signals from the ground station. Pilots could switch channels but were advised to keep messages brief and to listen out mainly on the station wave length.

Over the R/T Harry spoke to the other planes, urging the new pilots to make sure they never crossed the Straits of Bab el Mandeb into Djibouti or worse still into Italian Somaliland, both on the western side of the Red Sea. The British protectorate Somaliland stuck out as a peninsula into the Arabian Sea. People here would welcome British pilots but further south was the Italian Somaliland and no one knew what reception would await any downed British pilot. The four planes then flew back across the Gulf of Aden until they saw the rocky coast of Yemen when they turned to port and flew back to base.

Once back at base Sam and Harry headed for the mess for a quick midday meal, a change and a rest before going to keep their appointment with the C.O. He actually caught up with them as they were leaving the mess. 'Sorry, but something's come up. Could you both come and see me before dinner. If you're late down don't bother to change. Just come in your khaki drill.'

'If the C.O. says do this you do it.' was Sam's only comment. Harry merely nodded in agreement.

The afternoon session with the new pilots went much as planned. They flew north pointing out the various landmarks, the emergency landing grounds and making sure they knew not to land in Saudi Arabia without permission and not to land in Eritrea at all. When at last the day's flying was completed Sam and Harry walked together to the C.O.s office. They waited in the ante-room for his present visitor to leave. The door opened and the Medical Officer emerged, shaking a finger at them in mock admonition while the Duty Corporal went in to see the C.O.

'O.K. ask them to come in. You can go off now Corporal and get your evening meal.'

The C.O. welcomed them extending his hand to each in turn, not bothering to return their salutes. 'Come and sit down and tell me all about your trip to Luxor. I've had a look at your report and that of Cpl Jenkins. I've also seen the Emir and got his story. Anything you want to add – either of you?'

'No Sir. Not a thing. We're just glad it all turned out well.' Harry replied. 'No Sir. Not a thing. Its best forgotten.' added Sam.

'I'm glad you feel like that. It must have been a bit hairy at the time.'

'You're not kidding. You probably know that Jenkins does much neater stitches than I do.' Harry felt he should get this out of the way and possibly lighten whatever tension might arise.

'Yes. I even heard about that. But apart from that did you have a good time?'

'Well yes. We saw a few things we never expected to see and the Emir was very generous.'

'Do you have a copy of your report?'

'No Sir.' Harry sensed where these questions might be leading.

'Look. Sam and Harry. Its up to you if you want to take this any further. However if you decide to let it remain a closed book I know the Emir would be grateful.'

'Yes. We understand.' replied Harry. 'You're suggesting we turn a blind eye to what happened.'

Sam heard Harry's words and try as he would he could not stop the smile which turned into a chuckle. The C.O. watching both pilots closely for their reaction could not ignore the amusement on Sam's face. 'What's so funny?' he demanded.

'I'm sorry Sir but do you realise you've just asked Nelson to turn a blind eye. It's a pity his name is not Horatio although Harry does begin with 'H'.

'I see,' said the C.O., laughing. 'History repeating itself. You're not related to him are you Harry.'

'Not as far as I know Sir.' replied Harry. 'But I'm sure he would approve and maybe issue his famous signal.'

'Alright. I'm going to destroy this report. We will never need to speak of it again. The only other man on the station who knows about it is the M.O. and his only comment was "Well done". So to both of you my personal thanks for a job well done. Now shall we go in to dinner?'

On that happy note the incident was closed.

'Just one thing Sir. What about Corporal Jenkins?'

'Oh he's quite happy to forget about the whole thing. I may as well tell you what I have in mind for him. I gather from the M.O. he's quite a bright lad and dedicated to his job. I had a word with him this morning and apart from the initial shock in the plane when he didn't know whether to punch the Emir or not he's quite happy with the way things turned out. I haven't told him yet but I'm going to offer him promotion to Sergeant. This is not because I don't think he'll keep his mouth shut but because the M.O. thinks he deserves it. Unfortunately we don't have a spare slot for him here so it will mean he has to be posted soon. Perhaps he'd like to move on anyway.

'I'm sure he would Sir. He is a bright lad. He even looked after us when we were in Luxor.'

Sam joined in the conversation. 'Any chance of him being posted to Luxor Sir? I think he has been there before and there's a certain civvy nurse who might like him back there.'

'Oh is there? I'll see what can be done.'

CHAPTER 11

As You Were

In September 1938 the news from England seemed to suggest a major crisis had been averted. Earlier in the year German troops had marched into Austria in a bloodless annexation of that country. In April there had been an Anglo/Italian pact which among other things recognised Italy's sovereignty over Abyssinia. Emperor Haille Sallassie had been taken in secret to London in a British destroyer and Britain was forced to accept that Italy would now rule over his conquered nation. No one appeared to have glanced at the map of east Africa and seen just how vulnerable many independent and protected countries were or that they might be open to aggression from this new empire builder.

Both of these points had been argued at length in the officers mess. There had been more exchanges of information and visits between the various RAF stations at Aden, British Somaliland and Kenya. All RAF personnel took part in exercises between stations to see how easily and quickly they could support each other if attacked. London did not instigate these manoeuvres. They were devised by the local commanders and only towards the end of October when they began to exceed their budget did they have to answer to the Air Ministry and the exercises were stopped. Even so valuable information had been achieved in a relatively short time. It was to prove later that if only the local commanders had been in complete charge the outcome of conflicts in this area might well have been totally different.

During these exercises the planes often flew quite close to Italian spheres of interest and it was easy to see that in southern Abyssinia and in Italian Somaliland there were strong concentrations of Italian troops and equipment near the borders with the British colonies and protectorates. One squadron had been flown down from Egypt and another in stages from India. At one time there were so many squadrons at Aden there was scarcely room to park all the planes. Wg/Cdr Brandon obtained permission from the Emir to carry out practice attacks on the Island of Zuga, a few miles off the west coast of Yemen. Signals regarding the Italian build up and the reasons were dispatched to London but very little came of them. Certainly no reinforcements were sent out from the UK to the RAF stations.

Following the meeting in September between Chamberlain and Hitler at Munich it seemed that a guarantee had been received from the German leader that he would make no more territorial demands in Europe. In spite of the feeling of being let down, by the beginning of October, most people were glad that a war had been averted. Life at the stations began to return to normal. The support squadrons returned to their own bases and certainly at Aden thoughts began to turn towards Christmas. This really amounted to a decision as to who could go on leave and where and who should remain at camp.

The formal mess evenings were reinstated and at the first of these the Emir was the guest of honour and for the first time brought with him his young son, now fully recovered. After dinner the C.O. rose and gave his usual talk which included a passing reference to the recent emergency. As soon as he had finished he introduced the Emir saying that the local ruler wished to make a special announcement. Harry and Sam exchanged glances and together tried to catch the C.Os eye to no avail. They need not have worried. The Emir rose to his feet, one hand resting on his son's head.

'Good evening Ladies and Gentlemen. Thank you for inviting me here this evening. I do so enjoy these meetings.

Tonight I want to introduce my son, who some day will take his place at the head of his people. Unlike many people in this region we do not resent the British presence here. In fact we welcome it. We learn from you and we hope that you learn from us. As you know, at the moment we are happy to allow Aden and other areas to be developed as supply depots for coal, oil and provisions for ships passing through. Most of the people working in the harbour area are from the local population which brings welcome employment so we both benefit.'

'My main purpose this evening is to publicly thank this RAF station in helping my son in his recent illness. Your Commanding Officer, Wing Commander Brandon allowed two of your pilots and someone from the medical staff to fly me and my son to Luxor for an emergency operation. My son is here tonight to show you how successful that was. As a small appreciation of his gratitude and mine I present you with this Competition Cup. I have discussed this matter with your C.O. and he has suggested that it should be awarded annually on your sports day. I'm sure you can decide exactly how to compete for it but I hope each flight, the medical staff, the admin staff and the camp security group will all take part. Each year I have arranged for a small replica to be given to the winning team. The main cup will be suitably inscribed each year and will remain on display here in the mess hall.'

Everyone tried to get a look at the trophy – a huge silver cup on a mahogany base. Those nearby could see that the inside was gleaming bright gold while all round the outside rim a dedication had been inscribed *'To all ranks stationed at RAF Aden for assistance given to The Emir of Aden and his family.'*

The Emir sat down amid general applause while the C.O. stood up to thank him and suggested that starting next year the sports day should be held on Empire Day, thus allowing plenty of time for the various teams to get organised. Not long after this the Emir made his excuses and departed with the Prince.

January 1st 1939 was the beginning of a momentous year. While life at the RAF station went on much as before the Emir began to make plans for restoring peace among the various tribes making up the whole of the Aden Protectorate. For the most part its border with Saudi Arabia was never much more than 200 miles from the coast. However this coastline extended for more than a thousand miles. Much of the land was mountainous with communication between the various townships difficult. While still maintaining a friendly liaison with the RAF the Emir enlisted the help of a Persian army detachment to train some of his soldiers in communication techniques and engineering. In addition he asked advice from the British naval detachment on the purchase of a small flotilla of motor launches and patrol boats. The final part of this spending spree was to obtain a few old training planes and to invest in a squadron of fighters.

The long awaited sports day was scheduled for 1st May and although the previous weeks had been occupied with forward planning much of the final detail had to be left almost to the last few hours. For many this was a new venture into organising events on such a scale. For the other ranks and civilian workers who marked out the field events, erected marquees, ensured that adequate food and drink was available and that first aid posts were in the right place it was hard work. It was a change from the normal routine and everyone worked with a will and even those teams competing managed to get in a few hours practice.

May 1st started with a sharp rain squall which soaked everything but it also reduced the temperature and although clouds threatened by 11 o'clock when the first event took place huge crowds had arrived. From then onwards everything went according to plan. Everyone enjoyed the races and other field events but the competition which received most praise was the mock bombing attack. One plane from each flight attacked a target set out on the edge of the airfield with small bags of flour, each specially coloured to distinguish each team. Following this the event which won special acclaim from the crowd was the staged crash of an RAF plane and the rescue of its pilot by the medical team. The station itself provided four competitive teams and invited the army, the navy and other local groups to take part in three special events.

The day was an outstanding success but within two days the RAF base had returned to its normal activities. It seemed that in spite of worrying troop movements in Europe there would be no war. Although they did not know it at the time this was to be the first and last sports day that Harry and Sam attended for within a month they would both be posted back to England. On a Friday before the normal long weekend the various notice boards on the station contained long lists of personnel, aircrew, ground staff, medics and general duties staff. All were ordered to report to the main hall at 16.00 hours to be addressed by the C.O. Speculation was rife but no amount of questioning admin. staff who usually knew what was going on could determine the reason for this unusual order.

Harry first became aware of it when he saw many of his comrades clustered round the notice board in the officers' mess. Philosophical as ever he decided not to join in the speculation but to wait. Groups of airmen began to gather outside the hall and as soon as the doors opened they went inside and sat down. Amid noisy chatter the hall gradually filled up until just before 16.00 hours the C.O. together with F/Lt Goldsmith and the M.O. walked slowly from the back of the hall and sat down at a large table on the stage. The babble of voices slowly died down and when the C.O. got to his feet there was complete silence.

He held them in this unreal silence for several seconds, then 'Good afternoon gentlemen. Sorry to take you away from your work but I will not keep you long.' This suggestion of sarcasm was greeted with smiles and then laughter. He knew full well that most work stopped early on Fridays and they knew that he knew. 'I have some news which I think will surprise you and because I don't want strange rumours doing the rounds I have taken this unusual step to keep you all informed and if I can to answer any questions which may arise.'

'From time to time we all get posted to different stations. Sometimes this is because there is a need for specialists to go to some distant place no one's ever heard of. Some are posted to teach others elsewhere. We in turn get new blood which we will eventually turn into old sweats or even old wrecks. Some of course go because we just need to get rid of them. I hasten to add this is not the case this time.'

'To be honest I don't really know why so many of you are being posted at the same time and I don't suppose we shall ever find out. However, we have quite a few people being posted here. In fact from the numbers which F/Lt Goldsmith has received we are getting considerably more than we are losing. We are also getting additional aircraft. Some of these will be flying in at the end of the month. Others are arriving in boxes so many of you will enjoy putting them together. Make sure there are no bits left over.' The C.O. waited while the laughter died down. He went on.

'There's just one snag in this reshuffle, the new people will be arriving before you depart. In fact for at least three weeks we are going to be a bit cramped. Please make the newcomers feel welcome and help them to settle in quickly. Some are arriving on Monday. I hope over the next few weeks to see each of you who is leaving. For the moment thank you. Enjoy your weekend. Any questions?'

There was stunned silence and then a gradual murmur as the airmen began talking to each other. F/Lt Goldsmith stood up and repeated the question. 'Surely one of you would like to ask something.'

W/O Watson rose to his feet. 'Sir. You probably know that I'm supposed to retire in August having served my time. Do you know exactly where any of us will be posted. I was expecting to go home although I'm still young enough to do another tour overseas if I decide to stay in. I expect my long suffering wife would like to know if she can expect me soon.' Laughter all round the hall followed this totally innocent request.

'Yes Mr. Watson we are aware that you've got more service in than any of us. Over the next few days we shall be receiving specific postings. All I can say in your case is that if you really want to go home I shall make certain that you do. Any more questions?'

LAC Jones, whose close friends always called on him for advice regarding the interpretation of Air Council Instructions and Kings Regulations got to his feet. 'Sir. My name is on the list and I have only been here eight months. Is it possible for me to swap with someone else who really wants to go?'

The answer was not quite what he expected from the adjutant. 'You know what the service is like. You have a completely free choice, whether to join or not. Once you're in, you're ours to do with as we please. If there's some special reason why you want to stay come and see me next Tuesday. I'm not promising anything but we'll talk about it. That goes for anyone. I can't promise to change anything but you are all free to discuss your posting. Make an appointment through my office.'

Sam Jordan asked if the new aircraft would be Hurricanes. The answer given by the C.O. was 'No' but he did expect a few Vickers Wellesleys together with their crews and maintenance staff.

The C.O. dismissed the company and they went off talking in small groups towards the barracks and their respective

mess halls for the evening meal. The C.O. caught the eye of
Sam Jordan and spoke quietly to him. 'Sam could you and
the other pilots remain here for a while.'

'Yes Sir.'

Sam moved over to the group of pilots slowly edging their
way towards the main exit. 'Hold on chaps. The 'Old Man'
wants a word.'

As the hall gradually emptied the C.O. stepped down from
the stage and came over to the pilots now seated in the two
front rows. He began 'Half of you are in the RAF for a long
time. The others are on short service commissions of five or
seven years. We haven't received the full details yet but I can
tell you short service commission types that most of you will
be going back to the U.K. There are nine of you and I think
the Air Ministry wants to get its money's worth before they
let you go. My guess is that for the next year they are going to
train you as instructors and during your final year or so you
will be training a new batch of pilots. As far as I can gather
you will all go for assessment and aptitude tests. Those that
are suitable will go to one of the Flying Instructors Schools
and learn how to fly properly. Those who are deemed to have
different qualities will join another squadron probably in the
U.K. As for you old sweats we don't yet have anything definite.
I expect some will go home, a few will go to Palestine and
others will go to India or East Africa.'

'We are going to be a bit crowded for the next few weeks
but I expect you chaps to help the newcomers on a one to
one basis. Fly with these people. Show them the areas we
need to patrol and those that we shouldn't. O.K. Enjoy your
weekend.'

There was much to do over the next few days gathering
together various pieces of kit and obtaining replacements
from stores. During postings all airmen, officers and other
ranks had to depart with a full kit. During the course of
normal duty some pieces of kit were inevitably lost and these

had to be paid for. Old or broken pieces were replaced free. There were the usual routines of medical inspection though these of necessity needed to be completed at the last minute, only to be repeated as soon as airmen arrived at their new station.

Communal parties for those leaving were the norm especially when large numbers were posted. Those in the know were usually able to persuade the messes to come up with a special meal at a small charge. It was one of the few perks the catering staff enjoyed and everyone from the C.O. down knew about it.

CHAPTER 12

Roll on the Boat

For Harry the move came at about the right time. He, Sam Jordan and for that matter several of his friends had been overseas ever since they had got their 'Wings' so they began to look forward to a cooler climate with some relish. During his time overseas Harry had written home almost every month but it had become increasingly difficult to find some new topic which might interest the folks back there. For Christmas and birthdays he usually sent local trinkets, jewellery or clothing. Now he took time off to visit Aden to find something small but special for his mother and his sister.

The first five of the new pilots flew in on Friday about 15.00 hours. They just about had time to get themselves checked in with the M.O., find billets and join the others for the evening meal. The next day a further ten arrived by boat and were duly accommodated. Only five had to make do on temporary beds in an empty chalet. Over the next few days air transports ferried in more ground staff while two freighters unloaded more stores, equipment, the boxed aircraft and the remaining personnel.

In spite of the overcrowding the hand-over had gone smoothly with Harry and the others showing the incoming pilots their boundaries and pointing out from a distance the potential enemy airfields. The three weeks passed quickly. Then came the final evening meal for the personnel who were leaving. This time in the officers' mess the official send off was attended by the C.O. himself. Drink flowed freely and everyone indulged too much but now that the time had come everyone was relieved to be going home.

The boat was scheduled to leave on Monday although passengers could embark any time after midday on the previous Saturday. The 1500 mile voyage through the Red Sea would take a week, stopping at Port Sudan before continuing northwards and then though the Suez Canal. By dinner they had settled into their cabins, two to each and sorted out their kit. Their steward, who apparently looked after twelve cabins arranged for baggage required on voyage to be stored in the hold. At dinner they were ushered into the main dining room which covered the whole beam of the ship. They entered down a flight of steps into a spacious dining room. At the far end were two emergency exits, one port and one starboard. In between were two pairs of doors which led to the kitchens. Everywhere was spotless while four huge fans rotated slowly circulating the air and causing little flashes of light from the large chandeliers which hung down from the high ceiling.

Many of the other passengers were already seated and the murmur of voices lessened as the RAF officers made their way to three tables on the starboard side. Sam took it upon himself to utter a 'Good evening ladies and gentlemen and young people' on behalf of them all. Nods, a slight inclination of heads and indiscernible grunts greeted his salutation.

'So its like that is it' he murmured under his breath.

He had no sooner sat down than more passengers began to arrive. They were wives and grown up children of diplomats returning from posts east of Aden together with a few army officers. A Brigadier approached their tables. 'Good evening gentlemen. Don't bother to get up. Welcome aboard. Any of you play bridge?'

'Not very well Sir but we're happy to learn.' Harry stood up and made a quick introduction of those on his table.

The army officer introduced himself, 'Brigadier Meyrick, my wife and daughter. We're going home from Rangoon. See you later.' He and his party moved on to their table.

These introductions were greeted in silence by the remaining passengers as the waiters hurried to serve the first course. After dinner passengers were free to go ashore so Harry and his friends took the opportunity to visit Aden for the last time. They were just about to go down the gang-way when Brigadier Meyrick appeared with his daughter and another young girl. 'I say chaps. If you're going ashore would you mind taking the girls along and keeping an eye on them?'

Harry told the Brigadier that Aden at night was not the nicest of places for two young English girls but he was over ruled by comments from his friends. 'Yes Sir. We'll do our best. We'll be back long before the boat sails.'

During the many months they had been stationed at Aden they had rarely visited the town. Introductions on the quayside followed once everyone had left the gang-way and the girls turned and waved at the army man. The extended party walked slowly through the dock area and on towards the town which was no different from thousands of ports throughout the world. Harry and Sam walked with the two girls, Barbara, the older one and Sheila, whose father had apparently taken over the Brigadier's command and was remaining at Rangoon.

The two girls chatted to each other and after a while included the RAF officers in the conversation. Most of the talk was idle chatter regarding incidents which had occurred in Rangoon and other places where they had been based.

'You've covered a lot of ground in your young lives.' ventured Sam.

'Oh. I'm not so young.' replied Barbara. 'Guess my age.'

'That's not fair.' Harry suggested. 'If I say 19 and you are older you might be upset because I thought you were not worldly wise and sophisticated. On the other hand if I guessed at 25 and you are only 20 you would not be very pleased.'

By this time they had reached the first bar where they intended to call in for a farewell drink. The others in the party had already ordered a round and organized two adjoining tables. 'What will you two young ladies have to drink?' enquired Arthur Knowles.

'I'll have a gin with a dash of sherry and cherry on a stick.' replied Barbara. 'And Sheila will have a sweet sherry. Is that O.K.?'

'So how old are you then?' asked Sam.

'I don't mind telling you.' replied Barbara. 'I'm quite old really – 20. In fact I'll be 21 almost as soon as we reach England. Sheila is the baby. She's only 18.'

Silence greeted this statement. Then Barbara continued. ''So what do you all do? I can see you're all pilots. Are you going to Egypt or home?'

'Most of us are going home.' replied Sam so we'll see more of you. 'In fact some of us are learning to play bridge so we can beat your father.'

'You've got your hands full. He's quite good. Let's move on to another bar and Sheila and I will buy the drinks.'

'O.K. Where would you like to go?'

'What's the wickedest place in Aden?'

'No idea. We're all clean living boys but we can certainly find another bar. In fact there's quite a nice hotel run by a French woman.'

Having visited two other bars by 10 o'clock they were all glad to return to the comparatively sumptuous surroundings of the boat which was to take them home. For the next few days at least with no parades, no duties and virtually nothing to do it would be as good as being on leave. Breakfast was a more leisurely affair and on advice from the steward who called them at 7.30 with a cup of tea they changed into civilian clothes.

Tom Livingstone decided to take up the brigadier's offer of bridge. He bought two packs of cards from the small shop on board and borrowed a book on bridge from the ship's library. Although he had played before he needed to brush up on the finer points. By lunch time they had all dispensed with ties and even the Brigadier turned up in civvies though when he went on deck for a walk he wore his army issue sun helmet.

The RAF men were pleased that their C.O. actually came to see them off and had dinner with them on board that night. He seemed genuinely sorry to see them go and had a special word for Sam and Harry, asking them to keep in touch.

The ship slipped her moorings at noon the next day with most of the passenger on the main deck waving at no one in particular. After lunch they went below to escape the heat and Tom Livingstone began to instruct them, four at a time, on the basic principles of bridge. By dinner they thought they had mastered it enough to take on the Brigadier. 'You'll end up losers' was Tom's brief comment. 'We must have a few more practice sessions and maybe in a couple of days if the opportunity arises we'll let the army bod make the first move.'

'Good thinking Tom,' replied Sam.

As the ship steamed slowly northwards they settled into a routine of breakfast followed by a stroll round the deck three times and then bridge lessons until midday when they went up on deck for a drink at the bar before lunch. It seemed courtesy demanded such greetings were exchanged with those at the nearest tables and the RAF officers were happy to continue this custom. Meanwhile the unchanging scene of the Red Sea with occasional glimpses of the coast or an island did little to lift the monotony of the voyage. Now during the hottest part of the day they indulged in a siesta after lunch. Harry used this time to write a few letters before he finally succumbed to the oppressive heat and dozed.

Dear Mum,

If you haven't received a letter from me for some time this will no doubt set your mind at rest. I am coming home! We left Aden two days ago and I'm hoping to post this at Port Sudan (A new stamp for your collection). I'll write again from Port Said but at present I have no idea when I will actually arrive in the UK. Our party includes 15 pilots from our base at Aden but there are a number of military personnel from places further east and some civilians going home after many years overseas. Quite a few are returning from cruises in the Far East. I bet they wish they had gone via the Cape for this really is a slow boat although quite comfortable.

I haven't any special news although no doubt once I get home I shall talk non stop. It's strange to realise that only a few months ago Sam Jordan and I flew this same route when we went on a mercy mission to take a sick child to hospital. At the time that flight seemed to take ages although we shared the piloting. In comparison our present rate is oh so slow. However it does have its compensations and we are treating it as unofficial leave. I'm even learning to play bridge although even with the ship's ventilators at full blast its often too hot to concentrate. If we go on deck and the ship is at all close to the shore there are hordes of insects. Still the food on board is excellent.

One other thing. As far as I can tell (from my old C.O. at Aden) we shall all be in England for some time doing an instructor's course and if successful teaching chaps to fly for a couple of years before my time to leave the RAF comes up. It's surprising how much junk I have acquired in such a short time overseas. I have two large boxes in the hold, two kit bags and two cases. I have managed to get you and Molly some nice gifts. Please give her my love and say I shall be writing to her next. I'm off now for another bridge session (i.e. the card game. I'm not navigating the ship).

All my love,

Harry

On Thursday morning the slight motion of the boat had ceased and they awoke to find her moored at Port Sudan. A few passengers disembarked but instead of moving on as the stewards had anticipated the ship stayed for two days. Those who wished were allowed ashore between 9.0 a.m. and 8.0 p.m. each day. Only a few availed themselves of this opportunity although the RAF contingent did so en masse.

The two girls were invited and this time the Brigadier and his wife joined the party. Then just two hours before the ship was due to sail three troops of British soldiers in full marching kit with rifles and side-arms and a detachment of dark bronzed Sudanese troops embarked. They quickly disappeared below decks and were rarely seen again until they disembarked at Port Said. Soon after leaving Port Sudan the opportunity to play bridge with the Brigadier was taken. Sam and Harry played against him and his wife. Tom and an Air Force padre, who was returning from India, played against his daughter and an army officer while a third table involved two more RAF chaps, a navy man and Sheila.. If it did nothing else it passed the time and helped to keep their minds alert. They changed partners three times and then the voyage was almost over as they began the even slower passage through the Suez Canal. Interest in watching this important waterway took precedence over everything else as the boat eased its way northwards although there was very little to see.

Some of the British troops who had embarked at Port Sudan were bandsmen. Harry was surprised to learn that most could play at least two instruments. In addition to their usual military instruments many of them played the piano, saxophone and violin. It seemed that they were often in demand wherever they were stationed to play at camp dances. Now and for the next two evenings of the voyage they played in the dining room once all the chairs and tables had been moved to the sides.

Harry never found out who organised the dances although he suspected it was Barbara. The first night most of the army personnel and wives attended. The RAF pilots put in an appearance but were quite daunted by the Military Two Step and similar dances. The two girls tried to cajole them into joining in but they remained resolute in small groups at the side until the band leader announced a ladies Excuse Me dance. When the band began to play a slow waltz Barbara approached Harry while Sheila singled out Sam. As the ship moved slowly through the first part of the canal Harry held a woman in his arms for the first time in years as he stumbled through the steps.

Barbara was a sympathetic teacher and after the next dance Harry began to enjoy himself. He glanced across at Sam and Sheila. Sam too was enjoying himself and seemed to glide effortlessly among the dancers. Emboldened by his prowess Harry asked Mrs Meyrick for a dance which seemed to please her husband as much as her. It was a fox-trot but after a few faltering steps he managed to get into the rhythm.

The girls were having the time of their lives dancing with different partners throughout the evenings. When Harry was dancing with Sheila on the second night she remarked 'You know you've made a conquest with Barbara don't you.' Harry didn't quite know how to respond but felt he should make some reply. 'Well she's a lovely girl and I've no doubt she's got lots of boy friends.'

'You're quite wrong. She is a lovely girl but I think she wants to get married and settle down. I bet by the time you reach England you will be engaged. I'm quite sure her father would approve and you've already made a hit with Mrs Meyrick.'

'Good Lord. I only danced with her once.'

'Ah well I think you've been hooked.' The dance ended and Harry was glad to get away and go on deck for a breath of air.

The RAF contingent thought they would remain on board to continue the voyage home but this was not to be. Having reached Port Said they were disembarked and almost immediately departed in a number of RAF cars and trucks and headed back towards the large RAF base at Ismailia. Harry just had time to leave a note for Barbara before he left.

Harry and his comrades were dropped outside the officers' mess with their overnight items. The remainder of their belongings were promised for the following morning. Inside the cool mess servants hurried about dispensing drinks for those seated in the smoking room while others could be seen setting out the dining room for lunch. An RAF corporal in a short white coat approached the newcomers and with a deferential cough announced his presence.

'The bar is open if you'd like to partake of refreshments. Just leave your name with the Bar Steward if you haven't got the correct currency.'

'Thank you corporal. Any special rules apply to those in transit?'

'The duty officer will be around just before lunch at thirteen hundred hours. He'll put you right. I think everyone here is in transit. Will that be all Sir?'

'Thanks. What's your name?'

'I'm Corporal Hudson. I've been here since 1924 so it's no good me going home now. No one would remember me. I've got a room just inside the entrance. I'm usually around.'

'Sounds like a right creep to me.' remarked Sam once they had moved away.

'There's usually one around, but I bet he knows all the dodges.'

The remainder of their kit arrived the following day and was taken directly to their rooms. The accommodation was quite spacious – single rooms in a brick built bungalow predominantly painted white. For the next five days the routine for the RAF pilots was much the same. After breakfast each morning the duty officer appeared, checked names on lists and those who answered were told to report to the gymnasium. Each group was told what to do and what not to do when they were in town. 'Remember we are here as guardians and to advise. The Egyptians gained independence in 1922 but allow us to retain bases in certain areas. Some of you will be leaving for India on the next boat going south. Some will go to Palestine just round the corner. Those waiting to go to the UK may have to wait some time. If you haven't gone within the next four weeks we will try to get you on RAF transports although your kit will follow by boat. In the meantime a few of you will be attached to one of the local squadrons based here on a temporary basis.'

For the rest of the day they were free to do whatever they wished. By dint of gentle digging and asking the right questions Sam Jordan found that he and his comrades were not likely to move for at least six weeks whatever the duty officer had implied. June gave way to July and the boredom of inactivity was not conducive to good discipline for personnel supposedly on active service. They were not to know that in just over two months time the same problem would descend on hundreds and then thousands of military personnel the world over. But for now in spite of rumours and disturbing news in the local papers the threatened war was confined to talk and denial.

The RAF base at Ismailia was well equipped with all manner of sports facilities. After a week of inactivity Harry visited the gym for a gentle workout each morning. He introduced himself to Sgt Harrison. 'Hope you don't mind. I don't want to do anything too strenuous but I'd like to keep reasonably fit. 'Very pleased to see you Sir. It's not often we get volunteers to do PT. Can you persuade any of the others?'

'I'll see what I can do.' Harry thought he could persuade most of his friends and maybe others would join in.

'We had a good fencing team here for years but bit by bit they all got posted. Now we only have one left. I don't suppose you'd be interested?' asked the sergeant.

'Sounds too dangerous to me.' was Harry's instant reply.

'You'd be well protected and it would certainly keep you fit.'

'O.K. you're on. So who is the expert around here? No don't tell me. It's you.'

'Afraid so Sir. On guard!' answered the Sergeant making an attacking move with his right hand.

This was Harry's first introduction to fencing and though he and most of the others made a complete hash of their first few lessons after a few weeks their efforts were rewarded when Sgt Harrison pronounced them no longer beginners. It certainly helped to pass the time and although still frustrated at kicking their heels they remained fit. The bridge school which they introduced was still flourishing when they finally left some time later. Harry decided to send home the gifts he had bought for his mother and sister. Cpl Hudson suggested he send them in separate parcels at least three weeks apart.

Sam thought he and Harry should make a direct approach to the Station Commander with a view to becoming attached to one of the squadrons on the base. It was easier than they had imagined. The C.O. was much younger than they had expected. Moreover he already knew of their desire to keep fit. Obviously a man of action, while they were still in his office he called in one of his squadron leaders and put to him the direct question. 'John. We've got two volunteers and possible more who are keen to get in a few more hours. Can you fit them in with your people?'

Sqn/Ldr Mason was equally forthright. 'Both A and B flights are short of pilots. Renwick has dislocated his shoulder and Smithers is off sick. Clements and Packard are grounded until we know the outcome of that flying accident.' Apparently at least another four pilots were unfit for flying for one reason or another. Harry and Sam glanced at each other and wondered what they might be letting themselves in for. They needn't have worried for the squadron leader's next words answered their question. 'You must think we're a right lot of slobs. It's just one of those things. We are normally so well covered we've sent people on leave and then in quick succession we are down to only two flights. Why don't you two come over to the flight office tomorrow morning. What experience have you had? What machines were you flying recently?'

Harry answered for both. 'We've both flown Harts and Gladiators in Kenya, Somaliland and Aden but we've also flown Oxfords and Envoys and Maggies.'

They joined 'A' flight on temporary secondment the following morning and told their new flight commander that at least six other pilots would like to be considered. The Sqn/Ldr himself checked them both out and during the latter part of the afternoon they found themselves airborne and being shown the various landmarks, the places they could fly and those that they shouldn't go near. 'Be specially careful not to go too far out into the Med. and when you come back don't go too near any navy ship. The navy gunners are trigger happy. They shoot first and then ask questions.'

July in Ismailia is not the nicest place to be so Harry and his friends were glad to join the squadron and be able to escape the oppressive heat by doing daily patrols. They were also allowed time off to visit the slightly cooler resorts on the coast. The Med. was all of 50 miles away along dusty roads in trucks driven at high speed by Egyptian drivers. The journey itself was hair raising but once there it was pleasant to bathe in the cool waters.

In four weeks all the regular pilots of the squadron were back in service so Harry and the others once more found themselves playing the waiting game, waiting for the boat which never arrived. There seemed to be new people arriving every week and very few departing. In August a new squadron was formed from various pilots and sent off to Cyprus together with its ground crews. Sam, Harry, Tom Livingstone and Alan Mackenzie were lucky enough to be included. So instead of going home they resigned themselves to staying overseas for a few more months. The only people who managed to get passage on a boat returning to the UK were civilians and time expired military personnel. Rather than take all his boxes to the new station Harry arranged for

Cpl Hudson to store them until he returned for he still hoped to go home.

At least the trip to Cyprus was fairly swift, 15 pilots being flown together in one RAF transport. With loading and refuelling the round trip of 600 miles took almost six hours. During the next four days three transports operated a shuttle service to transport enough stores, personnel and equipment for the new squadron to be self sufficient for two weeks. Further supplies arrived by sea. Everyone began to look for reasons for this sudden upheaval after so much inactivity. All that could be gleaned from Ismailia was that it had become overcrowded and that it was the Air Force policy to continue its expansion which had been started some years previously. At Akrotiri the newly formed fighter squadron shared the base with two fighter/bomber squadrons while a flight from coastal command, actually based on the coast, took meals with them in the mess.

Once settled in at the new base it was a relief to discover that the climate on the island was better than they had experienced in Egypt. There was little actual flying so apart from a daily flight to keep their hands in and the occasional bombing and gunnery practices the pilots had a very easy time. Harry and Sqn/Ldr Carter, the M.O. at Aden had maintained a fairly regular correspondence every two or three months. Now with so little air activity he wrote once more and broached a subject he had been considering for some time. In addition to the usual news his final paragraph was:

'With so little going on here and being frustrated at not returning to England to do my instructor's course I'm beginning to think I chose the wrong branch of the service. May I ask your advice about finishing my medical training and then transferring to the medical branch of the RAF.

Kind regards,

Harry.

P.S. I don't usually write post scripts but I think you'll like this one. I'm one up on Sam in aircraft types. I have actually flown a Lysander. As you know they are really army co-operation 'planes although we rarely see the army. Unfortunately there is still no sign of the really fast fighter aircraft. We are beginning to think that Hurricanes and Spitfires do not really exist.

Carter's reply came, surprisingly, within a week. It contained the usual news from Aden with a few anecdotes and towards the end of the letter an answer to Harry's question.

I cannot impress upon you too strongly not to become an M.O. in the RAF. My advice would be to continue as a pilot and as soon as your time is up get out fast. Then finish your medical training and as soon as you are qualified look for a nice practice in the west country as a G.P. As a local G.P. you will see a whole range of interesting cases and be able to help many people. Not so as an RAF doctor. More important, as a G.P. especially when your practice grows you will need an older partner and I shall be pleased to apply for the post when I leave the RAF.

By the way, remember Cpl Jenkins, now promoted to Sergeant. He also wrote a couple of weeks ago with a similar question. He would like to become a doctor in the RAF but of course, as yet we do not have any medical schools out here. Ah well. Here's to the future.

Kind regards to all. Michael.

P.S. Roll on the boat!

PART II

A Testing Time

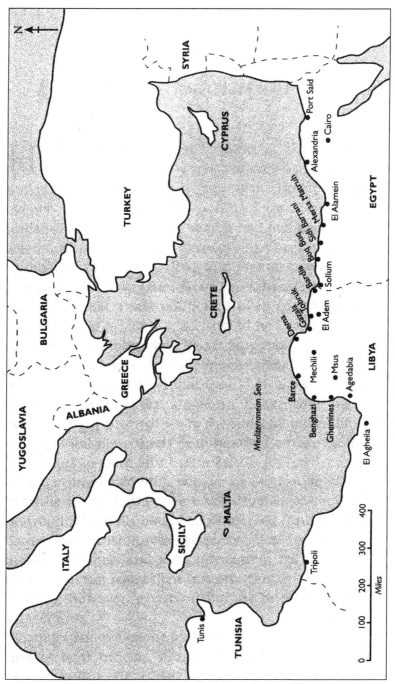

Map 2 The Western Desert

101

CHAPTER 13

Egypt and Preparation for War

Harry, Sam and the other pilots of the newly formed squadrons could only guess what was going on in the outside world. Although by no means isolated from world events rumours on the island were rife, each more unbelievable than the one which had just been discounted. There was no doubt that Germany had been re-arming for a number of years. The British and French governments were powerless to stop the German expansion. There were suspicions that a few politicians even considered that the German claim for more space should be accepted rather than let it provoke another war. Those supposedly in the know and others with relatives in the Foreign Office back home stated with absolute conviction that they knew the German military build-up in Europe was a gigantic hoax. Hitler had done it before and got away with it in the Sudatenland and in Austria.

Some local newspapers even reported stories brought back by visitors to Germany that a British Rolls Royce which, speeding round a corner, had hit a number of German tanks. They had been flattened as they were constructed of cardboard and plywood. The Rolls had been unmarked. And so the apathy continued. British forces overseas read of such events in the local newspapers and were not convinced but being so far away it was not really their concern. During the early summer months, however, events in Europe began to take a more sinister turn.

Sam Jordan, never one for beating about the bush, reckoned that at least officers should be told the truth if anyone really knew it. He asked his squadron leader to find out. Surprisingly, two days later, on 30th August, all officers above the rank of Flight Lieutenant were ordered to report to the station cinema at 09.00 hours. This very notice, in effect, caused a new batch of 'duff gen' to spread like wildfire throughout the camp. However on Wednesday the truth was revealed when the Group Captain spoke to his senior officers. He came straight to the point.

'There have been dozens of signals between London, Berlin and Paris during the past two weeks in an attempt to resolve the Polish problem. My latest information is that the Prime Minister will try right up to the last moment to stop the war which really does look imminent. The intelligence people are certain that this time Hitler is not bluffing. The military brass hats go along with this and expect that within a few days we shall be at war with Germany.'

He continued, 'The army is already on a war footing, the T.A. has been called up and reservists in the RAF have been recalled. The navy has been ready for the past month. Purely as a precaution I am suspending all leave until we know exactly what is going on. Any questions?'

There was silence for all of twenty seconds and then one after another the questions came in quick succession. 'Are we staying here?' 'Will some of us return to England?' 'Will we return to Egypt?' There was no satisfactory answer to any of them. Soon the Group Captain dismissed his officers who then had to bring this news to the attention of all other ranks. The immediate cancellation of leave did not go down well with everyone. During their short stay on the island a number of Cyprus friendships and even more amorous liaisons had been formed between the RAF personnel and local inhabitants. Even with the present crisis the ration trucks would still trundle into town to pick up supplies and the drivers could be persuaded to drop off messages to girl friends regarding the non appearance of partners for dates already arranged. For those who could not avail themselves of this facility there were usually ways of escaping from the camp and returning without using the main gate.

While Harry and the others who had originally been posted home still hoped to board ship at any time they were fast becoming convinced that it would not happen before Christmas. Then on 3rd September everyone knew that Britain and France were at war with Germany although no one expected the war in Poland to be over so quickly. As that phase drew to a close both squadrons were posted back to Egypt to a place no one had ever heard of – Fayid, actually just to the west bank of the Great Bitter Lake. Each squadron flew in three flights from Akrotiri direct to Ismailia where they refuelled before flying on to Fayid. Map reading was easy even for those who were off course when they crossed the Egyptian coast. Once refuelled they only had to follow the Nile south until they reached a particular bend in the river and they were at their new home where they were joined by another squadron the following day. For the first few weeks, even though now on a war footing, everything seemed much the same. The blackout conditions in England did not happen in Egypt although the aircraft were gradually painted in camouflage colours. As the months drifted by the phoney war in Europe had little effect on life in the Middle East.

New liaisons were formed with the local population and although at Fayid they were further away from the bright lights of the Egyptian cities it was not long before the enterprising locals had set up bars, cafes and trinket shops a few yards outside the RAF station. Just as they began to feel that they had settled in at their new camp Harry's squadron was moved from Fayid and located in what was no more than a landing strip in the desert about 50 miles west of Cairo. It was about 15 miles inland from the coast and first impressions of their new home were not favourable. The small tented encampment was a far cry from their usual accommodation. However within a few days of getting acclimatised to living 'rough' a few wooden huts began to appear. Then once the real potential of converting huge packing cases had been realised more spares were ordered, the idea being to create bigger and better huts. Within a month four blister hangers had been erected and a number of prefabricated huts had turned the site into home.

Then in May 1940 the speed with which the German army raced across Denmark, Norway and then the Low Countries was difficult to comprehend for those in the comparative quiet of North Africa. The collapse of the allies in France was even more difficult to accept while the huge RAF losses there meant that few planes could be spared for the Middle East. Now every available plane would be needed for the defence of Britain. The RAF and army units in Egypt began to realise that they might very soon be in deadly combat themselves against the Italians. The reality of war on a much larger scale could no longer be avoided.

Harry had resigned himself to never seeing a Hurricane and to some degree was comforted with the knowledge that the Italian Air Force was also equipped with single-seater biplanes of a similar speed to their own. The Gloster Gladiator had been in service with the RAF for a number of years and the pilots relied on its rugged characteristics. Harry still thrilled to the full throated roar as the Mercury engine carried him swiftly into the air.

There were snags. There always were. On the ground the enclosed cockpit still permitted countless sand particles to find their way inside and once airborne and in any upside down manoeuvre they showered down on the pilot. In the air even on a dull day the cockpit became too hot for comfort but when opened the noise from the slipstream drowned all but the loudest sounds. It was a choice between two evils.

The Gladiator had one other disadvantage. The big radial engine, efficient though it was, only managed to carry the plane at a top speed of 250 mph and with a maximum range of 430 miles it could not stay in the air for long. They began practising fuel economy exercises by flying out on practice raids at a fairly low speed which allowed them greater time over the target area and still left enough fuel to use full throttle in simulated attacks. Two accidents during these exercises convinced Harry of the value of an idea that had been at the back of his mind for some time.

They had taken part in a most successful practice session involving all three squadrons but on the return to base two aircraft had run out of fuel. Although both pilots landed safely miles apart they faced a long wait before they could be rescued and the planes recovered. Ground crews sent out in lorries took several hours to reach them. Having been refuelled the engines failed to start up. The problem lay in the air filters which had become clogged with sand.

The jokes which might have greeted the pilots when they returned the following day were somewhat subdued and it was the design of the filter which came in for well deserved criticism. For the ground crews it meant an additional routine inspection and it was several weeks before an improved filter became available. Harry discussed with his squadron leader the feasibility of providing a search and rescue flight using a Lysander from one of the reconnaissance squadrons. Harry explained his idea at some length and although it was supported by the Wing Commander it was not well received at headquarters. One high ranking officer even went so far as to complain about 'cotton wool pilots' and the fact that in his day pilots didn't get lost or if they did it was their own fault. Harry explained again in some detail that if each squadron or even each group had only one Lysander on strength it could be used for a variety of purposes and not only to go to the assistance of downed fighter planes. However the proposal was shelved.

There were still long periods when there was little to do so Harry, Sam and the others often went swimming. They were also still able to go on short leaves and weekend breaks but after a while the excitement and dubious joys of Cairo and Alexandria began to pall. Harry wrote to Cpl Hudson at Ismailia, enclosed some money and asked if he would send all his medical books currently in store. They arrived two weeks later and he and Sam continued with their medical studies, albeit only in theory.

As news of the Italian build-up in the west began to filter through the airmen took it in turns to go on leave. So as not to cancel all leave and thereby possibly warn spies in the big cities the commander decreed that only one flight from each squadron would be allowed on leave at any one time. This meant that Sam and Harry no longer took their leave together. Not keen to go into town on his next short leave Harry visited one of the Lysander squadrons and asked if he could fly one of their aircraft.

Having told them that he had already flown a Lysander he explained his search and rescue plan and that he wanted to see how feasible it would be. The squadron leader was not only sympathetic but impressed and immediately spoke to his superior about the possibility.

'You're in luck, Nelson. It's probably the one aircraft out here which we have plenty of. The C.O. thinks its a good idea and says you can stay here for a few days and learn more about the Lizzie. Who knows we may even let you go solo.'

Harry was delighted. 'Thank you Sir. I hope I'll be able to do something for you one day.'

He smiled. 'In fact you could do something tonight. It's F/ Lt Jennings' birthday and we were intending to give him a formal party in the mess. Unfortunately P/O Armstrong, who is the orderly officer this week, has broken his leg and is in hospital. We do have his stand-by but its his job tonight to be the toastmaster at the dinner. Could you be the duty officer for tonight and possibly tomorrow?'

'Sure. I'd be pleased to help out. Just tell me the routine here in case its different from our station. You do realise I'm only here for three days.'

'Yes. Thanks. P/O Andrews will take over the day you return to your squadron. Cpl Atkinson will accompany you while you're here so he will tell you exactly where you have to go to inspect and also where you can stay during your tour as duty officer. You'll have a few hours each morning when you can do your flying. I will let them know to expect you at the flight lines.'

'Thank you very much Sir.'

Not wishing to waste any more time Harry saluted and walked down to the airfield and introduced himself. One of the pilots, P/O Noland, volunteered to take him up and borrowed a parachute and helmet for his use. The Lysander had been standing in the early morning sun and the cockpit as they entered was unbearably hot. Once airborne the heat dissipated and Harry, standing behind the pilot was again surprised how roomy the cabin was and how good was the all round vision. He followed closely the pilot's movements on the controls as he executed a variety of manoeuvres before returning to base. Once on the ground Harry asked if he could take over the controls and do a take-off. The pilot, at first reluctant, gave in when Harry explained the real purpose behind his request in wanting to fly the Lizzie.

'O.K. I'll just clear it with the boss and you'll have to sign the log book.' Harry smiled his pleasure and looked forward to his flight.

Permission was given and having got into the cockpit, Harry strapped himself in and began to familiarize himself with the controls and instruments. Having started up the engine and received a green light from the control caravan he eased the throttle forward and took up his position for the take-off. Harry listened carefully to the instructions which came through his head set. The pilot, standing behind him, while a little apprehensive at first, soon gained confidence as his pupil responded quickly to each instruction. The aircraft gathered speed, Harry increased the throttle setting and soon the tail came up. A little more throttle and with a gentle pull back on the stick the aircraft was airborne and began to climb steadily away from the airfield. As on the previous take-off they were subjected to some turbulence in the hot desert air but once they had left the circuit and headed out to sea at 3000 feet it was another world, cool and calm.

The engine was remarkably quiet. The sea stretching out for miles below was like a mill pond and there was not a cloud in the sky. They flew parallel to the coast for some time until Harry recognised some of the land-marks and realised they were approaching his own squadron area and turned back. Under instruction from the pilot he put the aircraft into a variety of manoeuvres. Turns, dives, climbing turns, stalls and gliding were carried out with a competence that surprised even Harry. All the while keeping an eye on the altimeter, the fuel, the speed and the land below it was soon time for them to return to base.

'We'd better go back now. Shall I climb into the cockpit and you come back here for the landing.?'

'No. If its alright with you I'd like to try the landing myself. Don't worry. I'll be careful and if there's the slightest doubt I'll go round again and we can then change places.'

'O.K. Remember you signed for this aircraft.'

Harry was determined not to crash on landing and having made a mental note of where they had been heading, checked his map and headed for the base. Having joined the circuit he was relieved that no other aircraft were in the vicinity as he listened carefully to the instructions from P/O Noland. With the approach speed adjusted he put down a small amount of flap, levelled off at the correct height above the ground, applied a little more throttle and allowed the aircraft to sink gently on to the runway. With the throttle now back and the stick right back the tail came down and the plane ran forward to the end of the runway. A quick burst of throttle and left rudder turned the Lysander to the left and Harry began to taxi back to the squadron lines.

As they stepped from the plane he thanked P/O Noland who said. 'No problem. You made a better landing than I did the first time I flew one of these. We can do the same tomorrow if you like.'

'Sure thing. I owe you a drink in the mess.' replied Harry.

Harry managed to get in four more flights in the Lysander before his leave ended. Three were with P/O Noland and the final one with the squadron leader actually simulated a rescue mission for a crashed aircraft. There was no time for him to actually fly solo although he felt confident that he could manage it should the need arise and was pleased that his plan worked, at least in practice.

CHAPTER 14

Into Battle: June 1940

The Italian build-up had been going on for several months. At first it seemed no more than the normal supplies needed to keep military forces effective but in recent weeks this had increased considerably in Libya as well as in Ethiopia and Somaliland. Although their supply lines to reach their troops in the east were long the relatively short crossing of the Mediterranean Sea meant that they could easily replace all that they would use in North Africa. General Wavell's supply routes to serve his bases in Egypt were even longer because they had to come all the way from England. The grave situation in France and the threat of invasion for England meant he had to conserve his small force and supplies against the now inevitable Italian attack.

Harry and his squadron continued to do much as they had done at Akrotiri and before that at Aden but now they knew they were no longer merely training. The daily patrols continued with increased practice bombing runs and machine gun attacks. Here they flew over the desert to the west and headed northwards towards the coast. Although much of the sand below shifted from day to day many tracks in the inhospitable desert were not obscured by the wind and drifting sand. The map reading skills which the pilots had acquired in England were no longer valid. Here, as at other bases abroad, the roads and towns were scarce. They were forced to rely on other features as recognition points and unless they became totally lost in the desert map reading was fairly straightforward. The pilots surveyed the never ending scene below, added suitable notes to their maps and made sure they carried full water bottles and always took off with full tanks of petrol.

A few days before the Italians declared war it was obvious from their steady build-up over the previous weeks that they intended to attack Egypt. There was no other explanation for all their activity and the accumulated stores. In Ethiopia and Somaliland similar preparations could only mean one thing. The Italians would soon be on the move. If successful in Egypt they would be in a good position to join up with their forces in East Africa and Ethiopia. Looking further ahead they would then be in a position to infiltrate into the Sudan and Kenya. It was an inspired plan on a gigantic scale. These huge areas of land once captured and consolidated would be extremely difficult for the British to retake, given their limited forces available.

Wavell considered all the possibilities and quietly drew up his plans. The bars and night clubs in Cairo and Alexandria all had their share of German and Italian sympathizers. Even small towns frequented by the military could boast of eyes and ears which did not like the British. His mind made up, Wavell decided to allow leave and days off for his troops to continue as normal. He now guessed that the French in Tunisia and Algeria would not support him but hoped they would stay put.

Attack is sometimes the best means of defence. Italy declared war on Britain and France on 10th June 1940. Wavell took the initiative and on 11th June small units of the army moved forward across the wire into Cyrenaica. At the same time the RAF began their operations against the new enemy. It was a huge success and took the enemy completely by surprise. Harry and his squadron together with three others that had been brought forward took off within a few minutes of each other. They caught up with the bombers which had taken off earlier and escorted them to their target, the main Italian base at El Adem, south of Tobruk. They caused a lot of damage but the dump was so large they had to make several return trips before any reduction in size was apparent. On subsequent raids the Italian Air Force was waiting for them but they seemed disinclined to put up more than a token resistance. El Adem, at the time, was the largest Italian airfield in the whole of their North African Empire. On the ground, following these initial strikes, small British army units attacked, usually at night in a series of lightning raids. They captured a few prisoners and destroyed huge amounts of stores before being swallowed up by the desert and then returning to their own lines. Sometimes the ground raids lasted no more than a few hours. Occasionally they took place over a day or two.

Once they stayed in the desert for a week making nightly attacks before returning back to base. These hit and run tactics totally unnerved the enemy. All the time they were supported by the RAF and the navy. Because much of the fighting took place along the narrow coastal strip the navy was able to bring its big guns to soften up the enemy in advance of the ground and air attacks. It was a strategy to be employed much later with even greater success.

From 3000 feet above the desert it was difficult to distinguish friend from foe. Once when returning from a raid Harry edged out over the sea and failed to recognise whether the ships below were the enemy or the Royal Navy. He tentatively mentioned this on landing and was relieved that other pilots experienced the same difficulty. When flying at 1500 feet they soon discovered that some of the Italian gunners were remarkably accurate. By trial and error they found that the best height was about 500 feet. By the time they had been spotted they were over the target and away. The disadvantage was that targets came up quickly so they had to be extremely accurate in their map reading in a region with few distinctive land features.

Even with the excitement of winning, the continuous flying and fighting began to have an effect not only on the pilots but also on the ground crews. Their responsibilities were to prepare the planes, arm them and then be ready on their return. When they did so it often meant rapid re-fuelling and re-arming so that the attack could be pressed home. It also meant that quick and vital repairs were often needed for the aircraft. The ground crews worked quickly and efficiently but it seemed that no sooner had one squadron been made ready and sent on its way than another was preparing to land. It was exhausting work and many began to feel the strain.

The ground troops, among the most experienced in the British and Indian armies, took every advantage of their superior training so that in spite of being heavily outnumbered they were able to avoid meeting head on with Italian units. The success of the hit and run tactics was exciting but everyone realised it could not go on for much longer. Within a few weeks they had all returned to their bases in Egypt to await new supplies and to train the reinforcements which had begun to arrive from India, New Zealand, Australia and South Africa.

After the early brief period of skirmishing when a number of high ranking Italians were captured the fighting died down. Wavell had accomplished what he had set out to achieve. The RAF squadrons, although heavily outnumbered by the enemy aircraft, attacked whenever possible and because the opposing forces in the air flew comparable planes there were inevitable losses on both sides. Sam and Harry seemed to bear charmed lives while many of the friends they had started out with were killed, wounded or missing.

However they did not allow themselves to mourn even those who had been closest to them. This was a luxury they could not afford. As with all air crew they hid their feelings under a nonchalant exterior knowing that once they let their guard slip it would be all too easy for morale to plummet throughout the squadron. They concentrated on being glad to be alive even if they wondered to themselves how soon it would be before it would be their turn to be among the casualties.

Sam and Harry, both now promoted to the rank of Flight Lieutenant, occasionally met in the mess for dinner. For them and the other experienced pilots it was a busy time training new pilots who began to arrive in increasing numbers although there were no new planes. By early in September the Italians had recovered their nerve and began to replenish their stores. So it began to look as though they were building up for an attack. Reconnaissance flights and intelligence all reported that huge supplies were being assembled.

This respite for Wavell and his men came at exactly the right moment. Although his earlier raids had been successful with very few casualties he needed time to re-group and re-supply. For those recently returned from action it was an unreal peace. Apart from a few patrols the more experienced pilots spent many hours instructing the new ones. Although the novices at first seemed more interested in the personal accounts of the recent fighting both Harry and Sam agreed that the fledgling pilots knew far more about the theory of flight and aerodynamics than they had done when they first received their wings. However the real test would come when they needed to put the theory into practice. Harry concentrated on teaching them how to read the signs of the desert and the sky.

Everyone was allowed to go on leave for a week or a few days at a time. Sam and Harry decided to visit Alexandria. Suez at the southern end of the canal held no memories or excitement. Cairo, 100 miles from the coast, was the headquarters of the Allied military commands. Other pilots returning from there said it was impossible to find accommodation, that it was crowded with representatives from every nation supporting the Allies. Some hinted that there were even large numbers of Germans and Italians.

Even at Alexandria they couldn't find a bed in the
Officers Club or any nearby hotel but while sitting in a bar
and wondering what to do next Harry saw a pilot he had
known in Kenya when he had first been posted overseas. F/O
Anderson was talking to a pretty Wren Officer and stood up as
Harry approached. He introduced him to Pamela Selway, his
fiancée. After a quick drink and the usual small talk Pamela
invited Harry and Sam to return with them to a house a short
distance away. She explained 'It so happens that two of the
girls are away at present so you could have their rooms for a
couple of nights.'

The pilots were only too glad to accept this unexpected
hospitality and when they got there the couple revealed that
once every three months or so F/O Anderson came down on
leave for a few days from Palestine. They were then introduced
to three other Wren Officers and five Army nurses who also
lived there.

'Are you sure its alright for us to be here?' enquired Sam.

'Well we keep quiet about it. If we can't help out our own
airmen from time to time it would be a poor show.'

It was an easy going arrangement. At breakfast everyone
got what they needed themselves. The midday meal was
usually a light salad and cooked meat although most of the
girls were at work. It was the evening meal when most people
were present. The wine and spirits flowed freely and it was
late before anyone got to bed.

During the morning, before it became unbearably hot
Sam and Harry visited the many trinket shops and wandered
down towards the docks, expecting to be challenged at
any minute. It was a make-believe world. French warships
which had thrown in their lot with the Allies anchored close
to those of Vichy France whose crews had resolved not to
fight.

Their ships were impounded, their guns made harmless
yet their crews were able to wonder around at will.

Two days later Sam and Harry were able to move into the Officers Club for the remainder of their leave. Sam was relieved and remarked. 'You know it was good of Andy and Pam to let us stay there but I felt a bit embarrassed by it all.'

CHAPTER 15

Strategic Withdrawal

On 13th September 1940 the Italians crossed the border into Egypt in considerable force. Wavell had anticipated this Italian attack from reconnaissance reports and had stationed many of his long range desert groups to the south of the Italian thrust. They were under strict orders to harass the enemy but not to become heavily engaged. RAF pilots were under similar instructions to engage the ground troops but not to take unnecessary risks.

They allowed the Italians to go forward and to occupy Sollum on the way to Sidi Barrani, some 60 miles inside Egyptian territory but still a long way from Mersa Matruh, which appeared to be their first major objective. Having advanced a mere 60 miles the Italians called a halt and for the next two months extended the road and built a number of fortified camps. They then set about re-supplying their dumps ready for their final assault to capture Egypt and the fertile plains along the Nile.

The strategic withdrawal of the British forces had been accomplished with fewer casualties than had been anticipated. No one liked retreating but in the face of such overwhelming odds it was the only option. It made good military sense to withdraw and live to fight another day. It was once again an uneasy lull but for the British it came at a most opportune moment.

Wavell, however, was not resting. Once again his orders to his desert units were to keep watch and destroy any isolated enemy forces. For the RAF reconnaissance was their priority and to fight back only if attacked. While it was becoming more hazardous for merchant ships coming through the Med. to bring supplies for the British more arms began to arrive from India and the Far East. Additional supplies came on the long sea route round the Cape and up through the Red Sea.

Replacement aircraft remained a problem. They heard rumours of one ship bringing in a few Hurricanes yet when it finally docked at Alexandria only two planes were on board. The others had been needed for the defence of Malta. Harry, now sporting the rank of Flight Lieutenant on the epaulette of his khaki shirt, returned from a reconnaissance flight with his two comrades who made up B Flight of his squadron.

As he got down from the cockpit Cpl Rogers came over and offered to carry his parachute back to the 'den'. 'You're wanted Sir and I don't think you've got time for a wash. The Wingco asked me to tell you the moment you got in. Its important and you are to see him straight away.'

Having received such an intriguing summons Harry walked over to the group of huts which served as the squadron HQ in the desert. 'Good afternoon Sir.'

'Ah! Come in Nelson. Haven't seen much of you recently but I gather everything's alright.'

'Yes thanks.'

'Still belly-aching about the lack of Hurricanes?

'Well we did just about hold our own but it would certainly be nice to see one of these mythical planes.'

'I think we can do better than that. I've actually got two on strength as from now. I want you to go to Ismailia tomorrow and listen carefully to everything F/Lt Jones will tell you. If you feel up to it you can take one of the Hurricanes up on a flight and bring it back safely. If you prang it you'll be grounded.'

'Thanks for the opportunity. Who's going to fly the other one?'

'Can you suggest anyone?'

'Well there really is only one – Sam Jordan. I don't think you'll find a better pilot and he'll look after your precious plane.'

'Yes I thought you'd recommend him. Are you two in cahoots? I saw him not half an hour ago and he recommended you.'

'Well there you are Sir. As long as you're happy Sam and I will bring back your aircraft in one piece.'

'You aren't the only pilots going. Others from different squadrons will be joining you for about six days. Keep in touch. There may be more good news on the way.'

The following day Sam and Harry set off for Ismailia by lorry along the desert roads, stopping to pick up more pilots along the route. Four hours after setting out they arrived at Ismailia and could just make out two Hurricanes parked next to a blister hanger. It seemed that every airmen from miles around wanted to catch a glimpse of the new planes but six guards kept them all at a distance.

F/Lt Jones approached and welcomed the pilots as they got down from the lorry and struggled with their parachutes and bags towards a square marquee erected nearby.

'Good morning gentlemen. I gather you are the cream of the desert air force.' His words of welcome brought broad grins to the faces of the pilots and from the assembled ground crews.

'F/O Turner and I will take you in turns and tell you all we know about Hurricanes. Unfortunately we do not have a dual version but I can assure you they are not difficult to fly. Once you allow for the difference between this one and your present aircraft you should have no problems. Just remember you have a lot more horses at your disposal, the engine is in-line, its a much heavier aircraft, more streamlined and goes a good deal faster. Also it has an undercarriage which retracts but we'll come to that later. As you can see we only have two aircraft so there will be no breakages!'

'We've divided you into two groups, alphabetically. I will take the first half and F/O Turner will take the second. Over the next four days I expect you all to be able to fly these machines adequately. That's all I ask. Get up and down in one piece. Efficiency will come with practice and experience.'

The two groups of pilots now clustered round the two aircraft and over the next hour the instructors explained the various levers and instruments, spoke of take-off and landing speeds and stalls. By 11 o'clock both aircraft engines had been started up and the first of the pilots sat in the cockpit, the chocks were pulled away and he was allowed to taxi towards the take-off path.

Sam Jordan was the first pilot in the second group. He was instructed over the R/T to relax, release the parking brake and open the throttle sufficient to move the aircraft forward. He taxied left then right just as in the Gladiator to see where he was going but there the similarity ended. Even with only a fraction of the throttle forward he could feel the power of the Rolls Royce Merlin engine. He was instructed to taxi all round the perimeter and then line up into wind. His next instruction was to ease forward on the throttle and allow the plane to gather speed but not to take off. After 500 yards the tail came up and Sam felt that the plane was ready to take off. He was instructed over the R/T to throttle back and taxi back to the control box.

This process went on until every pilot had experienced their first thrill of sitting in a Hurricane. Lunch was a hurried affair and by 14.00 hours they were all back ready for the afternoon session.

'O.K. F/Lt Jordan. Do you feel confident to take her up. Say no if there's any doubt and we'll go through the procedure again.'

'I'll take her up.' was Sam's quick reply.

'Remember on your final approach if you are not happy go round again. I want you to do one circuit only. Do not retract the undercarriage. Leave it as it is. We'll do that tomorrow and then you'll see what this bird can really do.'

Sam strapped himself in, a mechanic cranked the engine into life and he went through the cockpit check as he had been taught. With chocks away and the brake released he taxied forward into wind. A 'clear to take off' message over the R/T and a green light from control allowed Sam to open the throttle and he was soon gathering speed down the take-off path. Soon the tail came up and he eased the throttle forward a little more and at the same time pulled back gently on the control column. In no time at all the Hurricane virtually took itself into the air.

He quickly reached 500 feet, the first turning point in the circuit. He was determined not to let the aircraft drift out too wide so he started to turn at right angles again and reached 800 feet and turned again, climbing to 1000 feet. At this height he levelled off and flew downwind parallel to his take-off path. He soon reached the point where he needed to turn cross wind and begin to lose height. Everything seemed to be happening twice as fast as it should but he was determined not to panic. He eased back on the throttle, allowed the nose to drop and maintained the speed in a gentle turning glide down to 500 feet. He was now on the final approach and his mind raced ahead of the actions he must take in order to make a reasonable landing.

Even in this short flight it was evident that the Hurricane was much faster than the Gladiator. He now needed all his concentration and experience to accomplish the landing, knowing that several pairs of eyes watched the plane's every movement. While it would have been nice to execute a three point landing he realised it would have to wait until he was much more familiar with this machine.

Sam levelled out at the recommended height and as the aircraft began to sink eased the throttle forward and allowed the main wheels to touch the ground. As soon as they had he throttled right back and pulled the stick back. The tail came down and he was running forward. A slight touch on the brakes virtually brought the aircraft to a stop and then easing forward once more on the throttle he taxied back to the control. Although sweating more than was occasioned by the heat of the day Sam felt he had accomplished a reasonable take-off and landing.

The next pilot took off and Sam walked over to the instructor to iron out a few problems. 'Very good for a first attempt but maybe the circuit was a little wide. Also full throttle for a smooth take-off. Keep your wits about you and I don't think you'll have any problems. Well done.'

Harry edged closer to Sam to glean whatever tips could be imparted for it was his turn next. 'I wouldn't say it was a piece of cake but I'll tell you this. We've both flown more difficult kites but everything happens quicker. No doubt the undercart also works like a dream. We just need to remember those little warning lights.'

'At least we get a warning note if it's not down when it should be. It'll be like the Envoy. I've managed to get a copy of Pilots Notes so we could spend some time tonight looking through it.'

By 1630 hours all the pilots had been up on one circuit and landing, known to all as circuits and bumps. Although some approaches were a bit shaky they had all returned safely and even though they were experienced pilots they were all as excited as schoolboys.

The pilots were getting ready to leave when they realised that F/O Turner the younger of the two instructors was getting ready to fly one of the Hurricanes. F/Lt Jones moved closer to the group. 'F/O Turner is just going to show you what to aim for when you get your own Hurricanes. He will demonstrate a perfect take off and three point landing and just in case you need to make a fast scramble just how quickly this can be done. He will also demonstrate a manoeuvre of which we do not really approve but I've no doubt some of you will try it so here's how it should be done.'

They watched as F/O Turner ran to the aircraft, his parachute already inside. As the engine came to life by one mechanic another was helping him get strapped into the cockpit and in no time at all the aircraft was speeding down the field. As soon as it became airborne the undercarriage came up. The plane climbed steeply with little attempt to execute the familiar pattern of the standard circuit. It quickly reached 5000 feet when the pilot did a series of rolls, loops and flick rolls. Then followed a screaming dive at the airfield. Although they appreciated it was a demonstration the watchers instinctively ducked as the plane screamed at them from 50 feet above ground. When they got up the Hurricane was streaking along the airfield at about 250 feet. The pilot then executed a slow roll, climbed to the correct circuit height and came in to make a perfect three point landing. Amid the babble of excited onlookers F/Lt Jones addressed the pilots.

'Gentlemen. That is what you must never do. Have a good night's rest. Swot up on Pilots Notes and we'll make an early start tomorrow. First flight will be at 0800 hours. Good luck.'

Over the next few days with varying degrees of competence they all flew the Hurricanes and with each flight gained the necessary confidence to carry out the instructions issued over the R/T. The next three days were given over to gunnery practice and without exception they all ran out of ammunition so quickly that had it been for real they would have had none left if they had been attacked. Each novice Hurricane pilot was accompanied by one of the instructors flying close by in the other machine.

They were instructed in the tried and tested method of firing in short bursts – a sighting shot then brief bursts not only to conserve ammunition but also to ensure greater accuracy. The two instructors seemed well pleased with the new Hurricane pilots who now wanted to know when more of these aircraft would become available.

'Not really sure but with the Battle of Britain virtually over we think Jerry has lost so many aircraft it will be some time before he attempts that again. Aircraft production in the UK is high. The only problem is getting them out here.'

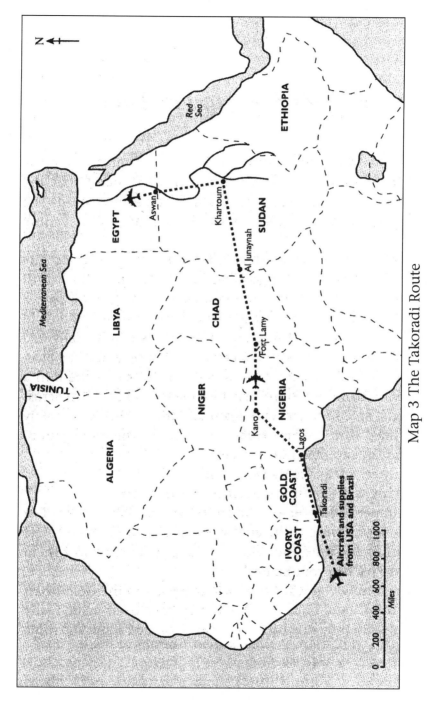

Map 3 The Takoradi Route

CHAPTER 16

*Fighter Pilot to Ferryman**

When the pilots returned to their own squadrons in the desert at the end of the week they found that the problem of aircraft supplies might have been resolved. The Wing Commander spoke to all of them after the evening meal.

'Anyone know where Takoradi is?' It seemed that no one had any idea. The Wingco continued. 'Neither had I until three days ago.' He uncovered a large map hanging over a blackboard. 'Here it is on the west coast of Africa, the Gold Coast to be precise.† Aircraft and supplies will be delivered there. Some will be boxed, taken to an airstrip and assembled. Others will fly off from an aircraft carrier. From there in a series of flights and stop-overs new planes will be flown across Nigeria, and on to French Equatorial Africa, which fortunately has sided with the Free French. From there the route goes to the Sudan and then north to Egypt.'

'Any of you like to fly Hurricanes?'

A chorus of shouts in agreement filled the air.

'I understand you all did pretty well on your course last week. If you want Hurricanes you must go to Takoradi to get them. By the time you return to Egypt you will know them like the back of your hands.'

'Tomorrow you will fly in two transports to the Gold Coast and from there once the Hurricanes have been made ready you will each fly one back. You will be briefed about the

---

* See also note at the end of this chapter.

† Takoradi is also known as Sekundi-Takoradi especially as the two towns have now merged into one huge area.

128

route and you must not stray from it. From Takoradi you will fly to Lagos in Nigeria where you will refuel and have a rest. Later that day you fly on to Chad in French Equatorial Africa and stop there for the night. The next day you cross into the Sudan, refuel at Al Junaynah and then fly on to Khartoum. The following day there will be two stages through Egypt before you land here.'

The Wing Commander went on to explain that the total mileage from Takoradi to Egypt was in excess of 3600 miles. The re-fuelling and stop-over points had been worked out and they should try to keep to them. They were not to stray from the agreed flight plan but if for whatever reason they had to make a forced landing they must give a map reference before they landed. They were reminded that they would be flying over really wild, inhospitable country and would therefore be carrying two water bottles, emergency rations, salt tablets, a first aid kit and a ground shelter.

He continued to hold their attention. 'That's the plan but like most plans on paper it may not work out quite like that. Don't take chances. We'd rather you arrive late than not at all. This will be a proving flight and no doubt there will be alternative stop-over points. You will gradually become familiar with the aircraft but it will be a tiring experience so I urge you to rest as much as you can and eat well on the route.'

'While you bring in these aircraft the RAF transports will be ferrying out more pilots to Takoradi. Once you get back here you'll have a couple of days off before you return again to the Gold Coast and return with more Hurricanes. Incidentally, the transports are not returning here empty. They are bringing in spares and vast amounts of ammunition and a few ground crews. Any questions?'

Sam wanted to know if new squadrons were to be formed. 'No.' Came the answer. 'The squadrons already here will remain. They will be re-equipped with Hurricanes. Moreover we are being reinforced by two New Zealand squadrons, three from Australia and two from South Africa.'

'You are not to read too much into these arrangements but it would seem to indicate that if the Italians attack again we shall be more than ready for them. I'll come and see you off tomorrow.'

The news was good and was received in almost total silence. Then as the truth began to sink in there were broad grins everywhere and a gradual murmur of voices until it reached a crescendo. It meant that at last the desert air force would be getting some modern planes even if the pilots had to go and get them.

'I thought they had ferry pilots to do this fetching and carrying.' moaned someone who was immediately shouted down before he could utter another word by the angry voices of his fellow pilots.

'Be your age. Ferry pilots do a good job but this way we get to know the aircraft before we have to go into battle. I think its a marvellous scheme. Good luck to the chap who thought it up.' Sam, as ever the optimist stated what most pilots felt.

The next morning they heard a steady throb of engines as the two transports joined the circuit and prepared to land. To Harry they looked the same as those which had brought him to Kenya, now a long time ago. Closer inspection revealed that they were Vickers Victorias. With two engines and a top speed of no more than 130 mph it would take them a long time to reach the Gold Coast and much depended on what airfields or landing strips they could find on the way. They were airborne by 0800 hours and the two planes flew more or less together in open formation. At the maximum speed of 130 mph the land some 5000 feet below seemed never to change.

For hour after hour, or so it seemed, the planes droned steadily southwards following the course of the Nile. Then having covered over 470 miles they landed at Aswan.

Civilization existed close to the banks yet a few miles from the influence of the great river the pilots knew that the featureless desert stretched for miles. It would not be a good place to attempt a forced landing. The short break for a meal allowed the planes to be refuelled but soon they were on their way hoping to reach Khartoum before nightfall.

Flying due south they covered another 675 miles, almost the limit of the transport's range, before the twinkling lights of Khartoum could be seen against the setting sun. Their landing ground was some miles west of the town and again little more than a bare strip cleared out from the scrubland. Even as they approached there were still native labourers who continued to move rocks and stones away from the path and stack them at the side. However, the flare path had been lit and a green flashed from the ground gave the pilots permission to land.

Behind a narrow belt of trees they came to a huddle of huts which appeared to have been newly erected. Once inside they sat down at four long trestle tables and devoured the food placed before them. It was a sort of stew with dumplings, potatoes and greens. It went down well although Sam voiced the thoughts of many when he declared. 'That went down a treat but I don't think we should ask too many questions as to what it was or where it came from.' The water on the table was warm and had a peculiar taste as though someone had put in too much chlorine. Then followed rice pudding, obviously made with evaporated milk which by now they mostly enjoyed. It was unsweetened although on each table were two large tins of jam.

Tea and coffee were available in urns at the back of the hut. Both drinks were very hot, almost too hot and both seemed devoid of actual taste. Towards the end of the meal an army officer greeted the assembled pilots.

'We apologise for the meal gentlemen. Didn't know you were arriving until three days ago and since then we've had to clear the site, erect the huts and try to get the place habitable. I guarantee on your next visit things will be much improved. I can't provide napkins but the meal itself should be more to your liking. We are awaiting the arrival of two field kitchens and proper provisions. Accommodation for tonight is in the three large huts. No beds as yet but they should be here for your next visit.'

Harry felt that some response was called for. 'Sir on behalf of everyone I'd like to thank you and your staff for making us so welcome and for providing such a sustaining meal under most difficult conditions.' Murmurs of approval amid applause came from the assembled company much to the pleasure of the army officer.

The transport pilots announced that the following day they hoped to reach Fort Lamy in the French colony of Chad. However as the distance was too far for the planes to make it in one hop they would have to land at Mahla Wells to refuel. This township was due west of their present position and still in the Sudan. However as they had received no indication that a meal would be available at Mahla Wells they would need to take sandwiches and flasks of coffee with them. The next morning, once they were airborne, the navigator in each plane sat at his small desk, worked out the estimated time of arrival, checked the drift as the aeroplane crabbed across the land below and worked out a new course to allow for the wind.

The landing strip at Mahla Wells was actually better than they had anticipated. Once on the ground and into the comparative shade provided by a hutted encampment and a few trees they started on their sandwiches and were assured that a meal would be available on their next visit. In spite of hearing the all too familiar excuse the pilots accepted the further delay with good grace. In fact three huge lorries carrying food and all manner of provisions arrived while they were still eating. The lorry drivers explained that the fuel expected at Fort Lamy had not arrived and as a consequence the RAF transports would have to spend the night where they were.

Now that the food had arrived they were assured of an evening meal and breakfast the next morning. In the meantime they settled down to play cards or wander around the small town until it was time for bed. More delays regarding the fuel kept the planes grounded until midday when they were assured that the fuel had arrived at their next staging post. However it would be at Arada, also in Chad, and not Fort Lamy, the old capital of the colony. So having eaten a quite passable lunch the ferry pilots were on board their transports and set off on the next part of their journey to Takoradi.

It was now 1400 hours and as the sun sets early nearer the equator everyone hoped that this leg of the journey would not be too far. In just three hours it would be getting dark as the planes droned onwards. The flight so far had been a new experience for most of the pilots who had never flown in RAF transports before, a busman's holiday in fact. They passed the time watching the ground pass slowly beneath them, interspersed with animated conversation regarding the new Hurricanes. Most of the time they just dozed.

The afternoon flight to Arada seemed endless. It could have been the aftermath of a large meal or maybe they were all just tired. Conversation dwindled into the odd comment. Then having flown another 375 miles during the afternoon they began to descend and in the distance they could make out the lights of a flare path dead ahead. If anything the landing strip was rougher than the previous one but both planes touched down safely. Once they had returned down the strip and parked for the night everyone got out. They were ushered towards a large hut where a meal was waiting for them.

This time it was braised guinea-fowl, potatoes, greens and gravy, followed by stewed paw-paw which many of the pilots had already tasted at previous stations. At the end of the meal a French army officer addressed them in almost perfect English. 'Good evening gentlemen. Hope you had a pleasant flight. There are four huts nearby where you will sleep tonight. Outside each is an ablutions block. Breakfast is a 0630 hours and I understand you will be departing at 0730 hours. I accept that conditions are a bit primitive at the moment but I can assure you on your next visit facilities will be much improved. Sleep well.'

Having checked over their sleeping quarters the pilots looked for the ablutions block. All along the outside of one hut there was a bench on which were placed at intervals small washing bowls. Three steaming cauldrons of water together with large ladles provided the hot water for a wash and a shave. The pilots went to bed early and were asleep within minutes. During their recent fighting against the Italians they had got into the habit of taking rests whenever the opportunity presented itself. It was no real hardship to sleep on straw-filled palliasses raised on bunks about 18 inches from the ground.

Another delay greeted the pilots as they woke on the third day. The need and the decision to set up the Takoradi route had taken everybody by surprise. It was a tremendous undertaking and would be some time before the system was fully operational. It was fortunate for the Allies that Chad was one of the few French African colonies that had decided to join the fight against Hitler. Now they went out of their way to help the RAF men. The enforced delay was put to good use by the fitters who had accompanied the proving flight. The transport pilots decided to wait until the next morning before continuing the journey. In the meantime French fitters joined in to assist in a rapid overhaul of the engines.

At last they received confirmation that fuel and provisions were available at all scheduled stops so a day later than intended the RAF transports set out on the last two legs of their mammoth journey. The next two days went according to plan. The first stop was accomplished in the morning, landing at Kano, a fairly large town in the northern part of Nigeria. A meal for the pilots and fuel for the planes was quickly done and they were soon airborne on their way to Lagos. As they approached the Nigerian capital the Atlantic Ocean was a welcome sight after the thousands of miles of inhospitable country they had flown over. From 5000 feet they could see the waves breaking on the shore while inland vast areas of low lying ground glinted in a variety of colours as the sun shone on large tracts of water.

The flight from Kano had taken four hours and once on the ground the men looked forward to an overnight rest. Journey's end was almost in sight while here in the capital the accommodation was the best they been offered throughout the trip.

A rain squall greeted them the following morning but it quickly passed to reveal a clear bright day. It was not long before they were airborne and in a few hours they saw their destination bathed in sunshine. The air was clear and they could see for miles as they flew westwards along the coast. If the hinterland north of Lagos had appeared water-logged the area inland from Takoradi was positively awash with water. The huge Lake Volta stretched for more than 200 miles making it appear that half the colony was under water.

The whole journey seemed longer although they had actually been in the air for a total of only 30 hours and refuelled six times when at last they arrived at Takoradi. Compared to most of the previous stop-overs it was a thriving city which they could see a few miles away as they came into land on the last leg of their journey. A few freighters were in port being unloaded and just off the coast they could see several warships including an aircraft carrier protected by a screen of torpedo nets and destroyers. They slept in barracks overnight that were like palaces in comparison to the sleeping quarters during their journey. After their evening meal and before retiring for the night they made the most of their improved conditions and began to unwind with a few drinks and a sing-song.

Early next morning at the nearby airfield all the pilots were given a resume of the Hurricane's capabilities and then allowed a familiarization flight lasting half an hour. Later in the afternoon they were all called to a briefing, given several maps and detailed instructions for the long trip ahead. As far as possible it seemed that the authorities had thought of everything to ensure a safe delivery of the precious planes to Egypt and the fighting which lay ahead.

Two days later they took off in their new Hurricanes at five minute intervals and were instructed not to close in on the aircraft ahead because the ground crews at each stop-over could only handle one plane at a time. The pilots nodded although all knew this was not the real reason.. If one plane had crashed on landing the ground staff needed time to clear away the wreckage before the next one arrived.

The Hurricane's top speed was 320 mph but they were told to fly well below that to conserve fuel. At 300 mph they could expect to cover 900 miles before refuelling so they anticipated fewer stops on the return flight to Egypt compared to those in the much slower transports on the way to the Gold Coast. Not all the stop-over points were equidistant and it was left to individual pilots to keep a check on their fuel consumption and make the appropriate landing long before they ran out of fuel. After that first proving flight there was never a shortage of fuel. A few air transports made sure that sufficient petrol was always available though soon large fleets of lorries took over the arduous task of carrying fuel and other supplies for this vital lifeline.

New refuelling and rest points were established along the route and because of their greater range the Hurricanes needed fewer. On one occasion Sam flew the old route while Harry tried out a new one. Harry parted company with Sam and flew to Al Junaynah just inside the Sudanese border and then on to Khartoum. They arrived at Khartoum within minutes of each other. The base at Khartoum expanded between each visit and within two months had become the largest staging post on the Takoradi route.

During October every pilot made two flights to Takoradi in the transport planes and returned to Egypt flying a much needed Hurricane. Once back with their own squadron they put in a lot of flying practice and gradually built up their expertise, not only in flying skills but also in gunnery. A few additional ground crews also arrived and they quickly set about instructing the others. By the end of October the newly equipped squadrons were ready for business.

November 1940 passed off much the same, each pilot making two more flights to the Gold Coast and back.

* Note. The full name is SEKONDI – TAKORADI although the town is usually known by its shorter version.

Once the route from Takoradi to Egypt had been proved it was used by the RAF and later by the American Army Air Force to ferry planes and equipment for several years from 1940 to 1945. As experienced by most military personnel during war time there were long periods of inactivity. While waiting for ships to arrive and aircraft to be assembled and tested time often dragged heavily for the ferry pilots at Takoradi. A variety of games helped pass the time. Apart from the usual card games and the Two Up gambling introduced by the Australians there was another which gained popularity. The dense forests which covered the route had many varieties of trees. Some were soft wood. Many were hard wood but all were slightly different in colour and in the grain. Several of the different coloured woods were machined into small oblong blocks, measuring about 1" x 4" x ½"

The game itself was simple, 48 different coloured blocks being used. Three were placed on their narrowest edge parallel to each other on a flat surface, usually the bar at a pub. Across these three more blocks were placed at right angles and so on until all 48 blocks had been used making a small tower of 16 stories. Then the first player had to remove one block from anywhere and place it at the top using only one hand. The next player did the same until, in theory, all single blocks had been erected one above the other and at right angles until 24 stories had been reached.

It doesn't sound too exciting but when one considers the amount of drinking that went on during such rest periods the pilots' hands were not very steady. Side bets were often quite heavy as teams competed. The secret of the blocks lay in the fact that each was marginally different in size although to the eye they all looked alike. The game was called TAKORADI.

A modern version may now be purchased from high class Games shops. It is called TAKERADI: an African game. Note the variation in the spelling.

CHAPTER 17

Attack! Attack!

Having nurtured his forces, put them through intensive training and built up supplies for the Army and the RAF, Wavell felt confident that he could now go over to the offensive, at least for a limited campaign of no more than five days. One of his aides, not within the general's hearing, suggested that the commander had so got into the habit of garnering his forces that he would be reluctant to go for an all out attack. But Wavell knew what was necessary and what was possible. Part of the reason for his action now would be an attempt to relieve the hard pressed British garrisons who had been forced to fall back when the Italians attacked in the Sudan, Kenya and British Somaliland.

The Italians were also attacking Greece from Albania and were not having it all their own way. By deliberately taking the fight to the Italians in Egypt at this time Wavell argued that the enemy might be persuaded to recall some of their troops from the East African campaigns as well as those which were now attacking Greece. In spite of their surprise attack against them the Greeks managed to stop the Italians but not for long.

Wavell continued the ploy he had used earlier to keep the enemy guessing. Leave for soldiers and airmen continued so that Cairo, Alex. and even Suez seemed to be full of British service personnel. As far as the men were concerned they too were unaware that the general was about to attack. The constant change of men going on leave every few days helped in this subterfuge and allowed the men as much time off as possible in war time. On one of these occasions Harry and

Sam met for the first time in weeks. After the brief exchange of news their talk was mostly about the merits of their new Hurricanes compared with their previous planes and they fell back into the easy relationship they had experienced since their early days at medical school.

Wavell's commanders in the field were experienced men: General O'Connor for the army and Air Vice-Marshal Longmore in charge of the RAF. Each realised the need for attacking now that they had new equipment although both doubted that their efforts would do much to help their comrades hundreds of miles away in the East African theatre of operations. They saw it as a golden opportunity to test their new tanks and aircraft and to promote a closer liaison between all three fighting services. Once again the Royal Navy was providing the heavy guns.

On 9th December 1940 General Wavell gave the start order for this limited attack and called on the navy for a supporting bombardment from the sea. The army had been reinforced by troops from Australia, New Zealand and South Africa and moreover they were now equipped with the new Matilda tanks. The RAF was also in an upbeat mood. Not only had the three original fighter squadrons been re-equipped with Hurricanes they also had two squadrons of Wellingtons and three of Blenheims.

The campaign started well. Diversionary attacks were delivered by the RAF desert force on Tobruk, Benghazi, Bardia and Derna. At the same time Wellingtons from Malta attacked Tripoli while the navy bombarded Sidi Barrani, Bardia and other coastal towns. Wavell's plan was not to saturate any one particular Italian stronghold but to allow the RAF to hit dozens of targets within a short space of time.

Longmore, the RAF Commander-in-chief, gave instructions for the bomber crews to drop a proportion of their load on nearby targets and then to fly on to release the remaining bombs on more distant Italian positions. This, hopefully, would make the Italians believe he had a greater bomber force at his disposal than was actually the case. In much the same way he deployed his fighter squadrons to escort the bombers and then to break away and attack enemy troop concentrations and other targets at will.

For the first few days the Italians thought they were indeed up against much larger enemy forces than was the case, helped no doubt by press releases to the Egyptian papers. The accounts there gave complete coverage of the British advances and the huge armies and RAF squadrons engaged. The navy too came in for its share of glory with exaggerated reports of the devastation caused by bombardment all along the Libyan coast. At the same time the British navy subs and surface vessels continued to sink Italian transports plying between Italy and Mussolini's North Africa Empire. By the time they realised they had fallen into a propaganda trap the Italians had already begun to retreat.

Sam, Harry and the other British pilots were relieved to be in action once more and knowing this time that they had the faster machines. Long gone were the leisure days when flying commenced at 06.00 hours and stopped at noon for a siesta because of the heat. Now it was a case of take off, complete the attack, return to refuel and rearm and then off on another sortie. In order to keep up the pretence that they had dozens of squadrons the fighters were ordered to return to different airfields to refuel. And it worked.

The first army units set off at 07.30 hours on day one, initially to destroy one or two of the enemy camps which the Italians had been building since they invaded Egypt in September. If the attacks were successful the troops were ordered to also pay attention to other forts along the escarpment and to shell the Italian barracks at Sidi Barrani and Maktila. The 4th Indian Division with their new equipment occupied Sidi Barrani on 10th December but once having consolidated the town and begun to settle in they were withdrawn. They were sent hundreds of miles to the east to mount an attack into Ethiopia. However their place was taken by the 6th Australian Division and by 13th December all Italian positions in Egypt had been overrun and thousands of Italians marched back into P.O.W. camps.

With the campaign going so well Operation Compass was extended beyond its original five days and the victorious British and their Allies advanced into Cyrenaica. Units of the 7th Armoured Division were on their way to Bardia and Tobruk. Sam and Harry met up again when their squadrons, returning from operations far to the west, were ordered to land at El Adem which had just been occupied by the army and cleared of obstacles. While waiting for their planes to be refuelled and rearmed they had their first sit down meal in days.

At first glance Sam merely nodded in Harry's direction, acknowledging another RAF pilot who looked as tired and dirty as he felt. Looking round he saw others who were in much the same condition, almost too tired to eat yet savouring each mouthful and hoping against hope that they could stay in the relatively peaceful surroundings for a few hours at least.

They were in luck. The order was given for the action to be called off until the following day when more supplies would have arrived and the whole area made more habitable. Victorious troops can keep going for a long time yet there comes a point when it is prudent to call a halt to recharge both men and machines. That time had come for the two Hurricane squadrons and the army units which had captured the largest airfield in the western desert.

Others, for the moment, would carry the fight against a faltering yet not quite beaten enemy. Almost as soon as they finished their meal and lay down to snatch a few hours sleep they heard the steady drone of Wellingtons and Blenheims passing overhead and the unmistakable sound of the other

Hurricane squadron escorting the bombers to their next targets.

After what seemed only a few minutes but in reality was six hours later Harry was gently shaken awake.

'Cup of tea Sir? There's hot water if you'd like a wash and a shave.'

Gradually coming out of a deep sleep Harry heard the words and their meaning seeped into his consciousness. He realised how thirsty he was, but there was something else. The voice was vaguely familiar. Suddenly everything clicked into place and for the first time in days he smiled.

'Corporal Hudson! Where on earth did you spring from. Thanks for the tea.'

Got fed up with Ismailia and when they asked for volunteers I jumped at the chance to see something other than barracks. We started out two days ago in a dirty great convoy and have been travelling ever since. We now have the job of cleaning up this place and looking after you. Begging your pardon Sir, but you really made an awful mess of this Italian airfield.'

"Never thought I'd see you again but I'm very glad. I think we can do with all the help we can get.'

Refreshed, Harry stood up and at Hudson's suggestion moved outside and into a huge tent which had been erected. Inside it was a hive of activity as men in various states of undress had their first wash and shave in days. Just arrived at the camp there was even a small stores unit where they were able to pick up a change of clothes, leaving their dirty ones in a bag with their names. These would be laundered and returned sometime in the future. Now that everyone began to look more presentable having washed away the dirt of several days there were smiles everywhere and gradual acknowledgement as comrades recognised each other.

'Breakfast is available for the next hour.' The announcement was greeted with cheers as the men, pilots and ground crews, made their way back to the large building where they had first arrived. There Sam and Harry met up again and for the first time ever actually hugged each other with tears in their eyes, happy and relieved that they were both alive. Over breakfast and between mouthfuls of bacon and eggs they exchanged their news. Their relief at seeing each other was tinged with sadness as they recalled those from their squadrons who had been killed or wounded.

'I suppose we'd better go over to the squadron office and see what they've got lined up for us.' Harry posed the question which was on everyone's lips. He hadn't seen his own Squadron Leader for several days although he knew he was still in one piece. The pilots from his own flight joined Harry as he and Sam walked over to the broken down building which for the time being served as their H.Q. The scene on the airfield was one of great activity.

Gangs of men, soldiers, airmen, and native labourers were clearing the landing areas of debris and on seeing so much rubble they thanked their lucky stars that they had managed to miss it when they landed yesterday. The sappers from the army had already made safe unexploded bombs and detonated huge stocks of ammunition of no use to the victors who now occupied the former Italian strong point.

Inside, pilots and aircrew sat on the few chairs available. Others squatted on the floor and awaited the arrival of the AOC and his entourage. They hadn't long to wait. 'Good morning gentlemen. I hope you all managed a few hours rest. Sadly some of your friends are missing but I'm happy to tell you that many are safe, some with minor wounds, a few with more serious injuries. Inevitably we have lost a few good men. Let us stand for a few minutes in silent tribute to them.'

They all stood up, silently remembering missing faces, recalling times spent together and wondering perhaps how long it might be before they themselves were being remembered.

'Please be seated.' After a brief pause he went on, 'As you know Operation Compass which was scheduled for five days was given a new lease of life. It will continue for a while yet. For the moment this will be our forward base and depending on what needs to be done we shall be returning here after each sortie.'

The next few days were busy with several flights each day though nothing like the frantic sorties of the previous week. Christmas came and went. By 6th January 1941 Bardia had been taken and almost without pausing a British armoured brigade had reached the outskirts of Tobruk. El Adem, although it still bore the scars of battle looked much better and the planes continued to take off and land without fear of falling into craters. Every few hours more lorries arrived with supplies and workshops were set up while fresh troops continued to pour in.

Everyone was fired up with the victories so far achieved but all the machines needed overhauling. The tanks had travelled far longer than was intended without major overhaul and replacement of vital parts. The aircraft too needed time on the ground for the fitters to carry out important maintenance. Even the supply trucks groaning under the weight of the stuff they carried needed a rest for their overheated engines trying to combat the heat and the sand.

If the machines needed a rest so too did the men. The aircrews had been flying more or less non stop for days. The ground crews had worked themselves almost to a standstill in order to keep the machines in the air. The soldiers checked their weapons, re-supplied their tanks, took what rest they could and awaited the next call to attack. Tobruk received more attention from the navy and the RAF and by 24th January ground forces captured this important Italian port. As soon as all the enemy POWs had been sent back east the cleaning up operations kept all units busy with little time for the rest and recuperation they needed. The call to arms came sooner than expected.

Intelligence reports confirmed that the Italians were about to withdraw from Cyrenaica altogether. If the Italians escaped into Tripolitania they might then shelter behind two rivers, which although only intermittently full of water, were nevertheless obstructions to be overcome by the British. Furthermore it was not known what military obstacles the enemy had managed to erect further west. One more important aspect was that Tunisia, ostensibly neutral, might allow the Italians sanctuary within its borders. It was well known that the Royal Navy had not stopped short of attacking the French navy when it refused to come over to the allies after the fall of France. Specific orders had come direct from Whitehall for this assault after much heart searching on Churchill's part.

This operation against a former ally had not gone down too well with the officers and men of the Royal Navy who carried out the orders. On land if the Italians were once allowed to take shelter in Tunisia it might well mean additional operations against the French and nobody wished to contemplate such a move.

Somehow the British had to win this race. In effect they had to move fast, much faster than the enemy, to overtake them and stop them in their tracks. With enough supplies for two days and barely enough petrol to get them to Benghazi the army set off from El Adem. As they passed Tobruk they waved to the victorious troops who had recently captured this stronghold and started out along the coast road in pursuit of the Italians. Meanwhile another British column had set out along an inland route, rested for a few hours at Bir Hakeim and then headed for Mechili on top of the escarpment.

CHAPTER 18

Down in the Desert

Although the RAF in the desert now had faster planes than the Italian Air Force it was still outnumbered even with the additional help of a squadron from the South African Air Force, and others from New Zealand and Australia. The three British fighter squadrons now operated from El Adem so Harry often met Sam on the ground and occasionally they were part of the same formation which either protected the bombers or acted as ground attack fighters. Whatever inter-squadron rivalry may have existed in the past the main purpose now was to get the next part of their war completed as quickly as possible and then have a well deserved rest.

There was no doubt that the enemy was on the run although the vast distances they needed to retreat in order to take advantage of any natural defences left the airmen at a slight disadvantage. They had to operate a long way from their base. Very occasionally, especially if they were escorting bombers far to the west they encountered tough enemy opposition. Over zealous RAF fighter pilots were held in check by their leaders with reminders to return to base long before they ran out of fuel.

It was on one such return trip that Harry had time to take stock of the landscape below where hundreds of enemy trucks and tanks moved slowly westwards like an endless snake. The land itself was dull, drab even, with little in the way of colour to break the monotony of the never ending sand. After rain it looked even worse while during a sandstorm it was impossible to see anything even a few yards away. For the aircrews when this happened the only possible navigating was to head for the coast and try to pick out landmarks in order to make it back to base.

In contrast the sea was a colour Harry had never consciously noticed before – a deep turquoise which looked totally unreal but very inviting. Apart from the few coastal towns and villages which boasted some vegetation the only green parts for thousands of square miles were the few inland villages built around oases. The contrast was striking and for a few moments Harry allowed his mind to shut out the war and imagined himself swimming in the cool clear waters below.

Orders were suddenly changed. In order to keep the aircraft airworthy two flights from each squadron flew on consecutive days. The third flight was grounded for maintenance which was welcomed by the pilots as a day off. With little to do such days were given over to sleeping and eating. The ground staff were kept busy the whole time. Only at night did they get any rest and even then they occasionally worked late into the small hours.

Derna was captured on 30th January and from them onwards the RAF used captured airfields rather than making the long flight back to El Adem. Harry was sent on a reconnaissance flight west of Derna and towards Barce where he came across huge concentrations of Italian troops and armour. Flying further west he reached Benghazi and after circling at a safe height he concluded that the enemy were getting ready to leave even that stronghold. Returning quickly to base he made his report and a small bomber force was despatched to try and delay the Italian departure so that British troops and armour could catch up.

A decision was taken for the troops harassing the Italians on the coast road to increase the pressure while those at Mecheli, which had recently been captured, would split into two groups. One column would move north west towards the coast. The second would attempt the more difficult terrain across country and try to reach Beda Fomm before the Italians.

In the meantime Harry's assessment of the Italian intentions having been confirmed, all three fighter squadrons were in action again escorting a mixture of Wellingtons and Blenheims. Half way between Derna and Barce the Italians sent up strong formations against the bomber force and some of the fighters had to break off the engagement in order to refuel. About half of the fighters with sufficient fuel remained while the others returned to base. After about two hours it looked as if the RAF had won the day again. Although they hadn't lost any planes many of the bombers bore scars from the Italian fighter attacks and anti-aircraft guns. They all made it safely back to base although four had to make belly landings as their undercarriages had been damaged.

Harry had been escorting one badly damaged Wellington back, looking out for enemy fighters on the way when he was told over the R/T 'Thank you. We can make it from here. See you in the mess for a drink tonight.' Breaking away Harry saw a Hurricane going down. At first he thought the pilot intended to ditch in the sea and headed towards the doomed aircraft. He then realised that the pilot was making for a level stretch of ground. The plane appeared to be not badly damaged. 'Probably run out of petrol' thought Harry. As he got closer he recognised it as Sam's aircraft by the number and tried to raise him on the R/T but without success.

Sam made an almost perfect landing and as the plane ran along the ground Harry breathed a sigh of relief which quickly changed to a gasp of horror as the little plane stopped abruptly. Almost in slow motion the nose dug into the sand and the tail stuck up in the air. Harry circled lower expecting Sam to scramble out of the cockpit but there was no movement from the pilot.

By this time his own fuel was getting low. He dared not risk a landing next to Sam so, having called him on the R/T

149

again with no response he climbed up and flew eastwards towards the temporary airfield.

He called base on the R/T. 'This is Blue Leader'

There was an immediate response. 'Hello Blue Leader. This is Solo. Pass your message.'

Harry gave his reply. 'Hello Solo. Blue Leader. Ask Sgt Watson to prepare Lizzie with fuel, blankets, water bottles and a medical pack. One of our pilots is down, Map Ref. ZX 1650 0055. I'll be landing back at base in approximately ten minutes. Blue Leader Out.'

The operator at base replied. 'Blue Leader. This is Solo. Wilco.'

Harry settled down to fly the 70 miles back to the airfield. He knew Sgt Watson would have the Lysander ready with the items he had requested, the plane itself checked and probably the engine ticking over. More than likely he'd want to accompany Harry to help the downed pilot. Harry had to wait his turn in the circuit before he could land but having got down he taxied quickly to the control cabin to book in and make his report. While he did so Sgt Watson transferred his parachute to the Lysander and within five minutes of landing Harry settled himself in the cockpit and began to familiarize himself with the layout of the controls and instruments.

'Sign the log book for me please Tom.'

'Sure. You want me to come with you?'

'Not this time thanks. You could have a good look at my plane. I think I've got a few bullet holes in the tail section.'

Receiving a green light from control Harry turned the aircraft into wind and took off towards Sam. With no armaments to ward off the enemy this time he gained height but only enough to enable him to recognise the landmarks and to identify the small bay near where Sam's plane had gone down. Flying westwards a hundred miles an hour slower than in his Hurricane Harry saw the main body of the retreating Italian army which seemed to have slowed down considerably. Many of the vehicles appeared to be badly shot up and even as he watched the whole column ground to a halt while tired soldiers manhandled a broken-down truck off the road.

Then the column started moving again. He estimated it was about 50 miles from Sam's position and at its present speed it would reach him in under three hours. Once having got his bearings Harry reduced height and about 18 minutes after take-off he circled the downed Hurricane fully expecting that Sam had managed to get out by now. However he seemed to be firmly strapped into his seat. Harry eased back on the throttle and allowed the plane to side-slip in order to reduce height quickly before finally straightening up for the final approach. Then he was on the ground which although hard underneath was covered with about two inches of soft sand. Remembering Sam's misfortune Harry pulled back hard on the control column to keep the tail on the ground and did not attempt to apply the brakes. The Lysander came to a stop within a few yards of the Hurricane. Harry kept the engine ticking over, clambered down and with increased concern for Sam struggled out with one of the water bottles, the first aid bag, a blanket and emergency rations.

CHAPTER 19

Rescue Mission

As soon as he reached the Hurricane Harry encountered his first problem and wished he'd accepted Tom Watson's offer to accompany him. He could see Sam slumped in the cockpit, unconscious. At least he hoped he was unconscious and not dead. With the tail stuck high in the air it was going to be difficult to get Sam out. He realised the first thing he must do would be to get the plane level. He tried reaching up to the tail and then jumping to get at it without success. The Hurricane's nose was not actually stuck in the sand but the sheer weight of the engine kept it firmly in its present position.

With some difficulty Harry scrambled on to the wing and reached the cockpit where he could see that Sam was wounded but hopefully still alive. The next problem was to get to the tail and hope that his weight would be sufficient to tip the plane level but not too quickly in case the sudden movement increased Sam's injuries. He needed to hurry but kept warning himself, 'Gently does it.'

Sitting astride the fuselage he eased himself towards the tail and pressing down with his hands rather like a game of leapfrog he slowly moved his body towards the tail. What with the effort, the need for urgency and the need for caution he was sweating by the time he reached the tail section and still the plane hadn't moved. If he stood up and slipped he might injure himself so he tried once more raising himself on his hands and letting his weight come down quickly. He felt the plane move so tried again but it was still not enough. He appreciated the plane would need to be repaired before it could be flown off so considered a little more damage would not really matter.

He stood up, balanced, jumped on to the tail plane and was rewarded by a definite movement. As he held on to the rudder he was gently lowered as the nose came unstuck and the tail wheel hit the ground and stayed there. Offering up a silent prayer he walked back to the front of the plane, put his foot into the familiar footholds in the fuselage and swung himself up to the cockpit. With the canopy already open he was able to reach in and check for Sam's pulse. As he did so Sam opened his eyes and said in a remarkably strong voice, 'What kept you?'

'Thank God you're alive. Are you O.K? God I thought you were dead. Are you badly hurt? Don't worry. I'll get you out. I've brought a Lizzie and I'll have you back at base in no time.' Harry realised he was babbling but it didn't really matter. He needed to keep talking to make his patient respond though in his heart he knew the real reason was sheer relief that his friend was alive.

'I'm going to release your harness and then your parachute.' Reaching down Harry removed the harness clip, then the straps from Sam's legs and shoulders and then hit the release mechanism on his parachute. The next problem was to get Sam out of the cockpit and on to the ground without causing him more injuries. He would face the problem of getting him across to the Lizzie and into the cabin later. Harry reached in and grabbed the lever which raised the cockpit seat and seeing Sam's eyes open again asked him where he had been hit.

'My left arm and I think my left leg although I can't feel it but I think I've lost a lot of blood.' was his weak response.

'Can you put your weight on your right leg and if I put my hands under your shoulders we'll try to get you out.' Harry sat astride the fuselage while Sam braced himself and together they heaved until Sam was able to put his foot on the parachute pack.

'You've put on a bit of weight. Its a good job you lost some blood.' Harry tried to joke and Sam tried to smile but was unable to prevent a groan of pain as he slumped back into the seat.

Harry took a breather. 'Right we'll try again. I don't want you to fall to the ground. Once you are out of the cockpit try to use the footholds and I'll be on the ground to take some of your weight.'

Sam was obviously in pain and worried in case the movement caused his wounds to bleed again. This time Harry got in front of Sam and helped to pull him from the cockpit. Sam was able to turn round and get his good leg outside and feeling for the footholds. Harry then squeezed into the cockpit and helped Sam get his damaged leg out.

'Wait till I get on the ground before you let go.'

As soon as they were both on the ground Harry cut away Sam's shirt and examined the wound, high up in the muscle of the upper arm. An entry and an exit wound indicated that the bullet had passed right through and fortunately the blood remained congealed. Harry didn't stop to clean the wound but put a pad over each hole and then a fairly tight bandage.

There was another wound in the same arm near the wrist and to Harry's inexperienced eye it looked the more serious as he thought he could see the exposed bone. He cleaned and then bandaged this and completed his work on the arm by applying a sling and a bandage around the body to keep the arm secure.

He then turned his attention to Sam's foot and as gently as possible removed his boot. He had to use some water as the blood had congealed on the sock but after a few minutes and many apologies to Sam he managed to expose the wound. It probably looked worse than it was but to Harry it looked a total mess and he wondered if Sam would ever walk properly again.

'Sam, I'm going to give you a shot of morphine. I think I ought to clean this up a bit before putting a dressing on. O.K.'

'Sure. It hurts like hell.'

'Here we go then as they say. It's only a little prick.' Sam actually managed a smile at the well worn joke. Harry worked carefully and as quickly as possible to get the wound cleaned and covered. At last he was finished and checked over the rest of the leg. 'Right my lad. That should do until we get to hospital. Have you got any more aches and pains. We may as well do the lot while we're at it.'

'No thank you doctor. That's the lot but your bedside manner leaves a lot to be desired.' Although still in pain and shock Sam entered into the light hearted banter.

Harry was quick to reply 'Well you see sir. I'm not really a proper doctor. I just get sent out on these nuisance visits. The real doctor can't be bothered. That reminds me I've forgotten to put a dirty big M on your forehead so here goes. Look Sam, I'm just going over to the Lizzie to make sure she's still ticking over.'

Gathering up his kit Harry walked over to the Lysander, slung the stuff into the cabin and then reached into the cockpit and gave the throttle a couple of hefty bursts. The engine responded immediately before settling back to a gentle tick-over and Harry went back to Sam. Together they hobbled along and although it was only a few yards it seemed to take for ever. Sam managed to get his good arm over the cabin entrance while Harry came from behind and heaved until his friend said he could manage and scrambled into the cabin, exhausted but relatively pain free as the morphine took effect.

'I'll just nip back and get your helmet and parachute. Then we'll be off. Don't go to sleep. Reach over and give the throttle a burst. There's water, a blanket and some emergency rations.'

Harry walked back to the Hurricane and reached into the cockpit for the helmet and parachute. Just as he was getting back down on to the ground he thought he saw a movement about 50 yards away in a small wadi. Then as he looked again he was convinced someone was watching but couldn't be sure. As far as he was aware no British troops had advanced this far west but the watchers could be local tribesmen or even the enemy. If he attempted to fly off in the Lizzie they might take a pot shot at him. On balance he considered it better to find out definitely especially when he realised that he still had his pistol strapped to him.

He moved towards the wadi in a wide circle, taking advantage of what cover he could find and was almost there when unmistakably he saw a body and then another. The first lay motionless but the second was definitely looking towards the plane. Harry drew his pistol and stood up. Later, he was never sure who was the more surprised, the Italians to see a lone airman, covering them with a pistol or himself to find five Italian soldiers, most of whom seemed to be wounded. There was one exception and he appeared to be very dead.

They all had weapons although it was obvious that they had no intention of using them as their hands shot up into the air. Harry put his pistol back in its holster and buttoned up the flap. He knew no Italian so he spoke in English. 'Good afternoon,' and held out his hands as a gesture that he meant them no harm. They were the first Italians he had seen close up apart from the thousands who were now prisoners of war. They talked quickly among themselves. Even if Harry knew the language it would have been too fast for him to understand. He next tried the only other language he knew – French.

Immediately there was a spark of recognition in one of the Italians. By question and answer Harry discovered that he had been a waiter in Paris a number of years before the war where he learned to speak French. Harry struggled to recall his schoolboy French and was surprised how much he remembered. Interspersed with the inevitable English words he gradually understood that the dead man was the driver of the staff car which had been blown over and wrecked by a shell from a warship. They had all managed to get away although the driver had died later. The senior officer was a brigade major while the speaker was his aide and the other two were private soldiers.

The speaker, who identified himself as Lt Ramonde Justie seemed to be the only one not injured. Harry could see they were frightened and needed help. He explained that he had some first aid kit in the Lysander but promised to return. All this had taken no more than five minutes and Harry hurried back to the Lizzie, retrieving the parachute and helmet on the way. He explained the situation to Sam who now seemed much easier and more comfortable.

'They're in a pretty bad way. Do you think I should do what I can to help or just leave them some water and first aid kit? We shouldn't stay too long for the Italian army is heading this way.'

'Yes. See what you can do for them. I'd like to think they'd help us if the roles were reversed.'

'O.K. then. I'll be as quick as possible. Give the engine a burst now and again.'

Harry hurried back carrying the medical bag, blankets, water bottles and emergency rations. On arriving at the group of soldiers he first checked the driver to make sure he really was dead and then started on the others.

'Tell your comrades I will make them as comfortable as possible. You may like to know that there is an Italian column of tanks and armoured vehicles heading this way. They will probably be here in about three hours so after I leave you may wish to go down to the road and wait for them.'

'Thank you. We are grateful.'

The first soldier had a shell splinter through his upper body. Harry removed the man's tunic with the help of the interpreter and set about removing the metal shard which

157

actually came away quite easily with clean blood seeping gently from the wound. Harry sterilised the wound and then applied a large pad and bandage around the man's chest. He did appear to be much easier although obviously still in shock. Harry gave him an ampule of morphine and wrote an M on the man's forehead to indicate that morphine had been administered. If the man ever got to a hospital the doctor would recognise the international code. He knew he was working in the dark and regretted that in all his medical textbooks he could recall no mention of how to deal with war wounds. He carried on with the assumption that all wounds however caused required much the same treatment.

The second soldier had a broken leg. Once his trouser leg had been cut away it appeared to be a clean break. He gave this man morphine also and explained to the lieutenant that when it had taken effect he would try to set the leg. The senior officer seemed to be in great pain and once he had been persuaded to remove his tunic Harry could see exactly what the problem was. His shoulder was badly dislocated but there appeared to be no other injuries. Harry checked his watch and was surprised that only fifteen minutes had passed since he had arrived. He explained through the interpreter what had happened, that he would try to put it right but that it would hurt for a while. If his manipulation was successful all would be well although it would feel like a bad bruise for some time. The brigade major understood all of this and gave a nodded acceptance of the proposed treatment. He was still concerned about Sam so dashed back to see if he was alright and then returned to the Italians.

Although he had never done this himself Harry had seen the manipulation performed a few times and hoped that he could manage it first time. With another silent prayer Harry grasped the man's arm and jerked quickly. Although the soldier was expecting it he could not suppress the cry of pain. His eyes filled with tears but his gestures and the torrent of words which spilled from his mouth were evidence of his gratitude to Harry.

Harry heard the unmistakable sound of a Lysander engine and looked up to see one circling overhead at about a thousand feet. As he watched it came lower and he waved hoping to attract the attention of the pilot. It flew directly overhead and Harry felt the pilot must surely have seen him before it headed off to the east. He turned his attention to the final patient, explaining he would try to reset the broken leg by first pulling the broken bones apart and hoping that they would go together neatly. He explained that it was important to do this as soon as possible and to make sure that the wound was clean. He would then apply two splints and bind the leg. He hoped that by now the morphine was taking effect but he dare not delay any longer. He had no wish to be captured by the Italian army. More important – he needed to get Sam to hospital as soon as possible. He already felt guilty at having kept him waiting even though Sam had agreed he should help the unfortunate enemy soldiers.

It seemed that everyone knew what was happening as he asked the lieutenant to help pull the broken bones apart. The poor soldier was aware of what needed to be done and for Harry it was a nightmare as he pulled the two pieces of bone apart and let them go again. He breathed a sigh of relief as they seemed to fit neatly together at the first attempt. The soldier was in pain although the morphine was doing its job and scarcely a sound left his lips. Harry worked quickly, making sure that the wound was clean and then applied two large splints. Having satisfied himself he had done all he could he suggested that they construct a makeshift stretcher and move down towards the road to await their comrades now heading their way.

CHAPTER 20

A Court Martial Offence

Harry prepared to leave his patients, waving aside their effusive, almost tearful thanks. He left them a full water bottle, two emergency ration packs and a blanket. From the wadi he made his way quickly back to the Lysander. Once on board he checked that Sam was alright, covered him with the remaining blanket and eased the throttle forward.

Once airborne he flew back over the wadi and then set a course for the temporary RAF base. After five minutes he saw the Italian army still struggling westwards and called base on the R/T to advise them. He also told them he thought it necessary to take Sam direct to hospital but would return to them as soon as possible.

'Good luck. Take your time. We're not going anywhere.'

Harry flew east for another 150 miles and then couldn't remember the call sign so decided to join the circuit and go straight in. He was immediately contacted on the R/T, asked to identify himself and explain his unauthorised entry of the circuit. Once he had given them the facts he was given permission to land though on his final approach he realised they were taking no chances. He was covered by a machine gunner all the time until he had taxied to the hospital tents, switched off the engine and got down.

Orderlies came running out and in no time at all Sam had been moved out from the cabin, on to a stretcher and into the hospital. Harry went inside and explained to a medic what the injuries were and what he had done. It seemed that they already knew the story as his R/T message to his squadron had been relayed to the hospital. Harry excused himself and went to report to the control cabin.

'You'd better get washed up and have a meal before you see the old man.' With this gentle reminder he realised it was some time since he'd last eaten and made his way over to the mess tent. A quick meal and an even quicker wash revived his spirits a little and he thought he'd better report to the senior officer. He was directed to Group Captain Holmes who was in overall charge of his and six other squadrons. He had only seen him twice before and Harry suspected that Holmes had never noticed him at all. The Group Captain questioned him at some length while a corporal took down everything including the position of the Italian army column. Harry had wondered for some time what he should do about the group of soldiers he had helped. Finally as the interview was drawing to a close he said.

'There's one more thing Sir. I came across five Italian soldiers sheltering in a wadi not far from the Hurricane. One was dead. Three were injured and the fifth acted as interpreter. I attended to their wounds as best I could and left them some water and a blanket. I also told them their army would be close by in about three hours.'

'I don't know that I want to know that. I'd rather you hadn't told me,' replied Holmes. 'However in the circumstances I rather think I would have done the same.'

'Do you have to include it in your report?' Harry was all for keeping the report brief.

'I'm afraid we must. Corporal, start a new page and report what F/Lt Nelson has just told us about the Italians. Of course sometimes reports get mislaid or lost. O.K. with you Nelson.'

'Yes indeed Sir. I hope they'd do the same for us.'

'Let's hope so. Now that we've got them on the run I see no harm in being charitable as long as the higher ups don't get twittery about it. Go off and see your friend. In the meantime

I'll get in touch with Sqn/Ldr Simpson. If its not too dark when you've finished maybe you could give me a lift over to your squadron.'

'Of course Sir. I'll need to take Sam his parachute and helmet so maybe you could get one for yourself before we set off. By the way Sir. I haven't seen Sqn/Ldr Simpson for a couple of days but if you can get him a few more pilots I'm sure he'll be pleased.' Harry thought he might as well let the boss know they were short of pilots.

Holmes just smiled and then said,' Just one more thing. Before you visit your friend you'd better call in at the stores and get a change of clothes. I don't think the hospital would approve of you walking around with all that blood on your uniform.'

'Right Sir.'

'Corporal, make out a chit for F/Lt Nelson for some clothes and I'll sign it.'

Harry took the chit, made his excuses and went off to get a change of clothes. At the stores they also gave him a large paper bag for his soiled clothes. This he deposited in the Lysander and then returned to the hospital. The same staff on duty recognised him and asked him to wait while they contacted the M.O. Half an hour went by during which time Harry found himself nodding off only to be woken up when his head fell forward. The M.O. arrived and sat down next to him.

'You look as though you could do with a good long rest.'

'You're probably right. Just taking forty winks to pass the time. How is F/Lt Jordan?'

'Bit too early to say yet. His upper arm wound should heal fairly quickly. His foot was a bit of a mess but that should be alright in a couple of months. The injury to his wrist is the worst. Small pieces of bone were broken. In time it will heal but he'll need a lot of exercise to keep the hand movements flexible. I've done the best I can but only time will tell.'

162

'Thanks Doc.'

'Your pal should be awake in about four hours so you'd better come back later.'

'Sorry I can't. I've got to return to my squadron and I'm flying the Group Captain there as soon as possible. Could you see Sam when he wakes up and tell him I'll be back as soon as I can?'

'Yes. Sure.'

Harry walked slowly back to the H.Q. tent and asked to speak to Group Captain Holmes. He appeared almost at once carrying a helmet and parachute. With him was also the corporal carrying a small bag, helmet and parachute.

'Have we got room for Cpl Stokes?'

'Yes Sir. The cabin is quite roomy. I'll just go and see if the Lizzie has been fed and watered and then we'll get airborne.'

'Carry on. We're right behind you.'

It was almost 16.00 hours by the time they were off the ground. Thinking back Harry tried to recall all that had taken place since mid-day and even before that. Two sorties in the morning, a quick snack while the Hurricane was being re-fuelled and re-armed. Then another sortie which was completed when he escorted the damaged bomber back to base. Then seeing Sam go down, the rescue flight in the Lizzie and the Italians. The flight to the hospital and now back to his squadron. No wonder he felt tired!

By 16.30 hours he approached his temporary airfield and called them on the R/T to explain that he had two passengers on board. As soon as they had landed Harry escorted his passengers towards the RAF Headquarters tent before returning to the control caravan to make his report. Once inside everyone wanted to know how Sam was and how he himself felt. Amid warm-hearted congratulations he made his report.

F/O John Humphries, one of his junior officers took Harry to one side. 'You could be in trouble Harry. Some Wingco flew in a while back and has been shooting off his mouth about a grounded Lizzie in enemy territory and that RAF flying crew were apparently tending some wounded Italians. He's breathing fire and talking about a Court Martial.'

Harry remembered the 'plane which had seemed to spot him, had flown lower as if to see if he needed help and had then flown off without any signal at all. 'Oh God,' he thought. 'That's all I need. Not much chance of a report going missing now. To hell with it.' He felt too tired to care.

As he turned to go he was confronted by a Wing Commander who had just come up the steps. Harry had never seen him before but gave a salute which was acknowledged though much smarter than Harry's somewhat casual one.

The Wing Commander spoke. 'Are you the pilot of the Lysander that has just landed?'

'Yes Sir.'

'What rank do you hold?'

'Sorry Sir. I had to change my clothes at the hospital but I've got them in a bag in the Lizzie. I'm F/Lt Nelson.'

'You could be anyone. Get some badge of rank and put your wings up. Have you been out here long?'

'Yes. Quite some time.'

'Flying Lysanders?'

'No. Flying Hurricanes.'

'Did you sign for that Lysander?'

'Yes Sir.'

'Sergeant. Let me see form 700 for the Lysander.'

'Here it is Sir with F/Lt Nelson's signature. He radioed in for the Lizzie to be got ready for him to rescue F/Lt Jordan.' The sergeant was trying to be helpful in giving the background information but the Wing Commander seemed not to be interested in any explanation.

The Wing Commander turned once more to Harry and went on. 'So who gave you authority to fly the Lysander when you should have been flying a Hurricane? Is this your signature?'

'Yes Sir.' The lie came readily to his lips as Harry was determined not to involve the sergeant. 'My Hurricane had a few bullet holes which needed to be repaired and I needed to try and rescue one of our pilots. I took the initiative myself. If there's a problem I'll take the responsibility.'

'I'm sure you will F/Lt Nelson. No doubt your rescue attempt to try to save another RAF pilot was very worthy. My real concern is that you were seen to give succour to the enemy. I cannot let that go unchallenged. It is a court martial offence and you will be placed under arrest. Have you anything to say?'

'Just one thing. If I am grounded will you fly the next patrol against the enemy as we are so short of pilots?'

'Don't be impertinent.'

By this time Harry, who was normally an easy going chap, lost his temper. 'Suit yourself. I'll collect my parachute and helmet then go and have a meal while I'm waiting for the MPs.'

The Wing Commander was becoming more flustered by the minute. He realised that he had overstepped the mark in his reprimand of a pilot in front of other ranks and that he had made a fool of himself but there was no way he could extricate himself. Even his aide looked helplessly on and suggested they move out of the caravan as murmurs of 'shame' and 'bloody cheek' could be heard from Harry's mates.

The Wing Commander suddenly turned towards the door. 'You'll be hearing from me.' He took the few paces to the door and in his anxiety to get away quickly practically ran down the steps. His rage did not help and he missed his footing on the final step and fell heavily, hitting his shoulder against a large drum of petrol. He lay on the ground in agony with a dislocated shoulder.

Harry was right behind him and guessed at once what had happened. He was on the point of continuing when compassion took the place of his initial intention to ignore the Wing Commander.

'Can I help you?'

'No. Clear off.'

Sergeant Watson arrived on the scene and spoke to the Wing Commander who was struggling to get up off the ground. 'Excuse me Sir. We can call up an ambulance but it may take some time before it gets here. F/Lt Nelson is also a doctor and he may be able to make you more comfortable.' Without waiting for the Wing Commander's reply the sergeant called after Harry. 'Hang on a minute Sir. I think we may need you after all.'

Harry returned to the officer who was now sitting up. 'Can you remove your tunic Sir?'

'Not easily.'

'No. I thought not. Let me help you and we'll assess the damage.'

Once removed Harry could see it was indeed another dislocated shoulder – the second he had seen that day and he wondered whether he should attempt to put this one back in place. He also wondered what were the chances of him succeeding twice in one day.

'Sir, you've dislocated your shoulder. I can give you a shot of morphine but its probably better if I put it right without. Initially it will hurt like hell but if I get it right first time it should be bearable and it will soon feel no worse than a bad bruise. By the way, what is your name?'

'John Price. Now will you just get on with it.'

For one moment Harry hoped he would not manage it the first time. He took a firm grip on the man's arm, looked around at the sea of faces and could not suppress a wink towards Sgt Watson. It was all over in a second and Harry stood beside his latest patient with a grin of sheer relief on his face. The sound as the shoulder blade popped back into its place was quite loud and was followed by cheers and smiles as the patient was obviously more comfortable. He offered a grudging word of thanks and then to the astonishment of everyone said, 'This doesn't alter anything.'

It was at this precise moment that Group Captain Holmes arrived on the scene. 'Ah, Harry. I see you're up to your old tricks. You must make up your mind whether you want to be a doctor or a pilot.'

'I think I'll stick to flying at least for the present.' Then in spite of himself Harry burst out laughing, breaking the tension all round.

'What's the joke?'

'That's the second dislocated shoulder I've set today. The next one will have to sort it out himself.'

'Who's this latest patient?' Enquired the Group Captain.

'Its Wing Commander Price. I think he's just visiting but he wants to make a complaint about me.' With that explanation Harry continued on his way back to the Lysander to retrieve his kit and to get his clothes cleaned and his badges of rank put on his new uniform.

CHAPTER 21

Promotion

Harry Nelson found the bag of washing he'd brought back and realised it was impossible to remove the blood from his shirt. Carefully removing the F/Lt tabs from the epaulettes and cutting away his wings from the shirt he threw the remainder into a bin for disposal and walked over to the small stores unit hoping to replace at least some of his clothes. There had been a number of calls on the stores but he was in luck and came away with a shirt, a pair of shorts, shoes, socks and some underclothes.

The stores clerk was very helpful. 'I've got one flying helmet left. If you are size 7 you're in luck. If not I'll try and get one for the next delivery.'

Harry said he'd manage with his own and thanked the man and then asked, 'Any chance of a towel and some soap. I could do with a good wash down.'

'If you don't mind doing it in the open we've rigged up a shower at the back. I'll get someone to let you have a couple of gallons of hot water but the rest will have to be cold.'

Harry didn't quite know what to make of this unexpected good fortune and thanked the airman again. 'You're welcome Sir. Keep up the good work.'

Within ten minutes, having enjoyed the quite efficient home-made shower Harry was more like himself and felt that things were looking up as he put on his new clothes and went off in search of an evening meal. The sun had now completely disappeared although only a few minutes earlier there had been the most spectacular sunset he had ever seen and there had been many of these during his time in the desert. Half an hour later, after a quite substantial meal, he bade goodnight to his dining companions and made his way to his tent for an early night's rest. Stopping only to remove his boots he slumped onto his bed and fell into an exhausted sleep. He was soon shaken awake by a corporal MP who enquired, 'Do you happen to be Sqn/Ldr Nelson?'

'Yes Corporal. What can I do for you?'

'Well Sir. Group Captain Holmes would like a few words with you before you turn in for the night.'

'O.K. Lead the way.'

Harry grabbed his hat, pulled on his boots and followed the military policeman to the Squadron Office. It hadn't changed much in the past few days although the front door was now back on its hinges and some of the damage to the roof had been repaired. Inside seated at a table was the Group Captain and next to him his squadron leader looking quite smart in his khaki uniform. His left arm was in a sling and his face was drawn as though in pain. On the table were several piles of papers and at the side sat Cpl Stokes with his typewriter.

It all looked very formal and Harry's first thought that he was going to be given a chance to present his side of the pending Court Martial charge. The Group Captain smiled and indicated for Harry to sit in the chair in front of the table.

'Good evening Harry. Did you enjoy your meal? Sorry we had to drag you out again.'

'Good evening Sir. Yes it was a good meal. I'm only surprised how well stew and dumplings go down in this climate. I do hope your injuries are not too serious Sir. I didn't know you'd been hit.'

The Sqd/Ldr smiled back to Harry. 'I'm afraid I'll be out of action for a while.

The Group Captain joined in. 'That's why I've asked you to join us. Sqn/Ldr Simpson was wounded this morning and he needs some time off. Our problem is that we need someone to take his place and he's recommended you. From what I've heard about you in the recent past I'm happy to go along with that. How do feel about Acting Squadron Leader?'

'I'll be glad to look after the boys until the Sqn/Ldr gets back.'

'Right. Cpl Stokes fill in the necessary documents and I'll sign them. You don't need to collect your new rank badges. We took the opportunity in order to save you the time. Congratulations Sqn/Ldr Nelson.'

Simpson stood up and shook Harry's hand. 'Look after the squadron Harry. I'll be back.'

'There's just one thing Sir. You are aware of the problem I had with Wing Commander Price earlier today. What is likely to happen? It's not going to look too good if a squadron leader is put on a charge and there's not much chance of the report going missing now.'

The Group Captain intervened. 'I think you can safely leave that for me to sort out. We are continuing operations against the enemy so first thing tomorrow get your chaps together. There are a few new bods coming over too. As soon as new orders come through you'll all be up there once more. One more thing. We can't have a new squadron leader flying without a gong. So in view of your past actions and your courage and initiative in saving F/Lt Jordan I'm recommending you for a gong. Any questions?'

'No Sir. I'm very relieved. Thank you. Goodnight.'

Cpl Stokes deliberately winked at Harry as he left the office. Harry returned to his tent absolutely drained. What a day! Two sorties in the morning followed by the rescue mission to bring back Sam and then the assistance to the wounded Italians. Then followed the trouble with the Wing Commander, meeting the Group Captain and now promotion and the possibility of a medal. He checked the date of this somewhat momentous day. It was 3rd February 1941.

Mulling over the events of the day prevented the sleep that he really needed for a long time. At last sheer fatigue took over and he slept until day break when the sound of aircraft engines roused him. By 7.0 o'clock he had washed, shaved and had breakfast. News had filtered through about his promotion and as he reached the squadron lines his pilots and ground staff applauded loudly. He thanked them, said that nothing would change in the squadron routine and that as soon as their old Sdr/Ldr had recovered he would be returning.

He went on. 'We haven't yet received our orders for the day but I understand we shall be pursuing the enemy for several days yet. For the moment, as I am acting as Squadron Leader, 'A' flight will be under F/Lt Smith, 'B' flight under F/Lt Bannerman and I shall command 'C' flight. As before we shall fly in fairly open formation with two planes closer together while the third about 200 yards away to starboard and slightly behind as the lookout man. Our new pilots will be close to each leader and as soon as we get a break in flying I will have a proper chat with them. That's all for now. Look out for each other.'

The crews dismissed and Harry walked over to W/O Kemp, the most experienced of his ground crew to discuss the state of the Hurricanes. It seemed that all the planes were ready. They even had three in reserve and four others being serviced. Fuel and ammunition were sufficient and they were expecting to be re-supplied each day for as long as necessary.

It was 10.30 hours before their first orders came through, the long delay because the navy had been in action once more throwing tons of shells along the coastal road which was crowded with retreating Italians. 'A' flight was ordered to fly well ahead of the devastation caused by the naval bombardment and bring back a recce report of any new positions where the enemy might make a stand. Although fully armed Harry warned his flight to withhold their fire unless attacked.

'B' flight left a few minutes later to intercept any enemy

bombers and to engage enemy fighters while 'C' flight had the job of attacking ground troops especially tanks. Each flight would be away for about 50 minutes giving the ground staff time for a meal and to get everything ready for when the planes returned. It would then be time for the pilots to snatch a meal before their next op. By 15.00 hours the whole squadron had been up three times and all had returned safely but their new supply of ammunition had not arrived. Headquarters advised them to stand down for the day so Harry took the opportunity to see his new pilots.

During the night new supplies arrived. The lorries had been forced to stop for several hours while roads and tracks were repaired. It was all very well delaying the enemy by bombing the roads but it also meant that the pursuing victorious allies had to make long detours to avoid the damage or stop and repair the roads. From then on it was agreed that bombers would be used only against major defences leaving the fighters to harass the enemy with machine-gun fire.

New orders arrived. One third of Harry's squadron was sent ahead of the troops advancing across country to report enemy activity on their intended route. Harry elected to go himself with this flight and in a few minutes they had caught up with the troops. From the air the route looked almost impassable and Harry could imagine the difficulty the tank crews were experiencing as they urged their vehicles along as fast as they dared. It was obviously necessary to conserve their engines and their tank tracks for the fight that was yet to come but at the same time they needed to be in place before the enemy retreating along the coast road could establish a defence system. As far as Harry could see there were no Italian troops anywhere in this inhospitable country or they were so well camouflaged as to be invisible.

From Bir Hakeim on to Mecheli along the top of the escarpment, some 85 miles, there was not an enemy in sight. Over the R/T he sent one of his flight back to base to report the situation while he and one of the new pilots pressed on to Msus. This was an Italian fort with a strong force. The Italians must have been aware that their troops on the coast were retreating but until they spotted the Hurricanes overhead they thought they were safe especially when no bombs were dropped and no bullets came from the British planes. In a matter of hours they were completely surprised when the first of the cruiser tanks appeared in the afternoon of 4th February. The Italians did not stay long to see how strong was the British force. They left the fort with the British in hot pursuit and this time the remainder of Harry's squadron joined in the fight.

In the meantime another Hurricane squadron supported the ground troops as they followed the Italians along the coastal road. By setting off at different times the groups of planes managed to provide cover for the British troops in case of surprise attack from the Italian Air Force.

CHAPTER 22

To Aid The Greeks

Having captured Msus, a major Italian strongpoint, more Italian prisoners were rounded up and had to be sent back east. For them the war was over but for the victorious British there was no let up. Snatching a brief respite and a quick snack from their diminishing rations they set off once more for Beda Fomm. Harry and his pilots were in action again, reporting enemy positions and supporting the ground troops whenever required. Nobody, whether in the air or on the ground could know that within a few days it would virtually all be over.

Australian troops pushing westward along the coast captured Benghazi and then moved steadily southwards towards Ghemines and Beda Fomm. In the meantime British troops had set an ambush across the road and hoped that their ammunition would last out. If not they were prepared to use bayonets. The Italian vanguard troops were utterly surprised when they realised they were not only pursued from behind but confronted by British troops in front who now barred their way to possible freedom. The Italians halted and decided on their next move. It was not long in coming. Using their few remaining tanks the Italians launched an attack against the British so fiercely there seemed every chance that it might succeed.

Equal to the occasion the British poured in a withering fire to such an extent that many soldiers were left with no more ammunition. The weary troops called once more on Harry for support although by now the two sides were so close it would have been difficult to distinguish friend from foe. As the

Hurricanes arrived it was seen that the efforts of the British soldiers had been enough. As the smoke began to disperse from the battle it was realised that all the Italian tanks had been destroyed and in the silence which followed white flags of surrender began to appear all along the Italian column. In effect they had little option as the Australians and other British troops now caught up with them from the rear. The battle was over and with it the Italian presence in Libya.

British troops took stock of their surroundings, waited a day for more supplies to arrive and then advanced on to Agedabia. In the process they captured two more Italian airfields. These were quickly cleared of rubble and the RAF were able to move into their furthest west temporary airfield. The buildings had escaped serious damage and when Harry landed he was able to secure quite acceptable accommodation for himself and his men. The air force Military Police arrived soon after and set about securing the airfield against any isolated groups of Italians who may have escaped capture. An hour later and the RAF admin. staff appeared and it was soon realised that here as in many other outposts the Italians had lived extremely well. The stores were stocked with enormous quantities of food and literally thousands of bottles of Italian wine.

'Excuse me Sir.' W/O Harrington saluted. 'I think we have a problem.'

'Carry on Mr. Harrington.'

'Well Sir. We've discovered all this food. Most of it seems alright, especially if you like Italian stuff but there are thousands of bottles of plonk. What shall we do with it?'

'If its all in one place put a guard on it. Better still sort out the food and keep what we can use and pass back east all the Italian stuff you don't want. I expect the POWs would prefer their own food. As for the wine we'd better keep most of it under lock and key. I think we all deserve a little celebration. As soon as the evening meal is ready give a bottle of wine between four men. The same goes for the officers. We don't want them getting too happy. There's still much to be done and we can do the same tomorrow if we are still here.'

'We've also got a few army bods arriving.'

'They ought to share in the spoils. Ask whoever is in charge to come and see me.'

'Thanks Sir.'

Within the next three hours Harry had delegated various officers to organise sleeping quarters, mess tents and cooking arrangements. A medical unit soon arrived. Then followed a small cleansing unit, workshops, stores and armaments groups. The army commander arrived and introduced himself as Major Edward Griffin. Harry explained what had so far transpired and the major was in full agreement and thanked Harry for the gift of wine. They agreed to share the food and wine and the major said as he had more men to spare he would provide guards for the camp as a whole but Harry insisted that the RAF should also share in guard duties.

Before darkness fell the routine of the camp had been established so that the army and the RAF looked forward to a few days rest. After the first few hours when food and sleep seemed to be the only requirements for the exhausted men Harry sensed a different atmosphere in the camp. It was an almost carefree attitude which he could well understand after the privations the men had experienced.

Harry felt it himself – the need to get away – be completely alone and do nothing. He realised that a fighting unit must keep itself in top condition yet he was almost reluctant to impose a rigid discipline on men who had responded so well in the recent battles. He appreciated that it would take a long time to return to normal and as yet no one could remember what normal was. It seemed that they had been in action for ever.

Still no signals came from H.Q. It was as though they were completely isolated. They had plenty of food and drink although they were a bit short of ammunition and spare parts for the planes and RAF transport seemed to be in short supply. Harry called a meeting of his officers and discussed with them the thoughts which had been idling in his mind.

'Good morning chaps. I want to discuss a few things with you.' He went on. 'We do seem to be out on a limb here. No communication from H.Q. and I gather the army bods are in the same boat. Its all a bit unreal after the hectic weeks we've been through. I'm not sure that all of the Italians have been captured. We are still many miles from the Tunisian border. In spite of the thousands of prisoners sent back there may still be many Italians to the west of this place. As soon as all the planes are serviceable and we've replenished our ammo I'm going to send up two flights as far as Tunisia. If we see anything we'll ask the army to support us but of course I'll clear it with H.Q. first. Can I have your comments, not now but in a couple of hours when you've had time to think things through.'

Major Griffin sent a note over to Harry asking if he and a few of his officers could meet. Harry replied by inviting them to a mess dinner that evening and also invited his pilots. It was a pleasant evening but as soon as the meal was over the army major got down to the real reason for the visit.

'I apologise for inviting myself over,' began the major. 'I've just received some rather worrying news and I wondered if you'd heard anything. I'm not sure how your commanders operate but our generals usually stay at a safe distance behind the lines. For a long time General O'Conner preferred to be with his troops but not having received any signals from H.Q. in the past few days he decided to go all the way back to Cairo and see Wavell himself. We are still waiting for him to return so I can't get the rumours verified or discounted. I do know that many of the units have been withdrawn and gone back east. At first I assumed it was part of a changeover for resting the troops and that fresh units would arrive to carry on the fight. I've been told by some transport people who bring our supplies that this is not happening and that most of the units are waiting in Egypt although a few have gone further east, possibly to help the Greeks.'

Harry and his officers were stunned by this news. He felt he had to make some comment. 'I thought the Greeks were holding their own. In fact we have only just heard that they have not only stopped the Italian advance but driven them back in Albania.'

'Well yes they had. Only now it seems that Jerry is on the move once more and is threatening them from the north. Rumour has it that they are coming right down through Yugoslavia, attacking Greece and if they manage to occupy Turkey they will threaten our oil supplies in the Middle East. Remember Syria is French so we shall get no support from that quarter.'

'Good Lord! I was about to send up a couple of flights to the west to find out exactly how many Italians are left in this area. I know we've captured thousands but I'm convinced there are still a lot here if they haven't already escaped into Tunisia. Thanks for letting me know. I'd better try and raise H.Q. and find out the score.'

'Might I suggest you don't use your radio. I have a sneaking suspicion that the Italians might be listening in.'

The army officers departed and Harry promised to keep them informed of any developments. Harry decided to remain at the airfield and to send one flight on a further reconnaissance to the west. The second flight would remain on standby. He also sent two Hurricanes to RAF Headquarters with instructions to go even as far as Cairo if they couldn't get any real information nearer. They were not to use R/T and would report directly to the most senior RAF officer they could find and confirm the news he had just been told.

Harry then called his senior NCOs and explained the need for all ranks to be on their guard against sudden attacks. In addition he gave instructions for all vehicles not needed in the day to day running of the camp to be made ready for a long journey eastwards. He then went over to the major to explain what he had done. Between them these two middle ranking officers established a plan to be prepared to move at a moments notice, or to repel any attack and if necessary to advance further westwards if that order came.

Two of the Hurricanes returned from the recce within an hour to report small groups of Italians in isolated pockets, some no more than 50 miles away while others were much closer to the Tunisian border. They appeared to be going nowhere and nor did they pose any threat when the planes flew quite low over their positions. The third Hurricane landed half an hour later. It had flown right up to the border and had not seen any troops even on the French side. About 110 miles away was the fortified town of El Agheila.

The Italians there posed the greatest threat to any further British advance. Harry invited the major and a couple of his officers over for an evening meal and reported his findings. They agreed that there seemed to be no activity contemplated by the enemy but Harry promised to send up a patrol three times a day just in case. After the meal Harry explained the procedures in place regarding the transport and stores. The major was obviously impressed and told Harry they had done much the same.

Before turning in for the night Harry took a stroll round part of the perimeter and chatted briefly to the RAF guards stationed every few hundred yards. About half of the perimeter was guarded by the army and as he came to their first post he stopped and introduced himself. In spite of the battles they had recently fought and the hundreds of miles they had travelled they seemed quite happy with their lot. 'Only another half an hour Sir and we'll be relieved. It gets quite cold here in another two hours.' Harry spoke for a few minutes then bade them farewell. 'Goodnight lads.'

On the way back to his own tent Harry stopped in between two of the sentry posts, marvelled again at the quietness and the gentle light which seemed to come from the stars high above in the heavens. It reminded him of the first time he had experienced this solitude – now eight months away almost to the day when they had first attacked the Italian positions. A lot had happened in such a short time. Now when just one more effort might clear the enemy from Libya once and for all it seemed that they might have to retreat once more. He thought briefly of Barbara and wondered if she was now safely in England. He couldn't write to her as he did not have her address. On the other hand she might get in touch with him although there had been no mail for weeks.

Tomorrow his planes should return from Headquarters. Then they would receive definite orders and with luck attack the few remaining Italian positions. For the second night running Harry had difficulty in getting to sleep. The events of the past few weeks, then the past few days and finally the lack of communication from H.Q. kept turning over in his mind. The last time he'd seen Group Captain Holmes everything had been going so well. He remembered part of the conversation when he, a newly promoted Squadron Leader had virtually been left in charge of this far flung unit with instructions to carry on as usual but he couldn't believe this would allow him to take the initiative and carry on with the attack. Nor could he recall any hint of withdrawal. Finally he got up, brewed himself a mug of tea and settled down to write a few more lines to his sister. After another hour he lay down on his bed and slept. Dawn came too early but after a wash and breakfast he prepared to face another day.

CHAPTER 23

One Final Effort

Major Griffin arrived just as Harry was finishing his meal. He greeted the army man. 'Good morning. Would you care for some tea or anything.'

'No thanks Harry. I've already eaten. I must say your meal looks more appetising than mine was. I also noticed on the way over here that you have quite a number of armoured cars. I never appreciated that the RAF had such vehicles.'

'Ah those. They are really a hang over from years ago. When the RAF was the police force in Iraq, Palestine and other places east of Suez nearly all the squadrons had a few of these to keep the jumpy natives in order. The RAF needed troops on the ground as support. Its only a small force really but extremely mobile and helpful in securing airfields.'

'Ah well. You learn something new each day.'

'My chaps haven't returned from H.Q. yet but I'm expecting them any minute. Have you got any more up to date gen?'

'No nothing since yesterday but I thought we should pool our resources and any ideas you might have come up with.'

'Sure. I've been thinking about our situation here. Its uncanny. We're the victors yet we still have to be on our guard and there's still no contact with H.Q. Its almost as though they have forgotten about this forward unit.'

Harry saw no reason not to tell Major Griffin what he and his officers had been considering. He went on. 'We know there are a few Italians about 50 miles from here. There is also a much bigger force at El Agheila. We wondered whether you would support us on the ground if we attacked them

181

from the air. At least it would secure our immediate front. In the meantime I've given orders for all our spare transport to be loaded up and ready to move back east if we receive orders to withdraw. Do you have enough transport for all your men?'

'That sounds like clear thinking. We'll do the same and if you can find room for about 70 of my men nobody will have to walk. In the meantime I'll split my force into three. One to go forward when the time comes, one to remain here to defend the camp while the third can be the reserve to go forward or back east as required.'

The next half an hour was spent in finalising the details of the plan. Griffin wanted to move his seriously wounded men to base hospital and Harry agreed to send one of the trucks and two medical bods for the journey. They also considered what to do if they received no orders.

Harry spoke first. 'I think being out here on a limb our number one priority is to look after ourselves and our men. With our recces in place we shouldn't be caught napping. As to orders I've only recently been promoted to Squadron Leader and my instructions were to carry on the fight. How about you?'

'Not so clear cut I'm afraid. On the other hand if I didn't use my initiative and pursue the enemy I could be in trouble. I could place myself under your command and then I'd have no option but to carry out your orders.' Griffin said this with a smile on his face but Harry realised he was quite serious.

'I don't think it need come to that. In any case you outrank me by date. When did you join up?'

'1938. I joined the T.A. Then when war broke out we went into the army proper and I came out here in February 1940. What about you?'

'I joined up in 1936, went overseas in 1937 and have never been home since.'

'Well there you are then. You have a longer service record. In any case I think we'll work well as a team.'

'O.K. We'll have a general meeting here at 11.00 hours with officers and senior NCOs. I think we must tell them together. Some of these old sweats are not only good at their jobs they would surely have something of value to contribute. Can I leave it to you to write all this up and let me have a copy – just in case we're regarded as a couple of renegades. If nothing untoward happens we can destroy the reports.'

'Marvellous. I'm glad we met.'

With that the two officers parted company to get on with the business in hand. On his way back to his tent Harry pondered over the meeting and the possible outcome which might follow. He told his second in command to pass on the word about the meeting and settled down to write a letter to Sam Jordan.

Dear Sam,

I'm writing this from somewhere south of Benghazi and hope before long to go east and have a spot of leave. I hope you are progressing well in your recovery and trust you will soon be completely well again. Sorry I haven't written too often but I'm sure you can imagine we've been a bit occupied. Now we have come almost to the end of the line and are taking a breather before pressing on or returning to H.Q. As a matter of fact we are on our own here, sharing a captured airfield with a few hundred army bods. With no communication from H.Q. for several days we, that is the army officer and I, are contemplating a joint effort to press on and clear the Italians from this whole region. However we are hoping that definite orders arrive soon before we put our heads on the block and take things into our own hands.

Its been an exhilarating experience to be on the winning side but sad to see the endless groups of dejected prisoners. We are sending back east a few of our seriously wounded army people so I'm taking the opportunity to send this letter and hope that they will be able to get it to you. I've put your last address but no doubt you'll have moved from there. I suppose its just possible that Sqn/Ldr Simpson may have been sent to your hospital as he was wounded some time ago so he may have already told you that he has temporarily put me in charge of the squadron.

One of our recce planes has just landed so I'd better go and see what's happening and the hospital wagon is just about to depart. I'm also sending a nice bottle of Italian plonk which we captured so think of us when you wet your whistle.

As ever,
Harry

Returning once more to the details of the proposed action Harry was surprised at the speed with which this joint venture was progressing, at least on paper. Two days ago the major and Harry had not met. Now they were contemplating an attack on the last remaining Italian stronghold and, moreover, without direct orders from H.Q.

Harry considered carefully his position. One more effort might well do the trick. On the other hand if it did not succeed he would most definitely face a court martial. He needed to ensure that he was victorious and with the minimum of casualties. Thinking about possible casualties almost decided him against the hazardous venture. If he did nothing and they were attacked they might suffer casualties in any case. On balance he felt he should continue with the attack rather than wait and hoped that his squadron would feel the same. He drove quickly over to the army positions and posed his thoughts to Major Griffin.

'We have been considering the same question here. Everyone is in agreement for this final push. If we are careful and attack with an overwhelming force we should accomplish our objective with no casualties whatever. With your lot making the attack just ahead of us the enemy may be so concerned with fighting you that our troops will encounter little opposition.'

'I agree. In fact we shall have all our planes up for the first attack and see how things progress. We must conserve our fuel and ammo but if the whole squadron is not needed we will return two flights to be on standby. They can be whistled up at a moments notice.'

The final plans were discussed. Harry agreed that the RAF armoured cars should remain behind to guard the camp leaving most of the army to take part in the assault. Harry then told the major.

'Our planes will take 20 minutes to reach El Agheila and I suggest we attack just ahead of your people. Although our attack will give some warning to the defenders we can attack from the west, north and south more or less simultaneously leaving you to arrive five minutes later from the east. I reckon you need to start four hours ahead of us.' Harry emphasized the need for precise timing.

'Yes I agree. We will not go more than two miles beyond El Agheila so you can attack anything on the ground further west. Once we've captured the place I call you up and you can then come in to land. We can then gradually move some of our stores to the new positions.

They shook hands and Harry returned to his tent to make the final preparations and to write a few more letters, one to his mother, one to Michael Carter and the third to Group Captain Holmes. This letter stated briefly what was he was planning in view of the lack of communications from H.Q. He began to worry about the two pilots he had sent back east. Both should have returned by now and he tried to put at the back of his mind the fact that they might have been lost.

Harry and the whole of the RAF contingent waved to Major Griffin and his men as they set out on their journey of just over 110 miles. If all went well they should be in position for the assault on El Agheila just as dawn broke. In their previous reconnaissance flights westward none of Harry's pilots had seen any indication that mines had been laid to impede ground troops. However it was always possible that nearer their fortifications the enemy would have laid them. It would be only prudent to slow down any attacking force. On the other hand the Allies had advanced to their present positions so quickly that the Italians may have been more concerned with escaping than trying to stop the pursuers.

Two hours after the army had set off Harry received his first encouraging signal. The Italian soldiers camped a mere 50 miles away had all surrendered without a shot being fired. For the pilots left behind the hours ticked slowly by. Their temporary base at Agedabia had been a refuge for a few days and Harry hoped he would live to return there. For many it was impossible to sleep but as the sun began to cast its glow across the desert aircraft engines were started up, pilots strapped themselves in their cockpits, the ground control fired off a green flare and the squadron took off into the lightening sky.

CHAPTER 24

Everyone Back

Harry elected to lead the first flight and flew well to the south of El Agheila and way beyond before coming back to attack the target from the west. The other flights attacked from the south and the north at five minute intervals. The planes attacking from the south then made a big sweep away and came in from the west. Harry returned, this time attacking from the north while the remaining flight made its second attack from the south. All planes then returned to base to refuel and rearm in order to continue the assault and harass any troops trying to make their escape to the west. In this way Harry hoped to convince the defenders that they were being attacked by an overwhelming force.

The Italian defences replied with some conviction against the initial attack but during the second and subsequent runs the planes encountered little in the way of effective fire. As Harry and his squadron circled overhead they saw Major Griffin and his small army advancing on a fairly broad front in five columns. Only from above could anyone see how small the attacking force really was. Just as dawn was breaking the small British force reached it's target.

Major Griffin made the most of his resources. His five tanks went ahead, guns blazing, while guns which he had mounted on some of his other vehicles stopped in order to improve their aim. From above it was easy to see that the concentrated fire landed bang on target. More vehicles followed behind the tanks. These contained the assault troops. The Italian gunners replied as the tanks got closer but their aim was poor and as the tanks reached the outskirts of the town the fire from the defenders ceased altogether either because they had been knocked out or because the gun crews were seeking to escape to the west.

A few did manage to get away but two army vehicles raced through the town and caught up with the enemy who were persuaded to return. Harry and one flight landed in the desert while the others returned to base. Griffin sent out a lorry to pick up the pilots and in the next half hour the army had secured the town. Less than three hours later everything was quiet. The prisoners had been disarmed and the British troops were settling down for a meal. Harry and Eddie met, shook hands and congratulated each other. Griffin voiced his main concern.

'The main problem now is what to do with all these prisoners. We haven't got enough transport to take them back. Moreover my chaps are tired and need a rest. Suppose I put a guard on all the fuel, ammo and food, gather up all their weapons, destroy them and put their officers on their honour to stay put.'

'Well its worth a try. Do you have anyone who speaks Italian?' Harry was well aware he couldn't do it.

'Well I'm not too bad. A bit slow but in previous encounters I've managed to make myself understood.' The major was obviously pleased with his language skills.

Harry accompanied the major when he went off to speak to the prisoners. He explained that the British troops who had captured the town was only the vanguard of a large army heading this way and that he would allow the prisoners as much freedom as possible if they promised not to escape. The senior Italian officer agreed and as a goodwill gesture Griffin handed him back his revolver, explaining that it was for his own personal protection in case he was attacked by his own men. He also said that if any did escape they would be recaptured and locked up or shot. He would also allow the prisoners to look after their own cooking arrangements.

It was still only midday by the time everything had been settled. Harry thought he ought to return to base and hoped that by now one or both of his pilots had returned from H.Q. As he bade goodbye to the soldiers he said to Griffin. 'Eddie, are you going to write a report on this engagement.'

'Yes. I think we'd better don't you. My adjutant has a gift for words. He emphasises the good parts and tends to gloss over the mistakes.'

'Well in this case there were no mistakes. Everything went according to plan and we had very few casualties.'

'Yes that's the best part. None of my chaps got killed and only a few wounded. Even those don't amount to much. Do you really think this war is nearing the end?'

'Let's hope so. As soon as I've got any definite news or orders I'll be in touch. Cheerio for now.'

With that Harry and his pilots were driven out to their planes and flew back to base. They were soon overhead and as he came into land Harry counted all his planes safely parked at their dispersals and was pleased to see two extra ones. There was one other, a Lysander. As he taxied in he saw Group Captain Holmes coming towards him. As he got down he came towards Harry with outstretched hand. Somewhat relieved Harry shook his hand, smiled and said. 'Nice to see you again Sir.'

'I understand you've been continuing a private war.'

Harry thought quickly. 'It was a joint effort between us and the army. You may remember your instructions were to carry on as usual. As we had no orders and no contact with headquarters I thought that was the best thing to do.'

'I might have known you'd have a good answer. It's another case of turning a blind eye but this time it's me. But well done. Good show in fact. Actually we do have orders now and you're not going to like them. Go and get cleaned up and report to me with all your pilots in, say an hour's time. No make that 14.00 hours and we'll all have a cup of tea. By the way Nelson are you sure you're not descended from our great naval hero!'

'Not as far as I know.'

As he left the Group Captain, two pilots, F/Lt Andrews and P/O James walked with Harry towards their billets.

'So what's going to happen. We gather from Bushell and McFadden, when they landed that something's in the wind but they've been told not to say anything until we're all told by Groupie.'

'Well I've no idea either but we'll soon find out. At least there doesn't seem to be any threat of a court martial. I think he would have told me. See you at 14.00 hours.'

A quick wash and change of clothes did wonders for Harry. Elated with the success of the day but tired with all the flying and concerned with the responsibility for his part in the battle he did feel a little easier in his mind. He worried about the forthcoming meeting and admitted that the Group Captain also seemed concerned. If the news that he was about to impart was that the war was over surely he would have blurted it out. No, it must be something quite serious. Maybe the rumours that Griffin had heard were true. Still no point in worrying. In a few minutes all would be revealed.

The officers drifted into the big tent now used for their meals and as the last one sat down Group Captain Holmes stood up. 'Good afternoon gentlemen. I have some rather bad news. There's no point in beating about the bush. We are all being posted. Well most of us. Three new squadrons will be taking over this sector. In fact they will have to look after the whole region from El Agheila all the way back to Egypt. You and most of the other squadrons are going initially to Egypt and then depending on the situation in Greece we may go there to help them. We shall join the army in one huge military base and from there be sent to whatever theatre of war we and the army are needed. I'm afraid there's more bad news. Bulgaria is likely to join the Axis allowing German troops to pass through its territory and invade Greece. Yugoslavia was invited to join the Axis but so far they have refused. For our part we are pledged to support Greece in order to honour an agreement made in 1939.'

So the Group Captain confirmed the rumours which had been circulating for the past few days. Everyone had assumed that if true the Germans would only give token support to help the Italians overcome the Greeks who had stubbornly resisted the initial invasion. Now, following the Allied success in the desert everyone had hoped for a long rest but it was not to be. The Group Captain continued with his dire account.

'The Germans have moved quickly, too quickly in fact. We should have seen it coming but we didn't. Personally I doubt if there's anything we can really do to help the Greeks but we are committed to try. As far as airfields are concerned there are very few in the whole country. If we'd gone in sooner and prepared them we might have made a difference but at the time we just didn't have the planes to spare.'

'Some replacement troops are being sent here but I understand that El Agheila is the furthest west position they will hold at least for the time being. From there all the way back to Egypt our recent conquests will be lightly held by troops with a few tanks and about 30 planes in support. For the past ten days our squadrons and the army units have all been gradually withdrawn. We are in fact very thin on the ground. However London insists it knows the score so who are we to oppose them. I'm sorry I have no good news. Thank you for all you have done. Keep in touch Harry. I too have been posted back to Egypt and must return now.'

There was much discussion as the full importance of the news was absorbed. As the Group Captain made his way out the officers, in small groups, began to disperse with mixed emotions. Some were relieved at going back to Egypt. Life in the desert had been grim for so long. Others looked beyond the immediate orders to what might happen if the enemy became aware how thinly held Libya would be once the bulk of the army had been withdrawn.

Harry caught up with Holmes. 'Excuse me Sir. I promised to let Major Griffin know as soon as I had any definite news. Would you mind if I flew over to El Agheila and told him personally. We were a good team and I'd like to keep in touch.'

'Of course. No problem. Please give him my congratulations on a job well done. May I suggest you stay here until Sqn/Ldr Harrison arrives to take over. He should be here tomorrow but the rest of your chaps can fly off to Cairo today if you wish. Keep in touch. Look me up at RAF Headquarters.'

'Thanks. Goodbye Sir and good luck. By the way, I sent off a letter to you giving an account of our recent action. No doubt it will catch up with you sometime.'

Although it would soon be dark Harry decided that the 20 minute flight to El Agheila and back, with a few minutes on the ground could be completed before the light finally went and the desert became dark and cold. He stayed only long enough to see the rest of his squadron fly off east and then he went in search of Major Griffin.

Griffin was pleased to see Harry. He and his small band of troops had got the barracks and the town in some semblance of order and so far the prisoners had caused no trouble. Harry explained briefly his own orders and that in general there was a massive withdrawal of all military units. Once settled back in Egypt the army would be able to repair its tanks and other vehicles. The RAF would be concerned with making sure the planes were in tip top condition. Perhaps while this was being done the troops might enjoy a few days leave and recuperation.

'I agree with you Harry. It does seem foolish to leave so few troops in such a vast area but presumably those in charge must know what they are doing. After all they have a more global picture.'

'I'm not so sure,' replied Harry. 'Past experience has often shown that those on the spot are better informed and better equipped to deal with local situations. There's little good in borrowing from Peter to assist Paul.'

'Thanks very much for letting me know the situation. You'll be glad to know that our communications have been restored. In fact we've just received a lengthy signal but its not yet been decoded.'

Griffin drove Harry out to his plane. His driver cranked up the Hurricane and with a wave Harry turned into wind, took off and headed back to base. He flew at no more than a thousand feet and at maximum speed. Only by looking far ahead could he make out any individual landmarks and at that speed as he reached them they passed by in a blur.

The attack when it came was sudden, unexpected and completely shattered his canopy though apart from small pieces it stayed more or less in place. The shock of feeling the blood pouring from his head wound left Harry momentarily stunned. His left eye was completely closed and although he felt no pain he didn't consider his chances of survival very high. His experience as a pilot came to his aid and he was able to trim the aircraft to fly more or less straight and level while he carefully removed his goggles and helmet. By reaching down into the pocket of his shorts he was able to reach his handkerchief and attempt to wipe away the blood. It seemed ages before he was able to staunch the flow but after a while when he removed the handkerchief it had eased up.

His main concern was to get down in one piece, preferably on a desert base which had medical facilities. With the imminent withdrawal of military personnel he wondered if he should try to fly well in front of the columns going to Egypt in order to reach a camp which had not yet packed up. With one hand holding the handkerchief to his wound, the plane continuing to fly itself, he picked up his helmet with his other hand and called up F/Lt Andrews, his No. Two in the squadron. There was no reply but his base, just a few miles away and still on air, was able to return his call. They were ready to move off but would wait until he landed.

With little regard for correct R/T procedure Harry advised them. 'I've been shot and am losing blood. I can still fly the plane, just, but can't see very well. Could you have the meat wagon standing by and I'll try to land. Should be with you in a few minutes.'

'Roger, Blue Leader. Wind is 045. Land as you can. We'll be waiting. Can you tell me the nature of your injuries. Out.'

'Not sure. Hit in the forehead. Can't see out of my left eye.'

'Roger, Blue Leader.'

Harry was surprised how much easier he felt knowing someone else was aware of his problem even though they could not at present do anything to help him. He could not imagine where the shot had come from. Perhaps he had been careless and not seen the plane that had attacked him and why only one shot. He remembered now that he had been looking to the right, far out into the desert where he had seen vehicles travelling east at speed along desert tracks. Then CRACK – his canopy had been shattered and he had been hit. He wondered now whether, coming in to land if he'd be able to open the canopy or whether the ground crews would have to cut it away once he was on the ground.

He began to feel a little light headed, whether from loss of blood he could not be certain but glad for the moment that he did not appear to have any other injuries. Then the airfield came into view and as he called up control he marvelled at how calm he felt and how remote it all seemed. He even remembered the correct call sign, flew the correct circuit, checked the wind sock, eased back on the throttle and with undercarriage down and locked managed a quite passable landing.

The ambulance and fire tender followed him along his landing and as soon as he had stopped and switched off willing hands were ready to help him from the cockpit. A little unsteady on his feet at first he was advised by the orderly to lie down on the stretcher. As soon as they had covered him with a blanket he was carried to the ambulance and in no time at all he was in the makeshift hospital being attended to by a surgeon.

Harry was conscious, not in any pain and not particularly worried. He had expected to be extremely agitated but everything appeared to be remote as though it was happening to someone else. Even the fact that he was wounded seemed unreal. He heard the murmur of voices, vaguely made out shapes of people looking down at him and tried to move but couldn't. He thought he must be going out under the anaesthetic but couldn't remember it being administered. Then he thought he was dying and soon after was convinced he had. In some strange way he felt happy, almost elated and he knew he needed a rest...

Three hours later he opened his eyes, had a horrible taste in his mouth and felt hungry. He was about to call out to someone passing by but felt himself drifting off again. He never knew how long he had been asleep but the next time he opened his eyes he felt a lot better although he still had the horrible dry taste in his mouth. He realised he was in hospital and smiling down at him he recognised Barbara in a nurses uniform. His voice croaked as he uttered 'Hello Barbara. Have you been here long?'

'Nice to have you back with us Sir. Yes I've been here on and off all night. But how did you know my name is Barbara?'

Harry, now a little more aware of his situation realised the nurse was not Barbara Meyrick. 'Sorry I thought you were someone I knew. I know another Barbara and she looked like you but not so pretty.'

'Oh come on. I can see we're going to have trouble with you. Would you like something to drink?'

'Yes please.'

'I'll help you drink some cold water now. After that you'll manage on your own. That's enough for now. Go back to sleep and I'll be back in an hour and we'll see if you can get up.'

'Thank you Barbara. Do I call you nurse or what.'

'You can call me Sister.' With that Barbara O'Leary, smiling to herself went on to see the next patient.

Later that day the M.O. who had attended Harry stopped at his bed during his rounds. 'Good afternoon Squadron Leader. Feeling a little better?'

'Yes thanks. Still a bit woozy but I now believe I'll make it.' He said with a smile.

'Yes I'm sure you will. We'll be sending you to Cairo tomorrow and you should be up and about in no time.. You might have headaches for a few days but they'll gradually subside and I think even the scar on your forehead will go in time.'

'Thanks for those comforting words. And thanks for looking after me. I still can't believe I never saw that other plane.'

'Well these things happen. Forget about it. You're here and in one piece. By the way if you're up to seeing visitors a Sergeant Watson from your squadron is here.'

'Oh yes. I'd like to see him. Ask him to come in please.'

Sgt Watson who had been waiting some time was ushered into the ward and advised to stay no longer than ten minutes. Harry was pleased to see him. They had known each other a long time and served in the same squadron ever since Aden.

'Glad you made it Sir.' His opening remark was frank but conveyed his concern for his squadron leader.

'You're not the only one. I suppose all the others have gone back to Egypt.'

'Yes. I managed to stop off just to see how you are. I gather you'll be going to Cairo soon and no doubt you'll be returning to the squadron when you're fit.'

'I haven't thought that far ahead yet. Just glad to be alive and in one piece. I was just telling the M.O. I still can't understand how that plane managed to get me. Momentary lapse I suppose.'

'Well Sir. I think I may be able to shed some light on that but I'm not sure you're going to like it.'

'Well Tom, after that intriguing remark you'll just have to continue.'

'Well Sir. It wasn't a plane. Once we'd got you out of the cockpit and away to hospital we went back to the plane to get it repaired. Actually we didn't have any spare pilots so we took the wings off and brought the whole lot back in bits. By the way what height were you flying at?'

'Don't remember. Oh yes, probably about 1000 feet. Why?'

'Well I think that might have been the problem. We found a bit of a beak and a few feathers in the cockpit. We think you hit a buzzard. It shattered your canopy and some of the splinters caused your wound. I gather the M.O. spent a long time getting them all out. Birds wrecking aircraft have been known before. These fly quite fast and if you were also flying at max that's probably what happened.'

Sgt Watson waited, wondering if he'd been right in telling Harry. Harry considered this revelation for a minute and then said. 'Thank you for telling me. I bet I never live it down.'

'It's happened to a lot of pilots and they didn't all live to tell the tale. The chaps were very concerned about you and much relieved when we knew you'd made it.'

'Where are we?'

'Well after you landed the other day we got you off to hospital. The ground crews and the medics waited till the new squadron arrived the following day. Our squadron is in Cairo at present and I'm going to join them. We are now at Tobruk. I managed to salvage a bottle of wine so this is from the lads. And this is a get well card. Its from all of us but Cpl Ramsey did the art work. I'll say cheerio now Sir. All the best.'

With that and a smile of thanks from Harry the sergeant left.

Harry put the wine on his locker and then looked at the card. It was quite large, obviously made from a carton and on the front cover was a copy of the squadron badge and number. At the bottom was a drawing of Harry's plane with a crumpled canopy and the words *Down But Not Out*. Inside were signatures of most of the ground crews accompanied by appropriate get well messages. On the back cover, in colour, was part of the fuselage of Harry's aircraft marked with a tally of the number of sorties he had made. The final one depicted a huge buzzard in Italian colours. 'Thanks Tom.' Harry whispered and lay back on his bed, his eyes filling with tears.

* * *

On February 12th 1941 Harry left Tobruk in an ambulance with five other wounded pilots on the long journey to Cairo. He had sought out the M.O. who had done the operation, thanked him and showed him the Get Well card. 'Yes. I'm glad you know. Wasn't quite sure how you'd take it. You've got a good bunch of chaps there. I've recommended that you have a couple of weeks off and then a check-over before you fly again. If the headaches persist see someone.'

Harry had also seen Sister O'Leary and thanked her for her administrations. 'Would you like me to contact your Barbara?' she asked.

'No thanks. I don't know her very well. Its just that you looked so much like her.'

* * *

On the same day some 500 miles west of Tobruk General Rommel arrived with a few staff officers to assess the Italian presence in Libya. Within a few days he had landed at Tripoli again and from then on for many months to come he and the Afrika Korps caused real problems for the depleted Allies in North Africa.

PART III

Desperate Hours

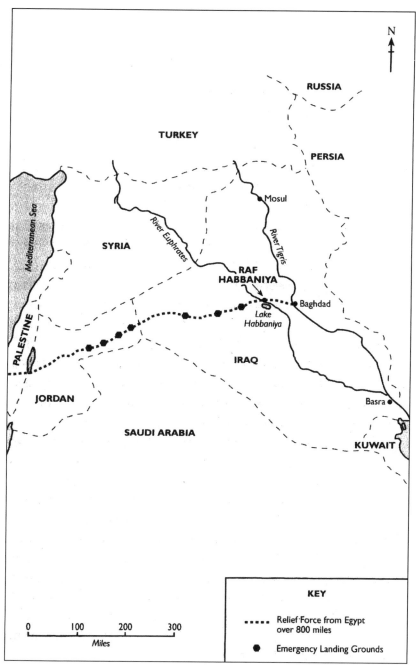

Map 4 IRAQ

CHAPTER 25

Convalescence

The journey from Tobruk to Cairo was slow. Although the road which hugged the coast was adequate and had been repaired many times the ambulance drivers were instructed to make the journey as comfortable as possible for their patients. It was a daily occurrence for the convoy of ambulances to make the 500 mile journey to Cairo. Their speed at just over 25 mph had been worked out so that they reached each stop on the way at the correct time. This speed also allowed faster moving convoys to overtake the slower vehicles and not clutter up the vital highway.

There were six patients in each vehicle and they came from a variety of regiments. A few were RAF pilots and there were two from the Fleet Air Arm. Although Tobruk was well provided with medical facilities the navy and the RAF preferred their people at Cairo. The army wounded were given first aid at Tobruk and the more serious cases were sent east to keep the local hospitals clear for new cases. It was a never ending process.

For the first few hours of the journey Harry was content to lie on his stretcher and listen to the swish of the tyres on the road. Occasionally there was the clatter as vehicles overtook or passed in the opposite direction making the ambulance shake while the noise was enough to startle the patients from their slumbers. Occasionally Harry opened his right eye but could see nothing apart from the canvas side of the ambulance.

After three hours the convoy stopped. The drivers got out to stretch their legs and have a smoke. The medical orderlies sprang to life and visited each patient offering words of comfort or a joke followed by a mug of water and food. Wounds were checked where necessary and after an hour the convoy moved off on its slow journey eastwards. The slight breeze caused by the forward movement was welcomed. Their midday stop had been unpleasant. The sun almost overhead burned mercilessly on men and vehicles alike in spite of the canvas awning which had been erected over the ambulance with an extension on the north side where the meals were prepared and where the drivers had tried to rest.

The evening stop just after 17.00 hours was better. Then after an hour the convoy set off towards Cairo which was reached 24 hours after leaving Tobruk. The patients were separated into their various onward destinations and an hour after leaving the convoy Harry and the others were being settled into the RAF hospital in Cairo.

A nurse in immaculate white uniform spoke to each one saying much the same thing. 'I hope your journey was not too exhausting. Would you like to go to bed now or would you like a wash and a meal.' When she came to Harry and saw his name tag she said, 'Ah. Sqn/Ldr Nelson. We have two of your friends already here. They will no doubt be round to see you soon but first you must see the doctor. Do you require anything?'

'No thank you but do tell me who these friends are. Is one of them Sam Jordan?'

'Yes it is and the other is Sqn/Ldr Simpson.'

'I'll look forward to seeing them tomorrow. I think I'll have a wash and go to bed now. I can manage on my own.'

'You'll do no such thing. Nurse come and help Sqn/Ldr Nelson to the bathroom and then see he's settled in his bed.'

Harry smiled his thanks and winked at the young nurse with his good eye. As he tried to get up from his stretcher he realised he wasn't as strong as he'd thought. 'Getting a bit too old for this lark.' he explained and was glad when the nurse helped him first to his feet and then into a wheelchair. 'Just wait here for a moment while I take your things to your bed.' When she returned she asked, 'Would you like a bath or a shower?'

'To be honest I'd rather go to bed.'

'I'm sure but Sister says you should have one or the other and what Sister says goes or I'll be in trouble. May I suggest a bath but don't go to sleep in it. I'll run it for you and stay to make sure you're O.K.'

'Thanks.' Harry felt tired out yet he'd done nothing all day. Maybe he was getting old. Even so once he had managed to get into the bath and settled down the warmth of the water began to soothe his weary body but as it did so he felt his headache returning. He made a half hearted attempt at washing himself and then the nurse discreetly handed him a towel and asked if he needed any help. 'No thanks but my head is beginning to hurt again.'

'We'll get you into bed and the doctor will be round to see you.' The nurse was very businesslike, practical, deferential almost and Harry felt he was being cosseted far more than the nature of his wound warranted. As she wheeled him slowly towards his bed he said 'I'm sure there are a lot of chaps worse off than me.'

'No doubt there are but you're all special so make the most of it. As soon as you're able to cope we'll let you go. Get some sleep. I'll see you later.'

Harry lay in bed and looked around. There seemed to be about twelve beds ranged down each side of a long ward with patients in various positions. Even at this late hour some were sitting up and chatting to their neighbours. Some had arms or legs or both plastered and held in awkward poses. Others looked deathly pale and a few beds had screens around them. With his single wound over his left eye caused by a buzzard he felt a fraud and resolved to get out of hospital as soon as possible.

He slept and was roused from a pleasant dream by a male voice and then a female voice which he recognised as that of the Sister who had admitted him. 'Ah. Sqn/Ldr. Had a nice sleep?' enquired the M.O.

'Yes thanks.'

'No don't get up. I just want to ask a few questions. I know you've had them all before but we must make sure your notes are correct and amend them if necessary. Any headaches? Any aches or pains anywhere else? Good. Right. Let's have a look under these bandages and see if we can't get rid of some of them. It seems you have been extremely lucky. A little bit lower down and I think you'd have lost your eye. A bit higher up and Lord knows what damage might have occurred.' As he spoke he removed the bandages and looked carefully at the wound, then took out a small torch and shone it in both Harry's eyes. The examination continued.

'Just follow my finger will you. Pulse O.K. Blood pressure not too bad. Temperature up a bit. Right Sister. I think we'll have those stitches out and then just a light dressing. I'll be back tomorrow and you can probably get up for a few hours. The nurse will bring you something for your headaches. You'll have those for a while but they'll gradually tail off. Welcome back into the land of the living.'

'Thanks Doc. When can I see my friends?'

'Soon. You need some rest first and no excitement.'

For the next two days the routine was much the same. The early morning bustle to get patients washed and fed before the doctor's visit accompanied by the ward Sister was accepted by the men with varying degrees of humour. Harry was keen to get out of the hospital as soon as possible and although he rested several times during the day he felt he was making steady progress towards recovery. Certainly he was steadier on his feet and the headaches not so painful. On the third day after the midday meal he was sitting outside on the veranda when visitors descended. At first, approaching tentatively, then as they realised Harry was awake, first Sam Jordan and then Alex Simpson, his old squadron leader, came over and shook his hand.

They fussed over each other in between reminiscences and mutual congratulations on surviving. Sam was full of gratitude to Harry for his rescue and insisted on recounting it in detail though to Harry's relief he left out all mention of the Italians. Soon a third visitor joined the wounded pilots. Michael Carter, now promoted to Wing Commander, came out to meet the comrades he first met when they were all at Aden.

'Good morning boys. Glad to see you all up and about. I'm here in Cairo as a member of the RAF Medical Board though only for two weeks so I doubt if any of you will come in front of me. Then its a spot of leave and back to Aden. I hope they're treating you alright here.'

This reunion was short lived as the Sister approached. 'Sorry gentlemen. I'm afraid I'll have to cut short your meeting. You're disturbing the other patients. And you Sir,' addressing Carter, 'should know better.'

'Sorry Sister. These are my fledgling pilots when we were in Aden together and if it hadn't been for two of them there might have been a real problem.'

'Very well. You may all go and sit in the hut over there but not for long and keep the noise down. In any case I want these patients back in the ward by 16.30 hours.'

'Thank you Sister.'

All four walked over to the adjacent hut and sat inside to continue their reminiscences. As they talked a cursory glance over each patient assured Michael that Harry and Alex seemed to be well on the way to recovery. Simpson no longer had his arm in a sling and although Harry looked a bit drawn the sparkle in his eye had returned. Sam's arm was also no longer in a sling although his hand was heavily bandaged. He walked awkwardly with the aid of a stick and Michael wondered if he might do better without it. He resolved to find out more about his injuries and the possible prognosis.

The medical officer left after about half an hour but promised to see them all before he went on leave. The days passed gently by and the three friends met each day after lunch and began to go for walks in the grounds. Sam got stronger each day and at the end of a week he was advised by the doctor to leave his stick behind for short periods. Harry suggested they take up billiards where there would be a fair amount of walking yet Sam could sit down whenever necessary. They roped in another pilot. He had been in one of the bombers when they first attacked the Italians in November 1940. He had crashed on a more recent raid and broken a leg. His leg was now as good as new but his shoulder and neck still hurt but he could hold a cue and at first he was better than any of them.

Michael Carter arrived one day with another medical bod, a certain F/Lt Sommers. He spoke briefly to the four billiards players and asked if they would mind being interviewed by Sommers. 'Anything for an old friend.' was Sam's quick reply.

'Well let me be honest and explain a little more. As I know most of you as old friends would you mind if we used you as guinea pigs. Ian has a little experiment he'd like to conduct. You've all been wounded and are recovering. Some of our other patients are not responding to treatment and we'd like to use you as controls to find out why that might be. You've probably guessed by now that Ian Sommers is a psychiatrist, a fairly new branch of military medicine.'

'O.K. as long as you don't start sticking needles into us.' replied Sam.

The questions started straight away. Sommers began, 'What I want to know is how soon you would all like to get back into the cockpit.'

Sam answered first. 'As soon as my leg is better I'm off into the pale blue yonder.' Simpson said he'd like to get cracking and take out the bloke who shot him down or someone like him. Harry, who superficially had the smallest wound said he'd just as soon take it easy for a bit longer. He went on 'You know in some ways I feel I could do with a long rest. Don't get me wrong. I like flying but I seem to have been doing nothing else ever since I got out here in 1937. I know that's my job but it does seem to have been a long time. I think I could do with a spell on the ground.'

Once he'd made this statement the others agreed roughly with his feelings. They all wanted to get airborne again sometime but didn't mind if their return to duty was delayed for a while yet. The questions continued for a few minutes and then Sommers said 'Thanks very much for your observations. As you'll have noticed I didn't take notes. I wanted to get an overall impression. Would you mind if I spoke to you individually only for half an hour or so. I promise your names will not figure on any report which may appear – only your answers. You may rest assured that you'll be helping a lot of chaps in the weeks to come.'

They all agreed and the last session ended just in time for them to return to their ward for the evening meal. Michael came back after the meal to thank them and explained that F/Lt Sommers was also on one of the medical boards which decided when pilots should return to active duty. 'Once you're pronounced fit you'll probably be given leave and then wait for a posting. Before you actually take to the skies again you'll all be given a flight assessment. In the past they often asked pilots to return to flying duties too soon sometimes with dire consequences. We don't want that to happen again.' They spoke briefly again of the time they had spent together at Aden. Then it was time for Michael to go. As he did so he said, 'One more thing. After you've been flying for a month or so could you drop me a line to let me know how you're getting on.'

'All part of your experiment is it?' Sam wanted to know.

'Well yes in a way but really I'd like to keep in touch with you chaps. Let me know if I can help in any way. Take care. See you sometime.'

On 21st February Harry was called before a panel of RAF doctors and one high ranking pilot. Michael Carter was also present. Much to Harry's surprise he asked how his medical studies were progressing and realised that none of the others present was aware of his earlier ambition to become a doctor. Harry thought for a while before replying.

'I've been a bit busy of late but no doubt if I ever get a quiet moment I'll take up medicine again.'

This reply caused a few smiles from the medical men but a frown from the pilot who looked as though he'd like to know more but thought better than to ask. With Harry's records in front of them giving the results of his physical examination that morning he was able to answer all their questions and they concluded that he was well enough to be discharged from hospital. He was told he would join a holding unit, put on so called 'light duties' and after 7 days would probably go on leave. Only after that would he be finally assessed for flying duties.

CHAPTER 26

Promotion Confirmed – and a Gong

Harry was sent to another base just outside Cairo. His 'light duties' involved nothing more than working in the admin. office, checking over personnel in transit, those going on leave and those scheduled for actual postings to different RAF establishments. It provided him with an overview of the military deployment as far as the RAF was concerned in the Egyptian sector though he knew that bits of paper provided little in the way of the reality which took place on the ground or in the air.

Alex Simpson had been two days ahead of him in leaving hospital and for his 'light duties' he became the Sports Officer while that officer went on leave for two weeks. They met occasionally, talked about old times and gradually merged into life on the RAF base.

A week later Sam and Joe Unwin, the bomber pilot who Harry had escorted in the desert, arrived. It seemed that Michael Carter was no longer on the assessment panel, having gone on leave. Sam looked pale and though he walked more easily his general appearance suggested he was far from well. Even so he seemed brighter in himself and the four of them took to the billiards table again. A couple of days later they borrowed a car and Alex drove them into Cairo.

There seemed to be more troops than ever and Sam remarked that the Egyptian traders were not as friendly as on previous occasions. They were still eager to take money from British troops yet the little friendly gestures of earlier visits had vanished. There was the usual gossip in the bars and hotels and everyone talked quite openly of events in Greece and the fact that Rommel, a new German commander, was gathering his forces in the western desert to launch an attack against the lightly held British garrisons. British officers, apparently in the know, countered this by declaring that it would take the Germans at least ten weeks to prepare an attack and long before that British reinforcements would be in place.

Simpson and Unwin were sent on leave, after which they were to report to RAF Ismailia. Harry, still in his temporary role as Admin. Officer, was about to send a clerk to put up new orders when he noticed his own name. His promotion to Squadron Leader had been confirmed and he had been awarded the DFC. The following day he received personal confirmation of this in a letter, together with a small length of DFC ribbon, sufficient for three uniforms. He had forgotten the Group Captain's remark about a possible gong and now wondered if he should tell Sam. He needn't have worried for Sam saw the notice later that day and offered his congratulations.

'Well done Harry. The Groupie told me he'd put your name forward for a medal. If it hadn't been for you I wouldn't be here now. Let's go out and celebrate.'

Whilst in the desert they had little need of money and their back pay had built up into quite tidy sums. Sam decided to open a bank account locally and deposit his cheque. Harry did the same and enquired about sending money home on a regular basis and then wondered why he'd not done it before. These transactions and a bit of shopping took care of most of the morning and it was lunch time before they got back to camp. On the way they decided to forego their celebration for the time being until they went on leave and they really felt up to it.

The following day they were sent on leave. They both felt really tired and wondered if they were going down with some dreadful desert sickness. 'You know what it is,' remarked Sam.

'It's the old body telling us to take things easy. In fact that's why they're sending us on leave, not to enjoy ourselves but to get better and quicker so that they can get some more flying out of us before we croak.'

'You can be a cynical bastard when you try.' was Harry's reply. Yet he worried a little for it had never been in Sam's nature to be so.

Sam replied. 'Tomorrow we'll go to Alexandria for our leave and call on a friend.'

'You've got no friend in Alex.'

'That's where you're wrong old boy. When we were there earlier I got to know Joyce Young pretty well. She said anytime I was this way to let her know.'

Harry remembered the Wren, a dark haired girl, always immaculately turned out. She arrived and departed from the communal house at such odd hours he doubted if he'd exchanged more than a couple of sentences with her. 'I know who you mean. Wasn't she in signals?'

'That's the one. Several times when you and the others were out or when I got up early she had just come off duty. We just got chatting.'

'Nothing else?' was Harry's question but he knew Sam would never attempt anything beyond the bounds of acceptable behaviour.

For once the journey into Alex was quick. Sam couldn't remember the telephone number of the house so they took a chance and after two errors of navigation finally hit upon the correct street and found it. As they got to the front door two army nurses came out and looked enquiringly at the two RAF officers while Sam asked. 'Do you happen to know if Joyce Young is at home and if not what time is she expected.'

'She has in fact just come off duty. You'd better go through and find her. Make sure you shut the door.'

Once inside they called out. 'Anyone at home.' Under the circumstances it was not really the most appropriate of calls.

A chorus of answers came from every corner of the house and not long afterwards Joyce Young came down the main staircase and greeted the two airmen. She didn't recognise them immediately and it wasn't until Sam called her name that she responded with a smile and added, 'Oh. Hello Sam. Give me half an hour. I'm just going to have a bath. Go into the lounge and introduce yourself.'

'How are you Joyce? Sorry I couldn't let you know I was in town. I lost your phone number.'

'Not to worry. I'll be down soon.'

They went into the large front room but none of the other residents was there so they passed the time by glancing through the magazines and catching up to date with news in the papers.'

Joyce reappeared much sooner than the anticipated half an hour and said she was about to cook a late breakfast and invited them to join her.

'No thanks. We've eaten.' replied Sam. 'We're on leave for a few days so I thought I'd see how you're getting on. Now why don't you chat to Harry and I'll cook you a meal. What were you going to have?'

Surprisingly Joyce accepted. 'That's marvellous. Scrambled eggs, bacon and tomatoes.'

Sam disappeared into the kitchen and Harry found himself talking to Joyce Young. 'I never realised Sam was handy in the kitchen. Before he comes back let me tell you he's been very ill.'

Concern showed in her face immediately and Harry continued. 'He was badly wounded and has only just got out of hospital. He's been passed fit but he's lost a lot of weight and I think it will be some time before he's back to his old self.'

'I won't ask about the details. He'll tell me if he wants to. I'm only glad he's alive and in one piece. I see you've been promoted since you were here last.'

'Well yes. When Sam was wounded our squadron leader was also out action for some time and I was given temporary command of the squadron. Until they could find someone else to take over they allowed me to keep the extra ring.'

'I also notice you've got the DFC. Do you have to hand that back as well?'

'As I recall, the officer, who asked me to look after the squadron said something like, "We can't have a squadron looked after by someone without a gong so I'll see what I can do." and that was it. I've only it had a short while.'

Joyce was not convinced by this casual explanation but she didn't press the point. Sam called from the kitchen. 'Five minutes. Harry put out two extra cups for tea.' They got up and went through the double doors to the slightly larger room which served as the dining room. Sam came in from the other end with a tray on which was a plate of scrambled eggs, bacon, tomatoes and mushrooms which he placed on the table. He went back to the kitchen and returned this time carrying another small tray with the tea pot, jug of hot water, sugar and milk.

Joyce smiled her thanks and added. 'I really am impressed Sam. I was really whacked and almost decided not to bother with a meal.'

Sam poured out three teas and Harry couldn't help noticing the look which passed between them as Joyce took a cup from him. He was suddenly aware that they were more than friends and wondered how long they'd been in love with each other. He couldn't understand it, felt a little awkward as though he was intruding upon their special moment together and decided to leave as soon as he had drunk his tea.

'Sam, Joyce. I hope you don't mind but I've got a couple of letters to write. We only came over on the off chance to see if you and possibly Pamela were still in residence. Sam can stay for a while and do the washing up and maybe we can make up a foursome for tomorrow.' It was obviously the right thing to do and neither Sam nor Joyce made any objections.

Joyce said. 'See you tomorrow then Harry. I'm sure we can arrange something special while you're both in town.'

Harry walked back to the hotel and did in fact write a couple of letters but spent the remainder of the day resting and eating. He didn't hear Sam come in but knew it must have been quite late. However the next day Sam was up early, called for Harry and they went down to breakfast together. In a most casual voice Sam said, 'By the way Joyce is off duty for a couple of days. She says she will organise a day trip, including a picnic and that Pamela and a friend would like to come with us. Is that alright with you?'

'Of course. I'm sure that'll be fine. She's rather nice isn't she.'

'Well nice is not the word I'd use. There is no single word to describe Joyce.'

'No you're right Sam. Sorry. I just meant she is out of the ordinary and you two obviously get on well together. I'm glad for you.' Harry thought he'd better stop looking for the elusive word to describe Joyce and change the subject. 'So what time do we need to be there?'

'Not later than 09.30 hours otherwise, apparently we'll miss the best time of the day on the river.'

When they reached the house it was obvious preparations were well in hand. Joyce had arranged for a taxi to take them to a small village a few miles to the east. At the river a small launch waited while they transferred two wicker baskets containing the picnic things. There was also a primus stove, kettle, tea pot, cups and saucers taken from the kitchen as well as a table cloth. Sam had guessed that a boat might be involved in the day trip and was relieved that it was a motor launch. He had not been looking forward to flexing his muscles with rowing just yet. The launch came complete with pilot and deck hand. Both seemed to be of Indian extraction, as like as not brothers. Just ahead of the small raised bridge the launch had been fitted with a deck canopy and beneath it were six easy chairs and a table.

Joyce, obviously pleased when she saw the admiration in Sam's eyes remarked. 'As in most things it's not what you know it's who you know. Let's hope the rain holds off. Welcome aboard the *Lotus Blossom*.' They cast off and in just a few minutes had left behind the factories and warehouses which lined the river bank. The river although placid was still swollen and as they chugged along at about four knots the threatening clouds vanished and they were transported into a world away from the war. The two girls chatted, Joyce and Sam spoke together in whispers and Harry made his way to the bow and sat quietly soaking up the tranquillity.

The picnic had been carefully planned. After an hour and a half there came a different noise from the engine as the throttles were eased back and the crew steered towards the bank. While one jumped ashore the other cut the engine altogether and threw a line to his mate who quickly secured it to a bollard. A second line was quickly cast ashore while the launch was pulled in and secured. The girls had obviously been on a similar outing before. They all disappeared below to emerge a few minutes later wearing swimming costumes.

'You're not seriously thinking of a swim in the river are you?' Sam wanted to know.

'No, not likely. We just need to get a bit of a sun tan.' Pamela went on to explain that the only swimming they did was either in the sea or the swimming baths belonging to one of the many clubs in Alex. Lunch itself was quite an elaborate affair. From a large thermos flask there was soup followed by cooked pieces of chicken, ham and small individual pork pies. There was also chopped tomatoes and cooked rice all washed down with white wine. A variety of sticky sweets followed and currant cake.

Harry could not resist asking if there was anything else to eat as he was hungry. Joyce replied, 'Let that lot get down first and we'll see. You never know what might be in store.'

'Only joking.' Harry was forced to admit. 'I can honestly say that was the most exotic picnic I have ever eaten. Congratulations. Do we wash the dishes?'

'Just rinse them in the small galley and we'll do them properly when we get back.'

When Harry returned to the deck he found the others in various poses of sleep. Pam and Thelma were near the bow and just shaded from the sun by the awning while Sam and Joyce sprawled close to each other on the deck itself on top of cushions. Harry managed to ease past them and slumped into one of the armchairs, surprisingly comfortable, and in a very short time everyone appeared to be asleep. The two crewmen had gone ashore probably to visit one of their families. Everyone in Egypt seemed to be related to someone else, a distant cousin or a friend of a brother.

There were no actual snores coming from the sleeping bodies but heavy breathing indicated that the large meal had done its work or maybe at last they were all able to relax and experience a really deep sleep. The past few months had been a tiring time for all. Sam and Harry flying most days until their wounds prevented them but that only left them with other problems to cope with. The girls, too, worked long hours. Two of them were nurses, working odd hours in difficult situations while Joyce, who also worked shift hours, had the exacting job of sending and receiving signals and then decoding them.

The two crew members returned to the launch and as they stepped on board the slight movement roused the sleeping bodies. After a few moments everyone was awake and Joyce suggested they all go ashore for a brief stroll but first they must change back into their dresses and take sun hats with them as they walked towards the village. It was an unreal afternoon in a make believe world as the five friends walked slowly towards the white walled cluster of houses. No one stirred. Even the dogs which slept in whatever shade they could find near the houses could not be bothered to investigate the intruders. The only thing which shed any light on the real situation was a flight of bombers high up in the sky flying to the west and even they seemed to be affected by the heat of the day.

On the other side of the village they came across a small clump of palm trees. The air here was much fresher and soon they saw a well but even this was deserted. They flopped down onto the ground. No one spoke until one of the girls saw a beetle and hastily got up. The spell was broken and they turned back and headed towards the river and the launch. Harry and Sam walked together. 'Wonderful outing.' Harry could think of nothing more to say but he would remember this day for a long time to come.

Back on the launch Joyce made some tea and they each ate a few more cakes and then it was time for the return trip back to Alex and soon back to the war. The crew released the ropes, jumped on board and headed upstream for a short while before turning round in a wide sweep and allowing the river to carry the launch back towards the sea. Once at its mooring they unloaded the picnic baskets while Joyce phoned for a taxi to take them back to the house. The sun was beginning to set as they carried the baskets indoors. The two RAF pilots stayed on for another couple of hours, thanked the girls for arranging the picnic and promised to think of something they could arrange in the future. Sam and Harry walked silently back to their hotel.

Their leave was coming to and end. Sam spent most of his time with Joyce. Harry went to a cinema one evening with Pamela and was surprised to find inside there was air conditioning. The next evening she met him at their hotel and together they went to a night club where there was dancing. Pam had not mentioned Andy and Harry wondered whether that romance had finished. At last he asked the direct question and she answered, 'Andy has been posted a bit further away and its not so easy for him to get transport but we are still engaged although I've no idea when we'll get married.'

'I'm glad. And thanks very much for taking pity on me these past few days.'

'It's not a question of pity. I was very glad of your company.'

It would soon be time for them to make their way back to Cairo and then probably be posted to Ismailia. Harry went round to the house to say goodbye to the girls, expecting that Sam was already there but as he wasn't Joyce managed to get him on his own.

'You are a naughty boy. Why didn't you tell me?' and she came forward and kissed him. 'Thank you so much Harry for saving Sam. When we get married we both want you to be our best man.'

'If at all possible I shall be delighted. I expect to be posted soon. When are you getting married?' Harry didn't really know what to say. Was he supposed to know about this secret or was Joyce making it up. No it couldn't be that. He had seen them together and although Sam hadn't said anything he knew how much he liked Joyce.

'We haven't discussed it yet and you are the first to know so look surprised when Sam tells you. We have to see if we can get our leaves to coincide. Don't tell anyone else.'

'It'll be our little secret. I really came to thank you for making this a leave to remember and to remind Sam we ought to be getting back to base and then on to Ismailia. Where is Sam? Out buying an engagement ring?'

Joyce blushed. 'I don't really know but we did look at some last week.'

While Harry was having a farewell drink Sam came bounding up the front steps with a great big grin on his face.

'I'm glad you're here Harry. It's about time we got moving. I'll just go and collect my stuff.'

Joyce followed him upstairs. A few moments later he came down with most of his kit while Joyce followed carrying a small attaché case. She made a mock pretence of keeping her left hand covered but Harry had seen the engagement ring which Sam had just given her. His hearty congratulations to Sam and a brief kiss to Joyce helped to cover his confusion. 'You kept that pretty quiet Sam. You must take things easy from now on. No more getting into scrapes. I'm so pleased for you both.'

'Take care you two,' were her final words as she kissed them both before turning hurriedly back indoors.

The following day Harry and Sam returned to Cairo. Between 21st March and 24th they had their final assessment and Harry was passed fit for duty. The M.O. suggested that Sam should continue to take things easy and that he too should be fit for duty in ten days' time. On 26th March they arrived at RAF Ismailia to await a further posting.

CHAPTER 27

No. 4 F.T.S. Habbaniya

The journey to RAF Ismailia was hot and sticky and although less than 80 miles they were glad when it was over and they were able to relax inside the cool bungalow. Harry's days of light duties had ended and he merely waited for a flight assessment before taking to the skies once more. Sam still had some way to go before he would be pronounced fit but he was definitely making good progress. Largely on the influence of Michael Carter he had been allowed to proceed to Ismailia at the same time as Harry.

It was not long after they had settled in that Group Captain Holmes appeared on the scene and discussed with Harry the possibility of going on an instructor's course. 'I see that according to your records you were due to return to England to do just that. I'm afraid that's not possible at the moment. We might be able to get you on a boat going the long way round but I wonder if you'd like to continue your convalescence at a flying school out here, doing a few lectures and possibly a bit of flying. As you know we have No 4 Flying Training School at Habbaniya, Iraq and I think your experience in the desert would be invaluable to the trainee pilots. As far as I know none of the instructors there has flown a Hurricane so you could bring them up to date as well.'

Harry considered this suggestion for a while. He, personally, would prefer a little longer on the ground before he got into the cockpit again. This way he could ease into it gradually whereas if he was posted back to a squadron he realised he would be thrown in at the deep end. On the other hand, he thought, that might not be a bad thing. He felt fit enough though still a little weary. He suddenly realised that Holmes was not giving him the choice. It had already been decided so he smiled and said. 'That's just what I need Sir.' The Group Captain continued, 'Good. Go there. Don't go line shooting but give them the truth. It will give you the chance to prepare some lectures and no doubt the CFI will let you have a few flights. It will be a nice way to get back into the saddle. As soon as there's a place on a boat going home I'll let you know.'

Harry was posted to Habbaniya on 28th March 1941. Sam came to see him off and carried some of his kit to the waiting Anson. Harry expected to be a passenger in the aircraft but as he reached it the pilot, F/Sgt Joe Erskine, was standing outside with a clip board in hand, checking off the passengers as they entered and the packages as they were stowed on board.

'Good morning Sir. If you don't mind it would help if you could sit up front with me and wind up the undercart once we're airborne. It's 125 turns of the little handle. It would also help if you could do a bit of map reading for me. Although I've done this trip many times I need to keep a lookout for Polish airmen. They have a habit of shooting anything that flies slow.'

'No problem. It's time I started to earn my keep again.'

Harry took a good look at Erskine for the first time. Probably younger than himself, his eyes had a weariness beyond his years as though he had done too much flying. Harry knew only too well that feeling. He also noticed that just below his wings Joe Erskine wore the DFM ribbon, the equivalent of his own DFC. Harry also knew that despite the usual comments that such medals were issued with the rations it was usually a question of sour grapes. He didn't doubt that Erskine deserved this one. He climbed on board sat in the other seat next to the pilot, adjusted his parachute harness, strapped himself in, put on his helmet and plugged in the R/T.

No matter what rank he held and irrespective of who was on the plane the pilot was always the captain and in sole command even as in this instance the observer was a squadron leader. The last piece of luggage was secured and the pilot got one of the mechanics to crank up the port and then the starboard engines. Soon both were running smoothly and Erskine did the usual cockpit checks and then taxied to the beginning of the runway awaiting clearance from ground control.

Erskine acknowledged the clearance and the plane began to move forward gathering speed until it became airborne and slowly gained height. Joe carried out the correct circuit procedure and then headed west for Cairo. 'Could you start winding up the undercarriage now.' As soon as Harry had finished Joe went on to explain, 'From here we go first to Cairo to drop off some mail that some clot forgot and then we go more or less direct to Habbaniya. We must refuel at Cairo to make sure we've got enough to get us to Iraq. Once we leave Egypt you'll see several landing grounds indicated on the map. For us they are emergency stops in case we have to divert or need additional fuel.'

'Why might we need to divert?'

'Well the Jerries are pressing on and there have been one or two attempts to put Mosul out of action. In fact I think the squadron that was there has gone to Greece so we need to keep our eyes peeled.'

'O.K. I get the picture. Is there any ammo in the gun turret?'

'Oh yes. Never go anywhere without it.'

The stop-over at Cairo was brief. Having switched off the engines the fuel was topped up while Joe went to the control tower to deliver the mail. The two other passengers also got out and followed him. In less than half an hour they were airborne and soon passed over the familiar landmarks of Ismailia and then they were flying over new ground as far as Harry was concerned.

'Do you do this trip often?'

'About once a week ever since I got here about two months ago. Before that I was with Coastal Command patrolling part of the Indian ocean. If you'd like to fly this kite Sir you have control.'

'Thanks. Better keep my hand in though I've never flown an Anson.'

'You don't need to fly them. They fly themselves. It's just the sodding undercart that's the problem.'

'The engines seem similar to Oxfords.'

'Absolutely identical. Ansons are a bit slower but they carry quite a bit. I seem to have spent a long time in them. I suppose you're going to be an instructor in Iraq.'

'Not quite. I'm supposed to be going home to do an instructor's course. This posting is just for a short while to recuperate or until a place is available on the boat.'

'I've heard that one before. Not much chance of recuperating at Habbaniya or Shaiba. The temperature in the summer is well over 100.'

'Thanks for warning me but I don't think I'll be there that long.'

They lapsed into silence until they prepared to land at one of the desert landing grounds.

'O.K. Sir. I have control. We'll just stop here for a short while to offload a couple of packages and see if they need anything. They're a bit isolated and they like to see someone from the outside world once a week. After this its on to Habbaniya. Ever been there? It must be an important base. They've got an Air Vice-Marshal there as well as the station commander.'

'No this will be my first visit and I guess I won't see much of him. Is it a big camp?'

'Oh yes. Its the biggest in Iraq. In fact its like a small town with far more amenities than you'd expect. They seem to have dozens of tennis courts and of course they play rugger and soccer. I've also seen a golf course and I believe there are riding stables.'

'You must be kidding. What's the snag? There must be one.'

'Two main ones. Its hot and there are no women apart from a few nurses. Lake Habbaniya is not far away and it has fresh water. Flying boats use it a staging post and I believe RAF personnel can go yachting on it.'

'Sounds good to me.'

'Let me know how you feel after you've been here a month. Mind you there's always something going on. Its a large depot for all the RAF in Iraq and has huge workshops.'

'I'll certainly look out for you when you next visit. Thanks for the info.'

'Mind you. I've never been posted there – only stayed a couple of days at a time. So maybe its better than I've suggested.'

'Or it could be worse.'

'Well yes although I doubt it. Anyway the food is good. Better still in your mess. Even so its a strange place to send anyone to recuperate. I understand the maximum posting there is two years. After that people go mad.'

They lapsed into silence while Harry absorbed the news about his latest posting. A few minutes later Harry lowered the undercarriage and F/Sgt Erskine eased back on the throttles while he prepared to land at another of the outposts. The emergency landing ground was little more than a strip of desert made reasonably smooth. A few natives wandered about picking up stones from the landing area and as the plane came into land the dust showered them but they seemed oblivious and merely carried on with their work. A cluster of huts and a few tents were all the dwellings he could see in this outpost of the Empire. An armoured car became visible as they taxied towards the huts and Harry could also see what appeared to be a boundary fence running for miles. In the distance he could just make out a series of stone cairns which he later found out marked the oil pipeline through which flowed much of the oil used by the military forces in the Middle East.

The ground staff at the desert landing ground were obviously pleased to see Joe Erskine. He switched the engines off just long enough to take some mail to the control caravan and returned with two small cases to be delivered to Habbanyia. With no visible instructions being issued the ground crew started to top up the fuel. Joe chatted briefly to a corporal while the refuelling was completed and then they were on their way on the last leg of this particular trip.

Sqn/Ldr Harry Nelson landed at Habbaniya just six weeks after being wounded and just a few days after being passed fit for flying duties. He had been warned to expect headaches occasionally and not to fly as a pilot for at least another week. He said farewell to Erskine and made his way to the officers mess, reported for duty and was given a room in one of the many bungalows on the base. Harry was prepared, for the moment, to accept his temporary role as a ground instructor for a few weeks but looked forward to the time when he would be fully recovered and able to rejoin his squadron – or better still return to England. Emerging from his room after a quick shower and having changed into his new khaki drill uniform he went along to see the Chief Flying Instructor, Wing Commander Lang.

'Glad to have you with us Sqn/Ldr Nelson.' The CFI welcomed Harry on to his team. 'We can do with some up to date gen on fighter combat experience to stimulate our pupils. Most of us here saw action many years ago. The pupils here are in various stages on their course. All have flown solo and about half are on the advanced stage of their training and are now flying Oxfords. Have you flown them?'

'Well not many hours. However I have flown an Envoy which is very similar.'

'No matter. We'll soon get you checked out. In the meantime I'd like you to give a series of talks, lectures really, about combat experience, survival techniques, emergency procedures and the like. Let me have a rough draft of what you intend to say but I leave the content entirely up to you and you can get stuck in the day after next. Here is the general time table of the course. You'll see that some lectures are given first thing in the morning and others just before the evening meal. In between it gets very hot here so you may find that the pupils are not wide awake for the early lectures. Those at the end of the day are also subject to lack of attention because the pupils are tired. That's the way it is I'm afraid.'

Harry felt the interview was at an end, stood up, saluted and returned to his billet. He began to wonder what ramshackle establishment he had been posted to and resolved to make his lectures interesting enough to keep his audience awake. He had never done anything like it before but thinking back to similar lectures he had attended when he was a pupil pilot he remembered how boring and badly structured most had been. He began to rough out a course of lectures and became so absorbed that he quite forgot the time and where he was. A discreet knock on the door and a voice called to tell him it was time for the evening meal. He called out his thanks and tidied away his lecture efforts.

He met a few more instructors at dinner and though they wanted to discuss with him his experiences in Libya he excused himself, saying he must get an early night. In reality he continued with drafting out his lectures and was extremely pleased with his efforts when he finally went to bed. The following afternoon he went along to see the CFI and to show him the first batch of lectures. Wg/Cdr Lang asked him to wait while he read the outline and Harry could see by the expression on his face that his lectures would be accepted.

'Nice work. I like these. Not too formal yet the meat is there. I think the pupils will be pleased you've arrived. I don't propose to listen in on the first but once you've got into your stride I'll probably drop in on one or two. I might learn something to my advantage. We can all get a bit stale doing the same thing day in and day out.'

'Right Sir and to be honest I'd welcome your criticism. I've never done this sort of thing before. You do know that I'm supposed to be going on a proper instructors course back in England.'

'Oh yes. All of us here have been through that and although the principles remain the same I'm sure the method of delivery now recommended is better. That goes for flying too. I understand they now record your voice and if its not clearly understood you don't pass. O.K. Your first lecture is the day after tomorrow. Best of luck. Let me know how it goes.'

Harry spent some time preparing his first lecture which was about checking aircraft before take off and equally important to report to the riggers and fitters on return anything wrong with the aircraft. He remembered to put in a few anecdotes but when he stood in front of the class he was totally unprepared for the chorus of questions aimed at him. After a few minutes he realised that most were trivial aimed at wasting time in order to drag out the lesson until it was time for them to go to their next lecture.

He stopped talking and kept them waiting for a full two minutes and then said, 'I realise I'm new here but it's my job to instil some sound advice into your tiny minds. Now I don't really mind when I do it. So if we haven't completed this lecture in the allotted time you will return here after dinner tonight and when that is done you will stay here and each write a five hundred word essay on wasting time. Moreover if I don't like any one essay you will all walk round the perimeter in full pack. Make no mistake I can be a right bastard if I wish. Shall we get on? What I'm about to tell you may save your life one day.'

The remainder of the lecture passed without incident. The class was quiet and Harry wondered if he'd gone too far. After all these were not young school kids. They were potential pilots and had actually volunteered. He would have to tell the CFI what had happened. The pupils began to show an interest in what he was saying and towards the end of the lecture sensible questions were asked. Harry felt he had won the first round but could not for the life of him understand why he had acted in such a manner. Maybe he had learned an important lesson too – how to exercise control.

He was down to give four lectures each day and as he prepared each talk it gave him an opportunity to look back over what he had achieved since 1936 when he first put on an RAF uniform as a rookie. His next lecture was about map reading and finding one's way home. This was to be followed by emergency landing procedures. These would be followed by bombing techniques and then fighter tactics. After the fiasco of his first lecture the class had settled down and Harry could tell that what he had to offer was well received. Questions were answered truthfully, often with a personal anecdote of his own experiences.

The Chief Flying Instructor did attended one lecture and afterwards congratulated Harry on his delivery. 'I've got another job for you if you don't mind. The M.O. has asked if I can spare a pilot to take a pregnant nurse and another patient to hospital in Basra. The only trouble is that P/O Tomlinson who normally flies the Anson is off sick. Could you fly the kite if one of the advanced pupils goes with you as navigator and operates the undercart?'

'Yes I don't see too much of a problem. I'd like to do a circuit and bump first just to get the feel of it.'

'Sure. LAC Porter will come with you. He's quite good on Oxfords and has also done a few hours in the Anson. He flies a bit left wing low but is otherwise very sound.'

'Can't you get him to fly straight and level?

230

'Sorry. You misunderstand me. Haven't you come across that expression? Let's just say that some of them would prefer to carry a handbag rather than a wallet.'

Suddenly the meaning dawned on Harry and he felt himself blushing. For all his experience as a pilot in some areas he realised he was decidedly naive. The CFI continued.

'We have at least three on the base but so far they have caused no problems and they all happen to be good pilots.'

'O.K. Sir. We'll see what we can do. If you tell me what time to take off I'll be ready.'

'Thanks Harry. I'll organise the flight plan and get clearance. All you need to do is deliver the two patients and bring back any mail. Shaiba is the nearest RAF base. If you leave just after lunch you should be back before dark.'

Harry spoke to two instructors at lunch who assured him the Anson was an easy plane to fly and when he said that LAC Porter was accompanying him he was relieved that they both agreed he was the most promising of the pupil pilots on the senior course. He was also told that at both Shaiba or the other RAF base, transport would be laid on to take the patients to the hospital. He was also advised to make sure that if he himself wanted to go into town if might be better to rely on local taxis.

The flights to Shaiba and return were accomplished with no attendant problems. Harry found himself taking a closer look at the pupil pilot than he might otherwise have done. He was a big lad, spoke only when spoken to and carried out the navigation and handling of the undercarriage with efficiency. On the return flight Harry asked him to take over the flying while he checked the back of the plane including the gun turret. Once back in the pilot's seat Harry allowed his pupil to continue to fly the plane. In no time at all they were back at Habbaniya and preparing to land.

'O.K. I have control.'

'You have control Sir. Let me know when you want the undercarriage down.'

As soon as they had landed Harry reported to Lang and felt obliged to comment on the competence of LAC Porter. The CFI nodded his agreement and then went on, 'Do you mind doing another trip tomorrow?'

'No. It's good to keep my hand in although I've been used to flying fighters. Same place?'

'No. This time I need you to go to Baghdad and take some important documents to the Ambassador from the AOC here. He needs to let the Ambassador know the situation here and is asking for reinforcements in case the Iraqis start any trouble.'

'So tell me Sir. What is the situation here? I hadn't realised there might be any trouble.'

'Well as you know we have been here for a number of years and more recently given the job by the League of Nations of mandating this whole area. With the outbreak of war the German Legation was closed but we know their business was carried on by the Italians until they came in. The trouble is because Iraq is really an independent country and neutral there is very little we can do legally to stop them assisting anyone. There has always been an element of local unrest and we now believe it might erupt into open revolt. However for the time being we must sit tight and wait for them to make the first move.'

Harry felt there was more to this than the CFI was letting on although he supposed this sort of warning was all that he could expect. He resolved to ask a few more questions whenever the opportunity arose. If he managed to get out into Baghdad he felt sure someone there would know. Wing Commander Lang's next words put paid to that idea.

'You can take Porter with you again but he must stay with the plane while you go by RAF transport to the Embassy. On no account are you to stop off in the city. You must deliver the documents directly into the Ambassador's hands and to no one else and you are to await his reply.'

'What about my lectures?'

'Do two in the morning then after lunch you can go to Baghdad. See you back here for the evening meal. Let me just say it's important for the flying and training here to carry on as normal. That's why I can't spare any other instructor and in any case your rank is sufficiently high to get you out of any situations which might arise.'

At 13.30 hours the Anson lifted off from Habbaniya and headed for the airfield just outside Baghdad. Harry had to wait over half an hour before a car was available to take him to the Embassy and once inside the British compound he had another long wait. At 15.00 hours there seemed to be a general movement in the large waiting room. People scurried around with bits of paper or small cases and Harry looked out for the attendant who had first told him to wait. He never appeared but a tall young woman, immaculately dressed, came through the front door and was met by an attendant who took her case, umbrella and coat.

The woman glanced at Harry, acknowledged him with a smile and proceeded to walk up the wide staircase which led to the main offices of the first floor. She returned soon afterwards and came towards Harry. 'Sqn/Ldr Nelson, I'm sorry you've had to wait so long. The Ambassador is having a particularly difficult day, fraught with problems.'

'Don't we all?' remarked Harry. He was not used to being kept waiting and after all he supposed the documents he carried were of some importance so why the long wait!

'Yes. I suppose so. Can I help?'

'Sorry, No. I've been instructed to hand these documents only to the Ambassador.'

'I imagine they must be important otherwise they wouldn't send a squadron leader. I'll see if I can squeeze you in. While waiting would you like some tea?'

'That would be most acceptable.'

'Follow me then. I'm Jane Templeton, actually a niece of the Ambassador. I'm on my way back to England from Calcutta and this is as far as I've got. I'm in the diplomatic corps.'

'Well I'm glad you came in when you did otherwise I might have been here all night and I really ought to get back.'

'I think it's possible that you will be here overnight. I'll arrange an overnight stop for you here. I'm so sorry,' she said with an apologetic smile.

Harry found himself smiling back and in a less impatient voice said, 'I ought to let LAC Porter know that we won't be returning tonight and could you also let Habbaniya know.'

'Of course. We'll have tea first.' The clock on her office wall slowly changed from 3.15 to 4.00 as Harry waited and in spite of two calls to the Ambassador on his behalf it was 5.00 pm before Harry was finally ushered into the Ambassador's room.

Cornwall came forward to meet him. 'I do apologise for having kept you so long Squadron Leader Nelson. It's been one of those days. I imagine what you have in that case is also part of the problem. Excuse me for a moment while I read through the documents.' He broke the seal, read through the papers quickly and then again slowly, making notes. He looked at Harry. 'Do you know the contents of these or even the gist?'

'No Sir. I'm just the messenger.'

'Well it's no secret really and I guess if things get worse everyone will know. There have been several rumours for weeks that Rachid Ali wants to take over the country and throw in his lot with the Germans. At the moment he's being a bit difficult.'

For one moment Harry thought the Ambassador was going to tell him the whole problem between Iraq and Britain. It was almost as though he wanted to unburden himself on to some outsider he thought he could trust. However, to Harry's relief he didn't. Diplomacy came to the rescue and then the telephone rang. After taking the call and saying to whoever was at the other end that he would call them back the Ambassador continued his problems with Rashid Ali.

'Well I know he will not permit additional troops to be stationed here so I'm going to tell him they will merely be passing through on their way to Egypt. If you can stay overnight I may have an answer for you to take back directly to Air Vice-Marshal Smythe at Habbaniya.'

The Ambassador had obviously come to the end of his history lesson and pressed a bell on his desk. Miss Templeton came in and said. 'Yes Ambassador. I've already arranged for Sqn/Ldr Nelson to stay here.' Jane Templeton remained quietly while her uncle made a few more notes.

'Ah.' The Ambassador turned to look at his niece and Harry sensed there was a question mark in that single word. 'We'll talk again Sqn/Ldr Nelson. Miss Templeton will look after you now.'

CHAPTER 28

Diplomatic Diversion

Jane picked up the phone and said, 'Mija, could you go into my office please. I'm leaving the Ambassador's room now. Sqn/Ldr Nelson will be with me.' Harry followed her out and they went along the corridor and entered another room almost as large as the one they had vacated.

'So what position do you hold here at the Embassy if, as you say, you're only passing through?'

'It's a long story. I am waiting to go home but as we are short staffed here I have been temporarily seconded to this Embassy. I'm acting Second Secretary. My uncle's right hand man at this very moment is trying to negotiate terms with Rachid Ali, the Prime Minister.'

A discreet knock on the door was followed immediately by it opening and a tall, smiling young man entered. 'Yes Madam. What can I do for you?'

'Sqn/Ldr Nelson cannot return to his unit so will be staying here and has not brought any overnight things. Could you organise some and if possible a shirt, tie, lightweight suit, shoes and shaving things.'

'Yes Madam. May I borrow a car and would the squadron leader care to accompany me so that we can get the correct size.'

'That is not possible. He has some work to do here. I'm sure you can obtain something to fit. A nice plain grey, I think. Do you agree Mr. Nelson?'

Harry didn't know what to make of this sudden change of plans. He'd never had anyone choose his clothes for him and this casual assumption that he should be kitted out without any real referral to himself definitely went against the grain. He decided he didn't like this woman. She might be efficient at her job. She might be the Ambassador's niece but he'd be gone in the morning and he saw no reason for this unnecessary expense. Even so she was decidedly pretty, beautiful even as she issued her orders to Mija with great charm. Clearly the man wanted to please and even Harry felt he was under her spell. He could scarcely believe he had made no objection.

As soon as Mija had left Harry ventured a comment, 'Thank you very much Miss Templeton but I do not need any new clothes. I know I must look a bit weary but a bath and some food would soon revive me and who is going to pay for the clothes. I didn't bring much cash with me.'

'Do forgive me. I do tend to get carried away. I'll explain. The Ambassador likes to maintain a semblance of decorum even in wartime and tonight he is hosting a gathering of local dignitaries. There is to be a small dinner party, nothing too elaborate, followed by a dance and general small talk. I hope you'll be able to attend and if you do it would be best if you were not in uniform.'

'Surely if what Ambassador Cornwall said earlier is true some of the guests may well be sympathetic to the other side.'

'True but we can give as good a performance as them. In uniform you might have given the wrong signal. In civvies no one will question a new man stopping off on his way to Calcutta.'

'So you've got it all worked out. If I'm to pose as a diplomat you'd better fill me in a little. I'll do my best.'

'I do apologise for not telling you sooner. The idea only came to me while my uncle was talking to you. In any case I'd like to find out a little more about you. I hope you're a good dancer.'

'Well you're unlucky there. I can fly any number of different planes but dancing is not one of my good points.'

'We shall see. I'll just get someone to show you to your room. You can have a rest until 7.00 when there will be a few drinks while the guests arrive. Dinner is at 7.30 and the dancing starts about 9.30.'

Harry could scarcely keep the sarcasm from his voice as he remarked. 'I can see why so many people want to be in the diplomatic corps. They have such an austere and difficult time.'

Jane Templeton smiled. 'At last you've been provoked. I was beginning to think you couldn't be bothered. Tell me what you really think.'

Again Harry was at a loss for words not wishing to offend yet more than a little cross that he hadn't foreseen her game. 'Well Miss. You certainly had me fooled. Is that part of your training?'

'Of course. I'm glad you are staying over even if you can't dance or were you trying to fool me.'

'No I do dance of course but not very well.'

Jane held out her hand. 'A pleasure to meet you Squadron Leader Nelson. I bet you're a ladies man deep down just like your namesake. Shall we start again. I really do need your help. I'll see you later.'

Harry realised he had been dismissed. Strange woman. Another knock on the door and a servant entered. 'Here is your key Sir. If you'd care to come with me I'll show you to your room. Mija will call by soon with your wardrobe. If they are not to your liking tell him and he will get others. The ante-room for drinks and the dining room are both on this floor. Go back to the main staircase and turn left. The dining room is immediately ahead.'

'Thanks.'

'My pleasure Sir.'

It was all so civilised. Harry could scarcely believe he was in the midst of a possible coup and so far he had seen no outward signs. He only had the word of the CFI at Habbanyia and the British Ambassador at Baghdad to go on. Surely they must have some firm evidence.

A few minutes later his clothes arrived. The suit was quite well made and fitted. In fact all the clothes fitted so well Harry wondered how many other men Jane Templeton had kitted out. It had all gone so smoothly he doubted that it had not been well rehearsed and done many times. There was little time to get ready for the evening festivities but with a few minutes to spare he made his way to the ante room where drinks were being served. Already young women and older ones in flowing evening gowns and a few young and middle aged men were talking animatedly to each other, recognising a few acquaintances and being introduced to newcomers. Queening it over all was Jane Templeton or that was how it seemed to Harry as he made his way forward.

By her side stood the Ambassador, looking tired, bored even but putting on a brave face. He did look as though he carried the world's troubles on his shoulders and Harry wondered if things had suddenly got worse. Harry nodded to a few people who he was sure he'd never see again and edged closer to Jane Templeton. 'Good evening. Nice to see a friendly face.' He commented.

A friendly smile greeted him in reply and she introduced Harry to a middle-aged Indian saying, 'I think you two may have something in common but do circulate and keep up appearances. Do be careful.' This was her parting shot as she left the two men to ponder.

'What can she mean?' Harry questioned.

'I think Jane was warning us that everyone here is not really who they pretend to be. I'm Major Ebn Singh of the 4th King's Own Royal Rifles.'

'I'm not who I seem either. I'm really Sqn/Ldr Nelson. Have you known her long?'

'Not really. She stopped off here on her way home and as the Ambassador had lost one of his senior staff she stepped into the breech. I gather she's very efficient at her job and on these occasions she's a godsend. By the way could I scrounge a lift back to Habbanyia when you go?'

'Yes. I'm sure we can squeeze you in. With luck I should be returning tomorrow. I've left the plane at the airfield with a pupil pilot in charge. As soon as we're ready tomorrow we can go. It's only 50 miles so it's hardly worth flying. On the other hand I gather it's pretty awful by road.'

'Yes it is. It's bandit country really. I'll tell you later why I need to get to Habbanyia. In the meantime we'd better circulate.'

With yet another cryptic sentence left unfinished Harry wondered what he had let himself in for. A gong sounding the call to dinner shattered his thoughts and everyone made their way into the dining room. It was obvious that many guests had been here before as they went directly to their allotted seats. Others looked for their names at the place settings while Harry was surprised to find his and Singh's opposite each other at the bottom of a long table. As they sat down Harry ventured a quiet comment. 'I see we're not considered very important.'

'I'm sure it's all been carefully thought out. And wait till you see who occupies this chair at the end between the two of us.'

As soon as everyone was seated the Ambassador took his place at the top leaving Jane to sit at the bottom of the table. During the meal she shared her conversation with her two male companions and the two ladies sitting next to them. Harry was puzzled about the two other women. They both spoke perfect English but he completely failed to guess their nationality. The conversation ranged initially about children, and the arts and commerce but never once was the weather or the war mentioned. The meal itself was the most varied he had ever eaten. The lady on his right was glad to tell him what each course was and even suggested that he might not like one or two. Drink seemed to be confined to a variety of cordials and when the meal finally ended they were offered very strong coffee and sweets.

The whole affair was beautifully orchestrated. At a sign from the Ambassador, Jane got to her feet and without banging on the table or ringing a glass she got immediate silence. 'Has everyone finished? The more energetic of you may wish to go along to the ballroom. Some may wish to see the Ambassador privately and I will try to arrange this. If any of you require transport now please let me know. I know some of you have little ones to care for. Thank you so much for coming. The Ambassador is so glad his friends are able to come to these occasional dinners. Thank you.'

She laid a hand on each of her companions' shoulders. 'Please remain here until everyone has left if you wish to chat to each other.' Harry and the major wandered out on to the balcony. The heat of the day had gone and although still warm outside the air was much fresher. They had only been there a couple of minutes when someone greeted them. 'Now come along you men. We can't have you outside while some young ladies require dancing partners.'

They turned and recognised a member of the embassy staff, looking a lot older than her forty odd years and regaled in a long flowing flimsy dress. As they got back inside the dining room she whispered. 'Sorry to drag you in but would you mind circulating. I'm afraid my dancing days are over but some of the young ladies would welcome a turn round the dance floor.'

As she moved away it was obvious that she walked awkwardly and for the first time they noticed that she carried a small slim walking cane. Feeling somewhat taken aback they escorted her to the dance floor and sat her at a table where she chatted with friends. Harry took the bull by the horns, said cheerio to the Indian major and walked across the ballroom to ask one of the ladies for a dance. 'I'm afraid

I'm not very good but maybe you could teach me a few steps.'

The woman, whom he assumed to be Italian or of Italian extraction, answered in perfect English. 'You are so kind to ask a young widow.' She rose quickly and Harry escorted her on to the floor. She smiled as they set off and said. 'I gather you are not on the embassy staff here but are on your way to India.'

Harry almost lost his footing as he was concentrating on his dancing but he recovered and answered quickly. 'It will be my first posting east of Aden.' He was surprised how easily the lie escaped his lips and then realised that in a way his present posting was in fact the furthest he had been east of his old RAF posting in Aden. 'May I ask what you do here Madame?'

'I don't really do anything. My husband was in banking in Basra but when the war started for Italy in 1940 he was in Rome and has not returned. I had a letter saying he had been killed not by bombs but by a German staff car. So you see I'm not very pleased with Germany.'

Harry had not expected such frankness. 'I am so sorry to hear of your loss. It is no consolation but these things do happen in wartime. Surely if you don't do anything the time must drag for you apart from attending these functions.'

'Well sometimes. The Iraqi government allows me to remain here. I think they expect me to provide snippets of information which might help them in some way and thereby assist the Germans. But I know nothing and nor do I intend to find out. My husband was a lot older than me and when this war is over I shall no doubt marry again. In the meantime I just pass the time. It's an idle life really but there's nothing else to do.'

They danced well together and Harry realised that she was not only an accomplished dancer but that she was virtually guiding him and correcting the small errors he made. He was sorry when the dance ended and he escorted her back to her friends. In just a few minutes he had obtained a potted history of her life. He looked up and caught Jane's glance. With an almost imperceptible movement of her head she suggested he move over towards the doorway and as he walked back across the dance floor he noticed she moved along the back so that they reached the door at the same time supposedly by accident.

'Good evening Mr Nelson. I hope you are enjoying yourself. I see you have met the merry widow.'

'She speaks excellent English.'

'Well she would. She is English. Married her husband in 1938 and came out to Italy for the honeymoon and they moved here six months later. He was an Italian banker, a lot older than her and very well liked by all accounts. He was killed while on a visit to Rome in 1940 but she remained here.'

'I'm intrigued. Do tell me more. Would you care to dance?'

'Thank you. I thought you'd never ask.'

Harry took her hand and they walked slowly on to the dance floor as the band began to play a waltz. Although he felt his dancing was passable he wanted to make a good impression. Once round the floor and Harry realised that Jane, too, was an accomplished dancer and, remarking on her skill, almost at once regretted it.

'What did you expect,' she replied. 'We diplomats are expected to be accomplished in all aspects of the social graces. Sorry that came out differently from what I intended. Please excuse my bad manners. I didn't mean to be so rude.'

'You're forgiven. You must remember I'm just a lonely squadron leader who is happy to be dancing with the most glamorous young lady in town.'

'Now don't go overboard or I shall not believe a word you say.' But she smiled and Harry sensed that she was pleased with his compliment. The dance ended and Harry asked if he might have the next.

'I'm so sorry. I must speak with a really horrid man. He's probably the most ruthless man in Iraq but for the moment we must not do anything to offend him especially while he's within the British compound.'

'Would you like me to follow him when he leaves. As a new diplomat who is soon going to India I could claim diplomatic immunity when I bump him off.'

Jane smiled. 'I don't think that will be necessary and I see it doesn't take long for rumours about you to circulate. I'll see you in the morning.'

Harry sought out Major Singh and together they found the Ambassador and asked if they might be excused as they hoped to make an early start in the morning.

'Yes of course. This will go on for another hour and then I have some urgent work to complete. I hope to have an acceptable answer for you to take back to the AOC. In the morning get hold of Miss Templeton and she will arrange to slip you into my office. Goodnight.'

Harry made his way to his room and was glad to flop down on the bed. He noticed that the covers had been turned back and there was also a dressing gown on the bed and a pair of slippers on the floor. Both looked new and when he opened the wardrobe he realised that his uniform had been cleaned and pressed. He wondered if he'd been singled out for this treatment or if it was accorded to all embassy visitors. Almost for the first time he took a good look round the room. It was large with windows from floor to ceiling which opened out on to a balcony below which was the back of the embassy gardens. Next to the double doors of the wardrobe he noticed another door which was locked when he tried it. He wondered where it led and resolved to find out in the morning. For now he would sleep.

A gentle knocking on his bedroom door awoke Harry from a deep, untroubled sleep. The door slowly opened and the first thing Harry saw was a tray upon which was a cup, teapot, milk, sugar and a hot water jug. They were carried by an Indian servant he had not seen before who set the tray down on a small table. He said 'Good morning Sir. It is 7.30. Breakfast is at 8.30.' and then went out, closing the door behind him before Harry could even say 'Thank you'.

Harry was left to ponder the mysteries of wartime diplomacy which extended to such luxuries. He was about to drink his second cup of tea when he heard the unmistakable sound of a key being turned in the lock next to the wardrobe. Then followed a very quiet knock and the door opened slowly. 'Good morning Sqn/Ldr Nelson. I hope you slept well. Are you decent?'

'Yes. Come in Miss Templeton. I'm just on my second cup of tea. Don't usually experience such luxury.'

'I do apologise for this unorthodox entrance. I just wanted to acquaint you with the situation here without prying eyes.' She continued.

'I don't suppose you are privy to the note you brought from the AOC, Habbanyia yesterday. The Ambassador has asked me to tell you the gist of it. Your Air Vice-Marshal Smythe is very concerned that the Iraqi government is becoming increasingly difficult and even insisted that the training at the base is curtailed and that only take-offs and landings are permitted. No cross country flights may be undertaken except in emergency and then at the express approval of the government. The AOC had requested additional troops be flown in but all efforts by the Ambassador so far have proved unsuccessful. They really are being difficult. King Faisal is only four years old so the Regent rules in his place and until recently he has supported Britain. Rachid Ali, the Prime Minister, is the real power behind the throne and is pro-German. At present all British military units here come under the RAF and they in turn come under the Indian Command. We are not allowed to increase the size of our military units and because we have requested to do so Rachid is using this as an excuse to curtail any troop movements and to restrict the flying training.'

Harry listened to this catalogue of problems in silence. Some he had already suspected but he hadn't realised how much pressure was being exerted on the Ambassador. He was obviously aware how sorely pressed the British forces were and to Harry it seemed that the only reinforcements available would have to come from India. 'Thank you. Is there anything else I should know?'

'Well Major Singh will be flying out with you later, in civvies, to assess the situation and see if there is any way round this impasse. That is why you were both in civilian dress last night. We did not want to give the wrong impression. We are aware that some of the guests last night would like to see the back of us. It really is a difficult situation. After all it is their country and sooner or later they will rule it themselves.'

'Yes I can see that but it would have been better if you had told me sooner.'

'If I had you might inadvertently have given the game away.'

'Scarcely a game. However I'm in your debt for the clothes. What shall I do with them?'

'Well you might just as well take them with you but your night things can stay here. Who knows you may well be staying here again. I will see you at breakfast and after that I'll take you along to see the Ambassador. I hope you will not be too late getting away.'

Breakfast was a hurried meal and then Harry went along to the main waiting room to await his interview with the Ambassador. He quickly realised that something important was happening. The usual hushed tones and quiet efficiency had been replaced with a buzz of conversation. Even this early the room was full of people and by their raised voices and gestures he guessed that the news, whatever it was, was not good.

He needed to contact Jane but when he tried the internal phones they were all engaged. He spoke to the soldier on guard just inside the embassy main door. 'Is it alright if I go outside for a while?'

'Yes Sir. I'll give you a re-admission card but my advice would be not to go too far and to get back here inside half an hour.'

Harry took the card, thanked him and went in search of a phone in the nearest hotel which was less than a hundred yards from the embassy. He was put though straight away and asked to speak to Jane Templeton. 'Sorry to be so mysterious. I'm phoning from outside but I'll be back in a few minutes. Could you see me please.'

'Yes. Go to your bedroom and I'll try to get there by 11 o'clock. When do you have to leave?'

'Early afternoon. Maybe we could have lunch together.'

'Maybe. It will have to be a snack. We are inundated with requests for asylum and exit visas. Take care and get back inside as soon as possible.'

Just after 11.00 Jane came to his room and carried with her a tray on which were two cups of tea and a plate of biscuits. 'I've literally got no more than five minutes. Someone will come for you soon and take you to the Ambassador. The news is not good. The Regent has decided to call it a day and left his post. He may already have left the country. There's more. Rachid Ali has declared himself President of Iraq and Chief of the National Defence Government.'

Harry sensed there was more so said nothing.

'Our signals people have intercepted a message from Ali to the Germans. He is meeting with Ribbentrop on the 5th and we understand he has been promised military support if he will declare war on the British.'

'That is serious. Are the Germans able to muster enough troops?'

'Well we don't know. They certainly have their hands full but with our own limited resources they may have enough. We have only just got this news yet somehow many people already know what's afoot.'

'You must have more spies in your midst than you thought. What are our military people doing about it.?'

'Well they can't do anything really. In spite of being at war we are obliged to adhere to the agreement. Sorry I have to go. After you've seen the Ambassador give me a ring and I'll try to get here for a quick lunch. Take care Mister Nelson.' She placed emphasis on the mister.

'And you too. Let me know if there's anything I can do.'

Harry had just returned to the waiting room, hoping to glean more information, when someone came to take him to see Jane's uncle. Ambassador Cornwall repeated more or less what Jane had told him and added that he had been obliged to reject the local military request for additional troops as to have allowed them would have worsened the already tense situation. However he had sent another urgent signal to London advising them of the situation and asking for a decision. In the meantime it seemed that Rachid Ali, anticipating victory, had eased up a little and was now prepared to allow mercy flights to proceed without prior approval. Harry was given a small document case to deliver to Air Vice-Marshal Smythe at Habbanyia and then with a quick handshake he was dismissed. He felt it imprudent to question anything which the Ambassador was doing although he was fuming when he got back to his room. He realised that Cornwall must adhere to the treaties but couldn't understand the man's insistence that nothing could be done. Didn't he know that Britain was at war and fighting on her own!

Lunch, when it came, was even quicker than breakfast. Harry sensed that Jane, for all her outward calm appearance, was very concerned. They spoke little. Harry packed his uniform in the small case and prepared to say goodbye. 'I hope we'll meet again soon. If I can manage to get here may I call you.'

'Yes I'd like that.' She held out her hand and Harry grasped it in his and drew her towards him. A quick kiss on her cheek was all he intended and having done that he kissed her full on the mouth.

Jane smiled. 'I hope you don't do that to all the women you meet.'

'No only the pretty ones.'

Major Singh was waiting outside and they travelled to the airfield, talking over the events of the past few hours. When they reached the Anson it had already been checked over by Porter who made sure it was refuelled and had also obtained the latest weather report. The 50 mile flight back to Habbanyia took less than half an hour including the take off and landing.

CHAPTER 29

The Nelson Touch

Having spent much of the night thinking through all the wild plans which kept crowding his mind Harry rose early the next day and sought out the CFI long before any flying was due to take place. He wanted to see the AOC but felt that a direct approach would be refused or at least delayed. He needed to get the CFI to pave the way. He guessed that Air Vice-Marshal Smythe must be fully aware of all the problems in Iraq so he would need to choose his words carefully. The news of the change in Iraqi government and head of state was all over the base yet no one seemed very concerned.

'Hello Nelson. I gather your trip was longer than anticipated. Nice to have you back. What's your lecture on today?' The CFI seemed pleased to see him.

'That's partly why I wanted to see you early. I had planned to talk about taking the enemy by surprise. You probably know that in the desert we did that in June 1940 and again in November.'

'That sounds exciting. I gather you were in both shows.'

'Well yes I was but I wanted to ask you about the situation here. When I was in Baghdad there seemed to be all sorts of unrest simmering beneath the surface. The Ambassador is very concerned but there is little he can do. I wondered if you could get me an interview with the AOC. Maybe you could come with me. I think we are likely to be in the thick of it here.'

'I'll certainly do what I can and let you know. I doubt if he will see us this morning. As far as Iraq is concerned its technically a non-belligerent neutral although we are aware that a certain section of the population would like the British out.'

'I'd like to have a word, unofficially, with the AOC. Something the Ambassador said to me set me thinking.'

'My, my. We are flying in high circles. Go and give your lecture as planned. With a bit of luck he may be able to spare us a few minutes before lunch but I'm only guessing. Can you give me the gist of what you propose saying to him.'

'Well yes of course. In any case I would need your approval to put any of it into effect. Briefly, if the Iraqis attack here we have virtually no defence and we should be prepared to counter attack. Better still if we were in a position to take the initiative we might prevent any coup ever taking place. So first we need a fighter squadron here on the base. Second we need a bomber squadron and third we need ack-ack. Finally we need more ground support troops. If we can't get any of these we must improvise and hope that we'll never need to use them.

'Just how do you propose we go about all this?'

'Well if we could bring forward the advanced gunnery and bombing practices for the senior pupils and at the same time increase the weight of the practice bombs in use it would seem to any outside observers there had been very little change to the normal routine. And if we subsequently change the practice bombs for real ones and at the same time put guns into as many aircraft as possible we would at least have a fighting chance. Finally we need to organise all our aircraft into active squadrons. If these measures are not needed we have lost nothing except a few hours work in modifying the existing trainers.'

'I'll say this Nelson. You've got a vivid imagination. You've been in Baghdad recently and I'm sure you wouldn't suggest anything like this unless you really thought it could happen.

I'm prepared to give you the benefit of the doubt but I can tell you the AOC will be no push over. If things went disastrously wrong it would be his head that rolled.'

Harry, by now warming to his subject, felt like saying that if nothing was done all their heads might roll. Instead he said. 'Thank you Sir. I would be most grateful if you could pave the way for me'

Harry went to breakfast and then, having collected his notes and borrowed a large map of North Africa made his way to the lecture hall. As he entered he noticed that all the pupils were seated on one side of the room while all the flying instructors and ground staff lecturers sat on the opposite side. As he made his way to the platform the CFI got up from his seat and spoke quietly to Harry. 'There's to be no flying today so I hope you don't mind if we sit in.'

Harry commenced his lecture. 'Good morning gentlemen and young sirs. It's not often we have a full house. At the end of this talk I'll pass the hat round so that I can have a really good leave.'

A murmur of quiet laughter and smiles greeted his words. Almost from the beginning Harry discarded his prepared notes as he relived the hectic days of the desert warfare. He sensed his audience, even those few pilots who had been in action some years ago, appreciated the first hand account he was able to provide. He kept to a minimum the more gory parts of the campaign, interspersed with humorous anecdotes and then reminded his audience never to underrate the enemy. He reminded them that the early British machines were similar to the Italians although the enemy had the faster machines and there were many more of them. Even the enemy bombers were slightly faster than our own and they carried twice the bomb load. He then went on to explain how they had managed to overcome the deficit. He ended by saying, 'Its my impression that the war in the air is changing. We are becoming more aggressive and so too is the enemy.

But be careful. If we become too aggressive we shall make mistakes.'

When he had finished the applause was loud and sustained and then came the questions thick and fast. Finally the CFI stood up. 'Thank you very much Sqn/Ldr Nelson. We have just time for one more question.'

A commander of one of the armoured cars got to his feet. 'I don't wish to embarrass you Sir but I understand you have been shot down. What effect did that have on your morale?'

'Well some pilots have told me they feel inadequate, others wanted to pack it in altogether. A few sought revenge at the earliest opportunity. For myself, in hindsight, its laughable and I can now see the joke – just. I was returning to base after we had captured El Agheila, flying quite low and fast. I never saw what hit me and I was wounded just above the left eye but managed to reach base. The ground staff, after they'd got me to hospital found a bit of a beak and a few feathers in the cockpit. I'd been shot down by a buzzard. So be on your guard. Look out.'

The CFI moved towards Harry. 'Marvellous. I've just had a note. We can go over and see the AOC now.'

They went over in the CFI's car and Harry was introduced to Air Vice-Marshal Smythe who was not only in command of the Habbanyia airfield but also the ground troops and the many civilians who lived and worked at the base. Harry explained how he had become party to the knowledge he was about to impart and that if it were true and the British authorities could do nothing to implement their forces there might, with a little ingenuity, be a way that they might be able to counter any threat which the Iraqis posed. The AOC listened as Harry outlined his plan. He made a few notes and when Harry had finished he turned to the CFI.

'And do you go along with this?'

'We live in difficult times Sir and I think it would be wise if we prepare for the worst.'

'Well, Nelson. I can see you have given this some considerable thought. What do you expect me to do or more precisely what do you want me to do?'

'Well Sir. I'd like you to reassure me that I've got it all wrong. If I haven't then, hopefully, you can seek reinforcements from London or wherever. Maybe the Iraqis are bluffing but I think we should be ready and should call their bluff. In spite of the treaty things have changed. We are now at war and we should be entitled to bring in additional troops. You can be sure that if the Germans were in our position they would not hesitate.'

'Well, Nelson you put your case well. I am aware of the situation as you call it and I have made London aware of it as well. I have also put the Ambassador in the picture and asked him to let London know how we are fixed. In addition I have already asked for reinforcements and have been advised that they are not necessary. I'm sure you know only too well it's seldom the military who have any say in what goes on. We do just what we are told.'

'Yes I agree but in this case as in so many others I think the military on the spot should act first. We should get additional troops and if they are not needed little harm would have been done. If there really is no help from outside then I think we should do what we can ourselves.'

'Alright leave it with me and I'll see what I can do.'

Harry and the CFI were dismissed and they drove silently back to the mess. As they got out of the car the CFI said, 'The reason there was no flying today was that I received a note from the P.M., not Winston, the one here, forbidding it and suggesting that flying training should be curtailed. Well they may have the treaty on their side which stops us from flying in reinforcements but by the same token they can't stop flying training. It will recommence within the next half hour and we'll go on a bit later to make up lost time.'

After lunch Harry met Major Singh and put him in the picture. Harry felt that in the Indian major he had an ally, someone who appreciated the real problem they faced not only at Habbanyia but also in Basra and the British compound in Baghdad. It was obvious that he, too, had given serious thought to the problem as his next words revealed.

'I've been turning over in my mind a wild plan. There are nearly 9000 people in this campus. If the Iraqis attacked we have very little in the way of defence, apart from the few RAF armoured cars and some mortars. There are also 1200 levies. Would they help us out of loyalty or would they go over to the Iraqi camp.'

Harry had the answer to this problem 'You don't need to worry about the levies. I've discovered that they are Assyrians and hate the Iraqis almost as much as they dislike the British. The trouble as I see it we are such a long way from Egypt even if they could send us troops. In any case they are busy sending them elsewhere. How long would it take to get reinforcements from India?'

'Difficult to say. First we'd have to get permission. Although the Indian Command is more or less autonomous they would never go against a direct order from London. What we need is someone to give the order without London knowing. Obviously they don't tell London everything so it might just be possible.'

'Come over to the classroom. We'll have a look on the map and work out times and distances.'

Spread before them was a huge map covering Egypt, the Red Sea, North East Africa and the Middle East. Palestine, also under British mandate, looked vulnerable. There was also Syria, now in Vichi French hands. South West of Iraq lay Saudia Arabia while to the north lay Bulgaria, Rumania and Russia with Turkey as a buffer state.

Major Singh spoke. 'When you see it spread out like this its frightening. If the Germans move down and occupy Greece they only have to persuade Turkey to allow them passage through and they'll be into Iraq no trouble at all. With the French in Syria we really are up against it.'

Harry considered the possible moves by the enemy. If the Germans were successful in such a move and in addition had the Iraqis waiting as their allies the British would have no option but to surrender. 'My mind is made up. I'm going to seek another interview with Smythe. In the meantime I'm going to see the ground staff and engineers to see if we can't modify all the planes here to carry arms. If we need more guns and turrets I'm prepared to go to the other RAF bases to scrounge them. Trouble is I have no authority. I think the CFI would back me and I hope Jane Templeton would put in a good word.'

'If you're going to put your neck on the block I'm not going to let you do it on your own. Count me in. In the meantime I'm off to India to see if I can get some troops.'

Like two small boys planning how to break out of school after dark they went over the plans together again. Some ideas were changed, others scrapped completely and a few new ones emerged. As many aircraft as possible would be armed with bombs or guns. Harry would fly to nearby RAF bases and borrow as much equipment as possible and bring back as much spare ammunition as he could. They would involve as many officers as possible in order to get the work done quickly and it would be done under the cloak of speeding up the course as Harry had originally suggested. The additional air activity necessary to practice with additional armament would be explained as necessary because of the speeded up flying course.

For his part Major Singh agreed to seek out the commander of the Assyrian levies and sound him out regarding his loyalties. Furthermore he agreed to send a signal requesting additional troops be flown in from India and if this failed he would fly there himself and get them. They felt like conspirators, which of course they were. They could find no flaw in the overall plan except that it contravened the 1930 agreement and consoled themselves with the fact that if it all went wrong it would be themselves, two lowly placed officers who would bear the blame and not the Ambassador or a high ranking RAF officer. What they really needed was the support of someone with real authority like Wavell or even at a much lower level someone like Wing Commander Holmes. Unfortunately Wavell had moved to India but Harry wondered if it was possible to contact Holmes.

Harry acquired a large scale map of the RAF base at Habbanyia and was surprised at just how big it was. Its perimeter of just over seven miles was patrolled each day and he decided to make overtures to the armoured cars commander to see if this could be extended. Once he had explained his reason for such an unusual request F/Lt Hooper not only agreed but said he would extend their route outside to include several forays into the hinterland to check likely sites for an ambush. Harry also persuaded F/O Richardson, who did the daily met flight to check if weather conditions would allow the pupils to fly, to keep a good lookout for Iraqi troops which might be gathering for an assault on the base.

Within the camp boundaries all the RAF personnel and quite a few families lived fairly comfortably in what really amounted to a small town. A few shops, a cinema and recreational facilities made life bearable in an otherwise harsh environment. The 1200 levies also lived on the base as well as the armoured car crews and of course the pupil pilots in fairly comfortable barracks near their lecture rooms. He also discovered that many ponies were stabled on the campus and that Habbanyia not only had a polo field but also a large golf course inside the fence. Everyone, including the ponies, had to be fed and watered so the maintenance of such a large number of people was a major undertaking. Hence the large fleet of transport vans and lorries. Finally he was pleased that the well-equipped hospital which served everyone on the base had ample staff and space to cope with casualties if the worst came to the worst.

Following his second interview with the AOC Harry felt a certain sympathy with his stand but it soon became clear that Air Vice-Marshal Smythe was adamant. He could not move without approval from London and did not wish to complicate matters by flying in additional troops. In any case, he explained, none could be diverted from their present commitments. On the other hand Harry got nowhere when he suggested that it was only good military practice to be prepared. However, although he must have been aware of what Harry was planning, he never directly forbade him. This was enough for Harry. Between 10th April and 19th he got permission to borrow the Anson and with Porter in the other seat made several trips to the other RAF bases in Iraq. At each station he went to the chief engineering officer and explained that the CFI at Habbanyia was advancing the bombing and gunnery practices for the pupils and needed to borrow additional gun turrets and larger bomb racks for the aircraft. Some of these he took back with him. The larger pieces of equipment were picked up later by RAF lorries.

Two of them made the round trip to Baghdad twice a day. Others took the slightly longer journey to another RAF base while two others managed a single journey each day to Shaiba and back. The crews enjoyed the novelty of the longer journeys instead of the usual routines. The armoured cars continued with their normal patrols and the extended trips into the desert and swamp areas.

The CFI went along with this deception, hoping that it would never be needed but soon felt obliged to let senior officers in on the act. Without exception, once they realised the importance of the work they joined in. One even went so far as to indicate the most likely pupils on the senior course who should be asked to volunteer if the time came to go into action. An engineer officer, Wing Commander John Henty, who had many years before been a pilot prior to re-mustering, suggested that he should get in few more hours flying time so that he would be ready, should the need arise. He also offered to organise the aircraft into three squadrons. And so the plan took shape.

Before he flew again to the capital Harry needed to speak to Jane Templeton and wandered into the RAF post office on the base and made enquiries about a private call to the embassy. The corporal wanted to know what the call was about.

'Oh its really to do with a visa for my sister.'

'I think that will be alright. Do you know who you want to speak to?'

'Yes. Its Miss Jane Templeton. I think she's the deputy or whatever they call the number two over there.'

'It's ringing for you now Sir. Take number 3 over there.'

Jane answered and was surprised to hear his voice. 'Is this an open line?'

'Yes I think so.'

'Put me back to the man in charge please.' Harry called the corporal over and he spoke into the phone. 'Yes Ma'am. What can I do for you?'

'Can you put Sqn/Ldr Nelson into a private office and put this call through your scrambler?'

'Yes that's no problem.' The corporal beckoned to Harry and said. 'We'll go in here Sir. Speak quite normally but don't be too long in case we get urgent traffic from H.Q.'

'Thank you Corporal. Very efficient.' As soon as the connection had been made he spoke quickly.'

'Look Jane. I'm flying into Baghdad this afternoon. Have things quietened down a bit? May I call to see you.?'

'Yes and yes to both questions. Change into civvies as before and we'll have dinner at the embassy. See you soon. Take care.'

'You too.'

259

Harry left the post office with a grin on his face.

Harry took one of the modified Oxfords on his flying visit to Baghdad. He convinced himself that he needed more practice on this aircraft as he would be flying it in any forthcoming battle. In spite of its slow speed in comparison to his Hurricane it really was a comfortable kite and during the 50 mile flight he indulged in some fast diving and really tight turns. The ground staff were surprised to see him step out of the Oxford with its gun turret. Half an hour later he was inside the British Embassy. The staff recognised him immediately and soon Jane came down to meet him. 'They don't know whether you're a special messenger or whether you come only to see me.' Was her greeting. 'You're just in time for tea.'

They walked together up the main staircase and along to her apartment.

'Can you stay for dinner?'

'Yes but I must return tonight. I've actually come over in an Oxford. It has landing lights so I should get down safely without the need for them to lay out a flare path.'

'You live in another world Harry. We have our own problems here but yours sound much more exciting. Do be careful.' Jane tried to keep her concern out of he voice.

'I will. If things get worse it may become more exciting than we would wish..' Harry sought to reassure Jane that he realised the risks involved but would be careful.

Jane shrugged her shoulders and said, 'You just stay here. I'll just go and clear my desk and we'll have a meal earlier than usual. I'll be back in half an hour.'

'Anything I can do?' asked Harry.

'No. Just rest.' And with that Jane went back to her work and Harry went to her sitting room. It was a comfortable settee and he quickly fell asleep. At 5.30 Jane came back and smiled as she saw his slumped figure at one end of the settee. He looked so peaceful she hadn't the heart to wake him so she got on with preparing the meal. She changed her clothes and at 6.0 o'clock gently dropped a knife on to the table. Harry woke up, slightly bemused and apologetic.

Jane smiled as she said, 'Don't worry. I thought you needed the rest.'

'Sorry I must be more tired than I realised.'

'Well you take it easy while you can. It's when you're tired that things can go wrong.'

'May I go along and freshen up?'

'Yes. Use my bathroom.'

When he returned the meal was ready and Jane said, 'No wine tonight Harry as you're flying but we'll have two bottles next time.'

'Right and this can be one of them. A little gift for you.' Harry proffered a rather nice bottle he had bought at the mess.

'Thank you. I'll keep this till next time.'

'Can you keep this with it.' Harry gave her a letter addressed to her. 'Don't open it now. Only if I don't come back. I'm not being morbid only practical and there may be difficult times ahead. Now let's forget about everything else, have a meal and talk about us.'

Later that evening Jane sat next to Harry in the back seat of the embassy car as the driver took them to the airfield. She watched as the Oxford carrying Harry and Pupil Pilot Porter took off and stayed watching until its small white tail light could no longer be seen. It was quiet, peaceful even, as she returned to Baghdad.

CHAPTER 30

New Planes for Old

Slowly the work proceeded and slowly in spite of the additional ammunition being used up in practice sessions the whole stock-pile of bombs and ammunition grew. Harry continued with his lectures and wondered from time to time when he would be warned to stop his other activities. It seemed that once his initiative had been taken and set in motion the project had a life of its own. Someone even suggested that it should have its own codename. Major Singh came up with one which had universal approval – *Deliverance*. It seemed that the AOC had decided to ignore what was going on or maybe he was relieved that someone else had virtually taken charge. Another case of 'turning a blind eye' Harry thought to himself with some amusement.

For the next seven days everyone was kept busy. The pupils continued their flying and lectures. The ground staff did their normal work and carried out the modifications to the aircraft. As each modification was completed Harry or one of the instructors took the plane up on a vigorous flight test. In spite of the long hours Harry revelled in the work. He was back doing what he liked most – flying. But there was something else. He enjoyed the excitement of doing something which was clandestine and certainly without approval. He consoled his occasional stabs of conscience with the fact that it was necessary. He marvelled that everyone worked so well together. Maybe they all realised the potential danger they were in. Maybe some had already seen it coming and were at last glad to be doing something about it.

In checking the available aircraft he came across some old Fairey Gordons. He remembered them fondly as another of the aircraft he had trained on. It was not very fast, about 145 mph when new but it had two machine guns, one fixed firing forward and one in the rear cockpit. In addition it could carry up to 460lbs of bombs and had a range of 600 miles. Now its speed was much less. In theory it could stay in the air for four hours and as he considered this a plan began to form in his mind. He asked one of the fitters how difficult it would be to get the Gordons airworthy.

'No problem Sir. We have a few but they're only used for target towing. We could sort them out and get them serviceable.'

'That will be marvellous but I'd better clear it with your chief.'

'Sure. There's just one thing. If you need an extra gunner I'd like to volunteer and two other blokes in 'B' flight would be glad to get into the air again.'

'Thanks. I'll come and talk you later.'

He caught up with John Henty, the officer who had been a pilot sometime ago and they arranged that once the Gordons were serviceable Harry would give him a few refresher lessons. They then discussed how the work was proceeding. By simply borrowing from Peter to pay Paul they had managed to get at least four more planes airworthy. Number One squadron would have nine Audaxes. At one time these were front line fighters in the Royal Air Force. Now they were used as advanced trainers and were still quite fast. Two would be capable of carrying two 250 lb bombs. Five others would have four 25lb bombs and the others would carry two 112lb bombs. All would have machine guns, one firing forward by the pilot. The other would be operated by the gunner in the rear cockpit.

The second squadron would also be Audaxes, twelve in all, and carrying eight 20lb bombs each as they had not been able to get enough carriers for the larger bombs. However it was agreed that the gunner in the rear cockpit would have a supply of bombs with him and throw these out by hand. It was a makeshift arrangement but it had been done before.

Squadron No 3 would have Oxfords, all 27 of them. The 10lb practice bombs which were used on three aircraft as part of the training were replaced by larger carriers capable of carrying 25lb bombs. By using the bombsight in the nose of the aircraft they should be able to bomb from a greater height and with greater accuracy, the pilot making corrections during the run up to the target as given by the bomb aimer. Two Oxfords were designated as Command Aircraft so as to provide a running commentary, one being in the air as far as possible at all times. Six Oxfords had been fitted with a gun turret and these also had carriers for bombs so they took off with a crew of three. It was expected that twelve Oxfords might be in the air together and when these landed to refuel the pilots and gunners would merely transfer to another Oxford and take off. The first Oxford was then refuelled and re-armed awaiting the return of another crew. The 'odds and sods' aircraft would also be part of this squadron. They included the Gordons, a few Gladiators with a top speed of 250 mph and some Maggies.

By careful housekeeping they were able to get ready a total of 64 aircraft and it was decided to keep in reserve those not designated for immediate use by the squadrons. The mood of the pilots was upbeat but down to earth. If the Iraqis attacked they hoped their small air force would be victorious but they never lost sight of the fact that they might suffer some losses.

At that time the Iraqi Air Force was also equipped with Audaxes, purchased from Britain although an upgraded version of those based at Habbanyia. They also had some twin engined Italian Savoias. It was appreciated that the Luftwaffe was not far away and could easily bring in their much faster planes to support the Iraqis. With each passing day the war news from more distant areas was not encouraging for the Allies. The garrison at Habbaniya began to feel more isolated than ever.

Harry took up several Audaxes on test flights and still marvelled at the power of its in-line engine and the capabilities of this plane. By now virtually obsolete, he remembered with affection the first flight he had in one as a pupil pilot but he longed for a few Hurricanes and some comrades from his old squadron. As for the Oxfords although he had only a few hours in them he came to appreciate their own graceful lines. They needed to be rugged for teaching purposes as not all landings with pupils at the controls were smooth. They were in fact very streamlined and at only 188 mph the second fastest of the planes at Habbanyia. Once airborne, by altering the petrol mixture to lean the two engines gave the plane a range of over 900 miles. Including the instructors and those pupils on the senior course who had been earmarked to fly there was a total of 39 pilots.

The instructors, all excellent pilots in their own right, were aware that it was many years since some of them had seen action against local tribesmen. A few had never flown in action and they all needed concentrated practice sessions to sharpen up their skills. Harry discussed with the CFI how the pupils should be selected.

'We'll give them the advanced gunnery and bombing practices but leave it to the last possible moment before we ask them to volunteer.'

Harry would have preferred to tell them now. 'I'm convinced that most on the senior course will cope very well and the others will make excellent gunners and bomb aimers. Will you clear it with the AOC.'

'Not yet. I have spoken in general terms of what we intend but he doesn't want to know. He hopes it will all blow over.'

'I just can't understand some people. Here we are surrounded by a potential enemy. We are receiving massive support from all the RAF bases in Iraq and yet the top man can't be bothered. For that matter the top man in Baghdad is almost as bad. He says his hands are tied. Actually, his niece, Jane Templeton, has got more guts and has helped in letting me know a little of what is going on. In fact if it hadn't have been for her I doubt if we'd have known anything until it was too late.' Harry was feeling frustrated and didn't mind who knew it.

On 13th April Harry made another flight to Baghdad and as he came in to land noticed another Anson being refuelled. He reported to the control and saw Joe Erskine who at first didn't recognise him although when he did so his face lit up.

'Hello Sir. How's it going?'

Harry didn't answer that question at once. 'How long have you got before you go back? Can you have lunch with me?'

'Sure. I gather you have learned to fly Ansons.'

'Well it was a case of having to. That's what I want to see you about. I'm really glad I bumped into you.'

Joe accompanied Harry as he went to the maintenance hanger and when the engineering officer saw them his face dropped. He spoke directly to Joe. 'You're not on the scrounge as well are you?'

'Not that I know of but I'll take anything that's going.'

Harry intervened. 'No he doesn't want anything. He's a pal I met sometime ago and we've just bumped into each other again. We're off to lunch. Can you join us?'

'Yes I guess so. Give me a few minutes.'

'Good.' replied Harry. 'Can we go in your car and I'll buy you both a slap up lunch. I owe you both. You for all you've done and you Joe because I've got a favour to ask.'

'Well I'll have the lunch and then I'll consider the favour.'

'O.K. by me.' was Harry's reply.

Sqn/Ldr Young brought his car round and F/Lt Jefferson was already inside. 'Do you mind if Jeff comes as well.'

'No of course not. I should have included him anyway.' Introductions followed all round and soon the car was heading towards Baghdad.

'You know your way around here better than I do so pick a nice place but I'd rather not go right into town.' Harry felt he shouldn't go right into Baghdad.

'That's alright. There's a nice restaurant in the hotel just round the corner and the food's quite good. We go there most weekends.'

Over lunch in hushed tones Harry explained the aircraft modification programme for the benefit of Joe. He thanked the other officers for all their help and they hoped it would never come to the point where they would have to employ the upgraded aircraft.

'And where do I come in?' Joe wanted to know.

'Well I'm getting nowhere trying to get reinforcements. I want to get hold of Group Captain Holmes. He should be in Cairo but I daren't send him a wire and I don't really want to send a letter though the mail. Could you take a letter for me and deliver it to him. I'll let you see the contents just in case you want to say no. Basically it is asking him to send a fighter squadron or whatever he can spare when I send him a certain signal.'

'No problem.' replied Joe. 'Only too glad to help. I know the bloke. In fact I was talking to him only yesterday and he asked after you. But of course I haven't been to Habb. since I delivered you there.'

They stayed at the hotel longer than they intended and after Harry had paid the bill they set off back to the airfield. 'I don't think I need to scrounge anymore from you chaps. In fact we haven't got any more aircraft to modify but if the worst comes to the worst we should be able to give a good account of ourselves.'

'I thought you were supposed to be resting.' ventured Joe. The other officers wanted to know why and Joe was only too happy to tell them of Harry's previous exploits. Apparently Holmes had related most of the story to Joe. Harry was a bit embarrassed and sought to turn the tables on Joe by demanding to know how he had been awarded the DFM. Joe had no intention of telling them and muttered an apology to Harry for letting out his story. Half an hour later Joe took off and promised to call in at Habbanyia on his way back to Cairo in two day's time. Harry changed into civvies and hired a taxi to take him to the British Embassy and dinner with Jane Templeton. He didn't know what reception to expect but he knew he wanted to see her and it might be for the last time.

The moment he saw her he knew she was equally pleased to see him and later in the confines of his room kissed him briefly. 'That is in exchange for the more formal greeting we had earlier. So what have you been up to. I saw Major Singh the other day and he intimated that things were going well with you. He didn't go into details but I imagine that you now have an Air Force larger than the Iraqis.'

'Well we are merely preparing for the worst. I really hope it will never be needed. I suppose the Ambassador hasn't been able to get any reinforcements yet.'

'No. I do assure you he has told London so many times I think they are fed up and ignore him. I can also tell you that the German army is definitely moving down through Greece. In spite of us being isolated we still have our sources of information and as long as the Germans don't change their codes we can still monitor military traffic.'

'All part of the service is it?' enquired Harry.

'We do try to keep an eye on what's going on. We have a duty to look after our own nationals and there are quite a few of those in this country. But enough of war for the moment. Let's go and have dinner and then can tell me all about yourself.'

Dinner was a much more casual affair than on his last visit with just the Ambassador and two other members of the staff. After the meal they all made excuses to leave so Harry and Jane were left by themselves to go to the small drawing room. They spent some time talking, getting to know each other and Harry felt himself becoming more and more emotionally involved. He felt more at ease with Jane than he'd felt with any woman before. He was physically attracted by her beauty and delighted with her quick wit and ready charm. He sensed a warmth and vulnerability about her which totally belied the cool, distant demeanour she had shown when they first met. At 11.0 o'clock Jane said she must get some sleep before facing the problems of the next day and said goodnight with a passion which surprised them both. Harry thought he would not sleep but he did and was awake before his early morning cup of tea arrived. He saw Jane at breakfast and as they kissed goodbye he wondered when he'd see her again. So much had happened since he'd arrived at Habbaniya and although everything on the surface appeared quiet he felt it could not go on for much longer.

He returned to the airfield and then took off for Habbaniya with the final load of bombs and ammunition. Once down on the base he went to his room and started to write the all important letter. He composed it with great care. He felt that if anyone could bring pressure to bear in the right quarters it would the Group Captain. In as few words as possible he explained the problem as he saw it and the measures taken to make a stand if the Iraqis attacked. He added that he was the sole instigator of this enterprise. Other people were also involved once they could see the possible dangers when he had discussed his ideas with them. They may not have realised that he did not have the proper authority to ask for the help they had given. He would take full responsibility for all that had been done in the hope that if the need did arise everyone would be prepared, given the limited resources they had been able to acquire. His final paragraph ended,

> I hope, Sir, that you do not think I habitually flout authority but I am convinced we must be able to defend ourselves. If there is no attack no one need ever know. I am writing to you now in the hope that you will be able to assist if the time comes. Would you be able to spare a squadron of fighters or a few bombers. If you agree I will send you a signal if these are really needed. W/O Erskine is aware of the contents of this letter but no one else knows that I have approached you in this manner. If at all possible I would welcome an acknowledgement of this request even if it is only to say no.'

Signed H. Nelson Sqn/Ldr.

Joe Erskine flew into Habbanyia on time but stayed only long enough to pick up the letter. Harry was not sure when they would meet again and was surprised to see the Anson coming in to land a few hours later. He wondered if Joe had already been to Cairo and back but realised there had not been enough time. He made his way to the control tower and waited for the plane to taxi in. As soon as the props stopped turning he went out to meet it. As he reached the plane the door opened and Joe stepped down. He looked different but as soon as he recognised Harry he smiled and exclaimed, 'Am I glad to see you. Can you give us a hand.'

One look inside the cabin was enough for Harry to signal the ambulance which always stood ready at the control tower. The crew were a bit slower than usual in getting off the mark as no pupils were flying and they had received no call over the R/T. Even so within half a minute they were by the Anson and came running out with a first aid kit. Joe was sitting quietly on the ground and Harry directed the medics inside the plane where they were as surprised as Harry had been. Seated inside was a German pilot, obviously wounded but whose wounds had been seen to. What really surprised them was that he was not only strapped into his seat but his hands and feet were securely tied together.

Harry left the medics to deal with the prisoner while he went to speak to Joe. 'Take your time. Are you O.K? If so we'll walk slowly towards the control tower. Tell me about it if you like but first we must get some hot sweet tea inside you and make sure you're alright.'

Joe answered in a soft, slow voice as though he wasn't quite sure what had happened. Then as they got closer to the building his voice became stronger and he became more animated. 'God that was a close call. I'll try to remember in sequence what happened.'

With each step Joe recovered his composure and by the time they were inside the building he was able to walk up the stairs to the first floor where he slumped into a chair. Harry asked for two mugs of tea and as that commodity always seemed to be on hand they were placed in front of them in no time at all. Joe sipped his tea and then asked for another while he began his story.

'As you know I left here about 15.30 for Cairo but I'd only got as far as E.L.G.8 when I could see there was trouble on the landing ground. Although I hadn't intended to land I thought I'd better go and see but as I approached they fired off a red Very so I started to go round again. Just as I did this joker comes tearing in from the north and starts shooting at me. I got the undercart up as quickly as possible, slammed the throttles beyond the wire and got right down on the deck.'

'He followed me down and each time I flew straight he fired. By this time I was almost as far as E.L.G.7 and as I didn't want him attacking them I started to come back this way. He got a couple of shots into the cabin so I thought it was about time I landed. I remembered a fairly level region not far from the swamp, managed to put the kite down and kept the engine running. By this time I was really niggled so I got into the turret and waited for him to come close enough but the silly sod decided to land beside me.'

271

'He got out of his plane and came walking slowly towards me and as he got closer he drew his pistol. I suppose he thought I was wounded or dead. I can tell you I was very much alive. Once or twice he stumbled on a few stones and then he kept his eyes on the ground. I waited until he got within a hundred yards and opened up with the machine gun but my shots were just in front of him. He threw himself to the ground but of course he'd got no cover at all so I then took careful aim and fired single shots. About the fifth one hit his right arm. Two more shots and I'd managed to hit his foot. He then threw away his pistol so I went out to get him.'

'I bandaged his wounds as best I could and then made him hop along to the Anson. Once inside I sat him in a cabin seat and bound his hands and feet. Poor bugger didn't know what I was going to do. Nor did I. Anyway I don't think he's badly injured. I went over to his plane, took out all the maps I could find and switched off the engine. Then I came back here. On the way I saw another German plane on the ground burning so I reckon the chaps at the landing ground had shot that one down.'

'Congratulations Joe. I think you should stay here tonight and if you're up to it tomorrow we'll get someone to fly you back to Cairo. In the meantime we'll get someone to check your plane over and repair the damage.'

By this time the prisoner had been taken to the hospital, checked over and placed in a small room with a guard inside and another outside. The M.O had been to see him and then phoned the CFI, not knowing quite what to do next but realising that the prisoner should be questioned. In the meantime Harry and Joe had gone quickly though the maps and found nothing of any real interest. Wing Commander Lang arrived, took charge of the maps and said someone would question the prisoner later. Harry arranged for Joe to spend the night in the room next to his and then telephoned Cairo to let them know that Joe had been delayed.

The next day Joe appeared to be none the worse for his adventure and after breakfast he and Harry went down to the hanger to check the state of his plane. Even on such a large base as Habbaniya the news of Joe's capture of a German prisoner and his plane soon spread. Everyone they met slapped him on the back or congratulated him. The perspex side panels where the bullets had entered had been replaced. So too had the seat where the German had sat because blood had seeped though the hastily applied bandages. Joe was able to provide a fairly accurate map reference where the plane had landed and one of the armoured cars set off with spare fuel, a mechanic and one of the instructors who reckoned he could fly it back .

Joe, when questioned, said he had never seen the German plane before. He reckoned it was not much faster than the Anson. It had a single in-line engine and was a high wing monoplane with two machine guns. It was a single seater, maybe a reconnaissance aircraft and also had small bomb racks under the fuselage. A few minutes spent on aircraft recognition cards revealed it as probably a Focke-Wolf FW 56 Stosser, an advanced trainer though why it was so far from home was a mystery.

Harry would have liked to accompany Joe back to Cairo but had to be content to let another instructor take him. So for once Joe sat in the other seat and operated the undercarriage. Harry made sure Joe still had his letter and was quick to point out that when he met Wing Commander Holmes he should also relate his own adventure as it would lend considerable weight to the problem faced by Habbanyia and the other RAF bases in Iraq.

CHAPTER 31

Help from India

The events of the past 48 hours were, if not a thing of the past, quietly put to one side. The wounds sustained by the German pilot were not serious and the M.O. thought that in a few day's time he should be able to walk with the aid of a crutch or a stick. Questioning by a couple of officers had revealed nothing as to why he was so far from home. It was therefore decided to send him to Cairo for further interrogation. One of the RAF transports, taking four high ranking army officers from Calcutta to Cairo, stopped off to pick up the prisoner and two guards.

The German plane was checked over and flown back to Habbanyia by F/Lt Kelly, one of the instructors, and once there it was identified as an advanced trainer. There still remained the mystery of why such a plane was so far from Germany where most flying training was carried out. The Emergency Landing Ground which had been attacked had re-established contact and confirmed that there had been two planes in the attack. It had happened suddenly with bombs and machine guns and on the second attack the ground defences had managed to shoot one plane down. The gunners had actually witnessed the attack on the Anson and then seen both planes go down somewhere in the desert a few miles away. They were relieved to know that Joe was safe.

Life at Habbanyia returned to normal or as normal as it had been before the incident. That morning, Harry returning to the mess after his lectures, met up with Major Singh, now once more in uniform. 'I'm going back to Baghdad this afternoon. Can I scrounge a lift?'

'Not sure. I'll have to ask the Old Man. I suppose I can get time off immediately after lunch so that I can be back here before nightfall.'

'Come on Harry. Don't you want to see the Merry Widow again – or Miss Templeton.'

'Now there's a thought. I wonder if it might be better if you asked the AOC directly. I really come under the CFI but the AOC carries more weight. I'm not really in the boss's good books at present and I don't want to cross his path too often. You could suggest to Smythe that your trip is more urgent than it really is otherwise he might tell you to go by road.'

'I'll remind him it's bandit country out there, which it is or might be soon.'

After lunch Singh found Harry in the lounge. Air Vice-Marshal Smythe had agreed that Harry could take him providing he had no other commitments. They had just agreed on a take-off time when Harry was called to the phone in the mess ante-room. He was wanted at the post office to receive an incoming call at 15.00 hours. Harry could only think that Jane wanted to reach him so he got there in plenty of time. The same corporal was on duty and told Harry to go to the same room and wait for the call.

At 3.00 p.m. precisely the phone rang and Harry picked it up but didn't recognise the voice at the other end. Certainly it was not Jane Templeton. The voice enquired, 'Is that Sqn/Ldr Nelson?'

'Yes. Who is calling?'

'Harry, this is Gp/Cpt Holmes. I got your communiqué and Erskine filled me in on more recent matters. I gather you have been enjoying yourself. I hope you're not going to start another war. We are only just about holding our own is this one.'

'Nothing like that Sir. I just happened to come into possession of certain facts and it seems that the diplomatic and military hands are tied so nothing could be done to counter a potential attack. I think we really could be up the creek here so I've tried to do something about it and I've received a good deal of help on the way. Hope I haven't embarrassed you too much.'

'No. Now listen carefully. We really do not have any planes to spare – nor troops for that matter. Apart from our commitments elsewhere we are holding back three fighter squadrons and a few bombers, mainly for local defence. Until we get reinforcements we are in much the same position as you. However if the Iraqis mount an attack send me a signal at once and I will do what I can. I suggest you send your own codeword *Deliverance*, followed by the time and date you need help. Have you got that?'

'Yes Sir, and thanks. I'm in your debt again. May I ask one more favour? Would it be possible to get some recommendation for Joe Erskine? What he did was quite a remarkable achievement under the circumstances. I saw him soon after and would be glad to write it up. Also the people at the ELG 8 witnessed it.'

O.K. Harry. I'll certainly pass on your recommendation. Good luck.'

'Good luck to you and thanks.'

Harry immediately found Singh and explained that he thought it best if he remained on the station in case Holmes wanted to reach him again. He managed to get another instructor, F/O Steadman, to take Singh to Baghdad where, with a bit of luck, they should be by 16.00 hours. As soon as they had landed Major Singh lost no time in hiring a taxi to take him to his RAF and army contacts in the city. The next day he flew in an RAF transport the 1500 miles to Karachi. It was the first time he had seen a Douglas Dakota let alone been in one. With a top speed of 230 mph and a range of over 2000 miles it did the long flight over the Indian Ocean in under seven hours. He was very impressed and discovered that No. 31 Squadron had only taken delivery of them at the beginning of April.

He made his way to the Indian Army H.Q. and put his request for additional troops to Col. Sutton. In his account of the defences at Habbanyia and the other RAF bases he tended to play down their actual strengths and the fact that they had modified their training planes. He slightly exaggerated the potential for an Iraqi attack and expanded the story of the German presence in the region. The two German aircraft had turned into a whole squadron, or so he believed, although this had not been confirmed. He banked on the fact that no details had been released so far. Nor did he mention the loyalty factor of the Assyrian levies thus allowing the colonel to assume they were a potential danger.

He did explain the embargo on any additional troops being stationed in Iraq. Col. Sutton brushed that aside. 'Don't worry about that. We'll just say they are in transit on their way to Egypt. I can't let you have too many. We'll send 200 troops by boat with all their transport and equipment. Another 200 can go by air if we can find the planes. Will that be enough?'

'Yes. Thanks. I wish you were coming with us. There's just one other thing. One of the people at the British Embassy in Baghdad was concerned about the number of civilians at Habbanyia. I wondered if once they'd set down the soldiers the planes could take back to Baghdad any women and children who wished to be evacuated. Earlier on some people were evacuated to Habb. but they may wish to return now as it might be safer in the city.'

'I'm sure that can be arranged. Since you seem to be well in with the RAF I'll leave it to you to sort out. Get back here as soon as things have quietened down. We'll probably have to send more troops to Egypt in any case and probably to East Africa as well. I'd like you to go with the Egyptian lot once it's been approved.'

Singh hadn't exactly been dreading his interview with Col. Sutton but the ease with which he had accomplished all he had wanted left him feeling elated although there was no one with whom he could share the excitement of what he had just achieved. Four hundred highly trained Indian troops would be a very welcome support for anything which the Iraqis might throw at them. All he had to do now was to find transport to get them to Iraq.

The next day he reported to the barracks and began to choose the troops he required together with their equipment and supplies. Although there were plenty of vessels going to Basra or in that direction none had enough spare room to accommodate 200 soldiers and their baggage. He was forced to split the men into platoons and let them go in several ships sailing at different times and travelling at different speeds. It was not good practice to split the troops in this piecemeal fashion but he had no choice. He comforted himself with the fact that, in theory at least, they would be arriving on friendly soil and the delay in meeting up would not jeopardise his expedition.

The RAF transport proved easier. Five planes were available each carrying twenty men and their personal equipment. The large transport planes were twenty times faster than the slowest ship. Moreover they would land precisely where they were needed, at Habbanyia, rather than at the port of Basra. With luck the troops going by transport plane would arrive at their destination within seven hours. That is if everything went according to plan. Even the stop-over on the return flights to off-load the civilians would only add an extra hour. Half his troops could be deployed and dug in within 24 hours of leaving Karachi. The remainder with the bulk of the heavy equipment and supplies might take anything up to a week. Once having disembarked at Basra some would have to go by road but if the RAF could spare the planes some could be flown the short distance to Habbanyia. It all began to take shape. And it all looked too easy. Something was bound to go wrong. It often did. Major Singh decided not to tell Harry what he had managed in the way of reinforcements just in case things did not work out as planned.

On 22nd April Harry received a letter which did not come through the normal mail but was delivered just after lunch by special messenger from Baghdad. He knew before he opened it that it was from Jane but was concerned that she had chosen this way of getting in touch with him. He had never before hesitated about opening any correspondence. Would it be good news or bad. He knew he must open it and quickly. The first word sent his heart beating a little faster.

> My Dear Harry,
>
> As it is such a long time since my uncle and I had the pleasure of your company we wondered if you would like to come and spend a few days here in Baghdad. The hectic days of the past week or so have slackened off so now we are only busy but at least we manage to have the evenings free.
>
> I know you will be amused when I tell you we have temporarily mislaid Mr. Singh. He is such a thoughtful chap and plays chess so well against the Ambassador we would like to invite him as well but don't know where to contact him. If he is with you could you pass on this invitation to him. Try to persuade him to join us tomorrow for a couple of days.
>
> We understand a transport plane is dropping off some material at Habbanyia before coming here and could easily bring you and Mr. Singh so that you would not have the rough journey by road.
>
> We look forward to seeing you both tomorrow.
>
> With kind regards, Jane Templeton
>
> P.S. It will be quite an informal gathering so we shall expect you both in civvies. There is no need to reply to this letter. If you cannot make it we shall understand.

It was, on the surface, just a polite letter for friends to meet in the comfortable quarters of the British Embassy for a few days away from the bustle of camp life. But if it was only that she could easily have telephoned. No. Harry was convinced there was some hidden meaning somewhere. He wondered whether to call Jane but the P.S. suggested she didn't expect a reply. He felt quite sure she also knew where Major Singh had gone and more than likely knew he would not be available to play chess with her uncle. Also he could not believe that all the problems at the embassy had more or less been overcome. He read the letter several times and wondered after each reading what clues he had missed and finally decided it must be a straightforward invitation. Yet it was such an innocuous letter it was hardly worth bothering to send by special messenger. He decided he understood neither the ways of women nor those of the diplomatic corps. He would take the letter at face value and see what happened. That's if he could get the time off at such short notice.

There was not a great deal of time if Harry was going to Baghdad. He walked over to the control tower and enquired about a transport stopping off tomorrow on its way to Baghdad. 'Yes. Here we are Sir. Due here from Cairo at 15.00 hours. Stopping at Baghdad to refuel on its way to India, Karachi, actually.'

'Do you know what its carrying?'

'The manifest includes some Browning guns and ammo, ten bags of mail, six anti-aircraft guns and shells and a few sets of tools. Must be a big plane unless this list is wrong.'

'Thanks very much. I've just had note to say that I should be on board and report to Baghdad. I don't suppose you know anything about that do you?'

'No Sir, but it should be easy enough to get a lift. Will you be coming back?'

'I hope so.' The information about the additional guns was encouraging. He wondered who had sent them. No doubt all would be revealed in time. He returned to the mess intending to have a drink at the bar. The CFI was also there with some of his staff. 'Can I have a word Sir?'

'Sure. Come and join us. Don't often get the chance to get together these days and when we do its usually about the students.' Harry joined them and the CFI bought him a drink. 'I ought to buy you one Sir. I need a favour.'

'Fire away.'

'Would it be alright if I had a couple of days leave. Sorry if its short notice but if things are likely to get a bit hairy soon I thought I'd better make the most of it now.'

'Yes. Can't see any problems. We're all back to strength and it will soon be the weekend. When do you want to go?

'Well I think I can get a lift in a plane going to Baghdad tomorrow afternoon. I should be back on 25th and I don't have any lectures after tomorrow morning.'

'That's O.K. Things have quietened down now. Still you never know with this lot.'

Harry stayed long enough to stand his round at the bar and then quietly slipped away to his bed still wondering about hidden messages in Jane's letter.

CHAPTER 32

Final Preparations

When he woke the next day he was no wiser but carried on with his lectures and even prepared two others to be given on his return. With regard to the anticipated attack by the Iraqis he had worked out roughly how his forces should be deployed. The airfield was outside the camp itself and was somewhat exposed. At the very edge on the southern side of the airfield was a fairly high ridge. To the north there was nothing but desert and swamp until a few hundred miles away lay the oil fields. He looked again at the polo field and golf course, both inside the perimeter, and wondered just how often they were used. If the two areas could be bulldozed together a second airfield could be constructed for the 'fighter' planes. If that were possible would many people really object and could the recreation area be restored once the emergency had been resolved!

Wg/Cdr Henty, the engineering officer, who had taken up Harry's offer of a few flying lessons was obviously the chap to contact. There was certainly no shortage of labour on the base. The Assyrian troops seemed to have plenty of time on their hands. There were also a few thousand civilians who could be redirected from their normal work for a short time. He caught up with John Henty briefly at lunch and put his idea to him.

'It's just an idea at present. I wonder how feasible it is. The main reason is that if an attack comes it will happen quickly and we might need to get the planes away as fast as possible. In any case if we had another airfield we could split the squadrons between the two. The enemy would obviously bomb the airfield outside the camp but we might be able to get the planes on this second airfield airborne before the Iraqis realised what we were up to.'

Henty quickly grasped this new idea. 'Leave it with me, Harry. In theory there is no problem. The bunkers on the golf course are not very deep. We could put tarpaulins or canvas at the bottom and fill in with any stuff lying around, add hardcore and bring it level at the top before adding grass. We can get that from almost anywhere such as it is.'

'Marvellous. I get these harebrained schemes from time to time but don't always know how to carry them out. Have you got enough barrows and shovels?'

'Well I'm sure there are some but these guys can make anything. Wooden barrows will be no problem and the chaps in the armoury can turn out shovels in no time once we've got the right template. The polo pitch will present no problems but we must get permission from the AOC. How long have we got?'

'Your guess is as good as mine. I'm going to Baghdad this afternoon, probably for two days. Maybe I can tell you more when I get back. Can I leave you to organize what you can?'

'Yes. Sure. Maybe we'll also have time for a few more flying lessons when you get back.'

'That too though I don't think you need any more. On paper we have 64 aircraft, all modified to carry armament of some kind. We have 39 pilots and I've included you among those. The CFI doesn't want to tell the pupils yet who will be asked to volunteer. I think they should be told now but he won't budge. The remainder will be asked to be bomb aimers or gunners. By the way three of your chaps would also like to be gunners. They are Sgt Green, Sgt English and Cpl Drummond. Is that alright with you but of course they'd like a few practice flights first.'

'Yes they did approach me and since I wanted to fly I couldn't very well say no.'

Harry then told John Henty about the transport arriving after lunch and its cargo. 'I can't think who the fairy godmother is but someone is sending ack-ack guns together with ammo and a few Brownings. Fighter planes and pilots would also be acceptable but I don't suppose they can be spared.'

After lunch they parted, Henty to consider the proposals regarding the airfields and Harry to finish the lectures he would be giving on his return and to pack his bag. He changed into civvies and waited in the control tower for the transport to arrive. And when it did he was as surprised as Major Singh had been when he saw his first Dakota. Pictures and articles had been in a variety of magazines but to actually see the plane was quite exciting even for a fighter pilot. As it came in to land Harry wondered how long it would take to stop and was surprised how short was the landing distance.

In just a few minutes its precious cargo was off-loaded through a side door and the guns, hidden from prying eyes under tarpaulins were spirited away to the armoury. A young pilot came into the control room, chatted to the duty pilot who signed for the goods and then said in a loud voice. 'I understand we have one passenger to be delivered to Baghdad. We'll refuel there before we go on to India. Anyone else care to come we have several spare seats.'

'Wish you'd told us sooner. We might have filled all of them.' replied the duty pilot.

The take-off in the Dakota was a lot shorter than Harry had imagined and as soon as they had set course for Baghdad he got up and walked along to the crew cabin, introduced himself and asked if he might sit in the second pilot's seat. Without a murmur the captain indicated that he could and the other pilot vacated his seat for Harry. The mass of dials confronting him was many more than on the Oxford instrument panel yet all the important ones were roughly in the same position.

'Do you want to fly her for a few minutes?'

'Yes please.'

'O.K. You have her.' Harry took over the half wheel control column and settled himself in.

'We're a little early. Do a few turns if you like.'

Harry was only too pleased, looked around, eased the throttles forward a little and executed an almost perfect turn to the left. Turning the wheel to the right he increased the throttle setting and made a much steeper turn but still managed to keep the nose level with the horizon. Then he was back on course, reduced speed and settled back at 200 mph. They flew at 5000 feet, a good deal higher than his usual flights to Baghdad so he was able to see more of the countryside. His stint as second pilot on the Dakota was short lived as the airfield came in to view. Harry thanked the captain and started to get up.

'Stay there if you like. Follow me through on the controls.'

'Thanks. You have control Sir.'

Harry stayed there until they had taxied to the control tower and the engines had been switched off.

'Nice aircraft. We could do with a few more of these. Thanks for the lift and thanks for letting me fly her.'

'You're very welcome. Have you done much flying?'

'Yes. I've done my share. Having a bit of a rest now though you might not think so.'

With a wave to the remainder of the crew Harry checked in at the control and then made his way to the guard room.

'Are you Sgn/Ldr Nelson?' asked the MP.

'Yes.'

'We have a message for you Sir. An embassy car will be here at 15.45 so there's no need to get a taxi.'

'Thanks.' Looking at the clock he saw he had only a few minutes to wait. In fact he had no time at all for the corporal called to him, 'It's here now Sir.'

The fact that Jane or someone had laid on a car made him realise that she was either really anxious to see him or that news of great importance had occurred. As they approached the city the streets were silent and bereft of people. He had never seen it so quiet, it seemed almost ominous and he was glad when after about twenty minutes the car stopped briefly outside the embassy gates while they were opened and then he was inside the safety of the compound.

He spoke briefly to the soldier outside the door, showed his RAF pass and was admitted. The guard inside called someone over and an embassy attendant asked Harry to follow him. He was shown into Jane's office and as soon as they were alone she came forward to greet him.

'Hello Harry. So glad you could get away and I do apologize for the cryptic letter.'

'No need to apologize. I was delighted to receive the invitation. I've no doubt you'll tell me all about it when you're ready. But for now just come here.'

She came forward, kissed him and then rested her head on his shoulder and held him. 'Oh Harry. I'm so glad to see you.' After a while she lifted her head and said in a weary voice. 'Let's have some tea and then I'll put you in the picture.'

As the tea arrived the phone rang and while Jane dealt with the call Harry poured out two cups. He heard her give instructions for no more calls to be put through and then she came and sat next to him on the settee.

'Thank you Harry. I see you're well trained. Have you got a wife somewhere?'

He tried to lighten the atmosphere with a flippant retort. 'No. Nor is there a Lady Hamilton for me but I could be tempted.'

Jane smiled and said, 'Touché.'

'Now, about my letter. You probably know my uncle has only been here a short while. The previous Ambassador was recalled earlier this month. We had a visitor yesterday,

Rashid Ali al Gailani to give him his full title. He wanted an urgent meeting with the Ambassador in private. That means no notes taken but whatever is said could be made to look binding. I was with the Ambassador to start with but left when requested. Back in my office I heard everything that was said and managed to take down the important bits.'

'He brought up the old points regarding the contents of the 1930 Treaty. Ali seemed to be under the impression that we had given permission for large numbers of troops to be landed in the country. My uncle said he knew nothing about it but said that as Britain was at war it would be natural for us to have troops in transit moving from one war zone to another. Ali said that was part of the trouble. As Iraq was neutral he did not want to give the Germans the impression that he favoured the British. The Ambassador said he realised the quandary that Ali was in and asked what he wanted him to do.'

'Well we did ask you to stop flying especially at Habbanyia.' was Ali's comment.

'Can't very well do that. You agreed and its part of the Treaty. In any case I understand they are so far behind with the present course they have actually increased their flying. However once the course is finished they will revert to normal flying hours and I believe they may close down the flying school altogether.'

'Ali seemed pleased about that but then enquired about a certain Indian, a Major Singh who often came in and out of the country.'

'Well you know more than I do. You are aware that the British military in Iraq come directly under the Indian Command so it would seem he has a perfect right to come and go. The treaty permits that. Leave it with me and I will find out precisely what is going on and let you know. Can you call again in two day's time?'

'Ali then said he'd had information about armoured cars scouring the countryside around Habbanyia, apparently looking for spies and upsetting local tribesmen. My uncle responded by reminding Ali that there were no local tribesmen within ten miles of the RAF base and that the cars were probably out looking for an aircraft that may have crashed. Ali left and promised to return in a couple of days.'

'Is there anything there that we didn't already know?'

'Not really but we intercepted another request from Ali to the Germans. It seems his earlier request for cash and military support, although promised, was being delayed. We have also monitored an enormous amount of traffic from the German army on their borders with Russia. It seems that dozens of divisions have been moving there over the past few weeks and even more during the past few days. Ali probably also knows this. Hence his request but he got no reply. His latest signal was an ultimatum. He says he intends to attack the British on 28th April, probably hoping to force the Germans into sending help.'

'Did he say where he was going to attack?'

'No but its most likely to be an isolated spot. We think Habbanyia. That's why I wanted to see you. We weren't sure if our signals were being intercepted so I decided to send you an invitation by special courier. By the way I do know where Major Singh is. He 's in Karachi and hoping to borrow some troops from India.'

'Yes he said he would but I haven't heard from him for several days. So things are hotting up. Ali is right. Our cars have been out patrolling further into the desert than they normally do but so far they have found nothing. Also our aircraft on their so called cross country training flights have been doing reconnaissance checks on Iraqi troop movements. There are small concentrations of Iraqi troops but nothing large enough to mount an attack on Habbanyia. They are probably planning an air attack.'

'So you are going to be in the thick of it at Habb. Do take care.' Concern showed in Jane's voice.

'Let me tell you what we've managed to do so far. We have converted all the training planes so that they are capable of carrying arms, either bombs or machine guns. All the instructors have been practising and the advanced pupils will be asked to volunteer. We have a total of 64 aircraft and 39 pilots. Just before I came here today an RAF transport delivered some anti-aircraft guns and ammo. We are considering making a second airfield within the camp perimeter in case the outer one is captured. If they attack we will try to evacuate the women and children. I know you are already crowded but they will be safer here than out in the country.'

'You're revelling in this aren't you?'

'No not really. But if we don't get help from outside we must look after ourselves. Everyone at Habb. has been marvellous and all the other RAF bases have contributed what they could. They are all so cross with London that they are prepared to go down fighting. By the way you will keep this to yourself won't you.'

'Of course. Let's go and have some dinner. There's nothing more we can do tonight. I don't normally panic but after Ali's visit I began to see what trouble he could cause and I began to worry and I think it was mostly for you.' They moved out of Jane's office and along the corridor to a suite of rooms marked 'Private'.

'Try not to worry. I've been in a few scrapes already and so far I'm still here. As you say let's have some dinner and then talk about the future or possibly dream of what it might be like.'

'Harry, make yourself comfortable while I prepare a meal. I have a small kitchen here. It wont be anything fancy but it will save going out. About half an hour. You can come and choose a bottle of wine and then go back to the living room and catch up on the world news. I'm afraid the papers are a few days old.'

Harry did as he was asked, chose a red wine from Jane's small supply and went back to glance through the papers. True they were a few days old and the news they contained was even older. Most of it was war news, reporting in some detail the German advances and putting a gloss on the withdrawal of the Allied forces. He couldn't really detect any bias either to the Axis powers or the Allied cause.

Jane called to him from the kitchen. 'Five minutes. Can you set the small table. We're having soup, a main course and a sweet. You'll find cutlery, plates and glasses in the sideboard.'

'O.K. Do you need a hand in the kitchen?'

'No thanks.'

A few minutes later Jane appeared with two bowls of soup and two rolls of bread, explained that more was available if required and set them down on the table. They exchanged toasts with the wine and started to eat. The soup was nothing more than tomato but after the first mouthful Harry realised it must be some special recipe. He was tempted to ask for more when he'd finished but decided to wait for the main course. It turned out to be a meat loaf, cut in generous thick slices with cold potato salad and a green salad.

'Hope you like this,' Jane remarked. 'If not I can do you an egg or there's cheese.'

'It's fine. In fact I didn't realise I was hungry until I started on the soup. So among your many talents you are also a good cook.'

'Well there's very little to go wrong with these but I didn't actually make the dessert. One of the cooks here did it for me but I think you'll like it. It's a butterscotch pudding.'

'I'm sure I shall. More wine?'

The meal came to an end and Harry offered to wash up. Jane declined his offer at first but then decided to let him help. It was quickly done and they returned to the sitting room for coffee. Once settled down Jane wanted to know more about Harry's life.

'So tell me Harry, what are you going to do when the war is over?'

'Not really sure. I started out intending to be a doctor, got side-tracked in 1936 and joined the Air Force. I can still go back to med. school and qualify and I suppose that is probably the thing to do. After all I can't go on being a pilot too long whereas I can be a doctor until I retire. What about you? Will you take over here from your uncle?'

'No chance. I'm too young and don't have enough experience. They'll send someone out whose been transferred from somewhere else. This is a particularly difficult station. I suppose if the war hadn't come the British might have moved out by now. I expect when there's a space on a boat I shall go back to England, have some leave and then be sent somewhere else.'

The conversation gradually diminished. Jane put her legs on the settee, stretched them out and lay down with her head on Harry's lap. Within a few minutes he felt her rhythmic breathing and realised she had fallen asleep, tired out. He tried to ease himself into a more comfortable position without disturbing her. Then he too, drifted off into a dreamless sleep. When he woke half an hour later he was stiff and as he tried to ease away, Jane stirred, looked up into his eyes and smiled.

'Enjoy your sleep?' asked Harry and he was smiling too.

'Yes I did. It's a long time since I've done that.'

'You looked very relaxed and I confess I dropped off too. No don't get up. I'll get more comfortable.' But the spell was broken.

'No. It was very nice and I feel much better but I've got a few things to sort out before I turn in for the night. Early morning start tomorrow. How are you getting back?'

'No idea, but I reckon those who summoned me here should provide transport to get me back.'

'Don't think I can't.' replied Jane.

'I'm sure you can do anything you set your mind to. I think I ought to get back by midday. If I can stay till about 11.00 we might have more definite news on the Iraqi front or even the Indian front come to that.'

'Yes. That's a good idea. I'll ring Shaiba and see if they can fly you. If not one of the embassy drivers can take you by road. It will take two hours but it might give you an opportunity to see just how rough the country is out there.'

'Good thinking. Well goodnight and thanks for the meal I really enjoyed it.'

Harry kissed Jane and as he pulled away she said. 'Would you like to stay?'

He was tempted but felt it would be wrong under the circumstances. He knew he liked Jane and it was obvious that she liked him but they were both under pressure knowing what lay ahead and therefore liable to let their emotions run away with them. Maybe she would regret such a liaison later. He knew he might regret not staying and tried to find the words to explain why he felt it best to leave things as they were at the moment. Finally he did speak.

'Jane I think I'm falling in love with you. I'm sure I am. I'm not sure how you feel but I'd hate it if we spoilt something precious by rushing into it before we're ready. Hopefully we'll have more time to ourselves soon when we can really get to know each other. Do you understand what I'm trying to say? Am I making a fool of myself?'

To his immense relief she said, 'I do understand. I really do. You go to your room down the corridor and I'll go to my bed. I'll see you in the morning. We can at least have breakfast together.'

They kissed and he left.

CHAPTER 33

A Calculated Risk

No further news had been received during the night. Jane had checked all the signals before breakfast and by the time she returned Harry had washed and dressed. Their breakfast together was quiet, neither knowing how to say what was uppermost in their minds. Finally, Harry said, 'I hope we're not going to talk about the weather.' It was the right thing to say for it broke the tension making Jane smile as she replied. 'I don't want you to go. You know that but I haven't been able to get you a flight so you'll have to go by road earlier than we planned – say 10.30. One of our more experienced drivers will take you together with some official documents and a guard.'

'O.K. I'll telephone you when I get there shall I?'

'Yes please and if the driver can't get back today can you find him a billet for the night?'

'Yes. No problem. Look Jane. About last night. I just wanted to say I felt so happy being with you, and I didn't want to spoil it. When all this is over I hope we'll have time to get to know each other properly.'

'So do I Harry. Don't say anymore. Just come back safely.'

The time passed quickly, then the car arrived and Harry was on his way back to Habbanyia. There were more people in the streets. That plus the fact that nothing new had been heard at the embassy was encouraging. Did it mean that the crisis had passed. Only time would tell but as they had already done so much at his base it would foolish not to complete their preparations.

Once clear of the city the state of the road gradually became worse although there was little traffic. The driver set a steady pace of 30 mph until after going for about an hour he was reduced to a crawl. The guard got out, waved down someone coming in the opposite direction and asked about the problem ahead. It seemed that two Iraqi army trucks had broken down and a third had crashed into them. Dense traffic on the road caused by an accident several miles ahead would cause delays for some considerable time.

When he got back into the car he said, 'I think we may have to make a detour Sir if that's alright with you.' He then went on to explain the problems ahead.

Harry agreed and with a quick word to the guard to keep a sharp lookout the driver took the car off the road and on to the desert. For a while the going was good in spite of having to go round several rocks and thorny scrubs until they came level with the accident. A crowd of excited civilians and a few soldiers surrounded the spot but once clear they were able to get back on the road and make up for lost time.

They got within five miles of the base when over the noise of the car engine they heard the unmistakable sound of gunfire. Harry couldn't believe the attack had already started but told the driver to stop. It soon became clear that the gunfire was not at the base itself but some way to the south. The staccato rattle of machine guns followed by the crump, crump of shells being fired made them all alert. 'That's a British twenty-five pounder' said the guard with so much authority that no one questioned him.

'Go forward slowly,' ordered Harry. So they went on again towards Habbanyia. Another two miles and the scene before them was puzzling at first. Three guns took it in turn to fire 25lb shells crashing into an outcrop of rocks about 2000 yards away. The gunners from the base were using the rocks as target practice. Just ahead of the guns but slightly to one side a couple of machine guns poured in a steady fire on to a similar pile of rocks about 500 yards away. Harry had to wait until after lunch for the real explanation.

The guns ceased firing and he then saw two of the armoured cars racing towards the rocks, each dragging a trailer. Once there the driver and his mate got down and started loading the trailers with pieces of rock and then shovelled in the smaller pieces. Then both cars dashed off at high speed racing each other towards the main gate.

Harry arrived at the camp about 13.00 hours, spoke to the guard and then explained to the MP in the guard room about the accident they had seen 20 miles from the camp. He also arranged for the driver and the guard to stay overnight if necessary. He invited them both to stay for lunch and left them to decide what to do. Before going in to lunch himself he telephoned Jane to say he had arrived and also mentioned the accident. It occurred to him that it might all be a plot to allow the Iraqis to get closer to Habbanyia on the pretext of helping their comrades. Then he dismissed that thought. They were not that subtle.

After lunch Harry asked to see the CFI and told him of the impending attack. Lang now accepted that the situation was really serious and called a meeting of all the senior officers for 16.00 hours. When they had all assembled he went directly to the problem. 'You will all know that there have been rumours of a possible Iraqi attack and that we have been taking certain measures to defend ourselves. It now seems that we were fully justified in taking those precautions. In fact from today we must double our efforts and complete our defences at this base. From various intercepts we understand that the Iraqis intend to attack the British on 28th April and it is likely they will attack isolated posts first. So we have three days in which to make this place ready.'

'I now propose to ask the senior pupils to volunteer their services and I expect all other pilots to take to the skies if necessary. Any questions?'

Wing Commander Henty spoke quietly, 'Just one. As you know I spoke to you about the possibility of creating a second airfield within the perimeter. This was not my idea but I expect you can guess who dreamed it up. We have made a few preparations. In fact we have jumped the gun a bit but merely to see how feasible it was. We have filled in five of the golf course bunkers although we haven't put down grass yet. All we want is your approval to go ahead with the rest and to use the Polo pitch as well. If the attack is planned for the 28th we don't have much time but we can make a start first thing in the morning. I've got all the material ready and all the necessary tools. I've also recruited sufficient teams to get the job done quickly and without getting in each other's way.'

'Right John, we really need Air Ministry approval for altering their camp. I'm going to stick my neck out and assume we have that approval. I'll also let the AOC know what we've done although he's not here at present. Start first thing tomorrow and we'd better tell the pupils then as well. Ordinary flying and lectures will be suspended in the morning but later we'd all better get some practice in flying as squadrons. I've asked Sqn/Ldr Nelson to say a few words regarding the formation of squadrons and I'm sure he will welcome any suggestions. O.K. Harry. The floor is yours.'

Harry explained what he had thought possible in view of their limited experience. Once the new airfield had been constructed it would be used by the lighter 'fighters' while the heavier twin engined Oxfords would use the main airfield as long as possible. He went on to explain that Squadron 1, flying Audaxes would be led by Wing Commander Henty, No. 2 Squadron, also using Audaxes would be commanded by Wg/Cdr Holdcroft. The CFI would be in overall command of these squadrons. Harry would take charge of the 3rd Squadron using 12 Oxfords. The remainder would be held in reserve. Depending on the nature of the attack they might have to modify their battle plans accordingly.

'In my experience it's best to keep the enemy guessing until he shows his hand. On the other hand a pre-emptive strike might prevent any attack ever taking place. If we adopt that course we have to get it right first time. And we must be prepared to change our plans. I would welcome suggestions. Let's meet here again tomorrow at 10.00 hours and again at 16.00 hours for an exchange of views. If we need to go on the attack we must organise the various crews and squadrons so we shall need to get in some practice. I think that's all for now Sir. Thank you.'

Wg/Cdr Lang dismissed the meeting and they dispersed in small groups, some to return to their normal duties and some to get an early drink at the bar. Harry caught up with John Henty and questioned him about the firing he had witnessed on his arrival. 'We needed a few tons of rubble to fill in the bunkers so we decided to knock hell out of the rocks as target practice. Everyone enjoyed themselves. We waited for the firing to stop and then collected the debris. Yesterday was even more fun. We got two of the met balloons, tethered them and sent them up a couple of thousand feet. Then we got the new ack-ack guns and used the balloons as targets until some clever devil burst them. By the way we have now sited all the guns. Three along the southern perimeter, one near the main gate and the other two on the eastern edge of the camp. All are protected by sandbags and linked to each other by telephone. There are also two machine guns to each site plus a platoon of soldiers in case they are attacked from the ground.'

'I can see you've all been busy and congratulations. The Ambassador is quite adamant that we must not fire the first shot. So a pre-emptive strike is out I'm afraid.'

'What! Even though we know the Germans may be involved!'

'Yes. Makes no sense but from what I can gather London is of the same opinion.'

After dinner Harry decided on an early night. The morning of 25th was just like any other. Harry continued with his lectures. Flying was resumed, with the pupils now realising that something serious was about to happen, especially as they were all summoned to attend a meeting with the CFI at 14.00 hours. Harry managed to take up John Henty for an hour's dual instruction and later they went in two planes with Harry giving instructions over the R/T. Harry watched from above as Henty returned to base and made a perfect three point landing. Harry's landing was not so well executed but he excused himself by saying he had recently been flying twins.

The meeting in the morning had produced a number of useful suggestions. Two officers volunteered to collate them and choose the best which might well form their battle plan. The second meeting at 16.00 hours was well attended. After much discussion Harry and F/O Kelly were delegated to sift through the suggestions and report to the meeting the following morning when lectures and flying training continued. On 27th reconnaissance reports from cross country exercises suggested that the Iraqis might be going ahead with their attack. Several large concentrations of troops had been seen, some as much as 100 miles away while others were no more than 50 miles from the base. All seemed to be heading towards Habbanyia. If the pupils could be believed the total was almost 5000 troops.

That afternoon a signal from Shaiba warned them that five RAF transports would be landing at Habbanyia and that some 200 Indian troops would need accommodation. In view of the report of advancing Iraqis the RAF admin. felt it was time to evacuate the women and children and send them back to Baghdad. On the ground preparations were made for the incoming troops. A few could be accommodated in huts but most would be living in tents although all could use the various mess halls for their meals.

The Dakotas of 31 squadron arrived at five minute intervals from 15.00 hours and as each plane was unloaded trucks took the soldiers first for a meal and then on to their billets or to the tents which had been erected near the main gate. Major Singh himself stepped out from the last plane and Harry who had expected him to be in the first waited with a borrowed car to take him directly to Wg/Cdr Lang. 'Nice work. Glad you could make it. Did you have much trouble persuading your boss that we need the troops.'

'No, not really. I took a leaf out of your book. I embellished the truth.'

By 16.00 hours the last transport had departed with the women and children for Baghdad. Harry managed to see the pilot who had earlier taken him to the capital and asked him to drop off a letter addressed to Jane Templeton. The Indian troops, so newly arrived, lost no time in inspecting their new surroundings and in spite of the coming darkness they had set up strong points around the perimeter and established patrols to supplement the Assyrian levies already in position. The following morning would be soon enough to check over the ground immediately surrounding the RAF base.

Before the camp was really awake that morning the early Assyrian and Indian patrols both reported the presence of 5000 Iraqi troops established on the ridge south of the base. As a precaution the patrols were doubled while those who had just come off duty were put on immediate standby. As yet the Iraqis had made no movement in the direction of the base.

The armoured car commander sent two of his vehicles out to investigate and made contact with the Iraqi commander. When asked why he was camped on the ridge he replied that he was on manoeuvres and would be sending a deputation to the base commander at noon. This was duly reported and the news spread like wildfire throughout the camp so that as noon approached quite a few RAF personnel found that they needed to take time off from work. In the meantime lectures and flying continued as usual. To all intents life on the base continued as normal.

On the dot of noon two army cars approached the main gate and were stopped by the guard. The officer in the first car never bothered to get out but gave a sealed document, addressed to the AOC, to the corporal. He returned soon after with an invitation for the Iraqis to enter the camp and they were escorted to Air Vice-Marshall Smythe's office in the H.Q. building.

What exactly was said was not known until much later but the substance was a demand from the Iraqi government that all flying should cease forthwith. The AOC had rejected their demands, pointing out that he had no authority to comply. It required agreement between the two governments involved to alter the terms of the Treaty but he would be happy to pass on their request. The delegation was escorted off the base.

The AOC immediately telephoned the British Embassy in Baghdad explaining what had happened. He was told that the Ambassador had been recalled and that his deputy, who had only just returned from India, needed time to catch up on routine matters before he replied. The AOC then sent a signal to the Air Ministry in London stating the situation and again requesting help. It was essential that they monitor all Iraqi movements. It was also decided to continue with the flying although the pupils were warned that at the slightest sign of aggression from the enemy troops they were to return to base or if that was not possible they should fly to another RAF airfield. So far the Iraqis had not moved. The work on the defences of the base continued with the construction of the second airfield almost complete.

The original plan of filling in the bunkers had not been changed. First a tarpaulin lined the hole and then rocks were piled in. It was finished off by shovelling in the sand which had formed the ridge around each bunker. It was then rolled, watered and finally grass turves were added and also watered in. It was hoped that when planes took off or landed they would not damage the bunker areas too much. An additional windsock was erected and a large letter 'T' constructed of wood and painted white and able to swivel round to indicate the wind direction. F/O Kelly volunteered to try out the new airfield and early the next morning he took off. In fact he managed to avoid all the bunkers but on landing decided he ought to test just how stable they were so he deliberately extended his landing run and ended up on one. Fortunately it withstood the weight of the plane and after a few more days he hoped they would all be as firm. Although he only did one circuit of the airfield he noticed that there were many more enemy troops on the ridge and he also spotted at least four field guns. It certainly looked as though the Iraqis were planning either an attack or a siege situation. As he taxied back to the new control cabin he wondered how long Habbanyia could withstand a siege if no more supplies were allowed in. When he mentioned this to one of the admin officers he was told, 'No problem. We have supplies of everything for at least six months, except by then fresh fruit and vegetables would no longer be on the menu.'

When the general meeting of officers took place later that day Major Singh was present and explained that he had managed to get 400 Indian troops, 200 of which were already deployed on the base. He had just heard that the first boat carrying 50 soldiers and their heavy equipment and ammo had landed at Basra. At first he wanted to test the Iraqi forces by getting his men to travel overland, a distance of 350 miles. With everything in his favour it might take them 14 hours but if they met with any opposition such a small force could do little to extricate itself. He therefore decided to wait another 24 hours in the hope that another contingent of soldiers might have landed from another ship. Shaiba, the RAF base, was only 30 miles away and under cover of darkness they could all move there and await transport by the RAF. It was just as well that they waited for air transport for the whole region to the north and west of Basra had been flooded as so often happened when the Euphrates overflowed its banks.

The flying training continued. If the pupil pilots were apprehensive they did not show their fears of the possible attack. Instead of lectures which had been cancelled for a couple of days the pupils spent the time belting up thousands of rounds of ammunition for use by the fighters and the gun turrets in the few Oxfords which had been fitted out. No other attempts were made by the Iraqis to further their demands. They seemed content to remain on the ridge and the British did nothing to move them on. However, each night the Indian soldiers sent out small patrols to seize weapons and on one occasion managed to spike three Iraqi guns and puncture several drums of petrol which leaked into the ground causing a potential hazard if anyone threw away a lighted cigarette.

So the 28th April, the day scheduled for the attack, came and went. No reply came from the signal which had been sent to London but quite out of the blue they learned that the AOC, the Air Marshall in charge of the whole of the RAF in the Middle East, had been recalled and that his place had been taken over by a more senior man.

Much closer to home the AOC at Habbanyia was also experiencing personal problems. With no direction and certainly no help from London he was very concerned with trying to keep within the letter of the Treaty with Iraq. At the same time he tried to ensure and encourage a proper defence in a friendly country where no defence was ever envisaged. He appreciated that the crisis would come quite soon but was unwilling to make the first aggressive move even though everyone around him seemed to be urging him to attack the Iraqis. With no support from Whitehall he felt he could no longer do his job properly. He, his wife and daughter flew to Basra.

302

CHAPTER 34

Pre-Emptive Strike

Preparations at Habbaniya continued. It was learned that another 50 soldiers had landed at Basra and then joined the others at Shaiba, awaiting transport. Reconnaissance flights by the pupils confirmed that more Iraqi troops seemed to be heading towards their comrades encamped outside the base. Three battalions were seen leaving Baghdad, ostensibly on manoeuvres but heading in the general direction of the isolated RAF base.

On the morning of 1st May it was obvious that the Iraqi troops on the plateau above Habbaniya had been reinforced. There were now more artillery pieces, more ack-ack guns and several light tanks. Urgent signals sent to London received no acknowledgement. Major Singh requested permission from the senior RAF officer to visit the Iraqi camp. He went in an armoured car driven by one of his own men. He asked if Harry would accompany him in a second RAF car. Once in the enemy encampment he explained to their commander that they needed to evacuate a number of civilians. For this operation two RAF transports would arrive in the afternoon and if he wished he could observe their departure. Fortunately the invitation was declined. The whole meeting was carried on with Singh speaking to the Iraqis in their own language.

Harry kept quiet during these delicate negotiations and although he understood not a word he sensed that the major had got what he wanted. On the return journey he questioned Singh. 'I didn't know you spoke their lingo. You realise I didn't understand a word.'

'Yes. Sorry about that. I needed you with me to give weight to my demands as it were. Fortunately they accepted my word. I'll let you into a secret. A few years ago I actually trained some of these chaps. I can't be sure but I think the Colonel we spoke to was actually on one of the courses. I was a good deal younger then but even if he'd recognised me he would not show it – mustn't lose face to the enemy.'

'You are a crafty old sod.'

'Yes I know but you have a very useful expression. "Needs must when the devil drives" At any rate we got what we wanted. I have no qualms about telling fibs to the Iraqis. I tried to have a look at what they'd got but its difficult to estimate their numbers. Even so they must have a few thousand troops so we'd better watch out.'

'Yes. My main concern is if they start a full blown attack on the base they could overwhelm us before we could get the aircraft off the ground.'

'I think our best bet at the moment is to nibble away at their outposts and hope that someone higher up sends us reinforcements. On the other hand diplomacy might win the day.'

Harry considered a third option and then replied. 'Or, we could attack first. If we could somehow get a couple of hours warning of their intentions, we could get airborne, attack them and take the sting out of their tail.'

'Well Harry. We have 300 troops and maybe a few more will arrive on the transports later. We have a few armoured cars and 1200 Assyrians. They would defend the base but 300 of us attacking several thousand of them is just not on. We could set up advance posts outside the perimeter to delay any attack but we must be able to retire to better defences here. We'll put down a few mines close to the camp so that any attacking force must find a way round. Our troops can set up some heavy machine guns and we should be able to hold an attack for some time. How quickly can you get your planes off?'

'We've virtually got two airfields now so they should all be airborne in about twenty minutes.'

'That should be time enough.'

Once back inside their own compound they parted company, Singh to have a final word with his officers and Harry to go for a late lunch. No doubt the Indian major would get a bite to eat at one of the many field kitchens that had sprung up around the base. As Harry made his way to the mess he reflected on the present situation. Here were two middle ranking officers who were organising the defence of an important RAF base. More than that they were actively planning to launch an attack against the enemy. A thought crossed his mind that maybe he attracted problems. He knew of people who always seemed to get into scrapes. Perhaps they couldn't help it. Perhaps he was one of them..

It was only a couple of months ago that he'd undertaken a similar operation in the desert in liaison with another army major. Then, against numerically superior odds they had won. Here the situation was totally different. They were far outnumbered in men. They were attempting to pit pupil pilots against trained soldiers and in addition they had several thousand civilians on the base who could not take part in the ensuing battle. He was under no illusion that it would come to a fight. And they had yet to meet up with the Iraqi Air Force.

For almost the very first time he began to have doubts. Was he seeing a crisis where none existed. If everything went wrong he had only himself to blame but he had involved others who might also suffer. Maybe the wound to his forehead which seemed to be better was actually worse. Maybe it had affected that part of his brain which allowed him to take unnecessary risks. These thoughts crowded in on him as he walked. As he got closer to the mess he met others going in the same direction and their greetings brought him back from his worrying uncertainty. By the time he was sitting down all his misgivings had vanished. After all he wasn't really alone in his fears about what might happen. Major Singh had agreed and supported his plan throughout so it must had some credibility and merit after all.

The feverish activity of the past few days suddenly ceased. Everyone had done all they could. By 18.00 hours all the mess halls were filled with personnel having their evening meal. An unreal calm could be felt. Everyone could see the Iraqi hordes on the plateau. Many had witnessed the surreptitious arrival of the last of the Indian troops and their British officers. Though glad that at least they had a few more fighting men everyone realised they were outnumbered.

Only four days earlier the dreadful news had been received that the British had been forced to evacuate Greece. They knew it was impossible for troops to be spared to help the isolated base at Habbaniya. They knew they were on their own and up against it yet somehow everyone remained calm.

It was decided to act normally so all the lights remained on in the camp until 'lights out' when those in the barracks were extinguished. By this time Major Singh and his men had laid their mines and established the forward and reserve posts he had mentioned to Harry. At 02.00 hours on the morning of 2nd May his forward posts reported increased activity among the Iraqis. They were obviously on the move. He sent a runner to warn Harry that the balloon was about to go up. Harry dressed quickly and telephoned the post office. 'I've got an urgent message to send to Cairo. I'm coming over at once.' The man on duty had everything ready and soon he had coded the signal WING COMMANDER HOLMES, RAF H.Q., CAIRO. URGENT REPEAT URGENT. DELIVERANCE 0205410500HN.

If Holmes received it and could act on it he would have three hours to organise the planes and get them over to Habbaniya. Harry knew he was cutting it fine but until now he had only been guessing that an attack would come. It looked as though the moment had arrived. He left it another hour before he told the CFI who was now officially in charge. He asked Harry to do the actually briefing. Wg/Cdr Holdcroft organised early breakfast for the whole camp, officers, airmen and pupils. By 0400 hours on the morning of 2nd May the pilots and aircrews were in the cinema being addressed by Sqn/Ldr Harry Nelson.

'Sorry to get you up so early. We have a busy day ahead of us. You all know what to do. We may be outnumbered – so what's new. A signal has been sent requesting urgent assistance from the RAF in Egypt. You all know what the problems are. They'll come if they can. In the meantime we shall keep the flag flying. The two Audax squadrons will be using the new airfield specially built for this purpose. The Oxfords, I'm afraid will have to make do with the old one but you all know your way around. Get up and down as quickly as possible. Remember surprise is on our side. The Iraqis think it will be a pushover. It's up to us and our soldiers to prove them wrong. The first planes should be airborne by 0500 and we should all be away by 05.30. You know what to do. Just imagine the enemy on the plateau is nothing more than the targets you've been hitting all the time during practice. I would only say BE CAREFUL. These targets may hit back. Listen out on the R/T for recall. Good luck.'

As he sat down a lone voice from the back of the hall said in a loud stage whisper 'It's not for nothing he's called Nelson. At any moment I thought he was going to say *"England expects..."*.' The hall exploded in laughter and even Harry couldn't help joining in. He hoped he hadn't gone over the top in what he'd said but at least morale was now at an all time high. Then for some reason best known to themselves the whole audience, pilots and ground crews stood up, clapped and shouted. Harry and the senior officers could only look on and smile as they made their way to the flight areas. The sky showed a faint glow in the east as the first engines were started. For those in the control tower it was an impressive sight. Virtually every plane at the base ready to do battle with the enemy. It would have been really impressive if they had been proper war planes. Above the roar of the engines a new noise could suddenly be heard – the crump, crump, crump of land mines being exploded. Then the first of the Audax squadrons took off quickly followed by the second and finally the Oxfords took to the skies.

The battle commenced as the first Iraqi tanks exploded the mines, not by running over them as they were clearly visible on the ground. They had been hit by gunfire from the leading tank which then veered off to the left precisely where the Indian troops were waiting. A devastating fire quickly put the tank out of action whereupon the others made it back in a long sweep to the relative safety of the plateau. One of the RAF armoured cars rushed to the crippled tank and rounded up the fleeing tank crew as they struggled to escape. This short engagement, almost standard procedure, was conducted with military precision. The only surprise was the fact that the Iraqis fell for it.

Suddenly the watchers on the ground heard another sound. A low rumble at first, the sound grew to a crescendo as ten small dots from the east slowly turned into ten Wellington bombers flying in formation at about 3000 feet. Dark against the sunrise they looked threatening and as they roared overhead a big cheer went up from the RAF base.

As one, the bombers wheeled round in a huge circle and came back over the camp. Now the onlookers below could see the bomb doors were open and as they watched 60 bombs came streaking downwards. Those on the ground began to take shelter, thinking that the bombs had been released too soon and would drop on the base but they landed on their intended target, the Iraqi army positions on the plateau.

The Iraqi ack-ack gunners had been well trained and those positioned away from the main encampment took their toll on the attacking aircraft. One Wellington was so badly damaged that it was forced to land on the airfield while ambulances and fire tenders rushed to snatch the crew to safety. The remaining bombers were all hit but managed to make it back to their base at Shaiba.

Then began the shelling. Almost the first to land on the base actually hit the crashed bomber and it blew up with its remaining bombs exploding in a spectacular display. The debris remained where it had landed for several days because it was too exposed for anyone to attempt to clear it away. In the meantime the first of the Audax squadrons arrived back and carried out their attack. They bombed and machine gunned the Iraqis and for a while the shelling ceased. Then, as they left the second wave of Audax aircraft arrived to repeat the earlier pattern. When they left the first flight of Oxfords could be seen high overhead. Flying very steady, the bomb aimers gave slight course corrections to their pilots and when the target came within their sights the bombs were sent crashing down while the aircraft wheeled quickly away or dived out of range of the guns.

Although they hit the targets and caused some casualties to the enemy the weight of bombs was nothing like as much as had been delivered by the Wellington bombers. Even so the Iraqi gunners took cover. Maybe they were conserving their ammunition for another Wellington attack. Soon another flight of Oxfords appeared overhead, released their bombs and flew away to the north.

The relief for the enemy did not last long. From two different direction more groups of Oxfords arrived, one flying at 3000 feet and the other at 5000 feet. They dropped their bombs and disappeared. Then it was the turn of another Audax squadron to come in for another attack and as soon as they had completed it they came in to land. The second squadron arrived soon after and it too landed safely. The Oxfords made their finally bombing runs and they too came in to land.

They, of course, had to use the main airfield and as they came in the Iraqi gunners took full advantage of their slow landing approach. One Oxford was shot down in flames and the crew killed. Four others were also hit but managed to land and quickly taxi through the gap in the hedge between the two airfields and get behind the hangers where the crews climbed out, excited and scared at the same time.

By now the first Audax aircraft to land had been refuelled and loaded up with bombs and ammo. A few bullet holes in their fabric had been hastily patched over although two planes were declared unserviceable and required further attention. Away they went and soon afterwards the second squadron was also airborne. Because of the Iraqi guns which might prevent the Oxfords from taking off the first Audax squadron was recalled to bomb and machine gun the Iraqi positions.

The ruse worked and all the Oxfords or those that remained serviceable got away safely just as the second Audax squadron arrived to carry out its attack. Harry flying in one of the Oxfords began to wonder how long they could keep this up. He also wondered if they would get more help from outside. He was grateful to the Wellington crews and sent a thought message of thanks to Wing Commander Holmes. Obviously his urgent request had been answered. Maybe it was time to send another.

The pilots and pupils at Habbaniya kept up the running attacks all day. Any pilot who could fly did so. When one plane became unserviceable they merely took another while the ground crews and armourers repaired what they could. Useable bits of aircraft were removed from wrecks and fitted onto less damaged planes. There had been no more attempts by the Iraqis to attack the camp. The mines had been replaced and the defenders of the forward positions relieved. Everyone, somehow or other had managed to get a midday meal. Some actually sat down in the mess but for most it was a hastily eaten meal delivered to the various posts around the base.

The hospital had been kept busy. Some of the injured airmen had superficial wounds but many were kept in the hospital to recover from more serious wounds. Three had really bad injuries and two more were treated for burns. By 19.00 hours on day one of the battle the weary pilots called it a day, had their last meal and went to bed. Some slept out of sheer exhaustion while others lay awake, going over in their minds the harrowing events of the day.

The senior officers held a council of war. Twenty planes had been lost or damaged. Some would never fly again although a few could be repaired. A third of their total strength out of action after only one day did not auger well. On the other hand they knew they had inflicted severe damage on the enemy forces both in equipment and men. So far no British airman had been taken prisoner but they had captured a handful of Iraqi soldiers.

Pilots and aircrews had suffered too. Out of the 39 pilots who started the day ten were either dead or seriously wounded and would take no further part in the battle. If they lost another quarter of their pilots the next day the end would soon be in sight. Harry thought he could come up with a new plan but he was so tired he needed just a few hours to get some rest. First he must send another signal to Holmes. At the post office he sent the following message. WING COMMANDER HOLMES, RAF H.Q., CAIRO. URGENT, URGENT, URGENT. DELIVERANCE 0305410700HN. He was surprised that apart from the Wellingtons which may have come in answer to his earlier request nothing had been received from the outside world.

For a while everything was quiet and the silence was eerie and unsettling. Most of the camp slumbered apart from the ground staff who carried on repairing the planes. Another pilot died during the night although two who had minor wounds declared themselves fit for duty. Then at midnight the shells began to fall on the RAF base. The barrage continued intermittently until 03.00. A few buildings were damaged. A few more holes appeared on the landing fields but little harm was done apart from depriving the British of much needed sleep.

The CFI, the most senior pilot and the most respected on the base took Harry to one side. 'I must tell you Harry, I was not too happy about remaining on the ground while my officers and even the pupils took to the skies. I'm going to fly tomorrow.'

'Yes I understand but we must have a senior man on the ground. Maybe one of the others would step down if you really insist.'

'I doubt it.'

Harry made one more attempt. 'Sir we all need you in command where you can look after us.'

'I hear what you say but my mind is made up. We need as many pilots in the air as possible. I'll tell the others of course but I shall fly tomorrow.'

Harry felt it was useless to pursue any further attempts to dissuade Wg/Cdr Lang and appreciated that the circumstances were such that even only one extra aircraft in the air might just make the difference.

CHAPTER 35

Desperate Hours

DAY TWO The morning of May 3rd started quietly enough. The sun still rose in the east and shed its early morning light. For the first time the beleaguered defenders saw the devastation caused by the shelling during the night. Although only two buildings had been hit the windows in many others had been broken. After a quick breakfast small groups of RAF personnel and civilian workers were organised into repair parties and by midday much of the debris had been cleared away. Some windows had been boarded up and a few had actually had their broken glass replaced. Other working parties were detailed to clear the airfields of rubble and fill in any shell holes.

While this work went on it was decided to get as many aircraft airborne as possible. So, long before midday the battle plan of the previous day was repeated although Harry and the senior officers thought they should modify their tactics as events unfolded. To some extent they were dependent on what the enemy did. Probing patrols of soldiers sent out from the base detected no signs in the enemy camp of an impending attack. Reconnaissance planes found no large numbers of Iraqis coming to reinforce their comrades on the plateau. In fact the inactivity of the enemy gave some cause for alarm. It seemed that they were waiting for something – but what!

In the general discussion that followed three possibilities were considered. The enemy had had enough for the moment and were waiting for new supplies of shells. They were waiting until all the British planes were airborne and away from the base before they started shelling or making a ground attack. The third option was that they would call in their air force or possibly the German Air Force.

It was a real poser. John Henty put forward a plan. 'Why don't we recall one of the Audax squadrons earlier than planned, get them to attack the Iraqis and then get the Oxfords to release all their bombs in one go. The fighters can give the bombers covering fire while they land and we'll see what happens. At least the initiative will be with us.'

When this had been agreed the first squadron was recalled and advised of the change in plans. The other Audax squadron was told to continue with its original orders, to bomb and strafe at 11.00 hours. These signals had just been acknowledged when those in the control tower heard the unmistakable sound of the Audaxes returning. But the low pitched snarl was coming from the wrong direction. It was Wg/Cdr Lang who first realised what had happened. His determination to join the fight arrived earlier than he had anticipated. Even while the desperate mini war was going on his day was full with the usual requirements of his office. Vital assessments and the paper work of running a Flying Training School still needed to be completed. He had expected to get most of it completed during the mornings which left the afternoons free to fly. Now all that had changed. He spoke with assurance.

'That's the Iraqi Air Force. They have quite a few Audax machines, purchased from Britain. They also have some Italian Savoias. We must alert our ack-ack gunners and delay our returning planes.'

'No. Let's leave things as they are but warn our planes. They obviously think all ours are away. We'll surprise them.'

As the only officer with recent battle experience, the others, including the CFI, seemed to look increasingly for Harry to make the decisions. He began to feel the strain of responsibility as he considered the few options open to them and there was little time for thought. It was action that was needed and at once. He gave instructions for control to advise the British planes that there might be enemy fighters overhead when they arrived back. The Oxfords were also warned to look out on their return, to continue with bombing and be careful not to fire on friendly fighters.

Wg/Cdr Lang spoke quickly to Nelson and to John Henty. 'We must be prepared to meet them with what we have here. If you could each fly one of the reconditioned Gordons, I'll take up the one of the Gladiators. I gather, John, that you've been practising on the Gordons.'

It was agreed that the Gordons would each have one of the volunteer gunners from the ground crews while the CFI had the much faster single seater fighter. The planes, already standing by, were quickly started up and the three took to the skies in a forlorn hope of meeting the enemy. Harry assumed, rightly as it turned out, that the Iraqis would come in at about 2000 feet so they needed to get above them as quickly as possible. The Gordon had a slightly slower rate of climb than the Gladiator but at 1000 feet a minute four minutes should be enough to be in position. The three aircraft gained height and from the north east the enemy could be seen approaching and flying in a tight formation.

Lang waited until the enemy was just below then waggled his wings and went into a screaming dive against centre of the formation. Nelson and Henty followed him down, each picking out a target on the edge. Lang got in a couple of long bursts from his forward guns and thought he had hit one and then as he came out of the dive and round in a wide circle he fired at the trailing enemy aircraft and let off the rest of his ammo. The leading Iraqi aircraft broke away and in doing so hit one of his comrades and the two planes locked together and fell to earth.

Harry and John, seeing the CFI in action followed suit and after diving into the formation came in from the right flank firing at point blank range. Then it was the turn of the gunners in the rear cockpits to let fly. They both claimed successful hits. The Iraqi pilots were far more experienced but had no wish to face up to these mad Englishmen and decided to break off the action. A second wave of enemy fighters appeared and sought to finish off the three British pilots. Just at that moment the British Audax squadron, which had been recalled, arrived over the base and quickly engaged the enemy. The British instructors and their star pupil pilots pressed home their attack. Two more of the enemy planes went down but several British aircraft had been hit.

Fortunately with their base so close they were able to land quickly. Then another piece of the battle plan jigsaw fell into place. As the crippled planes came in to land the Oxfords arrived and rained down their clusters of 20 lb bombs on the enemy positions. The Iraqi gunners, not wishing to hit their own planes, held their fire. Meanwhile the British and Iraqi pilots, both in virtually identical planes began a series of dog fights.

Suddenly the enemy planes began to edge away from the battle zone and break off the action. Maybe they were running out of fuel or ammunition. Maybe they had had enough. It didn't matter. The British pilots, inexperienced though they may have been were not drawn but returned to base after using up the rest of the ammo on Iraqi soldiers on the ground.

Suddenly a new sound could be detected this time coming from the west and as the dots in the sky got bigger the watchers on the ground realised that they were Bristol Blenheims. The fighter bombers screamed overhead and went headlong in pursuit of the retreating enemy fighters. While two of the new arrivals went in search of enemy formations to the north and south the third Blenheim caught up with two others in the east. The gunners got in two long bursts and one enemy fighter went down. The British pilot continued after the other, following it down to ground level and finally finished it off when it crashed into the River Euphrates.

The Blenheims landed at Habbanyia only long enough to refuel as they had to get back to Egypt. Over a quick mug of tea one of the pilots was heard to say, 'I got down so low my airspeed registered in knots, not mph.' This was an old gag indicating that he had flown very low over water and it was greeted with smiles and derision in equal proportions. By now all the Habbaniya aircraft had landed while those that could still fly were refuelled and re-armed ready for the next operation. The untried pilots and ground crews were learning quickly. The CFI went over to the Blenheim crews to thank them for their timely intervention and urged them to report the Habbaniya situation when they arrived back in Egypt. He explained that all their phone lines were either down or suspect.

The timely arrival of the Blenheims may have indicated to the Iraqis that the British still had more powerful planes which they could call upon. Three Habbaniya aircraft had sustained severe damage and would not fly again although some of their parts could be used to repair others. Luckily the pilots were all safe although badly shaken after the severity of the recent action. However once their nerve had recovered somewhat they all felt elated and took to the skies during the late afternoon in the final sorties of the day.

It was anticipated that the Iraqi Air Force would return, if not in force, at least on a reconnaissance flight but so far none had appeared. For a few hours the pilots and gunners rested. The ground staff repaired damaged planes and the pupils continued to insert bullets into belts for the machine guns. The evening meal was eaten in an air of unreal tranquillity yet at the back of everyone's mind was the thought that once night had fallen the shelling would begin again. The senior officers went into another huddle and considered what action they might take to counter this threat. One option was to get airborne at night and bomb the Iraqi camp but so few of the pilots had flown at night. They dare not lay out a flare path for it would give prior warning to the enemy who would no doubt begin shelling at once.

The Oxford aircraft, really the only planes equipped for night flying, could probably stay in the air for almost six hours so a take-off at 21.00 hours would mean a landing at 03.00 hours the next day when it would still be dark. To delay the take-off for a few hours might be getting to the time when the shelling had started the previous night. One aircraft would scarcely be enough to keep the Iraqi gunners in check. Three would be better and they could overlap their flying times. It fell to Wg/Cdr Lang, Sqn/Ldr Nelson and W/O Butler to fly the night shift. Major Singh offered a support plan to infiltrate the enemy lines and do as much damage as possible. The timing of these attacks would be crucial so that no Indian troops were engaged with the enemy when the bombers returned.

The plan was for each Oxford to bomb the enemy and stooge around for half an hour before coming in to land. This would give the ground troops time to return to the attack. Once the plane had landed the Indians would retire back to the base while the Assyrian troops would be in position to mop up any Iraqis who followed the Indians as they made their withdrawal.

The second Oxford would then take off while the combined ground forces mounted an attack on the enemy. Singh reported that when he had first broached this idea of a joint attack the Assyrians had reacted with surprised glee. It seemed they had long wanted to confront the Iraqis. Now they could argue that they were acting under direct orders from the British. Singh's final summing up of the situation was, 'Emergencies breed strange bedfellows.'

That was the plan. Only in the light of day on 4th May would it be known if it had worked. The troops mounted their first attack. On the far side of the hangers, out of sight from the enemy, the planes stood ready, fuelled and armed. Harry was the first to take off with LAC Porter as his bomb aimer. If Harry was injured Porter should be able to fly the plane back and hope that his luck would hold out as he came in to land. The plane showed no lights as Harry taxied the Oxford through the gap in the hedge and with an airman walking ahead showing the way with a shielded torch he was able to reach the take off point on the main airfield.

At five minutes past midnight Harry opened the throttles and the aircraft moved quickly across the field and was soon airborne. Harry thought he could see flashes on the ground from small arms fire and reckoned that Singh and his men were busy at work among the Iraqis. As the co-pilot's seat had been removed to enable the bomb aimer to crawl to the nose of the plane Porter sat for a time on the step just behind the pilot. They spoke to each other through the intercom.

'Sir. Keep on this course of 315. Gradually climb to 5000 feet and then level out. Continue on this heading for fifteen minutes at 130 mph.'

'Wilco.'

'Sir. I've written down all the instructions we had at the briefing so I know just what to do. At the end of this leg turn 90 degrees to starboard on to 045 for another fifteen minutes. Then turn 45 degrees to starboard and you should be flying due south.'

'Roger. Have you allowed for the wind.?'

'No Sir but I don't think there is any.'

'Well don't worry. After the second turn we'll fly for fifteen minutes then you can get down to the bomb sight. In just a few minutes you should be able to see the lights of the Iraqi camp. You'll be able to check for drift by picking out one fire. If we're too early we'll stooge around for a bit. Whatever we do we must not bomb our own chaps.'

'O.K. Sir. I've got all that.'

They flew on in silence. Even the engines seemed to sense the need for it. Although not normally a noisy aircraft at the moment it just seemed to purr along.

'Sir. It's time for the final leg. Turn on to 180 .'

'Thank you.'

Silence descended again. Soon would come the time of reckoning. Harry thought he could make out a few lights on the ground indicating the whereabouts of the enemy but they could be anything. The plane flew onwards towards its target. The actual bombing should prove to be no problem. It would be when they came in to land that the difficulties would present themselves. In the past few years Harry had done quite a bit of night flying and in coming in to land had used a variety of systems from paraffin flares laid out along the landing strip to a full night time system involving a flare path and glide path indicators which showed red if he was too low and green if his approach angle was correct. Tonight would be a first with nothing much in the way of an aid except the landing lights on the aircraft.

'O.K. Porter. Time for you to go.'

LAC Porter came and stood next to Harry, his headset still plugged into the R/T socket and Harry sensed he wanted to say something. After a moment or so it came.

'I'd just like to say Sir I'm glad I've flown with you. If we get down safely maybe we could do it again.'

For a moment Harry didn't quite know what to say. What words of assurance could he give this young man. He liked Porter and considered him to be an excellent pupil. It would be a great pity if he didn't live to get his 'wings'.

'You get on with your bombing run young Porter. Of course we'll fly again and then you can be the pilot and I'll try my hand at bombing.'

Porter unplugged his R/T, gave a thumbs up sign to Harry and with a happy grin on his face crawled down into the nose of the aircraft and settled himself at the bombsight.

Harry heard a click as his R/T was switched on and they were in contact once more.

'O.K. Sir. I'm ready when you are. We have five minutes to go. Looking through the bombsight there doesn't appear to be any drift so we should be able to go dead ahead to the target. I'll aim for the centre and the other planes can pick out each flank.'

'O.K.' Harry contacted base on the R/T and told them he was ready to commence his bombing run. Being on the same frequency the armoured cars would pick up the message and order the troops to pull back.

Harry maintained height at 5000 feet and the airspeed at 130 mph. Soon he could see flashes of gunfire and guessed that the Assyrian and the Indian troops were making their attack on the Iraqi positions. Suddenly the firing ceased. It was time to go in.

'Hello Sir. I've got a good sight. Can I drop the bombs all in one go?'

'Yes. Why not. Just make sure you're spot on. I'll keep the plane as steady as possible.'

'O.K. Sir. One minute to go. Target coming into view. The firing on the ground has ceased. See that big fire and the two little ones?'

'Yes.'

'That's where I shall aim.'

'O.K.' Harry wished he'd keep quiet and get on with it. Then came the instructions.

'Steady. Steady. Left. Left. Steady.'

Harry carried out the instructions from his bomb aimer.

'Dead ahead Sir. Steady. Steady. Bombs away.'

Harry felt the aircraft lift a little as all the bombs fell away. He banked slightly to the left then came back on his course. The bombs hit their intended target and although not a spectacular sight Harry was pleased for Porter that they had all gone home.

'Good work, Porter. Come up here again. We're heading home. This is going to be tricky and I want you strapped in for the landing. Sit behind me at the navigator's table.'

It took ten minutes for the plane to lose height and join the circuit. Whilst doing so Harry saw more flashes on the ground and guessed that the procedure was being repeated in order to get the second Oxford off the ground. Soon he sensed rather than saw it take off, flown by Wg/Cdr Lang. A few minutes later he moved the mixture lever to rich, lowered the undercarriage and prepared to land.

Fortunately the Iraqi ack-ack remained silent. At 100 feet Harry switched on his landing lights and as soon as the ground staff saw them they directed a searchlight beam along the landing path. Once the wheels had touched all the lights went out and Harry taxied as quickly as possible through the gap in the hedge and got behind the shelter of the hangers – all the while being guided by an airman with a shielded torch.

Once in the comparative safety of the dispersal he switched off and he and Porter got out of the plane. Several ground staff arrived to check over the plane, refuel it and prepare it for another mission. This was the danger point. If the enemy realised what had happened they could so easily lob shells into the camp hoping to hit almost anything. However the armoured cars had already travelled half way towards the Iraqis and were pouring in steady machine gun fire. The reply from the enemy was not very effective.

There was no way of knowing if Harry's raid had done much damage. At least the Iraqi guns were silent for the moment and if all went well in another half an hour the CFI would be paying them a visit. The third Oxford fitted with a bomb sight and flown by W/O Butler should arrive over the target at 03.00 hours. In fact he came over to join Harry and to ask just how difficult had been the landing. Harry felt the only thing to do was to be entirely honest.

'A bit more than hairy. The searchlight was a great help but if you're not sure go round again. You could always try a flatter power approach and landing.'

Harry and Porter went for a wash and a quick snack and then it was time to prepare for their next operation. As they walked towards the plane for the second time that night Harry posed a question. 'Well young Porter. Are you going to take her up this time?'

'No thank you Sir. I think I need a lot more night flying practice first. If its alright with you we'll go as before.'

'O.K. then. Let's dice.'

The mission was much the same as before and they landed safely although this time the ack-ack opened up but stopped after a few rounds. No doubt Singh and his soldiers had been at work again keeping the enemy busy. They hung around talking to the ground staff until the CFI had landed and then both crews waited until the final Oxford came in for the second time that night. W/O Butler was the first to make any real comment about the problems of landing. 'Thank God that's over. I'm never going to fly again at night unless we have a proper flare path.'

They all went in for an early breakfast, Porter feeling a little apprehensive about joining the officers and even W/O Butler was somewhat taken aback when Lang insisted that they all join him. The CFI gave them each a welcoming handshake especially for the trainee pilot. 'Well done Porter. I'm sure you'll get your wings. If not we'll give you an Observer's brevet.

DAY THREE. The second night of the siege merged into the third day and it was not long before the Audax squadrons were being made ready for their fighting patrols and bombing missions. All the spare serviceable aircraft were also prepared in case the Iraqi Air Force paid them another visit. The operational pattern of yesterday was repeated with varying degrees of success. By 11.00 hours it was a question of getting airborne as quickly as possible, strafing the enemy positions and getting back again. Any plane which landed with bullet holes was abandoned for the ground staff to repair. In the meantime any pilot who could still fly did so merely taking whatever plane was next available.

The defenders of Habbaniya received no more outside help but they had long since accepted that they were virtually on their own. By early afternoon Harry and the other night flyers had rested and joined in the fray once more. By now the pilots were doing really no more than extended circuits and bumps by flying a little further over the southern sector of the base and bombing or machine gunning the enemy positions and then making a quick landing, all the while hoping that the ack-ack gunners would not be too accurate in their fire. The enemy forces had made no more attempts to get close to the base. Maybe they were waiting for reinforcements. Maybe they were waiting for the return of their own aircraft or maybe they expected the Luftwaffe to join in. With all telephone lines to the base either down or deliberately disconnected Habbaniya was cut off from the rest of the world. Then just after 17.00 hours, when they were beginning to think of an evening meal, more Iraqi planes could be heard approaching.

Harry was in the air at the time. Flying an Oxford and with Porter in the nose of the aircraft they were flying at 5000 feet and just about to drop their load. He called to his bomb aimer, 'Get rid of those bombs as quickly as possible and then come up here and man the turret gun.' Harry called up base to let them know to expect visitors in a few minutes. As soon as Porter was in the turret Harry put the plane into a shallow dive and flew through the enemy formation just as they reached their target. Porter reckoned he hit at least two planes but it didn't really matter. The enemy having dropped a few small bombs made off. They were pursued by a few

British Audaxes which had been scrambled. The enemy lost another two planes on this raid. The British did not escape scotfree. One of the Habbaniya planes was shot down and its pilot killed. Another crashed on landing as its undercarriage collapsed but the pilot was alright although badly shaken.

Everyone on the base felt tired. The pilots, gunners and bomb aimers kept elated by the excitement of operations against the enemy felt the energy drain from them once they were able to relax, if only for a short time. The ground crews worked long hours to repair broken aircraft and then get them ready to fly again. They too were worried about the losses in aircrew and planes and they all suffered from lack of sleep. The hospital had coped well with the abnormally high number of patients but even the medical staff were feeling the strain. A few Indian soldiers and Assyrians had suffered minor wounds while those who had died in the conflict still awaited a proper burial. Added to all this was the knowledge that the enemy still remained on the plateau. It was as well they had not made a full scale attack on the base – a base without adequate defence, for victory to the Iraqis would then surely have followed.

Now there was another night to endure, not knowing whether the shelling would recommence and not knowing if the Iraqis under cover of darkness would make their final assault on the camp. Harry was also tired, almost too weary to sleep yet he knew that the following day things might be worse. He made his way to the hospital and spoke to each of the wounded airmen, enquiring after their health and trying to put a brave face on the situation. He also looked in on two other wards where the soldiers were being treated. Some were in bed but most sat in chairs at the ends of each ward and appeared to be in good spirits. What he found surprising was the fact that the Indians and Assyrians spoke in English not only among themselves but between each group. It was obviously a common language which they preferred.

He finally turned in himself but sleep would not come. Almost for the first time since the siege began he allowed himself a few moments to think about Jane. Communication with the outside world had been cut for the past two days and he wondered how she was coping. For all he knew the Iraqis may have already taken over the embassy. It would have been an easy thing to do with no more than a token force. The soldiers on duty inside could offer little resistance. He sent up a little prayer that she was safe and well and finally Harry drifted off to sleep.

CHAPTER 36

Final Account

D AY FOUR. During the night some shells had landed – a few at a time with a long wait until the next salvoes came over. It was obviously a ploy to keep the defenders awake rather than to cause any real damage. Apart from those who were actually on watch most of the others slept from sheer exhaustion. The roll call each morning began to show gaps in the ranks of the trainee pilots. Many appeared to have slept in their uniforms and the orderly officer who took the parade on 5th May commented on their untidy appearance.

'After breakfast I want you all to return to barracks, smarten yourselves up and be back on parade at 08.30. Flight leaders will see that their groups are well turned out. Don't forget most of you will be flying today and we don't want any slovenly pilots bending the King's aircraft. Dismiss.'

There were only a few grumbles of dissent. For the most part they realised they had let their discipline fall well below their usual standard. The CFI who witnessed this mild reproach called the duty officer over. 'Nicely done Mr. Thompson. For a moment there I thought you were going to put them all on a charge.'

'Oh no Sir. They're all good lads, just up against it at the moment but you'll see. They'll smarten themselves up and by tomorrow everything will be back to normal.'

'Let's hope so. I really do.'

The second parade of the trainee pilots that day was a much improved turn out. When the roll was called the duty officer was visibly shaken as the corporal recorded those present and those absent. 'Armitage.' 'Present sir.'

'Armstrong.' 'He's in hospital sir.'

'Brooke.' 'Present sir.'

'Christie.' 'Present sir.'

'Drummond.' 'Dead sir.'

'Duncan.' 'Sick sir'

And so the sad tale continued. The ranks of the instructors were not much better. At least three had been killed and four injured. Of the senior officers only Wg/Cdr Henty, the engineering officer, was still able to fly. Lang had been hit in an arm and was on his way to have his wound dressed when he had witnessed the earlier parade. Wg/Cdr Holdcroft had a more serious wound to his left leg and was recovering in hospital.

With their numbers so depleted Harry reckoned they only had one option remaining. While they could still put aircraft into the sky they must keep up the pressure on the enemy. It had worked so far and as a result there had been no major frontal attack on the base. So by 09.30, a bit later than usual the Habbaniya squadrons were airborne. A flight of Audax aircraft took off first followed by 9 Oxfords, all that remained serviceable. Then followed two more groups of fighters. While the bombers flew off to gain height before their bomb runs the fighters buzzed like bees around the Iraqi camp getting in short bursts of machine gun fire as they came within range and dropping a few bombs for good measure.

On one of these low level attacks one of the volunteer gunners, a corporal armourer, was hit by a stray bullet which came up from the enemy. The unlucky shot had come through the bottom of the plane, missed the gunner's body but grazed his forehead and like Harry's wound it bled profusely. He merely wiped away the blood with one hand and continued to fire his gun with the other. Once back on the ground he was treated at the first aid post which had been set up just inside one of the hangers. He refused to go to hospital and an hour later, his head swathed in bandages, he insisted on flying again.

Another more serious accident occurred just before midday in full view of everyone on the airfield. W/O Butler, taking off on his second sortie with bomb aimer and gunner burst a wheel on take-off. The plane had been checked on landing and appeared to be alright. However near the end of its take-off path and just about to become airborne one of the tyres burst. Butler did manage to get in the air but the accident had caused the plane to slew round a fraction and it lost a bit of impetus. In doing so it momentarily dropped and one wing hit the ridge at the end of the take off. With engines at full throttle the plane cartwheeled several times before it hit the swamp and all the crew were killed.

One of the armoured cars raced to the scene but could not save the crew. The accident itself was bad enough but the loss of three good men and the plane seriously reduced the fighting capabilities of the base. The frightful accident in full view of the airfield subdued the watchers. It was one thing to be told that an aircraft had crashed and the crew lost. To actually witness the event was quite another. It brought home to all their own mortality, how quickly death could strike and how precious life was.

Harry was in the next plane and continued taxiing to the take-off point and having received a green from control took off. He called up control and asked them to make a special search of the grass to make sure it was clear of debris. They could not afford any more losses like the one they had just witnessed. Slowly the remaining Oxfords took off and joined Harry who was flying in a large circle some 15 miles north of Habbaniya. Even the standby Oxford was pressed into service so now 9, all that remained of their original 27 took station as they waited for the Audax squadrons to join them. The CFI from his hospital bed had authorised the two remaining Gordons and the last of the Gladiators. Once the whole armada had joined forces, even though a motley collection, it was an impressive sight as they turned as one and headed back towards Habbaniya.

The order of battle, planned almost as a last ditch effort had been discussed at some length. They all thought that although their previous attacks had kept the Iraqis in check what was needed was a massive all out assault. What their bombs lacked in actual weight they would make up in quantity delivered in one fell swoop. Just prior to the attack Singh, his Indian troops and the Assyrians, supported by the armoured cars would launch a combined operation against the enemy It was intended to be a hit and run skirmish and to get out of the way before the planes attacked. Once the bombs had been released the ground troops would go in again while the planes landed.

On paper it sounded impressive although only time would tell. All went well as the troops went forward in their first attack and they even managed to capture a few Iraqi guns which the armoured cars dragged back to base. They would be used to good effect much later. The drone of the incoming planes could be heard above the noise of battle and it was a clear signal for Singh and his men to withdraw. The first of the Gordons detached from the force and came in low over the enemy positions with their forward guns blazing and as they passed their target the gunners in the rear cockpits let fly with their guns.

As soon as they had gone the bombers arrived, the two remaining ones with bombsights achieving a fair degree of accuracy while the others merely got close and dropped their loads. Finally the remaining fighters screamed down to create as much havoc as possible. The aerial attack was all over in less than five minutes after which the ground troops had gone in again and most of the planes had landed, the bombers using the main airfield while the fighters made do with the smaller one which had been constructed from the golf course and the polo field. They needed to be made ready in case the Iraqi Air Force returned. Part of the overall battle plan for the day was to maintain reconnaissance flights for as long as possible.

So Harry took off again with Porter and this time they took two flasks of coffee and some sandwiches to sustain them until relieved by one of the other Oxfords. Leaving their plane with the bombsight to receive a more thorough check they took one of the dual control Oxfords rigged so that the bombs could be released by the second pilot. It was to be a long day. Even at only 130 mph it is surprising how much ground may be covered. Although they flew in ever widening circles from Habbaniya they saw no trace of Iraqi troops or enemy aircraft. The steady beat of the engines almost induced the already tired Harry into a state of stupor. Porter took the initiative.

'Is it O.K. if I fly for a bit Sir? Harry was more than grateful for the intervention and readily agreed. 'You have control.'

With Baghdad only 50 miles away Harry was tempted to call up Shaiba, near Basra or the other RAF base nearer the capital. In the end he decided not to go beyond the 40 mile limit that had been agreed and to keep radio silence. He returned to base and his place was taken by the next reconnaissance plane and so the pattern continued until just before nightfall when they called it a day.

The Iraqis, still numbered in their thousands, remained on the plateau and although their inactivity indicated that they planned no immediate attack on the base it was decided to increase the lookouts leaving the majority at the camp hoping to get a restful night.

DAY FIVE. During the night of 5th and 6th of May the probing patrols of Singh and his men again infiltrated the enemy positions. Later patrols towards midnight reported that the enemy was breaking camp. At first it was unclear what their intentions might be. Singh himself went out and in what he freely accepted later as somewhat foolhardy actually spoke to a few Iraqi soldiers. 'About time too,' were his first words. 'We're just wasting our time here. It's about time we attacked.' 'Haven't you heard,' they replied. 'We're not attacking. We going back to barracks.' Much relieved Singh was quick to reply. 'I'm glad I bumped into you. We got our orders crossed.' With that he quietly withdrew and hurried back to Habbaniya.

He apologised for waking Harry with the news. 'No problem. I was only having forty winks. You must promise me you'll never do anything so stupid again. You're too valuable to lose.'

'I promise.' replied Singh with a twinkle in his eye and Harry knew that if a similar occasion arose again the Indian major would do exactly the same.

The duty officer was called and asked to alert the senior officers and to advise the ground crews but to make no move to get aircraft airborne. As dawn broke on 6th May the defenders at Habbaniya saw with utter relief that the Iraqis had left their camp. A short reconnaissance flight revealed that they were streaming back towards Baghdad. However a longer flight found several Iraqi battalions heading out from Baghdad in the direction of Habbaniya. Surely if the old troops were being relieved they should have waited on the plateau unless the whole thing was a deliberate hoax.

When he learned this latest news Harry consulted Singh who merely said, 'Here we go again. I always knew we couldn't trust them even when they're retreating. Mind you they've had quite a pasting and lost a lot of their equipment apart from that which we've pinched. I wonder what their next move will be.'

'Well we have also suffered but I think we can still put up a couple of squadrons, one of each. Let's have breakfast and then ask for volunteers to go after them one more time. I'm sure the young lads have had enough. We should maintain the initiative but it will be up to them whether we attack now or wait until the enemy attacks us.'

After breakfast all pilots and ground crews were summoned to the cinema. As the babble of voices gradually subsided Harry stood up on the stage. His opening words of 'Good morning heroes,' were greeted with whistles and cheers. 'We have received reports that the Iraqis have left their camp.' He waited until the cheers died down before continuing. 'They are on their way back to Baghdad.' Again the cheers prevented further words from being heard so he waited. 'Several battalions are on their way out from Baghdad and are heading in this direction so I thought I should warn you.' He waited until the groans became a quiet grumble and then someone in the hall said 'Let's get after them.' at which more cheering broke out.

'Quiet please gentlemen. You are a bloodthirsty lot. I agree with your sentiments but we don't need to go mad, that is not any madder than we already are. We need a few volunteers to go after the enemy and hopefully finish them off. I must emphasise it will not be easy and you have already done a marvellous job.'

One of the sergeant fitters got up. 'Sir if the lads are prepared to fly we'll keep 'em flying. We're all tired but we haven't come this far to stop now. Let's finish the job if we can and then we can all go on a week's leave.'

'Is that a condition Sergeant Rogers?'

'No Sir. Just wishful thinking.'

'O.K. thank you all. Please return to the hangers and get the planes ready. In the meantime any pilot who wants to volunteer please stay behind and we'll see how best we can fit you all in.' With a final cheer the ground crew began to disperse and Harry noticed that not one of the pilots or the pupil pilots got up. After all that these young men had endured it was an incredible affirmation of their determination to continue the fight.

By 10.00 hours all was ready at Habbaniya. With the aircraft numbers now so reduced the pilots were almost clamouring for a chance to get in one more blow against the enemy. Harry elected to circle overhead of the retreating columns and attempt to guide the fighter and bomber squadrons to vulnerable sections of the retreating Iraqis and to keep a lookout for any enemy planes which might put in an appearance. For once he was on his own, having persuaded LAC Porter to fly one of the Audax planes himself. Harry took off and a few minutes later the first flight of fighters became airborne. The young pilots were anxious to get to grips with the enemy but Harry ordered them to attack the front of the column. 'Knock out the head first and we'll worry about the tail later.' was his order. And so the battle was joined.

First the fighters came in low and attacked the already demoralised troops and when they returned to base for fresh ammo the next flight of fighters arrived this time loaded with bombs and once they had dropped their load they finished off by low level attacks with machine guns. From his overview of the battle Harry noticed that many of the gunners in the rear cockpits also dropped several small bombs on to the enemy below. A few of the Iraqis returned fire with their rifles but they appeared to be more anxious to escape than keep the aircraft at bay. There was a break for a few minutes which allowed the Oxfords, flying a bit higher, to come in and deliver their bomb loads.

The consternation on the ground was clearly visible. The vehicles, guns and troops which had been hit in the first attack had stopped in their tracks. Others coming up from behind were also forced to stop and became easy targets for the planes. And still the enemy retreated, finding a way off the road and on to the scrubland for a few hundred yards until they were able to get back on the road once more and increase the pace of their headlong flight. Even so they moved back towards Baghdad at no more than 10mph. At this rate it would be another four or five hours before they would reach the comparative safety of the capital.

Harry was still convinced that in spite of the losses they had already inflicted on the enemy they were not yet completely defeated. On the other hand instead of becoming more weary with each attack on the enemy his pilots appeared to be going in with renewed energy. Harry called on flight after flight of pupil pilots and the few instructors who were still able to fly. The ground staff did a magnificent job of refuelling and rearming each aircraft as it came in to land and even managed to stick patches over bullet holes which had torn the fabric. The pilots never bothered to get out of their planes and as soon as they got the thumbs up from the mechanics they were away.

By midday on 6th May the few serviceable aircraft at Habbaniya had flown 139 sorties and had lost only one Audax. But the battle was not yet over. The battalions of fresh Iraqi troops which had set out from Baghdad met those fleeing from the battle area on the road about half way between the capital and the RAF base. Their downfall was complete when neither force could move either back or forward.

Once more in a final effort the pupils of No 4 Flying Training School attacked and continued the destruction of the Iraqi uprising. Long before nightfall they had won the day but not without loss and the price of victory was high. Thirteen pupils and instructors had been killed and 21 seriously injured during the past few days. Four other pupils who had fought gallantly against overwhelming odds were so devastated by the experience they would never fly again.

As the aircraft came in for the last time the pilots weary with their efforts climbed down from their planes and while most of them walked back to their locker rooms carrying their parachutes a few just sat on the ground. Many were obviously thinking of the destruction they had inflicted on the enemy. It was an experience they would remember for a very long time.

Now that the battle was over the feeling of relief was mixed with one of anti-climax. Wisely the CFI decided to give the men a few days to unwind. Orders went out that only essential work should be done and that everyone should get some rest and recuperation within the confines of the base. Some spent long hours sleeping on their beds or lying in the sunshine while others wrote letters home which they knew would be censored but it was one way to let off steam. Many could not stop talking, going over each detail of the last few days. A few kept to themselves and strolled slowly around the perimeter. Others buried their heads in books and at night the camp cinema was crowded. Each found his own way back to normality and after a few days only three still attended sick parade. Sergeant Rogers did not get his leave until some time later. On 7th May the telephone lines were repaired and they learned that the British Embassy in Baghdad had indeed been occupied by the enemy. Generally the Iraqis there had behaved themselves merely cutting off the embassy from the outside world.

At the end of the week Wg/Cdr Lang called a meeting of the whole camp, thanked them for their efforts and said that camp life would now return to normal. He also informed them of war news in the world outside and none of it was good. The British were having a bad time everywhere while the Germans seemed to be victorious with each new venture they started.

The battle of Habbaniya could have been crucial to the Allies if it had been lost. Instead it became merely a footnote in the history of World War II.

On 11th May they learned that a hastily gathered force had started out from Palestine to come to their assistance. Composed of a variety of units, in fact all that could be spared, this relief force set out to cross the desert and swamps to reach Habbaniya, a distance of over 760 miles. On 17th May it was attacked by the Luftwaffe, then based at Mosul in northern Iraq. Once more the aircraft from Habbaniya took the initiative and although now up against superior forces took on the Luftwaffe and attacked their airfields.

It was some time later when they learned that word of their prowess and the stand they had made at Habbaniya had gone before them. The Iraqi press had completely exaggerated the number of RAF planes. Not only had the RAF suddenly acquired huge numbers if fighters and bombers but several thousand troops had landed at Basra and many more were on their way. None of it was true. A very small RAF force was all that could be spared from commitments elsewhere and they also attacked airfields which were occupied by the Germans.

To the Iraqi government in Baghdad it seemed that the RAF had mopped up their army and vanquished their air force. The press releases were an excuse for their poor showing virtually against untrained pilots. Had they but known it the defenders at Habbaniya were close to running out of bombs and ammunition while the RAF personnel were almost at the end of their resistance. If Hitler could have spared a few thousand troops and a squadron of fighters he could possibly have won a great victory in Iraq together with its vital oil supplies. As it was he had lost the initiative and never regained it in that region. His mind was on other places – RUSSIA.

On 12th May Harry obtained permission to go to Baghdad, having first telephoned the embassy and spoken to Jane. It was a subdued meeting, each thankful that the other had survived. He stayed for two days and was then recalled to Habbanyia but during those two days they made plans for their future together. In the meantime Rashid Ali had been captured trying to flee the country and with him they found enormous quantities of money which should have gone to pay his army.

Habbforce, the collection of army units which had set out from Palestine on 12th May reached Habbaniya on 20th May without being attacked any further. The march itself was an extraordinary achievement across most inhospitable terrain. They stayed at Habbaniya until 27th and then moved to Baghdad where they accepted the surrender of Iraqi forces and where the Regent was reinstated. Singh joined the parade of his men in the capital and while they went on to Basra he and Harry were entertained at the British embassy. Long into the night they told Jane about the five days and nights they had spent defending Habbanyia until Harry noticed she could hardly keep her eyes open.

'Oh. I'm sorry darling. How thoughtless of us to keep you up so late with our boring tales.'

'No. Its alright really.' She smiled wearily. 'I am interested. Its just that it has been a long day here too. In fact its been a long week.'

'No.' said Major Singh. 'Harry's right its time we all turned in. Good night my dear. Good night Harry.'

He closed the door behind him leaving Jane and Harry to prove their love for each other and give thanks that both had survived.

*   *   *

Happy Landings

Michael Carter returned to England but not as Harry's older partner. He retired from the RAF, married the widow of an old friend in Cheltenham and is quite happy pottering around his wife's comfortable farm.

Harry was posted back to Ismailia and subsequently went by boat to England where he was stationed at Montrose. This was No 2 Flying Instructors School. There he learned to fly all over again and then went to various flying schools throughout England teaching new pilots to fly Oxfords and other aircraft until the end of the war. Jane finally boarded a boat for home but after six months in England she was posted to Australia. She did not meet Harry again until 1944 when she returned to England and they were married.

Sam Jordan recovered from his wounds and was pronounced fit for active service. His wedding to Joyce was arranged for 7th June by which time Harry was expected back from Iraq. The powers that be had other ideas for 8th June 1941 was the date set for the campaign to wrest Syria from the French.

Sam, then given his own squadron, was among the first to begin operations. That bloody campaign saw Free French forces fighting against their own countrymen which ended in victory for the Allies. It took almost two weeks for them to occupy Damascus and another 18 days of hard fighting before Vichy French forces agreed to a ceasefire.

There were extensive casualties on both sides. When the fighting was over, the 40,000 French prisoners were given the option of joining the Free French or returning to France. Only 12,000 stayed to continue the fight against the Germans.

Fortunately Sam was spared and returned to Cairo. He and Joyce were married on 15th July with Harry as best man. Jane also attended as one of the bridesmaids before boarding the boat for England. Two weeks later Sam also returned to England and subsequently went first to Canada and when America came into the war, he was posted there as part of the RAF Liaison Mission.

When the war ended he and Joyce chose to make their home in Canada. He completed his medical studies there, became a surgeon and subsequently taught at McGill University in Montreal.

After the war, Harry also completed his training as a doctor and became a GP in Cirencester. The two families meet occasionally. One year Harry and Jane travel to Canada and a couple of years later Sam and Joyce return to the old country and stay with the Nelson family. Only occasionally do they talk about the war years.